She suddenly broke away from him and ran down the beach.

Turning, she kicked up a spray from the waves that had been washing over their feet. She caught him with a full body splash, and he yelped and laughed with surprise. Then he came after her. She squealed and turned to run, but he tackled her and bore her down to the soft, damp sand.

He leaned over her, looked down into her eyes and then murmured, "Good move. I just saw that goon up on the boardwalk. We are being watched."

He eased closer. "Can I kiss you?"

She tangled her fingers into the richness of his hair, pulling him in, and she kissed him.

Dear Reader,

Miami is my home, and has always been. In a nutshell, Scottish father and Irish mother met and married when both were working in Chicago; I guess they were both tired of the cold and the snow, and they moved to Florida.

Yes, it's wild. Like most other places, we have our very good elements, and our bad—such as the roads. Driving can be pure insanity. Every once in a while, you want to get out of your car and slap the person beeping at you from behind, because you really can't just run over pedestrians!

However...I love that we have incredible warm water that we can go in most of the time. (And when we can't, we can still offer a respite for our Canadian and Northern snowbirds!)

I love the diversity—in the same day, I can run into friends who are Cuban, Brazilian, German and British. I love that we always have flowers, and I have to admit, I simply take the color green for granted.

Our history, like all history, is varied. Visit Vizcaya, an Italian villa and the winter home of James Deering, built between 1914 and 1922 and still standing like an exquisite mirage on Biscayne Bay. Or stay at one of the most haunted hotels ever: the Biltmore, in Coral Gables, where Al Capone played, a henchman was killed and where many veterans, housed there after World War II, lived out their final days. (The hotel is truly beautiful now—I love it!)

Our zoo is fantastic, and we have Jungle Island, and the design districts, the art deco wonder of the beach, and... the list goes on.

If you've never visited, you must. Anyway, I hope you enjoy a little bit of my take on my home, Miami-Dade County.

Sincerely,

Heather Graham

New York Times and *USA TODAY* bestselling author **Heather Graham** has written more than one hundred novels. She's a winner of the Romance Writers of America's Lifetime Achievement Award and, in 2016, the ThrillerMaster award from International Thriller Writers. She is the founder of The Slush Pile Players, an author band and theatrical group. An avid scuba diver, ballroom dancer and mother of five, she still enjoys her South Florida home, but also loves to travel.

For more information, check out her website, theoriginalheathergraham.com, or find Heather on Facebook.

Also by Heather Graham

Harlequin Intrigue

Out of the Darkness
Shadows in the Night
Law and Disorder

MIRA Books

Echoes of Evil
Pale as Death
Fade to Black
A Dangerous Game
Wicked Deeds
Dark Rites
Dying Breath
A Perfect Obsession
Darkest Journey
Deadly Fate
Haunted Destiny
Flawless

Visit the Author Profile page
at Harlequin.com for more titles.

ISBN-13: 978-1-335-00820-6

Undercover Connection & Double Entendre

Copyright © 2018 by Harlequin Books S.A.

The publisher acknowledges the copyright holder of the individual works as follows:

Undercover Connection
Copyright © 2018 by Heather Graham Pozzessere

Double Entendre
Copyright © 1986 by Heather Graham Pozzessere

Recycling programs for this product may not exist in your area.

Printed in U.S.A.

New York Times and USA TODAY Bestselling Author

HEATHER GRAHAM

Undercover Connection
&
Double Entendre

CONTENTS

For Lorna Broussard—with love and thanks
for all the help and support for...well, many years!

UNDERCOVER CONNECTION

Chapter One

The woman on the runway was truly one of the most stunning creatures Jacob Wolff had ever seen. Her skin was pure bronze, as sleek and as dazzling as the deepest sun ray.

When she turned, he could see—even from his distance at the club's bar—that her eyes were light. Green, he thought, and a sharp contrast to her skin. She had amazing hair, long and so shimmering that it was as close to pure black as it was possible to be; so dark it almost had a gleam of violet. She was long-legged, lean and yet exquisitely shaped as she moved in the creation she modeled—a mix of pastel colors that was perfectly enhanced by her skin—the dress was bare at the shoulder and throat with a plunging neckline, and back, and then swept to the floor.

She moved like a woman accustomed to such a haughty strut: proud, confident, arrogant and perhaps even amused by the awe of the onlookers.

"That one—she will rule the place one day."

Jacob turned.

Ivan Petrov leaned on one elbow across the bar from Jacob. Ivan bartended and—so Jacob believed thus far—ran all things that had to do with the on-the-ground-management of the Gold Sun Club. The burning-hot new establishment was having its grand opening tonight.

"I'd imagine," Jacob said. He leaned closer over the bar and smiled. "And I imagine that she might perhaps be…available?"

Ivan smiled, clearly glad that Jacob had asked him; Ivan was a proud man, appreciative that Jacob had noted his position of power within the club.

"Not…immediately," Ivan said. "She is fairly new. But all things come in good time, my friend, eh? Now you," he said, pouring a shot of vodka for Jacob, "you are fairly new, too. New to Miami Beach—new to our ways. We have our…social…rules, you know."

Jacob knew all too well.

And he knew what happened to those who didn't follow the rules—or who dared to make their own. He'd been south of I-75 that morning, off part of the highway still known as Alligator Alley, and for good reason. He'd been deep in the Everglades where a Seminole ranger had recently discovered a bizarre cache of oil drums, inside of which had been several bodies in various stages of decomposition.

"I have my reputation," Jacob said softly.

Ivan caught Jacob's meaning. Yes, Jacob would follow the rules. But he was his own man—very much a *made* man from the underbelly of New York City. Now, he'd bought a gallery on South Beach; but he'd been doing his other business for years.

At least, that was the information that had been fed to what had become known as the Deco Gang—so called because of the beautifully preserved architecture on South Beach.

Jacob was for all intents and purposes a new major player in the area. And it was important, of course, that he appear to be a team player—but a very powerful team player who respected another man's turf while also keeping a strict hold on his own.

"A man's reputation must be upheld," Ivan said, nodding approvingly.

"While, of course, he gives heed to all that belongs to another man, as well," Jacob assured him.

A loud clash of drums drew Jacob's attention for a moment. The Dissidents were playing that night; they were supposedly one of the hottest up-and-coming bands, not just in the state, but worldwide.

The grand opening to the Gold Sun Club had been invitation only; tomorrow night, others would flow in, awed by the publicity generated by this celebrity-studded evening. The rich and the beautiful—and the not-so-rich but very beautiful—were all on the ground floor, listening to the popular new band and watching the fashion show.

Jacob took in the place as a whole, noting a balcony level that ran the perimeter, with a bar above the stage. But that night all the guests were downstairs, and Ivan Petrov was manning the main bar himself.

The elegant model on the runway swirled with perfect timing, walking toward the crowd again, pausing to seductively steal a delicious-looking apple from the hands of a pretty boy—a young male model, dressed as Adonis—standing like a statue at the bottom of the steps to the runway.

"I believe," Jacob told Ivan, turning to look at him gravely again, "that my business will be an asset to your business, and that we will work in perfect harmony together."

"Yes," Ivan said. "Mr. Smirnoff invited you, right?"

Jacob nodded. "Josef brought me in."

Ivan said, "He is an important man."

"Yes, I know," Jacob assured him.

If Ivan only knew how.

JASMINE ADAIR—JASMINE ALAMEIN, as far as this group was concerned—was glad that she had managed to learn the art of walking a runway, without tripping, and observing at the same time. It wasn't as if she'd had training or gone to cotillion classes—did they still have cotillion classes?—but she'd been graced with the most wonderful parents in the world.

Her mother had been with the Peace Corps—maybe a natural course for her, having somewhat global roots. Her mom's parents had come from Jordan and Kenya, met and married in Morocco and moved to the United States. Jasmine's mom, Liliana, had been born and grown up in Miami, but had traveled the world to help people before she'd finally settled down. Liliana had been a great mom, always all about kindness to others and passionate that everyone must be careful with others. She had believed that words could make or break a person's day, and truly *seeing* people was one of the most important talents anyone could have in life.

Declan Adair, Jasmine's dad, was mostly Irish-American. He'd been a cop and had taught Jasmine what that meant to him—serving his community.

They had both taught her about absolute equality for every color, race, creed, sex and sexual orientation, and they had both taught her that good people were good people and, all in all, most of the people in the world were good, longing for the same things, especially in America—life, liberty and the pursuit of happiness.

They sounded like a sweet pair of hippies; they had been anything but. Her father had also taught her that those who appeared to be the nicest people in the world often were not—and that lip service didn't mean a hell of a lot and could hide an ocean of lies and misdeeds.

"Judging people—hardest call you'll ever make," he'd told her once. "Especially when you have to do so quickly."

He'd shaken his head in disgust over the result of a trial often enough, and her mother had always reminded him, "There are things that just aren't allowed before a jury, Declan. Things that the jury just doesn't see and doesn't know."

"Not to worry—we'll get them next time," he would assure her.

Jasmine scanned the crowd. Members of this group, the so-called Deco Gang, hadn't been gotten yet. And they needed to be—no one really knew the full extent of their crimes because they were good. Damned good at knowing how to game the justice system.

Fanatics came in all kinds—and fanatics were dangerous. Just as criminals came in all kinds, and they ruined the lives of those who wanted to live in peace, raising their children, working…enjoying their liberty and pursuing their happiness.

That's why cops were so important—something she had learned when sometimes her dad, the detective, hadn't made it to a birthday party.

Because of him, she'd always wanted to be a cop. And she was a damned good one, if she did say so herself.

At the moment, it was her mother's training that was paying off. As a child, Jasmine had accompanied her mom to all kinds of fund-raisers—and once she was a teenager, she'd started modeling at fashion shows in order to attract large donations for her mom's various charities. She had worked with a few top designers who were equally passionate about feeding children or raising awareness when natural disasters devastated various regions in the States and around the world.

So as Jasmine strutted and played it up for the audience, she also watched.

The event had attracted the who's who of the city. She could see two television stars who were acting in a current hit series. Alphonse Mangiulli—renowned Italian artist—was there, along with Cam Li, the Chinese businessman who had just built two of the largest hotels in the world, one in Dubai and one on Miami Beach. Mathilda Glen—old, old Miami society and money— had made it, along with the famed English film director, Eric Summer.

And amid this gathering of the rich and famous was also a meeting of the loosely organized group of South Beach criminals that the Miami-Dade police called the Deco Gang.

They had come together under the control of a Russian-born kingpin, Josef Smirnoff, and they were an equal-opportunity group of very dangerous criminals. They weren't connected to the Italian Mafia or Cosa Nostra, and they weren't the Asian mob or a cartel from any South American or island country. And they were hard to pin down, using legitimate business for money laundering and for their forays into drug smuggling and dealing and prostitution.

Crimes had been committed; the bodies of victims had been found, but for the most part, those who got in the way of the gang were eliminated. Because of their connections with one another, alibis were abundant, evidence disappeared, and pinning anything on any one individual had been an elusive goal for the police.

Jasmine had used every favor she had saved up to get assigned to this case. It helped that her looks gave her a good cover for infiltration.

Her captain—Mac Lorenzo—probably suspected that she had her own motives. But he didn't ask, and she didn't tell. She hadn't let Lorenzo know that her personal determination to bring down the Deco Gang had begun when Mary Ahearn had disappeared. Her old friend had vanished without a trace after working with a nightclub that was most probably a front for a very high-scale prostitution ring.

She could see Josef Smirnoff in the front of the crowd; he was smiling and looking right at her. He seemed to like what he saw. Good. He was the man in charge, and she needed access to him. She needed to be able to count his bodyguards and his henchmen and get close to him.

She wasn't working alone; Jasmine was blessed with an incredible partner, Jorge Fuentes.

Along with being a dedicated cop, Jorge was also extremely good-looking, and thanks to that, he'd been given leeway when he'd shown up at the Gold Sun Club, supposedly looking for work. Jasmine had told Natasha Volkov—manager of the models who worked these events or sat about various places looking pretty—that she'd worked with Jorge before and that he was wonderfully easygoing. Turned out the show was short a man; Jorge had been hired on for the day easily. They'd cast him as Adonis and given him a very small costume to wear.

Jorge had been trying to get a moment alone with her as preparations for the fashion show had gone on. Jasmine had been undercover for several weeks prior to the club's opening night, and briefings had been few and far between. The opportunity hadn't arisen as yet, but they'd be able to connect—as soon as the runway show part of the party was over. She was curious what updates Jorge had, but they were both savvy enough to bide their time. Neither of them dared to blow their covers with this group—such a mistake could result in instant death, with neither of them even aware or able to help the other in any way.

Her cover story was complete. She had a rented room on Miami Beach, which she took for a week before answering the ad for models. She'd been given an effective fake résumé—one that showed she'd worked but never been on the top. And might well be hungry to get there.

After a lightning-quick change of clothes backstage, she made another sweep down the runway. She noted the celebrities in attendance. South Beach clubs were like rolls of toilet paper—people used them up and discarded them without a thought. What was popular today might be deserted within a month.

But she didn't think that this enterprise would care—the showy opening was just another front for the illegal activities that kept them going.

She noted the men and women surrounding Josef Smirnoff. He was about six feet tall, big and solidly muscled. His head was immaculately bald, which made his sharp jaw even more prominent and his dark eyes stand out.

On his arm was an up-and-coming young starlet. She was in from California, a lovely blue-eyed blonde, clearly hoping that Smirnoff's connections here would allow her to rub elbows with the right people.

Jasmine hoped that worked out for her—and that she didn't become involved with the wrong people.

Natasha was with him, as well. She had modeled in her own youth, in Europe. About five-eleven and in her midfifties, Natasha had come up through the ranks. One of the girls had whispered to Jasmine that Natasha had always been smart—she had managed to sleep her way up with the right people. She was an attractive woman, keeping her shoulder-length hair a silvery-white color that enhanced her slim features. She kept tight control of the fashion show and other events, and sharp eyes on everyone and everything.

Rumor had it she was sleeping with Josef. It wasn't something she proclaimed or denied. But there were signs. Jasmine wondered if she cared for Josef—or if it was a power play.

Jasmine had to wonder how Natasha felt about the beautiful women who were always around. But she understood, for Natasha, life hadn't been easy. Power probably overrode emotion.

The men by Smirnoff were his immediate body-guards. Jasmine thought of them as Curly, Moe and Larry. In truth, they were Alejandro Suarez, Antonio Garibaldi and Sasha Antonovich. All three were big men, broad-shouldered and spent their off-hours in the gym. One of the three was always with Smirnoff. On a day like today, they were all close to him.

Victor Kozak was there, as well. Victor was apparently the rising heir to receive control of the action. He was taller and slimmer than Josef, and he had bright blue eyes and perfectly clipped, salt-and-pepper facial hair. He was extremely pleasant to Jasmine—so pleasant that it made her feel uneasy.

She knew about them all somewhat because she had talked to Mary about what she was doing. She had warned Mary that there was suspicion about the group on South Beach that ran so many of the events that called for runway models or beautiful people just to be in a crowd. Beautiful people who, it was rumored, you could engage to spend time with privately. Mary had described many of these players before Jasmine had met them.

Before Mary had disappeared.

The club manager was behind the bar; he didn't often work that kind of labor himself. He usually oversaw what was going on there. He was like the bodyguards—solid, watching, earning his way up the ranks.

Still watching, Jasmine made another of her teasing plays with Jorge—pointing out the next model who was coming down the runway. Kari Anderson was walking along in a black caftan that accented the fairness of her skin and the platinum shimmer of her hair. Jorge stood perfectly still; only his eyes moved, drawing laughter from the crowd.

As Jasmine did her turn around, she noted a man at the bar. She did not know him, or anything about him. He was a newcomer, Kari had told her. A big man in New York City. He was taller and leaner than any of the other men, and yet Jasmine had the feeling that he was steel-muscled beneath the designer suit he was wearing. He hadn't close-cropped his hair either; it was long, shaggy around his ears, a soft brown.

He was definitely the best looking of the bunch. His face was crafted with sharp clean contours, high defined cheekbones, a nicely squared chin and wide-set, light eyes. He could have been up on the runway, playing "pretty boy" with Jorge.

But of course, newcomer though he might be, he'd be one of "them." He'd recently come to South Beach, pretending to be some kind of an artist and owning and operating a gallery.

The hair. Maybe he believed that would disguise him as an artist—rather than a murdering criminal.

When she had made another turn, after pausing to do a synchronized turn with Kari, she saw that the new guy had left the bar area, along with the bartender. They were near Josef Smirnoff now.

Allowed into the inner circle.

Just as she noticed them, a loud crack rang out. The sound was almost masked by the music.

People didn't react.

Instinct and experience told Jasmine that it was indeed a gunshot. She instantly grabbed hold of Kari and dragged her down to the platform, all but lying over her. Another shot sounded; a light exploded in a hail of sparks. Then the rat-tat-tat of bullets exploded throughout the room.

The crowd began to scream and move.

There was nothing orderly about what happened— people panicked. It was hard to blame them. It was a fearsome world they lived in.

"Stay down!" Jasmine told Kari, rising carefully.

Jorge was already on the floor, trying to help up a woman who had fallen, in danger of being trampled.

Bodyguards and police hired for the night were trying to bring order. Jasmine jumped into the crowd, trying to fathom where the shots had been fired. It was a light at the end of the runway that had exploded; where the other shot had come from was hard to discern.

The band had panicked, as well. A guitar crashed down on the floor.

Josef Smirnoff was on the ground, too. His bodyguards were near, trying to hold off the people who were set to run over him.

It was an absolute melee.

Jasmine helped up a young man, a white-faced rising star in a new television series. He tried to thank her.

"Get out, go—walk quickly," she said.

There were no more shots. But would they begin again?

She made her way to Smirnoff, ducking beneath the distracted bodyguards. She knelt by him as people raced around her.

"Josef?" she said, reaching for his shoulder, turning him over.

Blood covered his chest. There was no hope for the man; he was already dead, his eyes open in shock. There was blood on her now, blood on the designer gown she'd been wearing, everywhere.

She looked up; Jorge had to be somewhere nearby. Instead she saw a man coming after her, reaching for her as if to attack.

She rolled quickly, avoiding him once. But as she prepared to fight back, she felt as if she had been taken down by a linebacker. She stared up into the eyes of the long-haired newcomer; bright blue eyes, startling against his face and dark hair. She felt his hands on her, felt the strength in his hold.

No. She was going to take him down.

She jackknifed her body, letting him use his own weight against himself, causing him to crash into the floor.

He was obviously surprised. It took him a second—but only a second—to spin himself. He was back on his feet in a hunched position, ready to spring at her.

Where the hell is Jorge?

She feinted as if she would dive down to the left and dived to the right instead. She caught the man with a hard chop to the abdomen that should have stolen his breath.

He didn't give. She was suddenly tackled again, down on the ground, feeling the full power of the man's strength atop her. She stared up into his blue eyes, glistening like ice at the moment.

She realized the crowd was gone; she could hear the bustle at the doorway, hear the police as they poured in at the entrance.

But right there, at that moment, Josef Smirnoff lay dead in an ungodly pool of blood—blood she wore—just feet away.

And there was this man.

And herself.

"Hey!" Thank God, Jorge had found her. He dived down beside them, as if joining the fight. But he didn't help Jasmine; he made no move against the man. He lay next to her, as if he'd just also been taken down himself.

"Stop! FBI, meet MDPD. Jasmine, he's undercover.

Jacob… Jasmine is a cop. My partner," Jorge whispered urgently.

The man couldn't have looked more surprised. Then, he made a play of socking Jorge, and Jorge lay still. The man stood and dragged Jasmine to her feet. For a long moment he looked into her eyes, and then he wrenched her elbow behind her back.

"Play it out," he said, "nothing else to do."

"Sure," Jasmine told him.

And as he led her out—toward Victor Kozak, who now stood in the front, ready to take charge, Jasmine managed to twist and deliver a hard right to his jaw.

He stared at her, rubbing his jaw with his free hand.

"Play it out," she said softly.

The Feds always thought they knew more than the locals, whether they were team people or not. He'd probably be furious. He'd want to call the shots.

But at least his presence meant that the Feds had been aware of this place. They had listened to the police, and they had sent someone in. It was probably what Jorge had been trying to tell her.

Jacob was still staring at her. Well, she did have a damned good right hook.

To her surprise, he almost seemed to smile. "Play it out," he said. And to her continued surprise, he added, "You are one hell of a player!"

Chapter Two

"Someone knew," Jorge said. "Someone knew that Smirnoff came in—that he was selling them all out."

"Maybe," Jacob Wolff said. He was sitting on the sofa in Jasmine's South Beach apartment.

She didn't know why, but it bothered her that he was there. So comfortable. So thoughtful. But it hadn't been until now, with him in her apartment, that she really understood what was going on.

Two weeks ago, Josef Smirnoff had made contact with Dean Jenkins, a special agent assigned to the Miami office. Jenkins had gone to his superiors, and from there, Jacob Wolff had been called in. Among his other talents, he was a linguist, speaking Russian, Ukrainian, Spanish, Portuguese and French, including Cajun and Haitian Creole. He also knew a smattering of Czech and Polish. And German, enough to get by.

Maybe that's why she was resenting him. No one should be that accomplished.

No, it was simply because he had taken her by surprise.

"Maybe someone knew," Wolff said. He added, "And maybe not."

"If not, why—?" Jorge asked.

Wolff leaned forward. "Because," he said softly, "I

believe that Kozak set up that hit. Not because he knew about anything that Smirnoff had done, but because he's been planning on taking over. Perhaps for some time.

"Smirnoff came in to us because he was afraid—he'd been the boss forever, but he knew how that could end if a power play went down. He was afraid. He wanted out. Kozak was the one who wanted Smirnoff out. And he figured out how to do it—and make it look as if he was as pure as the driven snow in the whole thing himself. He was visible to dozens of people when Smirnoff was killed. He played his cards right. There were plenty of cops there today, in uniform. What better time to plan an execution, when he wouldn't look the least guilty? In *this* crime ring, he was definitely the next man up— vice president, if you will."

"The thing is, if Kozak figures out something is up, we're all in grave danger," Jorge pointed out. "Under- cover may not work."

"Jorge, undercover work is the only thing that might bring them down," Jasmine protested.

She was leaning against the archway between the living-dining area of the apartment and the kitchen. It was late; she was tired. But it had been the first chance for the three of them to talk.

After the chaos, everyone had been interviewed by the police. Stars—the glittering rich and famous and especially the almost-famous—had done endless in- terviews with the press, as well. Thankfully, there had been plenty of celebrities to garner attention. Jasmine, Jorge and Jacob Wolff had all managed to avoid being seen on television, but still, maintaining their cover had meant they were there for hours.

She'd been desperate to shower, and her blood-soaked gown had gone to the evidence locker.

In the end, they'd been seen leaving together, but that had been all right. Everyone knew that Jorge was Jasmine's friend—she'd brought him into the show, after all.

And as for Jacob Wolff…

"You shouldn't have made that show of going off with us in front of Victor Kozak," she said, glaring at Wolff. She realized her tone was harsh. Too harsh. But this was her apartment—or, at least, her cover persona's apartment—and she felt like a cat on a hot tin roof while he relaxed comfortably on her rented couch.

She needed to take a deep breath; start over with the agent.

He didn't look her way, just shrugged. "I told Ivan, the bartender, I wanted to get to know you. They believe I'm an important player out of New York. Right now, they're observing me. And they believe if they respect me, I'll respect them, play by their rules. I'm supposed to be a money launderer—I'm not into many of their criminal activities, including prostitution or any form of modern slavery. My cover is that of an art dealer with dozens of foreign ties.

"Before all this went down tonight, I was trying to befriend Ivan, who apparently manages the girls. I'm trying to figure out how the women are entangled in their web. Apparently, they move slowly. Most probably, with drugs. Before all this went down tonight, I'd asked about you, Jasmine, as if taking advantage of the 'friendship' they'll offer me. He said you weren't available yet, but that all good things come in time, or something to that effect. He'll think I took advantage of the situation instead—and that I'm offering you all the comfort a man in my position can offer."

"Really?" Jasmine asked. "But I was with Jorge."

Wolff finally looked at her, waving a hand in the air. "Yes, and they all know you two are friends, and that it's normal you would have left with Jorge. But Jorge is gay."

"That's what you told them?" Jasmine asked.

"I am gay," Jorge said, shrugging.

Jasmine turned to him. "You are? You never told me."

"You never asked. Hey, we're great partners. I never asked who you were dating. Oh, wait, you never do seem to date."

Jasmine could have kicked him. "Hey!" she protested. Great. She felt like an idiot. She and Jorge were close, but…it was true. They'd been working together for a while, they were friends. Just friends. And because of that, she hadn't thought to ask—

It didn't matter. They'd both tacitly known from the beginning as partners they'd never date each other, and neither had ever thought to ask the other about their love life.

She had to draw some dignity out of this situation.

"At least we did the expected," she said. "I guarantee we were watched. Oh, and by the way, Ivan Petrov controls the venue. But Natasha really runs the models. She gives the assignments, and she's the one who hands out the paychecks."

Wolff looked at her. "You're going to have to be very careful. From all that I've been told, she's been with this enterprise from the beginning. She may be almost as powerful as Kozak himself. When Natasha got into it, she wasn't manipulated into sex work. She used sex as an investment. She came into it as a model, slept with whomever they wanted—and worked her way up to Kozak."

"I am careful," Jasmine told him. "I'm a good cop—determined, but not suicidal."

"I'm glad to hear it. So, this is all as good as it can be," Wolff said, shaking his head. "What matters most here tonight is that we've lost Smirnoff, our informant. And we've still got to somehow get into this and take them all down. We have to take Kozak down, with all the budding lieutenants, too. My position with this group is pretty solid—the Bureau does an amazing job when it comes to inventing a history. But the fashion show is over. The opening is over. The club will be closed down for a few days."

"I'll have an in, don't worry. The last words from Natasha this evening had to do with us all reporting in tomorrow—for one, to return the clothing. For another, to find out where we go from here." Jasmine hesitated.

"They haven't asked you to entertain anyone yet?" Wolff asked.

"New girls get a chance to believe they're just models. After that, they're asked to escort at certain times, and, of course, from there…"

"We'll have this wrapped up before then," Jorge assured her.

"And if not, you'll just get the hell out of it," Wolff said.

"You don't have to be protective. I've been with the Special Investigations Division for three years now, and I've dealt with some pretty heinous people," Jasmine told him.

"I've dealt with them, too," Wolff said quietly. "And I spent this afternoon up in the Everglades, a plot of godforsaken swamp with a bunch of oil drums filled with bodies. And I've been FBI for almost a decade. That didn't make today any better."

"I'm not saying anything makes it better. I'm just saying I can take care of myself," Jasmine said.

She really hadn't meant to be argumentative. But she did know what she was doing, and throughout her career, she'd learned it was usually the people who felt the need to emphasize their competency who were the ones who weren't so sure of their competency after all. She was confident in her abilities—or, at least she had thought she was.

With this Fed, she was becoming defensive. She hated the feeling.

"Guys, guys! Time-out," Jorge said.

Wolff stood, apparently all but dismissing her. "I'm heading back to my place. Most days, I'll be hanging around a real art shop that's supposedly mine. Dolphin Galleries."

He handed Jorge a card, then turned to look at Jasmine. "Feel free to watch out for me. In my mind, no one cop can beat everything out there. We all need people watching our backs. I'm more than happy to know I have MDPD in deep with me."

His words didn't help in the least; Jasmine still felt like a chastised toddler. What made it worse was the fact he was right. They did need to look out for one another.

She wanted to apologize. They had met awkwardly. She wasn't brash, she wasn't an idiot—she was a team player. But despite his words, she had the sense that he was already doubting her.

"I'll be hanging as close as I can," he said. "The woman managing the shop, Katrina Partridge, is with us. If you need me and I'm not there, just ask her. I trust her with my life."

He didn't look back. If he had done so, Jasmine was certain, it would have been to look at Jorge with pity for having been paired with her.

When Jacob was gone, she strode to the door and slid the bolts. She had three.

"Jerk!" she said. She turned back into the room and flounced down on the sofa.

"Not really. Just bad circumstances," Jorge said, taking a seat beside her. "I, uh, actually like the guy."

She looked at him. "I don't dislike him. I don't really know him."

"Could have fooled me."

She ignored that. "Jorge, how did it happen? We were all there. The place was spilling over with cops. And someone shot and killed Smirnoff—with all of us there—and we don't know who or how."

"They were counting on the place being filled with cops, Jasmine. Detectives will be on the case and our crime scene techs will find a trajectory for the bullet that killed him. We do our part, they do theirs. Thing is, whoever killed him, they were just the working part of the bigger machine. We have to get to the major players—Kozak, whoever else. Not that the man or woman who was pulling the trigger shouldn't serve life, but…it won't matter."

"No, it won't matter," she agreed. What they needed to do was find Mary. She nodded.

He took her hand and squeezed it. "You're just thrown. We weren't expecting to take them all down tonight."

"We weren't expecting Smirnoff to get killed tonight. I—I didn't even know he'd gone to the FBI!"

"I knew but couldn't tell you. And I didn't know that Smirnoff would be killed before I had a chance to loop you in. I'm sorry—I put you and Wolff both in a bad position. At least you didn't shoot each other. You know you're resenting him because he had you down."

"He did not have me down."

"Almost had you down."

"I almost had him down."

"Ouch. Take a breath," Jorge warned.

She did, and she shook her head. "I worked with a Fed once."

"And he was okay, right? Come on, we're all going in the same direction."

"He was great. Old dude—kept telling me he had a granddaughter my age. Made me feel like I should have been in bed by ten," Jasmine said and smiled.

Jorge arched his brow at her.

"Okay, okay," she said. "I resent the fact he almost had me down. But really, I almost had him, too." She squeezed his hand in return. "How come we never have discussed our love lives and this stranger knew more about you than I did?"

"'Cause neither of us cares what our preferences are, and we work well together—and we enjoy what we're doing. And Wolff for sure had all of us checked out before agreeing to work with us. He'd need to know our backgrounds and that we're clean cops. Also, you're a workaholic and even when we're grabbing quick food or popping into a bookstore, we're still working."

"Not really," she told him. "Honestly, not until this operation."

He nodded. "Mary," he said softly.

"Jorge, I'm so afraid she's dead." She paused. "Even

more now. Do you have any details about the oil drums they found today? All I've seen is what has been on the news. Captain Lorenzo was even with the cops doing the interviews at the show, but I didn't get to ask him anything. Obviously, I did my best to be a near hysterical model."

"You were terrific."

She laughed. "So were you." Jasmine tried to smile, but she was searching out his eyes.

"Mary wasn't in one of the oil drums," he said.

"You're sure?"

"Positive. The bodies discovered were all men."

"Oh, thank God. I mean… I'm not glad that anyone was dead, but—"

"It's all right," Jorge assured her. "I understand. So, tomorrow will be tense. I'm going to get out of here. Let you get some sleep." He started to rise, and then he didn't. "Never mind."

"Never mind?"

"I'm going to stay here."

"I don't need to be protected," she said. "Bolts on the door, gun next to the bed."

"You don't need to be protected?" Jorge said. "I do! Safety in numbers. Bolt the door and let's get some sleep."

She rose. "Okay, I lied, and you're right—anyone can be taken by surprise. And I have been a jerk and I don't know why."

"I do," Jorge said softly. "You really shouldn't be working this case. You have a personal involvement. And in a way, so do I. I've met Mary."

Jasmine nodded. "I don't feel that I'm really up to speed yet, despite what we learned from Wolff. I'll get you some pillows and bedding," she told him.

"What time are we supposed to be where?" he asked her as she laid out sheets on the sofa.

"Ten o'clock, back at the club."

"I'm willing to bet half of it will still be shut down."

"We won't be going to the floor. We'll be picking up our pay in the offices, using the VIP entrance on the side to the green room and staging areas."

"You know that we can get in?"

She nodded. "I wound up with Natasha and the other girls in a little group when the police were herding people for interviews. Natasha asked the lead detective—Detective Greenberg is in charge for the City of Miami Beach—and he told her that they'd cordon off the club area until they finished with the investigation. Owners and operators were free to use the building where the police weren't investigating."

"Then go to bed. We'll begin again in the morning."

Jorge was clearly thinking something but not saying it.

"What?" she pressed.

"I didn't know until today that the FBI was in on this case—the briefing was why I arrived late. MDPD found the group operating the Gold Sun Club to be shady, as did the cops with the City of Miami Beach. But there's been no hard evidence against them and nothing that anyone could do. I know you've been talking to Captain Lorenzo about them for a while, but…we just found out today that Smirnoff was about to give evidence against the whole shebang. I'm just—"

"Just what?"

He grimaced. "I like the Feds. They have more resources than we do. They have more reach across state lines. Across international lines. And I don't know how long I'll get to be one of the models—if the big show ended in disaster, I could be out fast. And then I won't be around to help you."

"I'm willing to bet the Deco Gang will keep planning. Kozak will say that all the people who had been hired for jobs at the club will still need work. He'll go forward in Smirnoff's name—Smirnoff would not want to have been frightened off Miami Beach. We'll be in."

"You will be. I may not. So, I'm just glad that… well, that there's another law enforcement agent undercover on this case. Speaking of undercover…" Jorge grabbed his blanket and turned around, smiling as he feigned sleep.

Jasmine opened her mouth to speak. She shook her head and went to the bedroom. Ready for bed and curled up, she admitted to herself that she just might be glad for Jacob Wolff's involvement, too.

She had assumed the group was trading in prostitution, turning models into drug addicts and then trafficking them.

She hadn't known about the bodies in the barrels. And she hadn't suspected that Smirnoff was going to die.

So she was glad she would have backup if she had to continue getting close to these dangerous players. Otherwise she probably should back right out of the case.

Except she just couldn't. They had Mary. They had her somewhere.

And Jasmine had to pray her friend was still alive.

Chapter Three

Jacob could remember coming to South Beach with his parents as a child. Back then, the gentrification of the area was already underway.

His mom liked to tell him about the way it had been when she had been young, when the world had yet to realize the beauty and architectural value of the art deco hotels—and when the young and beautiful had headed north on South Beach to the fabulous Fontainebleau and other such hotels where the likes of Sinatra and others had performed. In her day, there had been tons of bagel shops, and high school kids had all come to hang out by the water with their surfboards—despite a lack of anything that resembled real surf.

It was where his parents had met. His father had once told him, not without some humor, that he'd fallen in love over a twenty-five-cent bagel.

The beach was beautiful. Jacob had opted for a little boutique hotel right on the water. Fisher House had been built in the early 1920s when a great deal around it had been nothing but scrub, brush and palms. It had been completely renovated and revamped about a decade ago and was charming, intimate and historic, filled with framed pictures of long ago. The back door opened to a vast porch—half filled with dining tables—and then a tiled path led to the pool and beyond down to the ocean.

Jacob started the morning early, out on the sand, watching the sun come up, feeling the ocean breeze and listening to the seagulls cry. The rising sun was shining down on the water, creating a sparkling scene with diamond-like bits of brilliance all around him.

It was a piece of heaven. Sand between his toes, and then a quick dip in the water—cool and yet temperate in the early-morning hour. He loved it. Home for him in the last few years had been Washington, D.C., or New York City. There were beaches to be found, yes, but nothing like this. So, for the first hour of the day, he let himself just love the feel of salt air around him, hear the lulling rush of waves and look out over the endless water.

There was nothing like seeing it like a native. By 9:00 a.m., he was heading along Ocean Drive. The city was coming alive by then; roller skaters whizzed by him and traffic was heavy. Art galleries and shops were beginning to open, and tourists were flocking out in all manner of beach apparel, some wearing scanty clothing and some not. While most American men were fond of surf shorts for dipping in the water, Europeans tended to Speedos and as little on their bodies as possible. It was a generalization; he didn't like generalizations, but in this case, he was pretty sure he was right.

A fellow with a belly that surely hid his toes from his own sight—and his Speedo—walked on by and greeted Jacob with a cheerful "good morning" that was spoken with a heavy foreign accent.

Jacob smiled. The man was happy with himself and

within the legal bounds of propriety for this section of the beach. And that was what mattered.

He stopped into the News Café. It was a great place to see…and be seen. Before he'd been murdered, the famous designer Gianni Versace had lived in one of South Beach's grand old mansions. He had also dined many a morning at the News Café. Tourists flocked there. So did locals.

Jacob picked up a newspaper, ordered an egg dish and sat back and watched—and listened.

The conversation was all about the shooting of Josef Smirnoff at what should have been one of the brightest moments in the pseudo-plastic environment of the beach.

"You can bring in all the stars you want—but with *those* people—"

"I heard it was a mob hit!"

"Did you know that earlier, like in the morning, three bodies were found in oil drums out in the Everglades?"

"Yeah. I don't think anyone had even reported them missing. No ID's as of yet, but hey…like we don't have enough problems down here."

People were talking. Naturally.

"Told you we shouldn't have come to Miami."

"Hey, mobsters kill mobsters. No one else was injured. Bunch of shots, from what I read, but only the mobster was killed."

Someone who was apparently a local spoke up.

"Actually, honestly, we're not that bad a city. I mean, my dad says that most of our bad crimes are committed by out-of-towners and not our population."

Bad crimes… Sure, like most people in the world,

locals here wanted to fall in love, buy houses, raise children and seek the best lives possible.

But it was true, too, that South Florida was one massive melting pot—perhaps like New York City in the last decade. People came from all the Caribbean islands, Central and South America, the countries that had once comprised the Soviet Union, and from all over the world.

Most came in pursuit of a new life and freedom. Some came because a melting pot was simply a good place for criminal activity.

While he people-watched, Jacob replayed everything he had seen the day before in his mind. He remembered what he had heard.

Witnesses hadn't been lying or overly rattled when they had reported that it seemed the shots had come from all over. From the bar, he'd had a good place to observe the whole room. And then, as Ivan had muttered that they could go closer and see, they had done so.

The shooter hadn't been close to Josef Smirnoff— Jacob had been near him and if someone had shot him from up close, he'd have known.

He was pretty sure that the shooters had been stationed in the alcoves on the balcony that surrounded the ground floor, just outside the offices and private rooms on the second floor. The space allowed for customers to enjoy a band from upstairs, without being in the crowd below.

When he'd looked up at the balconies earlier, he hadn't seen anyone on them. The stairs might have been blocked.

Would Jasmine have known that detail? Or would they have shared that information with a new girl?

Jasmine had, beyond a doubt, drawn attention last night. She had been captivatingly beautiful, and she had played the runway perfectly, austere and yet with a sense of fun. She was perfect for the role she was playing.

The band, the models, the excitement… It had all been perfect for the setup. It was really a miracle that no one else had been hit.

He had thought that Jasmine was going after Josef Smirnoff when he had seen her lunge at him—getting close to see that the deed was done, that he was finished off if the bullets hadn't done their work. He'd never forget her surprise when he had tackled her…

Nor his own shock when she had thrown him off.

He was surprised to find himself smiling—he wasn't often taken unaware. Then again, while he'd known that MDPD had police officers working undercover, he hadn't been informed that one of them was working the runway.

A dangerous place.

But she worked it well. She had an in he could never have.

He pictured it all in his mind again. There had been multiple shooters but only one target—Josef Smirnoff. Create panic, and it might well have appeared that Smirnoff had been killed in a rain of bullets that could have been meant for anyone.

Jacob paid his bill and headed out, walking toward Dolphin Galleries. He felt the burner phone in his left pocket vibrate and he quickly pulled it out. Dean Jenkins, his Miami office counterpart, was calling.

"You alone?"

The street was busy, but as Jacob walked, he was

well aware that by "alone," Dean was asking if he was far from those involved with the Deco Gang.

"I am," he said.

"They're doing the autopsy now. Someone apparently had a bead on the bastard's heart. It's amazing that no one else was hurt. Oh, beyond cuts and bruises, I mean. People trampled people. But the bullets that didn't hit Smirnoff hit the walls."

"They only wanted Smirnoff dead. Kill a mobster, and the police might not look so hard. Kill a pretty ingenue, a pop star or a music icon, and the heat never ends."

"Yep. I wanted to let you know that I'm on the ground with the detective from the City of Miami Beach and another guy from Miami-Dade PD. Figured if I was around asking questions I'd be in close contact, and you could act annoyed and harassed."

"Good."

"You met the undercover Miami-Dade cops, right?" Dean asked.

"I did. We've talked."

"Good. The powers that be are stressing communication. They don't want any of you ending up in the swamp."

"Good to hear. I don't think I'd fit into an oil drum. Don't worry, we've got each other's backs."

"Have you been asked to move any money for the organization yet?"

"On my way in to the gallery now," Jacob said. "I expect I'll see someone soon enough."

"It may take some time, with that murder at the club last night, you know."

"A murder that I think they planned. I'd bet they'll contact me today."

"You're on. Keep up with MDPD, all right? Word from the top. Both the cops and our agency are accustomed to undercover operations, but this one is more than dicey."

"At least I get to bathe for this one," Jacob told him.

"There's a bright spot to everything, huh?"

"You bet."

He ended the call, slid the phone back in his pocket and headed toward the gallery.

The sun was shining overhead. People were out on the beach, playing, soaking up the heat. The shadow of last night's murder couldn't ruin a vacation for the visitors who had planned for an entire year.

Besides, it was a shady rich man, a mobster, who had been killed.

He who lives by the sword...

Jacob turned the corner. Ivan Petrov was standing in front of the gallery, studying a piece of modern art.

MOE, CURLY AND LARRY—or, rather Alejandro Suarez, Antonio Garibaldi and Sasha Antonovich—were upstairs when Jasmine arrived with Jorge at precisely 10:00 a.m. the next day.

Alejandro was at the top of the stairs. Sasha was at the door to what had once been Josef Smirnoff's office and was now the throne room for Victor Kozak.

Jasmine had made a point of greeting both Alejandro and Sasha. She presumed that Antonio was in the room with Victor, which he was. She saw him when the door to that inner sanctum opened and Natasha Volkov walked out.

The door immediately shut behind her, but not before Jasmine could see that Victor Kozak was seated at what had been Josef Smirnoff's desk.

The king is dead; long live the king, she thought.

This had shades of all kinds of Shakespearean tragedy on it. Apparently, Josef Smirnoff had known that someone had been planning to kill him—he just hadn't known who. Maybe he had suspected Kozak but not known. And he probably hadn't imagined that he'd be gunned down at the celebrity opening for the club.

She knew that Smirnoff hadn't exactly been a good man. She had heard, though, that he wasn't on the truly evil side of bad. He'd preferred strong-arm tactics to murder. He'd rather have his debts paid, and how did a dead man pay a debt?

Jasmine couldn't defend Smirnoff. However, she believed that Kozak was purely evil. It made her skin crawl to be near him. She had a feeling he'd kill his own mother if he saw it as a good career move.

"Ah, you are here! Such a good girl," Natasha said, slipping an arm around Jasmine's shoulder and moving her down the hallway. She turned back to Jorge. "You come, too, pretty boy. You are a good boy, too."

Jorge smiled.

Natasha opened the door into a giant closet–dressing room combo. There were racks of clothing and rows of tables with mirrors surrounded by bright lights for the girls to use. Before the show the day before, the room had been filled with dressers, stylists and makeup artists.

"So sad. Poor Josef," Natasha said, admitting them through the door and then closing it. She made a display of bringing her fingers to her eyes, as if she'd been crying. Her face was not, however, tearstained.

"We are all in shock, in mourning today," Natasha added. "So, let me pay you for last night and we will talk for a minute, yes? Maybe you can help."

"Definitely," Jasmine said. "Talking would be good. Mr. Smirnoff was so kind to all of us. It's so horrible what happened."

"Terrible," Jorge agreed.

"So." Natasha grabbed a large manila envelope off one of the dressers and took out a sizable wad of cash. She counted off the amount for each of their fees. When Natasha casually handed it over, Jasmine saw it was all in large bills. It seemed like a lot of cash to have lying around.

Natasha indicated a grouping of leather love seats and chairs where models and performers waited once their makeup was complete.

Jorge and Jasmine took chairs.

"You—you were very brave," she said, looking at Jasmine. "I was behind the curtain, but I saw the way you protected Kari and tried to help poor Josef."

"Oh, no, not so brave," Jasmine said. "When I was a child… I was with my parents in the Middle East, and my father taught me to get down, and get everyone around me down, anytime I heard gunshots. It was just instinct."

"I tried to get to Jasmine," Jorge said, "because she's my friend."

"Of course, of course," Natasha said. "But you two and Kari were the ones who were out on the runway when it all happened. What did you see? Of course, I know that the police talked to everyone last night, but… we're so upset about Josef! Perhaps you've remembered something…something that you might have seen?"

Jasmine shook her head. "Oh, Natasha. This is terrible, but I was only thinking about saving myself at first. I didn't see anything at all." Jasmine wished that she wasn't lying. She could easily be passionate because her words were true. She wished to hell that she had seen something—anything.

She had just heard the bullets flying. And seen Josef Smirnoff go down.

"I'm so, so sorry," she said. "Of course, I suppose this means that... Well, if you need anything from me in the future, I'd be so happy to work with you again."

Natasha smiled. "Jasmine, you must not worry. We will always have a need for you. We are a loyal family here! And, Jorge, of course, you, too."

"Thank you," Jorge said earnestly.

"But nothing—nothing at all?" Natasha persisted. "Tell me about your night, from the time you stepped out on the runway."

"It was so wonderful!" Jasmine said. "At first, I could hear the crowd. We were having a great time on the runway, and I heard people laughing and having fun... and then, that sound! I didn't realize at first that I was hearing bullets. And then...then it was as if I knew instantly. My past, maybe," she whispered. "And I went for Kari, and when I saw Josef down on the floor, I wanted to help... He'd been good to me, you know? Then that man—a friend of Josef's, I think—thought that I was trying to hurt Josef, and he...he tackled me."

"And you were angry, of course," Natasha murmured.

"Well, at first, of course, but it was okay after. He apologized to me. He told me he thought that I wanted to hurt Josef. He was very sincere. So apologetic."

"He saw to it that we got back to Jasmine's place safely. I liked him," Jorge said.

"And you, Jasmine? Did you like him?" Natasha asked.

"After we talked, of course. He was very apologetic. He told me that he's new to Miami Beach—new to Miami. He was working up north, but he got tired of snow and ice and had some connections to help him start up in business down here, and so…he was sad that his first time really heading to a fine event ended so tragically."

"So. He made moves on you," Natasha said softly. She wasn't pleased, and Jasmine recognized why.

Jasmine was now a commodity—one controlled by Natasha—even if she wasn't supposed to really under-stand that yet. This newcomer needed to go through Natasha—her and Victor Kozak now—if he wanted to have Jasmine as his own special escort.

"Oh, no, he didn't make moves," Jasmine said.

"He was a gentleman. Almost as if he was one of your security people. He just saw that we got home safely," Jorge said. He looked at Jasmine. "I thought maybe he liked me better."

"Oh?" Natasha said. "Interesting."

"No, no, Jorge—he didn't like you better!" Jasmine said. She knew that Jorge was smirking inwardly, and yet he was playing it well. They were both saying the right things in order to be able to stay close with Jacob as they ventured further into the world of Deco Gang.

They needed everyone in on this—Federal and local. Jorge had been right.

"You found him to be a nice man?" Natasha asked.

"Very," Jorge said before Jasmine could answer.

"Jorge, I am sorry, I don't think that he's interested in you," Natasha said. "He did express interest in Jasmine. But we shall see. Be nice to him, if he should see you or try to contact you. But if he does so, you must let me know right away."

"Of course," Jasmine said, eyes wide. "I know that you'll watch out for me."

"Yes, of course. We will watch out for you," Natasha said. She smiled. "We are family here. So, now, come with me. There will be another event soon enough. We will mourn Josef, of course. But so many are dependent on us for a living, we cannot stop. We will have a memorial or something this weekend on the beach. You will be part of it. We are family, yes? We don't let our people…down. For now, you will give Victor Kozak your…condolences."

Give him their condolences. If this had been happening just years earlier, they might well have been expected to kneel and kiss Kozak's ring.

She and Jorge both smiled naively. "Definitely," Jasmine said.

They rose; Jasmine led them down the hall.

Antonio and Alejandro were by the door to the office. Jasmine knew that Sasha Antonovich had to still be guarding the door.

Natasha tapped on the door to the office. Kozak called out, "Come in," and they entered.

He was alone, poring over papers that lay on the table before him.

"We're so sorry for your loss," Jasmine ventured timidly when Kozak didn't look up.

"The police are still in the club downstairs," he said, shaking his head. "They want to know about the balconies. I want to help them. I want to find the person who did this to our beloved Josef. But the balconies were closed off. Just with velvet cords, of course, but... Ah, Jasmine! We were all so enchanted with your performance," he said, looking up. "And you, too, of course. You were the perfect foil for the girls," he told Jorge.

"Thank you," Jorge murmured.

"I don't know who was on the balcony," Victor went on. "We'd said there would be no one on the balcony."

"Maybe the police have ways to find out," Jorge suggested in a hopeful voice.

Victor Kozak waved a hand in the air. "Maybe, maybe not. We'll keep up our own line of questioning. Anyway..."

He seemed to stop in midthought and gave his attention to them. "Please, I know that you were hired by Josef, but...it is my sincere hope that you will remain with us. We pay our regular models a retainer, which you will receive while we wait for this...for this painful situation to be behind us. That is, if you still wish to be with us."

"For sure!" Jasmine said.

"Retainer? Me, too?" Jorge asked hopefully.

Kozak glanced over at Natasha. She must have given him her approval with the slightest nod.

"Yes, you were quite the centerpiece for our lovely young girls. We have a reputation for always having beautiful people in our clubs. All you need to do is be around, available to us, and maybe meet some people we'd like to introduce you to. Please, we will be in touch. You may come in tomorrow for your paychecks."

They both thanked him profusely. Natasha led them down to the street.

As they were going out, Kari Anderson was just arriving. She threw her arms around Jasmine, shaking.

"I don't think I had a chance to thank you. You saved my life!" Kari told her.

"Kari, I just made you get down," Jasmine said, flushing and very aware that both Natasha and Sasha were watching the exchange. "Instinct!" she added quickly. "And we're all just so lucky...except for poor Josef."

"I know, it's so terrible," said the young blonde, her empathy real. Jasmine liked Kari. She was an honest kind person who seemed oblivious to her natural beauty. "Josef was always nice. It's so sad. Terrible that people do these things today! Terrible that poor Josef was caught in it all."

Naive—just like Mary, Jasmine thought. Not lacking confidence but unaware of just how much they had to offer.

"Come on up. We will straighten it all out with you, Kari," Natasha said. "We will be all right. Victor will see to it," she added. "Now, you two run along and try to enjoy some downtime. Kari, come with me. We will have work for all of you—you needn't stress."

"See you, Kari," Jorge said, waving.

He and Jasmine started down the street while Natasha led Kari past Sasha and up the stairs.

"I worry about her," Jasmine said.

"I worry about all of us," Jorge said. "I was worried about the two of us unarmed during the show. We were taking a major chance."

"We knew there would be cops all over."

"Right. And Josef Smirnoff is dead and bullets were flying everywhere."

She couldn't argue that.

"So, tomorrow, we go back for our checks. Our retainer checks," she murmured.

"And you know we're going to be asked to do something for those checks."

"At least I don't think they're remotely suspicious of us," Jasmine told him.

"Not yet. We're still new."

"Kari came in just ahead of me," Jasmine said. "She…she was a replacement for Mary, I think."

"Here's the thing—what do we do when they want something from us that we don't want to do?" Jorge asked. "We haven't gotten anyone to admit to any criminal activity. If they ask you to be an escort, that's actually legal. So, you go off with someone they set you up with—and that guy wants sex. What do you do? Arrest the guy? That won't get us anywhere. And you sure as hell aren't going to compromise yourself."

"You may be asked first."

"I'm pretty—but not as pretty as you are."

Jasmine laughed. "Beauty is in the eye of the beholder, you know."

"Trust me on this. You'll be first. They'll tread a little more lightly with me."

Jasmine shook her head. "We have to get in more tightly, hear things and find something on them. You're right. They'll deny they have anything to do with illegally selling sex—I'm sure they've got that all worked out." She sighed. "I guess that our FBI connection will do a better job—he'll find out what they're doing with the money."

"How do we prove murder?" Jorge asked softly.

Jasmine lowered her head.

Jorge took her shoulders and spun her around to look at him. "We don't know that Mary is dead."

"I know," she whispered.

She was startled when her phone started to ring; it was a pay-as-you-go phone, one purchased in her cover name, Jasmine Alamein.

She looked at Jorge. "It's Natasha."

"Answer it!"

"Ah, Jasmine, my darling," Natasha said. "I'm so glad to reach you so quickly."

"Yeah, no problem," Jasmine said.

"We have a favor to ask of you. It includes a bonus, naturally."

"What is it?" Jasmine asked. Jorge was staring at her, wary.

"That friend of Josef's—Mr. Marensky. He is new in town. He has asked if you would be so good as to show him around. We'd be happy if you could do so— he came to us, instead of trying to twist our arm for a phone number. You will take him around town, yes? I said that wrong. He wishes to take you to dinner and perhaps you could show him some of the beach. And report to me, of course."

"Yes, for sure. Where do you want me to be when?" Jasmine asked.

"He will call for you at your apartment. Please, make sure your friend is not there when he arrives."

"What time?"

"Eight o'clock tonight."

"Thank you, Natasha. I will be ready."

"Wear something very pretty." Natasha didn't mean pretty. She meant *sexy.*

"I will. Thank you. Thank you!"

"My pleasure. Tomorrow morning you will come back in here."

"Yes, Natasha." Jasmine hung up. Jorge was staring at her. "My first date."

"I was afraid of this."

"She doesn't want you hanging around when my date comes for me."

"Like hell!"

"It's Jacob—*Marensky*."

"Oh." Jorge breathed a sigh of relief.

"I'm just a little worried," Jasmine said.

"About Jacob?"

Jasmine laughed. "Not on that account—I'm not sure he's particularly fond of me."

"You were acting badly."

"I was not—"

"You were."

"Never mind. I'm just wondering what good it's going to do if we just wind up watching one another."

"Trust me. That man has a plan in mind."

"I hope you're right. I'm so worried."

"Jasmine, we just went undercover. You know as well as I do that often cops and agents have to lead a double life for months to get what they're after. Years."

"This can't take that long," she said softly. She didn't add the rest of what she was thinking.

If it did...they might well end up dead themselves.

Chapter Four

Jacob arrived at Jasmine's apartment at precisely 8:00 p.m. She was ready, dressed in a halter dress and wickedly high heels. The assessment he gave her was coolly objective. And his words were even more so.

"You know how to play the part."

"Hey, I'm just a naive young model willing to let a rich guy take me out for an expensive dinner," she told him.

"Jorge?"

"They told me not to have him here."

"What is he doing tonight?"

"Catching up on his favorite cable show," Jasmine said. "Playing it all low."

"At his studio?"

Jasmine nodded and turned away.

Her captain had gone along with this at her say-so. But the FBI seemed to know way more than the police. She was certain that Jacob Wolff knew all about her fake dossier and Jorge's fake dossier, and she felt woefully late to the party.

"Hey." To her surprise, he caught her by the shoulders and spun her around. "This isn't a jurisdictional pissing match, you know. The FBI started planning the minute we heard from Smirnoff. You didn't know because we didn't inform the cops until it was absolutely necessary they knew we were in town. We had no idea you were in the middle of an undercover operation—we've had an eye on these guys for a while. Smirnoff coming in was the opening we needed."

He was right; they'd both had separate operations going on. And she'd wanted this case. She'd talked her captain into it being important. The bodies in the oil drums had proved she was right. Provided they could link them back to the Deco Gang.

"I'm sorry," she murmured.

"I worked something like this in New York not that long ago," he told her. "The Bureau crew I wound up working with hadn't known about me. It's always like that. A need-to-know basis. Fewer people to say things that might get you killed."

"Yes, but now—"

"Now, we're in it together. And now we need to head out. Where would you like to have dinner?"

"Wherever."

He grinned. "I'm supposed to be a very rich guy, you know. Oh, and with the power to push ahead at any given restaurant."

"How rude!"

"Yes, absolutely. But we're playing parts. And we need to play those parts well."

"How have your people gotten to so many restaurants?" Jasmine asked.

"They haven't," he said. "No one will say it, but everyone is afraid of the Deco Gang."

"Ah," Jasmine said. "Well, then, we're in the middle of stone crab season. I say we go for the most popular."

"Sure."

As they left her apartment, he slipped his arm through hers. Jasmine stiffened.

"Play along," he murmured.

"You think they're watching?"

"I think they could be at any given time."

She didn't argue that.

"I didn't bring a car. Taxi or an Uber?" he asked.

"I'm fine walking."

"In those shoes?"

She shrugged. "Not my favorite, but we're going about seven blocks. Over a mile in these? I'd say taxi or Uber!"

They walked past T-shirt shops and other restaurants with tables that spilled out on the sidewalk. It was a beautiful night. Balmy. It had to be in the midseventies. Jasmine could smell the salt on the air, and, over the music that escaped from many an establishment, she could hear the water—or at least she could imagine she heard the waves crashing softly up on the shore. Here where they walked, the sand and water were across busy Collins Avenue; the traffic was almost always bumper-to-bumper. She knew young people often came just to cruise the streets, showing off their souped-up cars.

She didn't get it; never had cared for fancy cars.

People in all styles of dress thronged the sidewalks. Some were decked out to the hilt, planning to visit one of the clubs or see a show. Others were casual, out just to shop or dine in a more casual fashion. While the South Beach neighborhood of Miami Beach was trendy and filled with great deco places, boutiques and more, heading farther north, one crossed Lincoln Road, a pedestrian mall and beyond that, a lot of the more staid grande dame hotels from the heyday era when Al Capone and his mobsters had ruled, and later the fabled Rat Pack had entertained, along with other greats.

The beach was like a chameleon, ready to change for every new decade.

At an old and ever-popular restaurant, known for its stone crabs while in season, they did find they were welcomed by a hostess and discreetly—but far too quickly—shown to a table. Jacob had managed, even with the lines outside wrapping around the building, to get them a private table in a little alcove.

Jacob made a pretense of studying the wine menu. He had known, she was certain, exactly what he wanted from the beginning. He wound up ordering champagne—and club soda, as well. She knew as the evening progressed, the champagne would disappear into leftover club soda.

The waitress was gone—they had both ordered the stone crab claws—and he leaned toward her, taking her hand from across the table, rubbing his thumb lightly over her flesh.

"You talked to your people?" he asked softly.

She nodded. "This afternoon. The three men in the oil drums…one has been there, they estimate, about three years. One several months…and one maybe two weeks or so."

Jacob smiled lightly, his expression expertly at odds with their conversation. "Do you know who they might be? They'll be testing, checking dental records. But so far, they don't match anyone reported missing down here." He hesitated. "We're a land of promise, but… people take advantage of that. I recently worked a case in New York… Here's the thing, and the cause of half the world's problems. When you have nothing at all, you have nothing to lose. People from war-torn countries might be desperate and can be drawn in and then forced to do just about anything." He was quiet for a minute. "Some wind up in oil drums."

"And some," she said, "just want more and more—like Victor Kozak."

"So it appears."

"What do you mean, so it appears?"

"Kozak became kingpin. But when Josef Smirnoff came in to the Bureau, he didn't know who intended to kill him. He just...he was afraid. He ruled so much, controlled so much, and yet must have felt like an ancient king. Someone wanted his throne."

"Just like an ancient king—who could plan to overthrow him unless they had a right to follow in his line?"

"That's true. But... I can't get over how lovely you look in that dress," he said suddenly.

She saw that the waiter had arrived, bearing a large silver champagne bucket filled with ice and a bottle.

"You clean up all right yourself," she said softly. And he did. He was wearing a casual soft taupe jacket over a tailored white shirt. He was a handsome man, she thought—with a bit of the look of a Renaissance poet, except she was certain that while his appearance was that of a tall lean man, he was composed of wire-tight muscle beneath.

The waiter smiled and poured their drinks, and they acted like a couple happily out on a date.

Jacob leaned closer to her again, smiling as he lifted his glass to her. "Josef Smirnoff admitted to dealing drugs, arms dealing, prostitution and money laundering. He swore up and down that he didn't order murder."

Jasmine lifted her glass with a dazzling smile, as well. "And yet, one of those bodies discovered had been there a very long time."

"So, someone might have been getting rid of people without Josef Smirnoff knowing."

"And how could that happen?"

"I don't know. We weren't able to get to Smirnoff for more conversation before he was killed. This had all just sprung into being, you know. It's been a complicated case for us. Smirnoff managed to get hold of an agent in the Miami office, but they didn't have anyone down here that they were certain couldn't be compromised—wouldn't be known by anyone. They appealed to the head offices in Virginia. From there, they called on me. I spent a week immersed in everything related to the Deco Gang, and we were lucky that we could arrange paperwork so it appears that I—as Jacob Marensky—own the Dolphin Galleries."

"So, you didn't know Josef Smirnoff?"

"I can't say that I knew him. But I know what he told people. And he was set up with the US Marshals' office—he would have disappeared into witness protection as soon as we had finished our investigation."

Their dinner was arriving.

"Do you really like stone crabs?" she asked him, hoping that her smile was flirtatious. "They're more of a local delicacy. And here's the thing—the crab lives! They take the claw and toss the crab back in. The claw regrows. That's why they're seasonal."

He lowered his head. His smile was legitimate. "Yes, I've had them, and I actually like them very much."

"Can I get you anything else?" their waiter asked.

They had their crackers, mustard sauces and drawn butter.

"I think we're just fine," Jacob said.

"Lovely," Jasmine agreed.

The waiter left them.

"So, you think someone other than Victor Kozak arranged the murder? You know that the press—and half the people in the country—think he was caught in another act of random violence."

He nodded. "And we have nothing to say."

Jasmine cracked a claw. A piece of shell went flying across the table, hitting Jacob on the left cheek.

"Oh! Sorry!" she said, somewhat mortified.

He laughed. "Not a problem."

"These really aren't date food," Jasmine said. "But then again, we aren't really on a date." She frowned, then made a show of dabbing at his face and laughing. "So, if not Victor Kozak, who would have the power to pull off such a thing as the murder of Josef Smirnoff?"

"It might have been Kozak. If not, there's Ivan Petrov, bartender and manager."

"You think he's high enough on the food chain?"

"Depends on who is in on the coup."

"The only people as close to management as Ivan are the bodyguards—I like to think of them as the Three Stooges."

"On steroids," Jacob said.

"Yes, deadly Stooges," she agreed.

"So, Victor Kozak, Ivan Petrov, Natasha Volkov—and the Stooges," he said.

"I just wonder about the bodyguards. The others are all Russian or Ukrainian, but Alejandro is Colombian, and Antonio is Italian."

"Half Italian," Jacob told her. "His mother is English."

"You do know more than I do."

"They are equal-opportunity crooks," Jacob said drily. "Any group down here can find power elsewhere—even elsewhere around the country."

"Their bookkeeper is from Atlanta," Jasmine murmured.

"Good old Southern boy."

"Girl."

"Pardon?"

"Good old Southern girl," Jasmine said. "And yet…"

"Yet?"

"I don't think she really knows about the criminal enterprises. She gets money after it's been laundered. As far as paperwork goes, they're enterprising citizens, paying their taxes."

"Well, Ivan is deep into it all," Jacob told her. "He was waiting at the gallery when I went in this morning. We made arrangements for the sale of one of the paintings in the gallery."

"As a way to move money?"

"Yeah. He paid way more than the painting is worth. The funds will go into an offshore account. It's all set up."

"So they believe in you?"

"For now…"

He had been studiously cracking a shell. This time, his piece of shell flew across the table—catching Jasmine right in the cleavage.

"Sorry!"

She caught the shell quickly before he could. But the gentleman in him came through; he started to move but stopped. The two of them laughed together. Honest laughter, and it was nice.

"Not really date food," he said. "Unless I were more accomplished at this, of course."

"I don't think you could be much more accomplished," she muttered, afraid that a bit of envy and maybe even bitterness might have made it through in her voice. She caught his curious look. "You speak half a dozen languages," she explained.

He shrugged. "I was just lucky. My family—much like yours—is a mini United Nations. Everyone from everywhere. And I love language. It gets easier to pick up another, if you know the Romance languages, the Latin base always helps for reading, even if it takes a bit. But all languages have rules—well, except for English! It's the hardest. Luckily, it was my first."

"Still…it's impressive."

"You speak Spanish."

"Picked up from growing up in South Florida. Half of my friends are Cuban, Colombian or from somewhere in the islands or South America."

"Or Brazil."

"I do also know a bit of Portuguese," she agreed.

They both smiled again. "So…we're equal-opportunity law enforcement, dealing with equal-opportunity criminals," Jasmine mused.

"So we are," he said. "Let's wander on down Washington Street. We'll stop and have dessert and coffee somewhere else."

"You think we're being followed?"

"I think we're definitely being watched in one way or another."

He paid the check and they left.

"You're from here, right?" he asked her.

"You know all about me, right?" she returned, looking at him.

"Well, I do now. I swear, when I tackled you…I didn't."

"You knew there were cops on the scene."

"They didn't tell me that one of the cops was a woman—modeling as if she were accustomed to the runway. But then you are, correct?"

"You received a full dossier on me after the fact?" Jasmine asked. "I wish that the powers that be might have returned the favor."

"I'm an open book," he told her.

"I'll bet."

"I knew from the time I was a kid I wanted to be in the FBI," Jacob told her. "I had a great uncle who was gunned down—for having the same name as a criminal. He was killed by mistake. Anyway, I got into a military academy, served time in the army and immediately joined the FBI. I've done a lot of undercover work. I seem to blend in well with an accepted and ambiguous foreign criminal look."

"Or latent hippie," she told him.

He grinned.

"If you want to see some of South Florida, I can show you around," she told him.

He smiled, lowering his head. "Great. I grew up here. But you know South Florida better than I do."

She grinned. "I was born here."

"Oh?"

"We traveled a lot—but always lived here. Well, not *here*, but in Miami, in Coconut Grove."

"There are so many areas… An amazing city, really. I think, just four decades or so ago, the population of the area was about three hundred thousand. Now, we're looking at millions." He cast a grimace her way. "Populations always lead to crime," he added.

He could be incredibly mercurial. He slipped an arm around her shoulder and pointed to a café before them. "They're known for their crème brûlée. Shall we?"

"Crème brûlée," she agreed, frowning slightly.

He lowered his head close to hers. "We are being followed," he said, pretending to nuzzle her forehead. "Ten o'clock, just down the street. Our dear friend Alejandro Suarez."

She was careful not to look right away, but let out a tone of delighted laughter and planted a kiss on his cheek.

"Let's have dessert," she said louder.

He took her arm and led her into the café.

"Well," she said as they sat close together. "I'm not sure if we've gotten anywhere, but the stone crab claws were delicious, and this is wonderful crème brûlée."

"Definitely better than some of the undercover work I've done before," he told her. He made a face. "Homeless detail. Sleeping in boxes—and for dinner, French fries out of the garbage."

"Yuck."

"You do what's called for."

"I would have…for this," she murmured.

"So, tell me about Mary. Tell me why you're on this case."

She stared up at him, startled. Somehow, he seemed to know everything. She hesitated and then shrugged.

"Our watchdog has stayed outside," he said softly.

She nodded. He was good at observation; she trusted him.

"Mary," she began. "The Deco Gang has been on

our radar for a long time—they've operated out of restaurants, bars and even dry cleaners, moving on all the time. My usual cases keep me on the mainland. MDPD comes in on cases in many of the cities—Miami-Dade County is made up of thirty-four cities now, with more incorporating all the time. Not all the smaller cities have their own major crime divisions, and so we handle a great deal of it. South Beach does have a major crime unit, but the powers that be approved of us taking over this case. Miami Beach cops had a greater risk of being recognized, even undercover. It's not that they tried to hand off work—it was just a better plan. And honestly, until the bodies were found...I might have been the detective taking it the most seriously. Jurisdiction on this is complicated. The oil drums you saw were discovered up in Broward County, by a Seminole law enforcement official."

"There's the Florida Department of Law Enforcement. They could have taken over."

"And those guys are great. But going in on this, it fell to something Miami-Dade would do. We were investigating a disappearance. We were suspicious of the Deco Gang. And when it came to finding a way to slip in and be close enough, the models the clubs use all the time seemed a good cover. I approached my captain about it."

"You were in."

She shrugged. "In all honesty, I was afraid if I mentioned that a friend of mine had been working with the gang's models and then disappeared, it would be a strike against me in terms of being able to take the case. But it actually worked in my favor—I really knew her, I could talk about her and maybe get some information from the other young women working with them. And Mary, well, she's one of the nicest people you'd ever hope to meet. She looks for the good in everyone. Since I'm a cop, she thinks I'm jaded—though I actually think I'm pretty nice, too. Cops don't have to be asses."

"No, they don't," Jacob agreed, clearly somewhat amused.

"But Mary's problem is that she does look for the good. She has to be slapped in the face by bad to see that it exists."

"She probably is a very good person."

"Kari Anderson—the girl on the runway with me when Josef was shot—reminds me of Mary. They're both natural blondes with huge blue eyes and a trusting manner to go with them. Mary was working dinner theater, but not making much money. She saw the ad for models. She did a few shows with the group—Smirnoff's group is behind a number of entertainment offerings. They've been doing legitimate business, too. They own a bunch of other nightclubs. Anyway, Mary got swept up with Natasha and Josef and what she was doing…and saw no evil in it. And she was excited to get paid so well. Florida is a right-to-work state, so dinner theater may be a group requiring Actors' Equity, but then again, it may not be. She was thrilled. She paid her rent two months ahead with her paycheck from one show. And then there was the regular retainer just for being at the clubs, filling them with beautiful young people… It was easy money at first."

"Did she say anything to you about being nervous?"

Jasmine shook her head. "Never." She hesitated. "The last time I talked to Mary, she was excited. She was going to be a star attraction, working their next show. Which was the opening of the club the other night."

"The one you starred in instead."

"Yes. Look, Mary never said anything to me. She wasn't nervous, as far as I know. She just disappeared. A few weeks ago, she was supposed to meet me for lunch. She didn't show up. Mary's parents passed away when she was eighteen. She's on her own, an only child. She and I have been friends forever—we went all the way through grade school and high school together. We have other friends, but no one else has any other information about her. I don't even know how long she's actually been missing. After she missed our date, I called and called. We had an officer from Missing Persons go in to talk to Josef and Natasha, and they both appeared mystified—according to the officer."

"Have you gotten anything?"

"Not yet. The girls are still getting to know me. No one expected what happened to Josef. But apparently, we're all on retainer. Including Jorge."

"Retainer," Jacob murmured.

"I'm not sure what's next. Jorge and I can go in for checks tomorrow."

"Good. I'll stop by at some point." Jacob leaned back. "Well, I believe I'm supposed to walk you back now."

She nodded, oddly sorry that the evening was ending. It was work. Dangerous work.

Work to find Mary.

"You think we're still being watched?" she asked.

"I do."

He paid, stood and drew out her chair. He very politely took her arm and opened the door for her as they exited the café. He slipped an arm around her shoulders.

"Alejandro still around?" Jasmine asked.

"I think he was sitting at one of the outside tables… that's the back of his head behind us. Nope, he's rising now. I'd say he's going to make sure that I take you home and then leave—not overstepping my bounds."

They walked at a lazy pace, his arm around her but with all propriety.

"Interesting," she murmured.

"What's that?"

"How I'm going to discover that they keep control. I mean, as far as they know, I'm just a girl trying to get ahead in modeling. What if I just liked you and wanted to be with you?"

"I don't know. But if I went outside the rules…"

"I'm wondering if we'd both wind up in oil drums. I can see how they'd blame you. You're officially on the inside. But—"

"You're just an innocent. Well, in their eyes."

They'd reached her apartment. She was in a charming place, ground floor, almost in front of the pool. He walked her to the door and then paused. She wound up with her back against the wall by her door. He had a hand on the wall and was leaning against her.

He lowered his face toward hers and gave her a slow careful kiss. She allowed a hand to fall on his chest, and she wished that she didn't feel that there was absolutely nothing wrong with him. His scent was clean and masculine, mixed with the salty cool ocean air. His chest was vital and alive and yet like a rock. His lips were…

He drew away from her.

"I think that was just right. You might want to smile and laugh and then go in."

"Alejandro is watching?"

"He's right out on the street."

"Lovely, what a lovely night," she said, letting her voice carry.

"I'm sure we'll see each other again," Jacob said. "If you're willing…"

"I just have to check my work schedule."

"Of course." He stepped back, and she turned and let herself into her apartment.

She swung the door shut and slid the locks. And then, she stood there for a long, long time. She brought her fingers to her lips. They felt as if they were on fire.

Chapter Five

"You will pay Mr. Chavez twenty-five thousand for the painting," Victor Kozak told Jacob.

They were seated in the office at the rear of the gallery Jacob was pretending to own. Jacob nodded sagely to Kozak. They had already been through the niceties. They both sat with little demitasse cups of espresso. Kozak had admired the shop. Jacob had expressed his appreciation for Kozak's patronage.

"I don't know this artist," Jacob said.

"Trust me. He is excellent."

"And my commission?"

"Fifteen percent."

Jacob let that sit. He smiled at Kozak. "No disrespect. Twenty percent." He was pretty sure that in all such haggling—legal and illegal—Kozak had a higher limit than the figure he'd started with.

"Eighteen," Kozak said.

"I'm looking forward to working with you. Seeing that wonderful art arrives in our country. But if we're to go forward in the future, I believe we need a set rate now. I will be an excellent gallery to procure all the right artists—but I need to survive. The overhead here is quite high," Jacob told him.

Kozak was thoughtful. "All right, then. Twenty percent."

He rose; their dealings were complete. Jacob stood as well and the two men shook hands.

"Have the police come up with anything as yet regarding the shooter? Or shooters?" Jacob asked.

"No, nothing they have shared. You said *shooters*. You think that more than one man was involved?"

"We both know guns," Jacob told Kozak. "Yes, the shots were coming from at least two angles, maybe three."

"Accomplices," Kozak said, shaking his head. "So much violence in this world." He sighed as he lowered his head in sorrow. "Josef was a good man." He shrugged, a half smile on his face. "A good man—for all that we are. He was simply a businessman, and he had integrity in what he did."

Drugs and prostitution, if not murder. But sometimes, even criminals had their ethics.

"All the security," Jacob said, "and still—"

"Don't worry. What the police don't discover, we will," Kozak assured him.

"Naturally," Jacob said.

"I'm so sorry that this happened. Josef…was your friend?"

"We had a few business deals years ago. Art, you know, is always in the eye of the beholder. He'd commissioned a few pieces through me in my galleries before. When I wanted to come south—no more chipping ice off windows, you know—I looked down here and saw that Josef was opening a club. It's always prudent to establish relationships before opening a business anywhere," Jacob said.

"Josef told me about you." Kozak smiled. "And we do nothing without checking out references. I know that

Josef trusted you. But now…his body will be released on Friday, they tell me."

"And there will be a funeral?"

"Yes, it will be at a little Russian Orthodox church in the city, not on the beach. A private affair. But you will be invited."

"I appreciate the honor and privilege of saying good-bye to an old friend," Jacob told him. "And with your permission, I will be by this afternoon with a small token for our new friendship."

"That will be fine. The club will reopen Friday night, but invitation only. A very small group to begin. We must show the world that we're now a safe place to be."

"This violence… It can happen anywhere. Lightning doesn't usually strike the same place twice. I believe the club will be fine."

Kozak gave him a rueful grin. "Sometimes, such events make a place a curiosity. Think back to the '80s. Paul Castellano and Thomas Bilotti were gunned down in a hit ordered by Gotti in front of Sparks Steak House in New York. The restaurant is still going strong. Down here, Al Capone was often in a suite at the Biltmore Hotel in Coral Gables. The suite is very expensive, and people still love to take it—even though Thomas 'Fatty' Walsh was gunned down at the hotel, supposedly over a gambling dispute." His smile deepened. "The hotel did go down after hurricanes and the Depression. It became a veteran's hospital. It was empty—and very haunted—but it's back to being very chic today."

"Let's hope we don't all have to go down first."

"Not to worry about us. Josef created a strong group of business associates. We will be fine." With that, Kozak took his leave.

Jacob walked him to the door. They both smiled at Jacob's "assistant," who was busy behind the old art nouveau desk that served as their register and counter. Katrina smiled back and waved.

She was a perfect choice for this role. Katrina Partridge had been with the Bureau for nearly twenty years. She was in her midforties, attractive and able to carry off both charm and a completely businesslike demeanor. She also knew the art world backward and forward.

When Jacob was gone, she shook her head, indicating they shouldn't talk in the gallery. She pointed to his office, and he followed her there.

"He was walking around a long time. I think he touched a few of the frames, and… I could be wrong. But he could have planted some kind of a bug."

"Good observation, thank you. So, we're being given our first commission," he told her.

"But that's not enough," Katrina said.

"We could bring him down," Jacob told her. "But there will be a work of art, and who is to say what a work of art is worth?"

"Someone who knows art," she said drily.

"But art is subjective."

"So true. Yes, you're right."

"We're after killers," he said softly. "That's what we want to nail them on."

"I know," Katrina said. "And hey, what's not to like about this assignment? I don't have much going on yet—I'm enjoying my downtime. Sand, beach, lovely weather…"

"Still, be careful, Katrina. We can never know when something may slip. They gunned down a man in a room full of cops and security."

"I'm always careful," she said. She smiled, indicating her back.

She was dressed in a fashionable skirt and blouse ensemble with a handsome tailored jacket. Despite the tailoring, he could see—when she indicated her back—that she was not without her Glock.

He smiled his acknowledgment but found himself worrying about Jasmine Adair.

Modeling. There was no hiding a weapon when dressers were around, making sure that a gown was being worn properly. And she was into it on a personal level—something that was dangerous from the get-go.

He had no right to interfere; her operation had begun before his and they were now required to work together. He had no problem working with police.

It was just that he was attracted to her. He didn't think it possible not to be. She was unique; elegant and a bit reserved, and yet when she smiled, when she laughed, she was warm, vibrant and sensual.

He turned his mind from thoughts of her.

"I'll bring the caviar over in about an hour," he told Katrina.

"All ready, in the container in back. I've dressed it up beautifully, if I do say so myself."

"I'm sure you did," he told her.

They moved back into the gallery. Jacob made a point of informing her that they were commissioning a piece, one that had a buyer already, who was in love with the artist's work.

She made mention of a local up-and-coming artist the buyer might like, as well.

A real customer sauntered into the room. Jacob returned to his office but found himself sitting and doing nothing but thinking.

He had to find a way in that was tighter; he had to be close to Jasmine.

He was still wary, of course. She hadn't turned him into a fool.

Maybe she had. Jacob hadn't felt such an instant attraction...almost a longing...in years.

Not since Sabrina.

"AH, YOU ARE SO beautiful, even in mourning," Natasha told Jasmine, admiring the way the draped black dress fell in sweeps to the floor. "Remember, at this, you will be quiet. You will help our guests with their drinks and food but keep a distance. Victor has ordered that this be a solemn occasion. You understand?"

"Yes, Natasha," Jasmine assured her.

Natasha looked over at Jorge, handsome in a conservative black suit. "You two will do well, I believe." She called to the little seamstress who hurried over. "I don't think that the hem needs to come up, but at the waist...a half an inch?"

"Yes, ma'am, of course," the seamstress said. She poked and prodded at Jasmine for a minute, pinning the waist and then nodding.

Jasmine thanked her. The tiny woman helped her slip out of the dress, and carried it away.

As Jasmine reached for her jeans and T-shirt, she was aware that Natasha was assessing her again—as she might assess meat in a market.

"So, last night, you were charming?"

"Yes, he took me for a nice dinner, and I told him about the beach."

"Very good. He likes you."

"I believe so."

Natasha turned away. "You could be asked to do much worse," she said, almost to herself, rather than to Jasmine. "So, now…jeans and a T-shirt. You must dress more…ah, how do I say this? Much prettier, to come in here."

"Business clothes."

"No, the halter dress you wore last night. Very pretty. And heels. No sneakers."

"Definitely, whatever you say."

"Victor would like to see you. I wish there was more time…time for you to go home. Ah, what am I thinking? I still have clothing from the show!" Natasha beamed, and caught Jasmine's hand. "No, no. Don't put your jeans back on."

"Oh…okay."

Natasha left her standing on the little podium where dresses were fitted and headed back to the racks of clothing that remained hanging in the massive closet space. She searched through the racks until she evidently found something that pleased her.

When she returned, she had hangers that bore a sleeveless silk blouse and a red skirt. "These will do," she said.

The skirt was short. Very short.

Jasmine donned the clothing. She smiled, hoping to show that she was feeling friendly with Natasha. "I don't think that the sneakers go with this so well."

"Ah, but of course not! You're an eight and a half, American size, in shoes?"

"Nine," Jasmine told her.

A very large shoe size, apparently, in Natasha's opinion. "Ah, well, you are tall."

She was five-ten. Natasha would be appalled by Jasmine's mom—just five-eight and she wore an eleven.

Natasha brought shoes—four-inch stilettos. "These will be beautiful," she said.

Jasmine slipped on the shoes. She was well over six-feet, now.

"So, come. Victor is happy with you." She turned to Jorge. "You—you will come on Friday evening. The service is at two. Josef will be interred after, and then we will be arriving here."

"Yes, ma'am," Jorge said.

Natasha studied him for a minute and then smiled. "We may have more work for you soon. Showing people Miami Beach—and all its pleasures."

Jasmine knew Jorge well. He didn't miss a beat. "Thank you," he said.

"And, now, you…" Natasha took Jasmine's hand. "Come and see Victor."

"For sure, a pleasure," Jasmine said.

"I'll wait here," Jorge said cheerfully.

"No, Jorge, you are done for today. Antonio will see you out."

Antonio was standing at the door to the large dressing room.

"Call you later!" Jasmine told him cheerfully.

She wasn't feeling so cheerful; she was caught here with nothing, no backup—and she was off to see Victor. She wasn't worried for her life. If she was going to be taken out, they'd have gone after Jorge, too.

Had she done too well with Jacob "Marensky"? Was

she now going to be asked to entertain another of their associates?

There was really no choice but to play it out. She had to wonder if this was where Mary had stood—right before she had disappeared.

With a smile, Jasmine watched Jorge go—and she accompanied Natasha to Victor Kozak's office.

Victor Kozak was not alone.

There was a man in his office. A tall man, he wore a designer suit in charcoal gray. He was perhaps in his midfifties, with iron-gray hair and mustache and watery blue eyes.

They'd both been sitting; Victor behind the desk, the new man in one of the upholstered chairs set before it. They stood politely.

"Ah, Jasmine. I'd like you to meet Mr. Connor," Victor said. "He's visiting from England and knows nothing about Miami Beach. He's hoping you will show him the beach, and to the finest hotel."

JACOB WAS ALREADY on his way to the club when his phone rang. He glanced at the number; he hadn't saved any in his contacts, but rather memorized the last four digits of those he needed to know.

Jorge Fuentes was calling.

"Where are you?" Jorge asked.

"Heading to the club. Why?"

"Head faster. I think they've taken Jasmine in to entertain a client. I mean, she can handle herself, but this is happening way too fast."

"Picking up the pace." Jacob moved forward quickly. "I'll be back in touch as soon as possible."

He didn't run; he might have been observed. But he

could walk fast as hell and he did so. He came to the corner of Washington Street and rounded it, heading to the employee side entrance to the club.

This time, Antonio was leaning against the wall by the door, smoking a cigarette, watching the day.

"Those things will kill you," Jacob said.

"Mr. Marensky. I don't believe we were expecting you."

"I have something for Mr. Kozak. He was just in the shop, you know. I need to get right up there."

Jacob didn't wait for Antonio to respond but hurried past him in a way that meant the goon's only action could be to physically accost him, and the man would still be trying to figure out if Jacob was important enough or not to get through.

Suarez was in the hall.

Jacob made a point of striding past him with a huge grin on his face. "Present for Victor!" he declared, lifting the ice chest filled with caviar that Katrina had so beautifully decorated with multicolored ribbons.

He burst into the office before he could be stopped.

Kozak immediately stood, reaching toward his jacket—and the weapon he surely carried there, Jacob thought. But he didn't draw the weapon.

Good. Jacob was trusted.

Jasmine was there, outfitted like the very expensive and exclusive call girl she was apparently expected to be.

A man had just been leaning over her—either inspecting her or seeking a better look at her cleavage. He was tall and solid, though his face was lined—perhaps from years of worriedly looking over his shoulder. His eyes were a strange, cool blue. Like ice.

"Victor! A present. Forgive me for interrupting. My

source delivered this just this morning, and after we spoke—" He paused. "Excuse me, sir. No disrespect intended. I was in a rush— Jasmine!" he said, breaking up his own run of words. "Hello, and thank you again for last evening. You were a wonderful tour guide."

"I was conducting business with Mr. Connor—" Kozak began.

Jacob brought a frown to his face, and then allowed himself to appear deeply disturbed. "No, sir," he said, addressing Connor.

Connor straightened and stared at Kozak. "Kozak, I want—"

"I'm afraid I already have an interest," Jacob said softly.

"She's just a woman," Kozak muttered beneath his breath.

Jacob was glad that Jasmine appeared not to have heard the words. "Forgive me, but, Mr. Kozak, you're a very busy man. This arrangement was made. Yesterday. And at the show, before he was killed, I received promises from Josef Smirnoff."

"Smirnoff is dead," Connor said.

"But not forgotten," Jacob said.

Kozak was, of course, in a tight position. If he hadn't murdered Josef Smirnoff and was taking over as a natural progression, he had to respect promises made by his predecessor.

"Not forgotten, no. And honored," Kozak murmured. Jacob had given him an out—and he was glad to see that the man wanted his "business" and was willing to take the out.

Jacob turned to Connor.

"I'm new, but…I understand this. Miss Alamein and

I had dinner last night and arranged for a sightseeing tour this evening. I had forgotten to tell Mr. Kozak about my tickets, but I'm afraid that I did specify this… young woman."

"I can make even better arrangements for you, Mr. Connor," Kozak said. "You must understand, we are in mourning right now. And in honor of Josef, I must follow through on all his promises."

"Fine. Call me when you have found a suitable companion," Connor told Kozak. He was looking at Jacob. Sizing him up. Apparently, he determined that the companionship of a certain woman was not worth a battle. He turned and left without another word.

"So, before you came to me…Josef had promised you this woman," Kozak said.

Jacob didn't look at Jasmine. Knowing her as he was coming to know her, he was amazed that she was managing to just sit still.

"When I saw her on the runway," he said, his voice husky, "I knew I wanted her at that moment. I believe she might have been his last promise."

"Then I will make no other arrangements. But you must remember, Miss Alamein is in my employ. And she will appear when she is needed."

"That is understood."

Kozak walked over to Jasmine. "You will honor this arrangement?" he asked her.

Jasmine stood. In the heels she was wearing, she was eye level with Kozak. She smiled sweetly. "As you wish, Mr. Kozak."

"Fine," Kozak said. "Just remember, you work for me," he added softly.

"Always," she told him earnestly. Jasmine's smile

deepened. "And thank you, sir. Thank you. Mr. Marensky and I were able to have the most delicious dinner last night. Far more easily than I might have ever imagined!"

Even Kozak seemed caught by her charm. "My pleasure. So, I believe that Natasha wanted to talk with you one more time. And…" he gave his attention back to Jacob "…Miss Alamein will be ready for you tonight, for these tickets you have."

"I'll wait and escort her home now," Jacob said. "Sir, if you have a minute, the present I brought… I believe you will enjoy it immensely. It is Almas, from the beluga sturgeon—supposed to be some of the finest caviar. I must admit, I am not an expert, but I have been assured by those who are that this is delicious."

"Then you must sit and enjoy it with me," Kozak said. He waved a hand at Jasmine. "See Natasha, see what she needs from you."

Jasmine was dismissed. She left the room.

Jacob looked at Kozak. "I thank you for respecting me—and Josef's memory," he said. "And I would like to do more."

"Oh?"

"I am not without certain skills. I would like your permission to look into Josef's death myself."

BREATHING WAS DIFFICULT.

Jasmine's heart was pounding. She'd been so sure of herself, even in Kozak's office with the very strange *Mr.* Connor all but pawing her, that she'd been figuring out ways to handle the situation herself. Alone with the man, she'd have figured out something…

And blown her cover. And all hope of finding out what had happened to Mary.

She hurried down the hall—smiling at Sasha, on duty there now—to the dressing room. Natasha was at one of the tables, studying her face in the mirror.

She looked at Jasmine, and as she did so, Jasmine had to wonder if the woman's eyes could stretch out of her head, or if she had ears that could extend down a hallway.

Natasha already knew what had happened.

"It's not good," she said. "It's not good at all. One man should not become so possessive."

Jasmine shrugged. "Does it matter?" she asked. "Does it matter if the money is the same?"

"Ah, child, you're new to this," Natasha said.

"Yes, I am. And I am ignorant but willing to learn."

Natasha seemed pleased with her reply. "He will start to think that he owns you and that he would be better off just spiriting you away somewhere. You must be careful and declare your loyalty to us at all times, do you understand?"

"Yes, Natasha. And I am loyal, I promise you."

"And," Natasha added, "you like this Jacob Marensky?"

"He's clean and he smells good. And he is younger."

Natasha waved a hand in the air. "Yes, he is clean and young and smells good. And young can be good. Old men, with their hopes and their prayers and their pills… They have no idea how often those they think they control sit there and do nothing but laugh at their faulty efforts." She shook her head; Jasmine had the feeling she had experienced the worst and earned her way out of it.

"So then, you may have your jeans and your T-shirt. Apparently, Mr. Marensky is a more casual man and you are going on a sightseeing tour." She shuddered as if a sightseeing tour might be akin to torture.

"Thank you," Jasmine said. "I must admit, the shoes…the heels are a lot."

"They make you very tall. Then again, Mr. Marensky is very tall." She waved a hand in the air. "Josef admired the man. Victor believes that he is an admirable man as well, who understands our business but demands that we respect his. You will, of course, report to me."

"Yes, I will."

Jasmine heard voices. A few of the other girls had arrived.

Kari Anderson came into the room, carrying a bundle of clothes. Behind her were Jen Talbot, Renee Dumas and Helen Lee. They were like a palette of beauty—Kari so pale, Jen olive-skinned, Renee almost ebony and Helen extraordinary with her mix of Eurasian features and lustrous long black hair. They were beautiful on a runway.

They had also been hired to please all tastes.

Thus far, though, she hadn't seen any of the women forced into anything. Just pretty girls with an understanding that they could be paid well for their company. She had sat silently herself as Victor had introduced her to Mr. Connor and informed her that he needed a guide and an escort for the evening. What if she had protested?

Had Mary protested?

"I'll just grab my things and change and get out of here," Jasmine said. "And hang these up."

She fled over to the hangers, finding that her clothing had not been hung—just folded as if with distaste and left on the shelving above the racks. She eased out of the shoes and slid out of the skirt.

Kari walked in. "I'm going to need that skirt, I hear," she said.

"Oh?" Jasmine handed her the skirt on its hanger and shimmied the blouse over her head.

"I'm going to go see Mr. Connor," Kari said. She sounded slightly nervous.

"Are you afraid of him?" Jasmine asked in a whisper. "If so—"

"No, no. He's supposed to be very nice."

"I thought he was new."

"No. Mary went out with him. Just dinner. She said he was very nice. Oh, sorry, you didn't know Mary. She was great, but…I guess this wasn't for her. Me, I want the runway. And if it means dating a few losers…" Her voice trailed. "Dating," she repeated drily. "Okay, having sex with a few repulsive specimens… Well, I managed to choose a lot of losers on my own! Might as well have it be worth something in the end, I guess."

"Kari?" Natasha called.

"Excuse me," Kari said to Jasmine. "I have to run!"

Jasmine caught her hand. "Kari—please. Will you call me tomorrow and let me know that you're all right?"

Kari seemed surprised. "Of course, I'll be all right. But thank you. And I will call you—we can maybe have lunch or something?"

"I'd love to have lunch," Jasmine assured her. She hesitated. "It's allowed?"

"Oh, yes. They like us to be friends. Sometimes…"

"Sometimes?"

"Kari!" Natasha called again.

"Later!" Kari told her, and with a swirl of blond hair, she was gone.

KOZAK HAD OPENED a bottle of his special "very Russian" vodka to go with the caviar. Jacob was careful to pretend to sip as much as the crime tsar but imbibe as little as possible.

His time with the man was proving to be very interesting.

Kozak talked about growing up in Russia—about the KGB coming for his father in the middle of the night.

"That must have been very hard on a child," Jacob said.

Kozak shrugged. "My father, he was a killer. When it all broke apart, though…everyone was running. The kind of crime was brutal, from all manner of directions. My mother, bless her, got us out. I never understood. Business is business, but…"

He paused and looked hard at Jacob, very sober despite the vodka he had all but inhaled. "You think you can find Josef's killer?"

Jacob weighed his words carefully. "There have been certain…events in my past that required me to take a closer look at them. I have a talent for uncovering things." He paused. "You really have no idea who killed him?"

Kozak frowned.

"No disrespect," Jacob said quickly. "I liked Josef. We did very good business together. But perhaps, something was going on with the group that was dangerous to all."

"You're talking about the bodies discovered in the Everglades," Kozak said. "There is talk of little but that and the shooting on the news these days. We have even ceased to care about politics, eh? When people are scared…"

He paused and shrugged again. "We had nothing to do with those bodies. Not Josef, not me. And I do not know who killed him. Me, I have kept my boys close—Sasha, Antonio and Alejandro. I have played the game, I have become the king. But you are a newcomer. Down here, that is. Josef trusted you. You know how to stand your ground. You tell me—who killed Josef?"

"I don't know, but as I said, with your permission, I will find out."

"You have my permission—and my blessing. What else do you need?"

"Permission to speak with your boys. And Ivan and Natasha. Whether wittingly or not, Victor, one of them helped the killers."

There was a tap at the door.

"It's me, Mr. Kozak," Jasmine said in a small voice.

"I will see her home," Jacob said, rising and heading to the door. "And I will begin tomorrow. I will find the killer, I promise you."

"Then most definitely, the woman is yours—along with my gratitude," Kozak told him.

Jacob nodded and opened the door. And capturing Jasmine's hand, he hurried down the stairs, Jasmine in his wake.

Chapter Six

"I should have gone with him," Jasmine murmured.

The look Jacob gave her could have turned her to stone. She supposed, in his mind, he had managed not only to save her from a fate worse than death—or actual death, for that matter—but to keep up their undercover guises, as well.

"No, no," she amended quickly. "You were wonderful, magnificent. I mean, you pulled that off, and normal circumstances—"

"Just wait. Wait until we reach your apartment," he said. "At this point, I'm pretty sure it's okay if I come in."

"Are we being followed?"

"Maybe. You never know."

She was surprised when he pulled out his phone. He had such a grip on her with his left hand that she could hear the voice of the man he was calling from his phone in his right hand.

"You got her out?" the voice asked.

Jorge.

"Yes." Jacob glanced her way. "I need tickets, fast. Some kind of sightseeing trip. First available."

"Call you right back."

"Tickets?" Jasmine murmured.

"Tickets."

They were almost to her apartment when the phone rang again. This time, Jorge was speaking more softly.

"Lincoln Road Mall," Jacob relayed.

"We can walk it," Jasmine suggested.

"Then keep walking."

He was angry; she hadn't had a chance to explain yet what she'd meant about wishing she'd gone with Mr. Connor. And on the street the way they were, unaware of how things might go, despite the stand Jacob had just made, he clearly didn't want her talking.

His pace was urgent; she had long legs, and she could trek it, but he was moving fast. They were some distance from the club on Washington Street when he finally seemed to slow—perhaps having burned off some of his energy.

She managed to retrieve her hand from his hold and slide an arm through his, drawing herself close and speaking softly, as if she whispered a lover's words.

"I may have found out how Mary disappeared—and with whom," she told him.

He turned and frowned at her.

"I finally got a second with Kari. She's probably going to wind up going off with this man, Connor. Jacob, Mary met with Connor. She met him—and then she disappeared."

"And you were willing to take that kind of a chance?"

Jasmine swallowed, leaning on his shoulder. "That's what I'm here for. But I didn't find out until after you came and got me out of the room. I saw Kari when I went back to get my own clothing. That's when she told me…and they're going to send her in to be his escort. Jacob, we have to find a way to follow that man. Maybe Jorge—"

"No, Jorge still has an in. And they'd wonder what he was doing. Let me call my office. They'll get someone on it."

He pulled out his phone again. They'd reached Lincoln Road Mall—a pedestrian walkway that offered dozens of shops and restaurants, fun places to dine and enjoy a coffee, a drink, entertainment or an evening.

"It's a private tour company," Jacob said, pointing to a spot by the theaters on Alton Road. "They'll pick us up there."

He veered in that direction, speaking quickly to someone on the phone and giving them the information they had on Connor. Jacob described him to a T. But Jasmine knew he had little else to go on.

She heard rapid questions in return, and then assurances.

"I believe that's ours," Jacob said, pointing to a limo with a sunroof.

The vehicle made a U-turn and pulled to the corner. The driver, a young man in a suit, hopped out and offered them a broad professional smile. "Marensky?" he asked.

"Yes, thank you, Jasmine and Jacob," Jacob said, sliding his phone back into his pocket.

"I'm David Hernandez, your guide for the day!" he said cheerfully. "I'm at your disposal. Now, I understand you're new to the beach, so I'll give you a few suggestions. My first pick is the Ancient Spanish Monastery, but that's north on the beach, so…"

"That's fine," Jacob said quickly. "Is that okay,

honey?" he asked Jasmine, and then he told their guide, "Jasmine knows the place. Me, I'm new."

"I love the Spanish Monastery!" she said. "But I'm not sure I'd be the best guide."

David looked at his watch. "Well, if we move, you can have a couple of hours there. Your assistant ordered a driver and guide until midnight, so—"

"We'll start with the Spanish Monastery," Jacob said.

They slid into the car. With the beach traffic, it was going to take them a few minutes to reach what Jasmine considered to be one of their most intriguing destinations.

"I grew up here, but not on the beach," Jasmine told David.

"Cool. I grew up in the city, by the old Flagler Dog Track—Magic City Casino now," David told them. "People say Miami is young, no history. But we've got tons of it. I could go on forever. But—"

"Please, do, go on forever," Jacob said.

He leaned back in the plush seat of the limo, closing his eyes for a minute. It was the only indication Jasmine had seen that his world could cause him pressure.

He had come in, guns blazing, for her.

She leaned back, as well. She really needed to talk to Captain Lorenzo and give her report. Lorenzo could get cops out after Kari and Connor.

"Of course, South Beach itself is a tourist attraction," David said. "Did you know that it was the original area that was populated? Believe it or not, the beach started out as farmland. The City of Miami itself incorporated on July 28, 1896. Julia Tuttle, our founding mom, had sent an orange blossom to Henry Flagler, convincing him to bring his railroad down—we were almost always frost free!

"The City of Miami Beach was incorporated on March 26, 1915. Now, Miami Beach is comprised of natural and man-made barrier islands. In 1870, Henry and Charles Lum—father and son, by the way, bought a lot of the bracken, sandy, nothing land that's worth billions today. There was a station to help shipwreck victims up north of where you're staying, closer to where we'll be today. They started off with a coconut plantation, but that didn't go so well. Enter some rich Yankees, and the beach started developing.

"Collins Avenue is so named because of an entrepreneur called Collins. He mixed up the crops and got things going. Then with Miami up and running, the railroad coming down and Government Cut created, people were on their way to thinking it would make a great resort area. Enter the Lummus family, who were bankers, and Carl C. Fisher from Indianapolis, who worked with the Collins and Pancoast group, and by the beginning of the twentieth century, Miami Beach was on its way."

David had a great voice—informative, interesting and soothing. Jasmine hadn't realized she had closed her eyes, too—until she opened them and discovered Jacob was looking at her.

"We're on it," he said softly. "The Miami office will speak to your captain and see that the police are aware of this new player."

"I just…" Jasmine paused, looking to the front.

David was going on, talking about the development of the area for tourists. The entrepreneurs had started off developing their crops—avocado, for one—and taking tourists on day trips from the City of Miami. Then came food stands and finally, the Browns Hotel, which was still standing.

"What if this man, Connor, is…a killer?" Jasmine asked quietly. "One of those men who can only get off if he strangles or stabs a woman. What if…?"

"He'll be followed and watched, Jasmine. And, they'll do the same with him as they did with me— just a date, first. Just a date. We'll find out about him, and Kari will be all right."

Kari would be all right. And that meant so much. But what about Mary? She'd been gone nearly a month now.

Jacob started fumbling in his pocket. She realized his phone was buzzing. He answered it in a quiet voice.

David kept speaking. "Collins needed money. He got it from the Lummus guys. He started construction of a wooden bridge. The beach areas went through a number of different names, but you can still find those founding fathers in street names here—and of course, we have Fisher Island, a haven for the very rich. If you really want to find a lot of these founders, we can do that another day.

"You should see the old Miami City Cemetery across on the mainland. It was north of the city limits in 1887 when it was founded. Julia Tuttle is buried there, and oh! If you like Civil War history, we've got some Confederates buried just feet from some Union guys—friends by then, I would think, since they died long after the war. Friends in death, if nothing else."

Jasmine looked at Jacob. He smiled tightly at her. "We have two guys on it. They're trying to dig up something on Connor, but we don't even have a first name for the man."

"He's English. He definitely had an accent."

"I told them that. Jasmine, they're watching Kari. She's at her apartment right now."

"She's an innocent… She's a Mary. She isn't worried about…about anything he might ask her to do. She said she's been with dozens of losers and might as well improve her career chances by going with men chosen for her by Kozak or Natasha. I'll never forgive myself if she gets hurt. I could have gone with Connor."

"She's going to be all right."

Jasmine nodded, taking a deep breath.

David talked on, telling them that when the South Beach area had fallen into a slump, Jackie Gleason had helped to change things doing his famous show from the beach, along with more entrepreneurs who saw the fabulous artistic value of the art deco hotels and buildings.

They were finally nearing their destination.

"The Ancient Spanish Monastery, known officially as the Monastery of St. Bernard de Clairvaux, is really—well, ancient. Construction began in northern Spain in 1133, in a little place near Segovia called Sacramenia. It housed monks for somewhere around seven hundred years, and then there was a revolution and it was sold and became a granary and storage and…not a monastery.

"It came to be here because, in 1925, it was purchased by an American—you guessed it—entrepreneur, Mr. William Randolph Hearst. For a long time, it was known as the world's biggest jigsaw puzzle, because it was shipped to the US as thousands upon thousands of stones.

"Well, then Hearst had some financial problems. He'd wanted to rebuild it at San Simeon, but some of what he'd purchased of the monastery was sold off. The crates—about eleven thousand of them—were in storage in New York. Not to mention there had been an outbreak of hoof-and-mouth disease in Segovia, which meant the packing hay had to be burned and the crates had to be quarantined.

"And then poor Hearst died! More entrepreneurs invested, and all the crates were taken out of storage. Took about a year and a half, they say, to put all the pieces back together. Two businessmen bought them, had them put together and then couldn't afford the fact that the monastery didn't make it right away as a tourist attraction. Financial difficulties again.

"In 1964, it was purchased by Bishop Henry Louttit, who gave it to the diocese of South Florida, which split into three groups. Then it was owned by a very rich and good man, a billionaire and a philanthropist, Colonel Robert Pentland, Jr. He went on that year to give the cloisters to the Bishop of Florida, and voilà! Finally, a church and a tourist attraction. And now, while the monastery is still a great tourist attraction, it's still also an active church. I love going there. It's like stepping back in time."

They arrived. David quickly arranged for their tickets, and Jasmine and Jacob were in, admiring the old stone cloisters and hearing about the historic instruments that were often used in services, seeing some of the artifacts that had come with the monastery—and the carved coats of arms and other relics that had come from other monasteries and venues around Spain.

Then they were out in the gardens, arm in arm, and Jacob was back on the phone again.

"I did get the autopsy information on Smirnoff from my Miami counterpart," Jacob told her as they strolled.

"I realize autopsies are important, but I'm pretty sure I know how Josef Smirnoff died—bullets," Jasmine said.

Jacob nodded. "Yes. But I guess he didn't know he had cancer—colon cancer. According to the ME, Smirnoff must have had it for some time without knowing. He wasn't looking at a long life, even if he'd gone for treatment."

"So, someone murdered him for nothing," Jasmine said. "Kozak was next in line anyway."

Jacob was quiet.

"You don't think it was Kozak?"

"He would just be so obvious. And he denied having anything to do with the bodies in the oil drums."

"Have they finished those autopsies?" Jasmine asked.

Jacob nodded. "They are still waiting on testing. They've gotten fingerprints on the most recent body, but the two other corpses were too decomposed. They think one of the bodies has been there several years."

"I'm assuming they're also trying to trace the oil drums and whatever remnants of clothing they can find?"

Jacob nodded. "They don't have much hope on the oil drums. They were apparently dumped by a major oil company years ago. They were headed to the closest landfill, I imagine. Nice, huh? Anyone could have picked them up."

"But you said they got fingerprints off the most recent corpse?"

He smiled. "As soon as I know, you'll know. Easy now that I've staked my claim on you."

"It does make communication between us a lot easier," Jasmine murmured.

"And hopefully keeps the wolves from baying at your door—and forcing you to show your hand." He grinned at her. "I can appear to be extremely possessive."

She was afraid that her smile was a little fluttery. Because something inside her had fluttered, as well.

His phone rang. He answered and listened intently. "Okay," he said, hanging up. He looked at Jasmine. "Apparently, Mr. Connor doesn't believe in being fashionably late Miami Beach–style. He's at Kari's apartment now."

"So, they're heading to dinner now. We should get back down there—"

"Jasmine, agents are on it."

"I know, but—"

Her phone rang then. She glanced at the number; it was the number that Captain Mac Lorenzo was using for the operation.

"Checking in—and watching out for a valuable asset," he told her.

"I'm fine," Jasmine assured him. "I'm touring the Ancient Spanish Monastery."

"I've spoken with Jorge. We're not pulling either of you out yet. But I also have strict instructions from way high above not to endanger an FBI operation."

"We're not endangering it."

"And you're not to endanger yourself," he reminded her.

"Never, sir," she told him.

"Just make sure you remember the FBI has taken the lead on this, and they're calling the shots."

"I understand." She was careful to keep any remnant of emotion from her voice.

"You're doing all right with interagency communication?"

Jasmine glanced at Jacob. "We're doing just fine, sir."

Jacob must have heard. He arched his brows in a question and reached for the phone.

"Captain Lorenzo, how do you do? Jacob Wolff. We're working on this together well. I don't think we could have planned this out any better."

Jasmine didn't hear what Captain Lorenzo said after that. Jacob handed the phone back to Jasmine and she quickly hung up.

"Thank you for that," she told Jacob.

He shrugged. "I think we are working well together."

"Yes, I guess we are."

"Hey, I'm pretty sure I would have liked you one way or the other. And I do admire your swing. That was a hell of a punch you gave me the other day."

"I didn't know—"

"Maybe that was better. That's the thing with undercover, really. Check in only when you need to or when you need help. Work everything on a need-to-know basis."

He was right, and she knew it. And she could have said she liked him, too. But suddenly, doing so seemed to be a very dangerous part of the operation.

She liked him too much.

Liked the deep set of his eyes, the tone of his voice… the way he touched her. She'd liked the feel of his lips on hers far too much… That brief touch was still a memory that lingered and haunted.

"I still think we should head back," she said.

He looked around. "It's beautiful here. Not just the monastery, I mean South Florida."

"Yeah. But how often do you get down here?"

"I go where they send me," he told her.

She nodded and turned away. Even with the undercover operation underway, they were ships passing at sea. It was disturbing that she was coming to care about him, and almost humiliating the way that she felt…

With him, she would have gladly taken a feigned relationship anywhere.

It was one thing to discover she found him attractive. More, even. Compelling, sensual…a man with the kind of masculinity that moved beyond sense and logic and simply reached into the very core of her being.

It just didn't work to be craving his touch while on the job.

"Well, we've checked in, Jorge knows I'm all right," she said, "and Connor will have Kari on the beach somewhere soon. I'd like to get back to South Beach."

"We can do that," he said.

He took her arm and they headed back. David Hernandez was waiting for them by the limo. Jacob told David he was great, and they would use him in the future, but for the moment, they'd decided just to head back to the hotel. They were going to wander the sand by night.

Hernandez thought that was fine, and he was grateful they'd call on him again. Of course, the man would be pleased. He had the night off now with full pay.

Jasmine and Jacob were both quiet during the drive back. When they reached the cute little boutique hotel where Jacob was staying, Jasmine admired the old lobby.

"You've never been in here before?" he asked her.

She grinned. "When I was in high school, we used to come out here and prowl a few of the clubs and maybe have soda or coffee at a few of the hotels. But I think I've only stayed out here a few times. I'm a native, but that doesn't mean I know every hotel."

"It's nice. Not a chain. And the owners seem to love the deco spirit of the place. I can have coffee on the balcony every morning if I want. I can hear the sound of the surf and watch the palm trees sway—before the rest of the world wakes up and the beach becomes crowded with bodies."

She smiled. "You will see some of the most beautiful bodies in the world out here, you know."

He was quiet for a minute.

"You disagree?"

He smiled awkwardly and shrugged, and then looked at her at last. His light blue eyes seemed to caress the length of her.

Her heart, her soul, her *longing* seemed to jump to her throat.

But he quickly changed moods. "Then again, it's not just perfect bodies. You know that, of course."

"You mean old and wrinkly? We'll all be there someday. I hope when I'm older and drooping everywhere, I still love the beach."

He laughed. "I'm with you on that. I hope when I'm creased and drooping everywhere I can still sit on the sand and watch the sway of the palms and not worry that someone is judging me. I believe everyone has to do what is comfortable for them—and that's part of what I love.

"Yes, there's beauty. Yes, there's the ridiculous. And

there are quiet times, when the sun is rising, when you can look out and feel you're in a private paradise. And then you turn around and the neon of the hotels and the rush of the world comes on in. This place is ever changing, plastic in so many ways and yet real when it comes to the feel of the salt air and those moments when you're in the water, and it's just you and the waves and the sea and the sky."

"Yes," she said softly.

"So, let's take a walk," he said.

They headed out to the beach. Jasmine doffed her sneakers and Jacob rid himself of his shoes and socks, too. They left them by a palm.

Jacob's phone rang.

He listened, and then he told Jasmine, "Connor has Kari out to dinner. He took her to Joe's Stone Crab. They're fine."

"I'm afraid for when they leave. What do we do now?"

"Wait," he said.

"So hard!"

He laughed. "I've been undercover for months at a time. Watching, waiting. And for this case, well, the watching and waiting is a hell of a lot better than usual." He was quiet for a minute. "I recently worked a case where immigrants were brought in and used horribly. It was long on my part, but when it broke, we moved quickly. This may be the same. Thing is, right now, we could get them, or Ivan at least, on money. Then again, they can employ the best legal team known to man. So, we have to take them down big-time—with evidence that prosecutors can take to court."

Jasmine muttered, "So...we wait."

"And play the part," he agreed.

Nightfall was coming in earnest. The sky was fighting darkness and the sun was shooting out rays that seemed to be pure gold and magenta.

Jasmine wasn't sure what got into her. She suddenly broke away from him and ran down the beach, turned and kicked up a spray of the waves that had been washing over their feet.

She caught him with a full body splash, and he yelped and laughed with surprise. Then he came after her.

She squealed and turned to run, but he tackled her and bore her down to the soft damp sand. He leaned over her, looked down into her eyes and then murmured, "Good move. I just saw Sasha up on the boardwalk. We are being watched."

He eased closer. "Can I kiss you?"

Role-playing…

She tangled her fingers into the richness of his hair, pulling him in, and he kissed her.

And then he broke away, laughing, and pulled her to her feet. "I think we gave Sasha a good show, eh?" he asked softly.

"Oh, yeah," she whispered. Once again, her lips were burning.

As they retrieved their shoes and decided on a restaurant for dinner, she couldn't help but wish that the FBI had sent down a much less attractive agent.

Chapter Seven

"His full name is Donald McPherson Connor," Jacob told Jasmine. "He's living at that grand old place down from the club just off of Washington Street—a quiet and dark intersection. The whole sixth floor is his apartment."

They were at her place. He'd done a thorough search for bugs and hadn't found any, and with the way this gang seemed to work, he was pretty sure he wouldn't find anything. In Kozak's words, Jasmine was "just a woman."

Jacob had a feeling that Kozak might be pretty surprised.

Just a woman. In any kind of a fair fight, Jasmine would take Kozak.

But for them, at this moment, it bode well that Kozak and the members of his gang still seemed to live in an archaic world of chauvinism.

"And what else?" Jasmine asked.

"Born in Yorkshire, and he has dual citizenship."

"How does he make his money?"

"He inherited a nice sum and knows how to invest in the stock market."

"So, an older Englishman-turned-American, rich, with nothing to do. Wife? Kids?"

Jasmine had changed from her salt-spray-and-sand-covered clothing to a dark silky maxi dress. She'd come to perch on the sofa by him, hugging her knees to her chest as she looked at him.

"Wife died about ten years ago. They had a daughter but I can't find much on her."

"Criminal past?"

"Nope."

"Any hint of anyone disappearing when he's around?"

"He's been living in Savannah. He's just been down here about two months. They're still looking into him."

"And the agent saw him take Kari back to her apartment and then leave?"

"Yes," Jacob said.

He didn't have to read from his phone; one of his assets was his memory. He could retain what was told to him, which was probably why languages came to him easily. Then again, he loved languages, and all the little rules and differences and nuances within them.

He wished at that moment, though, that he was reading. Because he was left to meet her eyes.

He'd been right that first day, when he'd seen her from afar. Her eyes were green. A brilliant beautiful green, like twin emeralds in a sea of gold. Her face was so perfectly molded he was tempted to reach out and touch it, as he might be tempted to reach out and touch a classic sculpture. Her hair was free, freshly washed and tumbling around her shoulders, still damp. And in the maxi dress, she seemed exceptionally alluring—though he was sure she had donned the article of clothing because it covered her entire body. It felt like a reaction to the skimpy outfit she'd been forced to put on for the "date" with Connor.

"But according to Kari, Mary did escort him," Jasmine pointed out, "and then she disappeared."

"You're going to need to get closer to Kari."

"Well, we're both supposed to report to Natasha tomorrow—Kari and I."

"And I have an excuse to go in. I've gotten Kozak's permission to investigate Smirnoff's murder."

"Have the cops gotten anything? I guess not. I'm pretty sure that, even though the FBI has lead, I'd know about it if anyone had been apprehended for the murder."

"From what I've heard, they're still pretty much in the dark," Jacob said. "Trajectory shows the bullets were fired from the balcony. But everyone working there swears the balconies were closed off. Someone is lying, of course. But no one knows who."

"No guns were found, no casings…no nothing?"

"Nope. And the gunmen—two to three of them, best estimate—entirely disappeared."

Jasmine leaned her chin thoughtfully on her knees. "We could see all the major players when it happened. You were out there with Kozak, Ivan Petrov and the goons, Sasha, Antonio and Alejandro. And Natasha was backstage."

"The killers were hired, obviously. And they were guaranteed a clean getaway. We dusted for prints on the rails and so forth, but there are hundreds of prints. Workmen were there, of course, before the grand opening. Anyone who so much as delivered pizza might have left a print. Smirnoff, from what I understand, loved showing off the place and brought everyone out to those balconies to let them see how they looked down at the floor and the main stage."

She shook her head. "So, we're nowhere."

"No. We're moving forward. You're just impatient."

"I guess so. I mean, I have worked undercover before. But often just for a day or so, getting into the right place, talking to the right people. I admit—it was never anything like this."

"We just keep moving forward."

She nodded. "I guess…I guess I need some sleep."

"Go on."

"You're staying here?"

"I believe I'm entitled now—and I don't want to disappoint anyone by not taking my full measure."

"Ah." She stood, almost leaping away from him. "Pillow and blankets. If I'd known I was having nightly guests, I would have asked for a two-bedroom." She smiled awkwardly and hurried into her bedroom. A moment later, she was back. She plopped down two pillows, sheets and a blanket. "Not sure if you need the blanket, I don't air-condition the place too much. But… Anyway, all right. I'll see you in the morning. Start coffee if you're up first!"

She spoke quickly, almost nervously. It wasn't like her.

"Good night," he said softly.

She left him, and he wished he wasn't playing a role. More than that, he wished he wasn't working. She'd closed the door between them, but he could still see her in his mind's eye.

See her laughter as she kicked up the salt spray.

Feel her beneath him when he tackled her in the sand.

He could see the emerald of her eyes as she'd looked at him before she pulled him in for that blistering kiss.

And he couldn't help but wonder, in his misery, if she just might…just might…be wishing a little bit herself that they had met under different circumstances.

He spent the next hour reminding himself he was a special agent, he loved his job and he had made a difference… They were professional. They played their parts. They brought down the bad guys.

He thought he'd never sleep. He wondered why the hell he had stayed. She could take care of herself. She was trained.

But despite the logic, despite what he knew, he was afraid for her.

He could have returned to his apartment. He knew being here had nothing to do with being professional. If it came to it, he'd give anything to save her life if it was threatened in any way.

Why? He'd worked cases with so many beautiful women and never done more than acknowledge that fact.

Jasmine was different. She had touched something else in him. Something that was more than attraction, even desire.

She was…everything. Everything in a way he hadn't known in over a decade. Not since his wife had died.

JACOB WAS UP when Jasmine emerged in the morning.

She'd spent the night…waiting. She'd thought the door to her bedroom might open at any time. She couldn't decide if she wanted it to or not.

But it did not, and when she finally rose, she found him already awake. He'd brewed coffee and was sipping a cup, leaning thoughtfully against the refrigerator.

He looked at her as she emerged, his eyes fathomless.

"Three more bodies last night," he said softly.

"What? Where?" she asked. Three bodies. Was one Mary?

He must have seen the fear on her face. "Three men

again," he said quickly. "And they weren't found in oil drums. This time, they were found south of the Tamiami Trail. Miami-Dade County, on Miccosukee tribal land."

"Three. Maybe the hired gunmen? If they weren't in oil drums, if they're new... It's possible it isn't related. Will we get identities soon?" Jasmine said.

He hesitated. "No. The bodies are missing heads and hands."

"Oh."

"Cause of death?"

"Unknown, at this point. In my mind, logic suggests they were shot in the head."

"Logic?"

"Execution-style—then the heads were removed. Dumped them in the Everglades." He hesitated. "From what I've been told, they were well ravaged by the animal life. Among other creatures, the vultures had a feast."

"There are few better places to dispose of a body than the Everglades," Jasmine agreed. "But they were definitely...male bodies?"

"Yes, definitely male bodies."

She wandered to the coffeepot and poured herself a cup. She was shaken, but she didn't want to be. She was a detective in a major crime division. But this was personal.

Maybe she shouldn't have been working this investigation. But there had truly been no one better suited to the task of getting in with the Deco Gang.

Jacob came up behind her and placed a hand on her shoulders. "Jasmine, I believe the men found might well have been the shooters. If whoever planned this wanted to make sure no one talked, they had to get rid of the people who actually carried out the deed."

"Yes, that's my gut feeling on it, too," she said. Her hands were still trembling slightly as she held her coffee cup. And she was ridiculously aware of him, right there behind her, the heat of his body, the scent of him.

She had to spin around, composed and determined. "So, today, you start questioning everyone?"

"Today I start questioning everyone."

He had barely spoken when there was a knock on the door.

"Excuse me," she murmured.

As she headed to the door, she was aware Jacob had already showered and dressed completely for the day. He had his hand behind his back, ready to draw his weapon if the guest at the door intended to offer any danger.

No danger was forthcoming; she looked through the peephole. It was Jorge.

She let him in quickly. "Hey."

Jorge glanced at Jacob. He seemed to accept the man's presence as normal.

"I was bringing you the latest news. Captain said he didn't think you should be calling in, even on the burners. Too easy for one of them to catch the phone and check out numbers and get suspicious when nothing on you had an easily trackable number. But I imagine you've gotten the latest?"

"The bodies in the Glades?" she asked.

He nodded and looked at Jacob. "Who do you think did it? Is it Kozak? Natasha? Ivan?"

"I don't know. But I intend to find out." Jacob smiled. "Breakfast first. Somewhere obvious. Somewhere anyone who wishes can see the three of us—me and my escort, provided for me with their blessing, and you, my new love's best friend. Plenty of places in the area. Let's go for a walk and find good food."

"Okay," Jorge said slowly, frowning.

"Then Jasmine needs to check in with Natasha and assure her of my happiness and her own satisfaction with the arrangement—and I get to question the goons."

"And…" Jorge pressed. "Me?"

"I think it's fine if you come in today, just a cheerful dude happy to be with a friend."

"It's a plan," Jorge said.

IT WASN'T DIFFICULT for Jacob to pretend to be out with friends. He liked Jorge very much and thought he was probably a damned good cop. He knew how to fit in to what he was doing, and he didn't need to take the lead. He'd set up the tour for them yesterday in minutes flat and had managed to introduce him and Jasmine on the floor opening night at the club—at the end of a spray of bullets—without giving things away. Jacob also just liked the man.

And as for Jasmine…

He had to be careful.

When they were seated, Jasmine and Jorge were talking about Miami, and Jasmine was telling Jorge about their tour guide.

"He was a great guy—a super guide, knew his stuff," Jasmine said. "Friendly and informative without being annoying."

"Hard to imagine this place as a coconut plantation," Jacob said.

"Hard to imagine the whole south of the state as a 'river of grass,'" Jasmine said.

Jacob noted that there was a man seated at a far back table, eating and reading a newspaper. Watching them.

Jacob picked up his coffee cup and said softly, "Antonio Garibaldi is at the back of the restaurant."

"We were followed here," Jorge said casually.

"And here's the thing," Jasmine said, running her fingers up Jacob's arm and smiling sensually, "we don't even know who else might be in the employ of the new boss, be he Kozak or even someone else."

Jacob leaned closer to her. "We need to find out who is calling the shots." He planted a quick kiss on her lips and looked at her lingeringly. Then he stood. "Think I'll visit the restroom."

He headed to the back of the restaurant and the restrooms. But he made a pretense of stopping, as if surprised and pleased to see Garibaldi.

"Hey! I guess I did choose a good place, if you're here," he said. He pulled out the chair on the other side of the table and sat.

"Yeah, they do a great breakfast," Garibaldi said. He was a big man with dark hair and a solid physique, built as a good bouncer should be. His eyes were quick and dark. His smile was pained.

"I'm really loving South Florida," Jacob told him. "And getting to work with Kozak. Of course, I'm as sympathetic as anyone over Smirnoff. He was a good man. What the hell do you think happened? I mean, forgive me, I know you guys are good at your jobs. But how the hell did shooters get up on the balconies?"

Garibaldi looked uncomfortable—he was on the spot. Then he leaned forward. "Hell if I know. Seriously. From the beginning, it was planned that the balconies be roped off. Crowd control. And that day... Smirnoff was giving us our orders. I was watching the front, Suarez had the stage and Antonovich was moving through the crowd. There were cops all over, hired for the occasion. I'll be damned if I can figure it out, and I've tried. Thing is, I was given my orders. The other guys were given their orders. We never saw anyone get up there."

"There has to be an entrance from the offices," Jacob said.

"Sure. There's a door across from Smirnoff's office. That way, when he chose to, he could be in his office, and when he wanted to be part of the crowd, he could come out on the balcony. The cops were all over it. But here's the thing. The door is kept locked. There's a key. And when the cops were all over the place right after the shooting, the door was still locked. Smirnoff kept the key."

"Duplicate keys can be made. I'm sure the cops checked on that," Jacob said.

Garibaldi shrugged. "Whoever may have had a duplicate key, I don't know."

"It was obviously well planned."

Garibaldi appeared to be honestly confused. "You know, sure, it could have been planned. But it seemed like one of those bad things, you know. Some disturbed person just out to hurt anyone—and getting Smirnoff."

"You don't believe that, do you?" Jacob asked.

Garibaldi's voice was soft and low. "I want to believe it," he said.

"But you don't."

"Kozak told us last night that he'd given you permission to question us, see if you couldn't figure something out. I'd like to help you. What do I know? I was in my position. And the shooting started. I was—well, hell. Hate to admit this. I was scared. I think I managed to get people out, get them down. But I got the hell out as fast as I could myself."

"You were armed?"

"I was. But the best gun in the world doesn't do you a bit of good if you don't know what you're supposed to be shooting at."

He seemed to be telling the truth. Jacob never took anyone at face value, but he also noted the man's expressions and body language. He'd have bet that he was being honest.

Garibaldi looked at him and seemed to judge him, as well. "I'm not in this for violence," he said softly. "The money is good…" He shrugged. "I mind my own business and don't care where it comes from. Drugs… People are going to buy them somewhere. The girls… They do what they choose. Natasha talked to Jasmine, and you all had an agreement. Cool. She seems to really like you. So, is that a crime? As for me, I do what I'm told and I keep my nose clean and stay out. I'm just security."

"So you're just supposed to report on us today?" Jacob asked him.

"Yeah. And it's cool. It's obvious you two have more than a business relationship going. That's the way Josef Smirnoff always rolled. Kozak said that it will be business as usual. Of course, he's scared now. Whoever killed Smirnoff could be gunning for him. That's probably why he said you could talk to people. Though, I already told the cops what I told you. The truth."

"Sure. Hey, next time you're watching us, just join us." Jacob shrugged. "She's a cool girl and I like Jorge, too."

"That wouldn't be the way the game is played," Garibaldi said.

"No, I guess not." Jacob stood. "You're a good-looking man with the right stuff. There are tons of other places on the beach that need bouncers, security. If this whole scene is too much for you."

Garibaldi shrugged. "I screwed up once. Didn't check an ID the way I should have. The girl's parents caused a stink. Josef gave me a job. Said I didn't need to ID anyone." He laughed suddenly. "Garibaldi. Nice Italian name. I was born here, my parents were born here and my grandfather came over from Naples to run a tailor shop. No mob ties whatsoever. He was in Worcester, Massachusetts. And didn't even have to pay anyone for a safe working environment.

"Alejandro Suarez, his family came over in the late 1880s. They were cigar makers up in Ybor City, Tampa area. And even Antonovich, he's a third-generation American. We're not…we're not mob. We're not mob-related. I'm here because I have a job. And I do it. Long hours, maybe, but so far, I haven't been asked to do anything other than protect people, watch people and break up fights."

"And what if you had to do something that was illegal?"

"It would depend on what that thing was." Garibaldi hesitated a minute. Then he said quietly, "Hey, man, you're buying art—that you haven't even seen. And we all know about your past."

Jacob nodded. "Yeah. But I play it the way Smirnoff

played it. I don't go in for murder. Gets messy—and gets the cops on you."

"Yeah," Garibaldi agreed.

"Sounds like you're a good man. One I'd like to have on my side," Jacob said.

"Thanks," Garibaldi told him.

Jacob left him and returned to his own table. Jasmine and Jorge were having a conversation about the best spas in the area. When he sat down, Jasmine played it perfectly, stroking his arm.

He wished her touch didn't seem to awaken every ounce of longing in his body.

NATASHA WAS WITH Kozak when they arrived.

Jacob was allowed admittance to Kozak's office. Jasmine and Jorge were directed to the dressing room, where they were alone.

Jorge found a stereo system and turned on music. Phil Collins, "In the Air Tonight." Fitting. Shades of the old *Miami Vice* that had really put the area—and many myths about it—on the map.

"Natasha is sleeping with Kozak," Jorge said softly. "She might have been sleeping with Josef Smirnoff, too. At any rate, she was with him for years and years. Trusted. She could have gotten the key and had a copy made."

Natasha came sweeping into the room. She saw Jorge and frowned slightly, then shrugged. "I suppose you say anything in front of Jorge," she said. "Oh, by the way, Jorge, a man has been courting our business, one who may need some entertainment."

"Ready when you are," Jorge said.

"Now, Jasmine, about Mr. Marensky..."

Jasmine smiled and then decided to go another step. She walked over and hugged Natasha.

The woman was not used to hugs. She didn't push Jasmine away, but she didn't hug her back. She awkwardly patted her shoulders. "So, all went well," Natasha said.

"He's lovely," Jasmine said. "Best way to make some money I've ever known!"

"Yes, I believe you. You're very lucky such a man is so captivated by you. It's not always the case, but for you… Yes, I am glad that such a striking man—one whom Josef approved and Victor seems to admire, especially—has taken such a shine to you. But you must realize, my dear, he may tire of you. And move on."

"I know that," Jasmine said. "But for now…he's fun. He wishes to please me."

"And he is far from repulsive in bed, I imagine," Natasha said.

Jasmine didn't let her smile slip. "Oh, so, so, far from repulsive."

"Ah, she's a lucky one," Jorge said.

"Then you will continue as you have been doing. Don't forget… Friday night. Friday is the funeral. And at the funeral, you will be a hostess here, and you mustn't cling to Mr. Marensky at the gathering after the ceremony. After tomorrow night, the club may reopen. The workers will have cleaned up. No bullet holes will show in the walls by the ceremony. Now, you do understand about Marensky, Jasmine? First, we need you to be working. Second, it's important he remembers that he is graced with your company through us."

"Definitely," Jasmine said. "Understood."

"Then you are free for today. You may go. You, too,

Jorge." She handed them each an envelope. Their pay-checks. They had no choice but to thank her and leave.

As they walked, they noted they were being followed. It was Alejandro Suarez on their tail this time.

"So, straight to my place, I guess," Jasmine murmured.

"I don't think they're following me."

"What about phones?"

"I have a new one."

"I need to know about Connor. About Connor...and Kari."

Jorge sighed. "Jasmine, we have to trust our fellows. They saw last night that Connor left Kari at her apartment. No sex, nothing. She was fine."

Aware of their follower, Jasmine laughed as if Jorge had said something great and grabbed his arm in fun—as a friend might do. In contrast to her actions, her whisper was intense. "But what are they doing about him?"

"Watching. And waiting," Jorge said. "Jasmine, you knew this wasn't going to be an instant fix, that we'd be out of the loop much of the time. And—"

They had only come a half a block from the club when Jasmine saw Kari headed their way. She released Jorge's arm and cried out with delight, running to see the other girl.

"Kari!" She hugged her. She pulled away and asked softly, "All is well?"

"Fine, it's lovely. Mr. Connor is an absolute gentleman. I'll be seeing him tonight." Kari grinned and said, "Oh, he isn't young and hot like Marensky. But he's fine, very nice. Polite and courteous in a way I haven't seen in years. Happy to have some arm candy while he's out on the town, you know?"

"Good. Well, I guess you knew that, from what Mary said."

"I miss Mary. She was the sweetest!"

"Did she ever say anything to you," Jasmine asked, "anything about going away or even…even about being afraid?"

"No. She was just with us, and then one day she didn't show and didn't come back. Natasha was very upset. She was very fond of Mary, too. Speaking of Natasha, I've got to get in. She wants to see me." But suddenly, Kari gripped Jasmine's hands. "I'm telling you, Mr. Connor is so kind and caring, wanting to know my every wish."

Jasmine realized then that it was the man's very kindness that actually frightened Kari.

Someone so nice. What happened when he wasn't? What might he really want?

Further determined, Jasmine smiled. "Great, Kari," she said loudly. "I guess Jorge and I are going to go home and binge on repeats of *Desperate Housewives.*"

"Have fun!"

"You're welcome to join us!"

Kari waved and headed off.

Jasmine headed back and grabbed Jorge's arm. "Something has to be done," she said firmly. "Before tonight!"

Chapter Eight

"I have had that door rekeyed," Kozak told Jacob. "The police asked about it, but it was locked. There was no sign that anyone had forced it. But…how? How did someone get through the balcony without being seen? There were dressers here, makeup artists… But when the show began, everyone was downstairs. Natasha was with the girls backstage. The band members were all downstairs. I didn't have the key! No one had the key—except for Josef Smirnoff."

"Someone obviously copied it," Jacob said flatly.

Kozak shook his head. "I have the only key now. No one knows where I keep it. And I don't intend to tell anyone. Including you. No offense or disrespect intended."

"None taken," Jacob said.

"You are free to look around, but I have to go. Josef's body is at the funeral home. I will make sure he is given the send-off such a man deserves."

"Where will the funeral be?"

"A small Russian Orthodox church, up the way on the beach. And then we will come here." Kozak hesitated. "Will you make the arrangements for it with me today?"

"I thought that I should stay here. We want to know what happened to Josef," Jacob reminded him.

"We do." Kozak sighed deeply. "Yes, you must speak with Antonio, Alejandro and Sasha. The thing is…"

"What is it?"

"They have their place. We work carefully. Of course, they are aware… But we never give them facts. They know people, they know who is important, but we have never given them much on the clients."

"They might have seen something," Jacob said. "Something they don't even know they saw. I've spoken with Antonio. You didn't tell me about the door and the key."

"I didn't. I had to make sure. Josef brought you in, and he assured me you were solid, that you were a powerful man with a long history. I had to come to know you myself." Kozak shrugged. "The police checked the door. They remain with nothing."

"But you know someone within your own ranks had to be involved."

Kozak looked unhappy. "Yes. But whoever did this, they were clever. They hired out. A man doesn't guard what he doesn't see to be in danger."

"No," Jacob agreed, trying to read Kozak.

"You must do what you will. I have hidden nothing on Josef's murder from the police. I will not hide it from you. But I must prepare to bury an old and dear friend."

It was evident that Kozak wanted company while he made arrangements at the funeral home. Perhaps it was even important to go with him.

"I will go with you," Jacob agreed.

As it turned out, Kozak didn't want a driver with

them. He had a big black Cadillac sedan, and he asked
Jacob if he would do the driving.

"You don't want one of the guys to come along?"

"A bodyguard?" Kozak asked. "I think you will do."

They took Collins Avenue north and reached the
funeral home. They were greeted by a solemn man in
a suit, Mr. Derby, the current owner of Sacred Night
Final Rest Parlor.

Derby expressed his condolences, offered them water
or coffee and then tactfully suggested they needed to
choose a coffin. The coffins ranged from a few thousand dollars to just about enough to buy a house—at
the least, a nice automobile.

Jacob was surprised to see tears in Victor Kozak's
eyes. He had either really cared for his friend, or he was
able to pull off a feat many a Hollywood actor could not.

Then again, business was business. He could have
loved the man—and still arranged for his death.

"What do you think, my friend?" Kozak asked Jacob.

"Personally?" Jacob asked. "I believe in a greater
power, but I don't believe the body is anything but a
shell. It makes no difference if a man is laid to rest in
the finest mahogany or the cheapest pine, or if he's cremated and his ashes thrown to the wind. But if you're
worried about the funeral, about our show of respect...
then I'd say this."

Mr. Derby, the funeral director, was eyeing Jacob
with anything but kindness. Still, he seemed to perk
up when Jacob pointed out a fairly expensive coffin,
one that was both handsome, staid and possessed just
the right amount of ornamentation.

"Perfect," Kozak said quietly. "This one is it, sir."

"All right, nice choice," Mr. Derby said. "Now, as to the wake—"

"No wake," Kozak said. "You will bring the body to the church. Closed coffin."

"Sir, my people have done an extraordinary job. You may have a wake. Mr. Smirnoff's face was not impacted, and his suit will cover—"

"No wake. No open coffin," Kozak said. "Josef will be honored and buried."

"As you wish, sir. As you wish. This is a painful time for you as a friend. I do suggest that you consider a viewing, for other friends—"

"No," Kozak said. "Our business is quite complete. We have our own cars for the services. You will bring Josef as arranged to the church. And arrange for the transport from there to the cemetery."

"Yes, Mr. Kozak. Arrangements have been made. He will be brought from the church to the cemetery. Now, the cemetery is over in Miami. You will need police officers for the journey as friends follow for the last services, something which, of course, we take care of for you."

Kozak waved a hand in the air. "Do what is needed."

He was anxious to leave; Jacob held back and assured Derby, "Someone will be by with the final check."

He then followed Victor Kozak back out to the car. The man waited by the passenger's side as Jacob clicked the door open.

Kozak was trembling when he sat. Jacob hurried around to the driver's seat. He didn't have to push; Kozak appeared ready to speak.

"It's not real—I was there. I was there for a hail of bullets. I watched my friend fall, I saw the blood. And yet, it's not real. Not until you see he is laid into the ground. Yes, it is indeed a hard time. You know this. You have laid a wife to rest."

Jacob was still a moment.

A deceased wife was in his fake dossier. It was always best, when creating such a lie, to incorporate many details of life that were real. That helped an agent live the lie that was being created.

"It was a long time ago, right?" Victor Kozak asked.

Yes, a lifetime ago. He'd fallen in love with Sabrina Marshall the minute he had seen her. It had been tenth grade. They'd quickly become an item; he, a high school jock, Sabrina the smart one. They'd married and gone off to college together, and even after graduation when they'd planned their perfect life, talked about starting a family...

The cancer had found her. It had cared nothing about youthful dreams.

"It was a long time ago, yes," Jacob said softly.

A long, long time ago. Many women in between; savvy, bright women, some in business, some in politics, but none in law enforcement.

None like Jasmine, someone he had seen from afar who had nevertheless seemed to enter into his soul. He barely knew her. Maybe, though, he knew her enough.

Maybe, when this was over... When this was all over, Jasmine would no longer be playing a role. She would go back to her passion, being cop in a major crime unit. And he would go where the Bureau sent him, because he was good at what he did, and he did believe, no matter what unbelievable things were going on in the world, that what he did was right. One good man, or maybe many good men, could make the world a better place.

Sabrina had believed that, too.

"I'm sorry," Kozak said.

"So am I," Jacob said softly. "So am I."

"But now, this woman, this Jasmine—she means something to you?"

"Yes," Jacob said simply.

"When Natasha brought her in, I knew, too, there was something about her. Women…most often, they are just part of business, and that's how it must be. So few have that inner fire. But, now and then…one enchants the mind, eh?"

"Yes," Jacob agreed. "This one in particular…there is something that appeals to me on many levels."

"She's all yours," Kozak said.

Jacob lowered his head. He was pretty sure he knew how Jasmine would feel about being granted to a man as payment for his friendship.

Heading back to Washington Street, Jacob cut down Meridian Avenue. As they neared the Holocaust Memorial of the Greater Miami Jewish Federation, Kozak made a little sound.

The memorial was a heart-wrenching, well-conceived artwork, created by survivors, respected and honored by a community. Statues and plaques told a story that tore at the human soul.

Jacob had been there several times through the years. His own past was a checkered piece of all manner of peoples, from the free world and from areas of great subjugation; his Russian mother had a background that included royalty, his Israeli father had parents who had barely made it out of Germany. Jacob was eternally grateful they had chosen the United States as a place to raise their own family—he knew he'd had a relatively easy and privileged start to life.

He was surprised when Kozak asked him to stop.

"You want to get out and walk around?" Jacob asked.

Kozak shook his head. "I just want to look."

Jacob sat next to him in silence.

"World War II. A brutal business. Hitler wanting to exterminate a race of people. Stalin…twenty million Russians were also killed, you know, between the enemy and Stalin."

"Yes, I am aware."

"Young people these days…they don't always know."

"Education is everything," Jacob murmured.

One of the sculptures at the outdoor memorial was especially poignant. It depicted a body, as many bodies had been found. Prisoners had not just gone to the death camps to be gassed and cremated; they'd gone to be a work force, and they'd been all but starved as they worked.

The body was skeletal and depicted in bronze. They were a distance from the sculpture and couldn't see it completely. But Jacob had seen it before. And he knew that Kozak had, too.

Kozak turned to Jacob. "My grandmother survived by hiding in plain sight in Berlin. My grandfather was a Russian soldier, hiding the fact that he was also Jewish. When the Soviet Army closed in on Berlin, my grandfather found my grandmother, who was terrified. She had been in living with a Christian German couple who were appalled by the death and terror around them. She'd been told, however, there was less torture if you quickly admitted what you were. When he found her, she said, *'Juden.'* But you see, my grandfather said,

'*Juden*, yes, I am *Juden*, too.' They were married, and they stayed married for the next forty years. They died in the same year. I believe he died of a broken heart when he lost her, because she passed away first."

"They had years together. It is still a beautiful story," Jacob said.

Kozak turned to him. "I have told you this story because maybe it will help you believe me. I don't kill people. I don't torture, and I don't kill."

Jacob couldn't help himself. Looking at Kozak, he said, "I beg to differ—slightly. Drugs kill."

Kozak waved a hand in the air. "Drugs kill, but people have a choice. But we do nothing where others have not made a choice. The addict must choose life. The drugs exist with or without my participation. We may as well get rich. Am I a good man? No. Am I a cold-blooded killer? No. Take what you will from that. But I did not kill my friend Josef."

Jacob nodded slowly.

Neither spoke for a moment.

He put the car back into gear and drove back south, to Washington Street and the club. They hadn't been away long.

"So, now," Kozak said, "you will find out what happened to Josef, yes?"

"I will do my damnedest," Jacob said.

JORGE REALLY DID put on a Netflix marathon of *Desperate Housewives*.

Jasmine nervously paced the room. "We should be doing something," she said.

"Jasmine, here's the thing. We are doing something,"

Jorge told her. "Okay, so, you're not a fan. What should we watch?"

"I can't. I can't sit still."

"You stink at this."

"Sorry!"

"All right," Jorge said. "I'll check in with Captain Lorenzo. Will that help?"

"Maybe."

He took out his phone and called. Jasmine watched him as he spoke, assuring Lorenzo they were both fine and they were proceeding with the work and their relationship with the FBI was moving along smoothly. Then he asked if anything else had been discovered, listened awhile and then thanked Lorenzo and promised he'd be the one in touch.

"Well?" Jasmine demanded, burning with impatience.

"There's a Miccosukee village where they sell hand-made clothing, arts and crafts—and have alligator shows," he said.

"I know. It's out on Tamiami Trail, just west of Shark Valley."

"There's a fellow who lives not far from the village. He raises alligators, sells them to various venues for alligator wrestling. Handles them from the time they hatch." Jorge stopped speaking.

"And?"

"One of his young alligators died, and he didn't know why, so there was a necropsy done on the gator."

"And?"

"They found a hand. He reported it. And it's been brought in to the medical examiner, and they believe it belonged to one of the dead men found out there.

They're hoping to get an ID. I don't know a lot about alligator stomach acids, but…well, they're still hoping to get something."

"I know what they're going to find," Jasmine said. "There won't be a match. I'm willing to bet that whoever is doing this is clever enough to have hired undocumented newcomers to do the deed."

"Maybe. Someone desperate and grateful for any work that doesn't go on the books."

Jasmine nodded. "Jorge, what do you think of Natasha?"

"She's all business."

"Yes. And she was in charge of the models. Of the show. And we all suspect she is sleeping with Victor Kozak, but—"

"Maybe she slept with Josef, too. And maybe she was sleeping with Victor because Josef tired of her, and maybe—"

"Maybe!" Jasmine said. "If only we had a definite."

She started to pace again, thinking, trying to remember every move Natasha had made on the day of the show.

Jorge groaned and turned back to *Desperate Housewives*.

"Hey," Jacob said to Alejandro Suarez. He was on guard downstairs, at the door to the club offices and staging area.

"Hey," Suarez said. He studied Jacob. He was puffing on a cigarette, leaned against the wall. He grinned suddenly. "Are you some new kind of enforcer?"

"I'm just an art dealer."

Suarez studied him. "Sure. But hey, I just work here. Kozak said you were going to talk to us."

"Do you remember anyone—anyone you didn't know—at the grand opening?"

Suarez laughed. "Anyone I didn't know? What? Do I look like I rub elbows with the rich and famous regularly?" There must have been something ominous in Jacob's look, because he quickly sobered up.

"Did you see anyone upstairs?" Jacob clarified. "We know that the killers were on the balcony."

"Yeah, that's what the cops said." Suarez sighed, reaching in his jacket pocket for another cigarette. He lit it with his current smoke. The man was a few years younger than Garibaldi and maybe a few inches taller in height. "I came in through the upstairs. We all reported to Josef, who said the balcony would be closed off. That would leave all of us down on the floor with the hired cops—you don't do anything that big without hiring cops."

"Right."

"When I checked in, the girls were all getting dressed. The band members were in the green room, making cracks about the girls. I guess they planned on having them in to party later. That idea went all to hell, huh?"

"You saw the band, Josef Smirnoff, Natasha and the girls. Anyone else?"

"Ivan was already down at the bar. The caterers were never allowed upstairs. Oh, Victor Kozak was downstairs already when I came in, seeing to a last-minute check on the place. When I joined him, he pointed out that the balcony stairways—there's one set near the entrance on both sides—were roped off with velvet cords.

They didn't want people up on the balcony. There's only one door up on the second floor, but it almost leads right into the office, and they didn't want anyone going up because of the office. And he didn't want anybody trying to grab selfies with the girls or the band or anything. If anyone headed toward the stairs, we were to politely stop them. And if they tried again, we were to politely escort them out."

"But no one tried to get up the stairs?"

"There were big signs attached to the velvet cords that said No Admittance. I think most people honor signs like that. Hey, it wasn't supposed to be… It was supposed to be a cool grand opening. No one expected any violence. If anything, we'd have had to throw out a drunk."

"But you saw no one. Nothing?"

Suarez shook his head. "No! I mean, I could have told you before the cops did their investigating that the shooters had to have been on the balcony. But there was a stampede. You know that. I admit, I froze for a second. Then I went to work getting people out."

"Was anyone on the back door—where we are now?"

"I'm assuming it was locked up tight. We were all on the main floor. But…"

"But?"

"I don't know what weapons were used. I was thinking that whoever was up there… Well, if they pocketed their weapons, in all the confusion, they might have come down the stairs and run out with everyone else. Or…" Suarez paused, shaking his head.

"What?"

"They could have come out the back, out of this door. But you see, I don't understand how that would be possible. Cops were already in here. They were crawling all over the area within minutes. I can't believe they wouldn't have seen three men with guns run out this door." Suarez seemed as mystified as Garibaldi had been.

Two down; one to go.

They were great liars—or they had planned their stories well.

Jacob thanked him, then turned and hurried back up the stairs. He found Sasha Antonovich outside the door to Kozak's office. Like Alejandro Suarez, he seemed at ease—bored, probably—as he stood by the door.

"My turn, eh?" Antonovich asked him. He shrugged. "We just look stupid. Kozak said you were going to try to do what the police seem be failing at. So. What can I tell you?"

"What *can* you tell me?"

Antonovich was older than both Suarez and Garibaldi. Remembering all the info he had been given, Jacob knew Antonovich had been with Josef Smirnoff the longest—well over a decade. His hair was beginning to gray, just at the temples. Fine lines were appearing around his light brown eyes, and he wore a weary look.

The man shook his head, his expression grim. "What do I know? That it wasn't just a random shooting? That someone was after Josef? I'm sure you believe that, too. How the hell did they get in? They had to have been on a guest list. I don't know who they were, what they looked like... There were hundreds of people here. They could have been with the caterers, they could have gotten in with the off-duty cops. The cops came from all over the city. Some of them, the Miami Beach guys, were naturally on duty, but in here... Josef wanted lots of security, so we hired people from all over the city. I've been thinking about it, too."

"A dirty cop? Is that what you're thinking?"

"Maybe. Or just someone dressed up like a cop. The other guys might not have known—they came from precincts all over the city. I keep thinking, though, that the guys investigating the shooting had to have thought of all this."

"I imagine they have. I would think they're working all angles."

"Three bodies found down off the Tamiami Trail—no hands, no heads. Sure as hell sounds like a hit to me."

"I agree. I'll bet just about all of law enforcement would."

"Definitely not just a domestic disturbance," Antonovich said, not amused at his own attempt at humor. "The door up here... I was the first one to check it, along with one of Miami Beach's finest. It was locked. If they came through that way, they had a key."

"It's been rekeyed."

"Yeah."

"Well, thanks," Jacob said. He started to walk away.

Antonovich called him back. "Hey," he said softly. "You get that son of a bitch. You get whoever killed Josef. He was all right. Yes, he sold drugs, he sold arms, he sold...women. But he was an okay guy, you know?"

"Sure," Jacob said quietly. He didn't agree that Smirnoff was "an okay guy," but he did believe that a murderer should be brought to justice. Antonovich seemed passionate about catching Smirnoff's killer.

"You're going to the funeral?" Antonovich asked.

"Yes, of course."

"I want to go over to the cemetery. It's old—and

pretty big. Angels and archangels…and small mauso-leums and large mausoleums."

"Places for a shooter to hide?" Jacob asked.

Antonovich nodded grimly. "I'll be checking it out," he said.

"Good. And good to know."

Jacob turned away. He knew the cemetery, on Eighth Street, or Calle Ocho, in the city. It was a beautiful cemetery. Gothic archways, handsome landscaping… and dozens of places for a shooter to hide—if Kozak was next in line, and there was still someone making a power play.

Antonovich appeared to be bitter about Smirnoff's death, as eager as any to pinpoint a killer. But Jacob just couldn't be sure what he felt he'd learned.

Either the goons were just hired muscle…or they had put together a trio of stone-cold killers, just waiting for the right moment to sweep in.

Which would mean that Victor Kozak was sched-uled to die, as well.

Chapter Nine

Jorge left Jasmine's apartment at about 4:00 p.m. "I don't think I'm supposed to be hanging around here forever," he told her. "Despite the amount of fun and entertainment you're providing me, I've just got to go."

"What are you going to do?" Jasmine asked.

He smiled. "Hole up in my room with computer files. I'd rather hang around the beach. Check out the scene, hear what I can hear. But I guess that will be nothing. Rats. Guess I'll be hanging out with my computer."

"You don't think that's dangerous?"

"No, Bernie in tech helped me out. I hit a key, and only a genius could find my erased history or files or anything. I'll be okay. You'll be with a hot guy—I won't." He grinned at her.

She didn't grin back.

He walked over to her and hugged her. "Partner, I can feel it. Mary is going to be okay. And you're going to be okay, and I'm going to be okay. Okay? Oh, and pretty man is going to be okay, too."

That one, at last, made her grin. "I'm sure. Fine, go work. And I'll—"

"Keep pacing."

"Yep, I'll keep pacing."

Jorge was gone; she was alone.

She found herself pondering Jacob Wolff. He seemed to know everything about her. Of course, he was with the federal government. She was MDPD—not any lesser, but still, a total difference in privileges and responsibilities. She was, however, sure that if the operation had been planned differently, she'd know much more about him. She didn't even know anything about the fake man, much less the real Jacob Wolff. She was probably lucky she knew his real name.

He probably even knew that her parents were working with a charity rebuilding houses down in Haiti.

She was working up a fair amount of aggravation by the time Jacob Wolff arrived at her apartment; she didn't notice at first that he seemed worn and weary when he walked in.

"Anything? Do you have anything at all?" she asked. "I believe that Connor will be with Kari again tonight— and I'm very afraid for what will happen to her after that."

"We've got field agents watching Connor. They can find nothing to suggest that he's a murderer."

"Oh, really? So, in your usual line of work, people advertise the fact that they're murderers?"

The way he looked at her, she wished she could swallow the words back.

"I don't know anything yet. I have a firm belief that the men just found in the Glades were the killers. I believe they worked for someone who copied the key to the balcony, and they didn't bother to escape that way— they just blended with a panicked crowd that was trampling one another. I actually don't believe Kozak called the shots, but I can't be sure. What have you got?"

"Why do you believe Kozak is innocent—of murder, that is?"

Jacob was looking straight ahead, at the television. "I think he would do a great deal to make money, but I think he's seen enough of death."

"What makes you believe that?"

He turned to look at her. "He has a past very much like my own. My father was born in Israel to parents who barely escaped the Nazis. My maternal grandfather made it out of one of Stalin's purges. I was lucky. I was born here. Almost right here—Mount Sanai. But my parents had to work hard. We were always just scraping by. We were here several years, and then in New York. I went to high school in Manhattan, and on to Columbia University with tuition assistance through the military—and then after my service, the FBI. I've been under the direction of great men with the Bureau for years, always FBI, but recently, FBI in conjunction with Homeland Security—and I've seen what's really, really ugly. So, I allow myself to be wrong. But I talk to people. I try to hear what's beneath what they say. I'm not perfect. I have been fooled now and then, but not often."

"So, you're the only one with a tough past, huh?"

He didn't reply. He looked away. "We'll need a place to go to dinner. We're definitely being watched, and while I'm not worried about our three stooges—who aren't all that stupid, I don't think—we're being watched by someone else, as well. I'm itching to get to the cemetery, but I know I have to trust others. I've called ahead. Miami field agents will be in the cemetery, in the mausoleums, around every angel high enough to cover a man. So, for us, for now…"

She sat next to him. He looked over at her.

She hesitated and then said, "I'm sorry. My past was a piece of cake. My parents are as sweet and kind as a pair of over overgrown lovebirds. I wanted to be a cop because my dad was a cop, and he was influential in catching a serial rapist at work on Eighth Street near Westchester. He somehow managed to teach us about the evils of the world and see the beauty in it, as well. He never whined about me becoming a cop because I was a woman, and neither did my mother. I never wanted for anything. I was helped through college. I… I'm sorry."

He reached across the sofa and took her hand. And they weren't playacting for anyone, because no one was in the room.

"I know," he told her. He grinned. "I've seen your file."

"And I haven't seen yours. I don't even know… Are you married?"

"I was."

"Divorced?"

"No."

"Oh. I'm…sorry."

"It's been a long time," he said.

"Still."

He shrugged and smiled. "You would have liked her."

"I'm sure I would have," she said softly.

He was studying her, to a point where she flushed. "What?"

"I'm a classic case—that's what an analyst would say, I'm pretty sure. Married young, the sweet love of youth, lost that love, plowed into work, kind of a loner. Way too much time undercover for serious relationships…"

She was definitely blushing by then.

"So I've read your file, but there's nothing in there that explains the you that Jorge knows—and told me all about."

"I'm going to kill him."

"Don't. He's your partner. And he loves you."

"Okay, so I don't have a haunted history. And I didn't lose anyone. I mean, I didn't lose a husband or a lover. I just…"

"Well, if you don't go out, you don't meet anyone."

"Seriously, I'm going to kill Jorge."

He grinned. "I really like Jorge. So?"

"Okay, I don't often work undercover. But I do work major crimes. And even though you have shifts with other officers and you work with other agencies, there are times you have to be dedicated to the case instead of getting to know the people you're working with. When you're the one a loved one of a victim is depending on, or you're the one who's gained the trust of a young witness, or…"

Her voice trailed. His elbow was angled on the couch and he was smiling as he watched her.

"Many men find female police detectives to be intimidating," she went on. "And many of those who don't are a little scary themselves. It's not that I don't go out, or I don't believe in going out—"

"Just haven't found the right guy?"

She shrugged, rising nervously. She hadn't expected the evening to turn into a tell-all, especially when she sure as hell couldn't tell the truth about her feelings regarding him.

She walked over to the door. "I guess we'd better go to dinner. Let's see…where haven't we been?"

He stood and met her at the entry. "I don't know. Where do you suggest?" They were facing each other, ridiculously close.

And then, they both heard a shuffling sound, just outside.

"Someone following you?" she mouthed to Jacob.

He carefully looked out. "Maybe," he mouthed back. He drew his gun. He checked the door, and she saw that he had double-bolted it.

To her surprise, he threw the door open.

Night was falling. But the way the apartment building had been laid out, the pool and patio area faced the west, and while the night encroached, the lowering sun created a sky of bold beauty. Soon, the radiant colors would be gone, and it would be the darkness that reigned.

"Ah, what a lovely night. Maybe later…" Jacob said, his voice carrying. And then, still speaking with a full rich voice, he turned to her. "On second thought, why don't we order in tonight?" he asked.

Was there someone out there? A figure, to the side in the shadows, hunkered down in a lawn chair?

The door was fully open. They were on display, and he was looking down at her with his brilliant blue eyes, so handsome and so startling against his dark hair and bronzed face.

Jacob pulled her into his arms and kissed her. And this time, he pulled her close. His mouth came down on hers while his arms encompassed her, his hands sliding down low against her back, drawing her ever closer, his tongue parting her lips and slipping deep within her mouth.

The door slowly closed behind them while they

backed inside the apartment, locked in the passionate embrace.

He was still kissing her as he eased one hand away, once again double-bolting the lock. She heard the sound as the bolts slid into place. And only then did his hold ease, his lips part from hers.

They were still so close. He looked down at her, and she could still feel the dampness of her lips, burning as they seemed to do when he touched her.

"I think..." she murmured, and he leaned closer, as if to hear her. His lips were almost upon hers again, his body was all but touching hers. To her amazement, she almost smiled, and she said softly, "Oh, screw this!"

She moved back into his arms. She was tall, but she moved up on tiptoe, the length of her body against his. She moved her mouth that one inch closer, found his lips and kissed him, parting his mouth, delving deep within it with her tongue, initiating all. She was stunned by her own movements, but more so by the depth of the longing and desire that was sweeping through her.

The kiss deepened and deepened. She pressed closer to him, flush against him, and felt his hands travel down the length of her body. The kiss broke, and he eased back slightly.

She felt she was panting like an idiot, and he had moved away. A flush of heat broke over her, and her limbs began to tremble. She had to force herself to bring her eyes to his, but when she did, she saw he was still watching her, intensely alert. He smiled slightly and said, "Ummmm." He was still holding her, and then he arched a brow and whispered, "Oh, screw this."

He swept her up, higher, into his arms. His mouth found hers again, but he moved as he kissed her, across the floor, toward the apartment bedroom. In seconds, they were lying down together on the bed. He braced himself over her, and said softly, "Only if it's what you really want."

She smiled. His pausing to question her, to be very sure, added to her sense of attraction and desperation.

She reached out, drawing his face down to hers again. She replied with her hands on his face, caressing his face as she drew him to her. "Yes. So much." They kissed again...just kissed, and then he straddled above her, doffing his jacket. The Glock he carried was evident then, and he reached back for the gun and holster, leaning over to set them on the dresser.

He looked down at her a moment.

"Mine's inside the bedside drawer, to the left," she told him. Now they both knew where to reach if they were threatened in any way at any time.

That solved, he struggled from his shirt; she rose up to help him. He was still in trousers, socks and shoes. He halfway rolled from her, divesting his clothing, and she slipped out of the cool knit dress she'd been wearing, as well as her bra and panties.

To her surprise, he suddenly made an urgent sound, almost like a growl, rising to meet her again.

Naked flesh against naked flesh, he whispered, "So wrong of me. I knew the moment I saw you on the runway that you were extraordinary, you were grace and laughter and beauty, and I wanted you, but I didn't know what it would mean when I knew you..."

When his mouth found hers again, she felt the burn that had teased her lips become something of a raging wildfire that snaked down the length of her body. She allowed herself to roam free with her hands, loving the curve of his shoulders, the clench of muscle in his shoulders and down his back. She felt his body harden against her own, and she couldn't wrap herself tightly enough to him, to be both almost in his skin and touch him just the same.

They fell back on the bed together and she lay on top of him, landing kisses on his neck and his shoulders, the hard planes of his stomach, and moving lower against his body.

His hands grabbed her back, and they flipped in the bed. His mouth fell upon her throat and her breasts and lingered and teased and caressed. Those kisses continued downward, and she arched and writhed against him, finding his flesh and returning each touch of passion and hunger and longing.

She thought she would burn to a cinder, she was so alive, burning with a need unlike anything she'd ever known, wanting the play to go on forever, yet desperate that something be touched, that he be within her, as well.

And then he was, and they were moving, and moving, and moving…

They rolled, their lips melded together again and the rock of his hips was incredible. The sense of him within her was almost more than she could bear, the absolute sweetness, the rise of that fire, that longing to be ever more a part of him. Rising…and bursting out upon her like a flow of liquid gold.

The night seemed to sweep in all around her for long moments as she felt little bits of ecstasy shoot through her, ebbing bit by incredible bit, until she felt the damp sheen of their flesh, still so taut together, the rise and fall of her breath, the rock-hard pounding of her heart.

And him, still holding her, still clinging in the darkness to the awesome beauty of what had been. So real, flesh and blood and pulse and their gasps for air…

They didn't speak at first; they just breathed.

And then he whispered softly, "I don't think I'll be putting that in the report."

She smiled and turned to him. "I understand you're often by the book. Forgive me."

"Forgive you?" He straddled her again, catching her hands and leaning low, his eyes alight with humor and tenderness. "Ah, my dear Detective Adair. It is I who must ask forgiveness. On second thought, no. Can't ask forgiveness. This was—"

"Incredible," she whispered.

"More than incredible. I don't know the words… Maybe there are none."

She pulled him back to her, and the kiss they shared was sweet and tender, and still, she knew, could arouse again at any second.

He pulled away and got out of bed suddenly. Light from the living room swept into the bedroom and she could see the full leanly muscled perfection of his tightly honed body in the doorway. He wasn't self-conscious as he padded out to the living room. Curious, she rose up on an arm.

Then he was back, every movement sleek and fluid, and he fell down beside her again. "Checking the door," he murmured.

"There's still someone out there?" she asked.

"Sitting by the pool. We'll order in," he told her.

He moved toward her and she jumped back suddenly, stricken. She'd been so enraptured with the man she'd been lucky enough to come to know that she had all but forgotten this wasn't an ordinary job.

She was looking for Mary. And even though Mary still seemed beyond her reach…

"Kari!" she exclaimed. "I'm worried, Jacob. What about Kari—and Mr. Connor?"

"I'll call in," he assured her. He found his jacket where he'd flung it earlier and dug his phone out of the pocket. After a minute, he had the info.

"Kari is back at her apartment."

"She's all right? And they're back inside?"

"Just Kari is back at her place. Connor took her out for a steak dinner and then a moonlit stroll on the beach. Then he brought her home. He left shortly, a smile on his face."

"Oh," Jasmine said. "Jacob, you don't think she'll be in any trouble with the gang for…for not sleeping with him?"

"No, I don't think she'll be in trouble."

Jasmine was still unsure. "He's being watched, Jasmine. Kari will be okay. Someone will get to Connor soon enough."

"Kari was worried though. I think she felt something was off. And I can't forget about Mary…"

"We'll find Mary. I swear it," he told her.

She believed him. And miraculously, she could move forward with her own night, grateful that the young blonde woman was all right. For now.

And there was nothing they could do. Not for the night.

She moved forward, catching his face, looking up into the dazzling blue of his eyes. "Thank you."

He kissed her again, that tender kiss… But the kiss

deepened, and then it began to travel, and he was kissing her breasts again, affording each the most tender caresses, and her belly and thighs, bringing that erotic fire with every touch.

She let the night seize her again, and she returned his caresses, unable to stop seeking more and more of him, know the taste of his skin, the taste of him.

They embraced tightly, and he was within her, and they rolled, and she was atop him, and this time they laughed and teased and whispered.

And then they lay together again, just breathing, still afrire, savoring the beauty of the darkness of the night, the coolness of the sheets beneath their bodies.

She was the one to sit up and straddle him this time.

He smiled, catching her hands with his. "Leave it to a cop to always want to be on top." He rolled her over, covering her with his body.

"And leave it to a Fed to think he must be in control."

"This Fed," he said softly, "is just happy to be with you."

She smiled back at him, wishing that the night would never end; that this was all they needed in reality and that the world would go away.

It could not.

He rolled from her, standing. "Food—we need to order food."

"I am hungry," she agreed.

She leaped out of bed, reaching to the foot of it for the caftan robe she kept there. He found his boxers but bothered with nothing else. He was already out in the living room, his phone drawn from his pocket. He looked at her. "I have a delivery service so, Chinese, Indian, Italian… Steaks? Seafood? What's your pleasure?"

You are my pleasure! she thought.

She managed not to say it out loud. "I'm easy. Food-wise," she added quickly. "Anything."

"Wow. I found one with pizza and champagne. Now there's an interesting combo. But I don't think that champagne… Not tonight."

"Not tonight," she agreed.

It was one thing to be drunk on desire when you were supposed to be drunk on desire. But quite another to have anything that might alter the mind with a goon outside on the porch.

"I don't believe we're in any danger, but I've seen things change quickly," he told her. "Ah, Thai food!"

"Perfect."

She stood near him and looked over his shoulder as he went through the offerings. They decided on one noodle dish and one rice dish.

Jasmine suddenly felt extremely awkward.

"Coffee!" she said. "I should make some coffee."

She started to walk into the kitchen. He caught her arm and pulled her back to him, holding her there, looking into her eyes. "Please, don't go away from me," he said softly.

She knew he didn't mean she shouldn't go into the kitchen and make coffee.

"I…it sounds like a line," she told him, "but I've never…in my life…just done this so quickly… I guess I don't know how to act."

"And I hope you believe me. I've always drawn a line. Until tonight."

She stood on her toes and kissed his lips lightly. "I won't go away," she promised.

She made coffee; Thai food arrived. Jacob made a

point of answering the door still clad just in his boxers. He was careful to double-bolt the door again, and
then to bring his Glock back out to sit on the table
while they ate.

"You know, I'm a damned good markswoman," she
told him.

He smiled at her. "I'd expect no less." He picked at
a strand of the noodles. "Oh, by the way, Kozak gave
you to me today." His smiled deepened as he saw her
stiffen. "Sorry. All in a role."

She hesitated. "But in truth, I give myself where I
choose."

"And so do I," he told her.

She laughed softly. Much of the Thai food went un-
eaten; they wound up laughing over a noodle they had
both chosen.

And then they wound up in one another's arms again.

THERE WAS A knock on the door.

Jacob rolled out of bed, instantly awake. He grabbed
his trousers and then his gun. Jasmine followed him
out of bed in a flash, slipping on a robe, going for her
own weapon.

He took a quick glance at the clock on the nightstand:
9:00 a.m. He headed out of the bedroom quickly, with
Jasmine on his heels.

But one look out the peephole had Jacob unlocking
the door. "It's all right. A friend," he told her.

Jorge stepped in, looked at both of them and then
smiled.

"Method acting!" he said. "I like it. Just wondering
what the hell took you two so long."

Chapter Ten

The funeral service was long. Speaking in Russian, the priest delivered the service with all respect and care—while the man might have known about Smirnoff and his deeds, he didn't judge when it came time for a man to meet his Maker. It was actually beautiful, though Jacob was sure many in the congregation had no idea what was being said.

Victor Kozak gave an emotional speech about his friend, and he did so in English for the benefit of the mourners who had gathered.

Many had come out to pay their respects—not so many would be invited to the celebration of life that would come later, at the club. Equally, not so many would travel with the funeral train that would follow the hearse to the cemetery.

Jacob had spoken with his Miami counterpart, Dean Jenkins. He knew agents were already waiting at the cemetery.

It would be a fine day for an attempt on Victor Kozak's life.

Jenkins also filled him in on what was happening with events at the morgue, and with the local crime scene technicians.

"They identified one of the dead men, from the hand they got out of the alligator's gullet. Ain't technology great? Although, to be honest, it wasn't fingerprints or anything like that. One of my guys working in Little Havana recognized the ring.

"The victim was Leonardo Gonzalez—an undocumented Venezuelan immigrant. He and a few of his fellows had traveled through Mexico and, according to our agent, onto a cruise ship and into Miami. He'd been a contract killer at home and was looking for work in Little Havana. He was happy to work for anyone but was looking for connections in the Little Havana area because he didn't speak any English.

"Anyway…according to our sources, he was the kind of really bad guy taking serious advantage of the criminal activity going on down there right now, but he might have crossed another crime lord, meaning it was time for him to get out. But he had his own little gang. I'm working under the assumption our other two headless bodies are associates of his."

"Thanks— Anything new on Donald McPherson Connor?"

"We followed him. He was a perfect gentleman with the young lady. And he left her at her door. An agent is still outside. He could have followed Connor, or he could have kept his eye on her. He chose to protect the one we know to be an innocent. Anyway, we have a new crew out on the streets today. Oh, they're checking in at your art gallery, too, making sure that Special Agent Partridge is doing okay."

"Thanks. Hey, should I be getting a new phone?"

"Not to worry, I'm listed as a local artist. You any closer?" Jenkins asked him.

"I don't know. I'm going to see what happens at the funeral."

They ended their call, and Jacob joined the mourners, making himself one with Ivan Petrov and the three goons.

Jasmine was not invited to this part of the day; she would be at the club, preparing to work with the food and drinks that would be served. He tried not to worry. He knew she was an accomplished policewoman, and he believed she was an excellent markswoman. She was also vulnerable, though he had warned her that she should be wary at all times—and armed if any way possible.

She knew that, of course.

Kozak hadn't asked Jacob to drive to the cemetery; he wanted him next to him in his car, behind the driver, who would be Antonovich.

Jacob couldn't help but wonder if Kozak was afraid that Antonovich could shoot them both if Jacob was driving—he'd be easy prey for a man sitting behind him.

They arrived safely at the cemetery. It was just west of the downtown area known as Calle Ocho. The cemetery had recently joined with two different companies that had been offering funeral arrangements and grave sites since the 1850s back in Cuba. It was at the edge of a neighborhood close to downtown known as Little Havana.

But like most of Miami, anyone and everyone might be here.

They entered through Gothic arches. The grounds were sweeping, well tended and beautiful. Trees cast shady spots everywhere, and the park stretched for long blocks. They drove around a winding trail until they reached the canopy that stood over the area where the body of Josef Smirnoff would be laid to rest.

The cars parked; Jacob got out and waited for Kozak to emerge from the car, as well. He looked around. A lovely marble angel stood guard over a nearby family lot; a small family mausoleum stood about fifty yards away. Another, about a hundred yards farther out.

They were under a gracious old oak, near to a grouping of military headstones. Down a bit farther was a large concrete memorial to a man who had been a Mason and with the Mahi Shrine. His memorial gave witness to the fact that he had spent forty years as a Shriner, dedicating his time to raising funds for the children's hospital.

Probably a great guy. Right now, Jacob had to be certain that his memorial wasn't hiding a sniper.

He continued his scan of the area. The large mausoleum with its beautiful stained-glass windows, known to house many, many bodies, was perhaps a hundred yards behind them. A great place for a sniper to hide.

He reminded himself that the Miami agents knew this cemetery, where to be and where to watch.

And still he was on high alert.

"There, Mr. Kozak," Antonovich said, coming around to Kozak's side. "The chairs in front, sir. Those are for you and those who were close to Josef."

Sticking to Kozak's side like a piece of lint, Jacob led the man to the chairs.

Josef Smirnoff might not have been a cold-blooded killer, but he sure as hell had been a criminal. Victor Kozak had taken over from him, and while he might not be a cold-blooded killer either, he was also a major criminal.

But the showing of respectable people at the cemetery was large enough; the local news media brought trucks to the winding road that led through the very large cemetery—another place for a shooter to hide. Politicians and other respectable citizens arrived to say goodbye to Smirnoff.

Jacob sat back as the priest gave the graveside prayers. He had to have faith in his fellow agents. But just as he had settled—still alert and ready—a latecomer arrived at the grave site.

It was the man who so disturbed Jasmine.

Donald McPherson Connor.

THE CLUB WAS a bustle of activity when Jasmine arrived, even though it was early. The catering company personnel included two chefs, two wine stewards and six members of a cleanup crew.

Jasmine and Jorge reported right away to the dressing room. The servers were suited out appropriately— men in tuxes, women in similar versions with short skirts instead of pants—and shown the various food stations and the additional bars.

"Remember, today, you serve quickly, politely and quietly. We honor Josef," Natasha instructed. "You all understand? Behavior is beyond circumspect."

Stopping by one of the makeup tables where Jasmine had just harnessed her own hair in a braid at the back of her neck, Jorge told her, "Five City of Miami Beach cops, all aware to watch for trouble—hired on by Kozak." He lowered his head to her, pretending to smooth back a piece of her hair. "The chef at the first table is a plant—FBI. We have representation from MDPD as well—Detective Birch. You've worked with her. She'll be on the arm of one of our young politicians."

"Sounds good," Jasmine murmured. "Then again, how many cops were prowling the show when Josef was killed?"

"There's a cop at the balcony door. If anyone is going to start shooting, it won't be from the balcony." He leaned closer still, pretending to flick a piece of nonexistent lint from her brow. "FBI is crawling over the cemetery, too. Thing is, the killer must know. Unless he—or she—is really an egotistical bastard, nothing will happen today."

Nothing would happen. This would go on...

Jorge grinned suddenly. "You look different."

"I don't dress this way often."

"No, it's the way your eyes are shining."

"Jorge."

"It's nice to see you happy."

She looked at him and then lowered her head, ruefully smiling. "I'd like to see you happy."

"Hey, you may. I'm not watched, not the way you are," he told her. "I had some dinner out last night. Sat on the beach."

"Jorge, you have to be—"

"I was careful. Trust me."

He grinned, and she knew it was the truth.

"Jorge, I need you!" Natasha called. "Now, you will take the large silver tray—you have nice long arms. Move through the crowd but offer up the food. Do not interfere with people who are talking. You let them stop. Think of yourselves as courteous machines."

Jorge moved on. Jasmine saw Kari at the next dressing table and she stood, heading over to her.

"Need help with anything?" she asked.

"Nope," Kari said, looking up. "I never can do false eyelashes right, but Natasha says we shouldn't wear them today."

"They're miserable things anyway."

"I agree."

"So, how are you?" Jasmine asked her softly.

"Good. Great, really."

"Great?" Jasmine asked.

Kari smiled. "I know that he's old, but honestly, if I were, say, forty-five instead of twenty-two, well... He has such a great accent. He talked to me about books and plays and he told me so much history about this place that I didn't know... He's kind, Jasmine. So very kind."

"Great to hear. I thought he made you a bit nervous. Are you okay with him now? When do you see him again?"

"Tonight. Later, of course. I told him—and I'm sure Natasha told him—that the club models were working the funeral, and we wouldn't be available until the entire celebration of life came to an end. He told me that, no matter what the hour, he'd like to see me." Kari hesitated a moment and then whispered, "I don't know why I was worried. Jasmine, we had the best dinner. Such a lovely night. He's truly so well educated. And then I thought he would want more. I thought he would want me to sleep with him. Oh! And he talked about Mary. He said she was such a lovely person—he was sure she went on to resume her education. They had talked about school and always having a backup to modeling or acting. He believes she might have headed out to California."

California? Or the pit of an alligator's stomach, somewhere out in the Everglades.

"I guess he's worked with or been a client of these people for a while," Jasmine said.

"Not so long. He told me that the group here—well, Josef Smirnoff first, and now Victor Kozak—knew how to find the most cultured women. He likes to go to the theater and the opera and art shows, and…he needs the right escorts."

"How nice."

"He loves music and musicals, voices!"

The opera…or screams as a woman died beneath a knife?

"Jasmine, he's really such a gentleman. I thought he might be the type to immediately demand that we sleep together, that…"

"What?"

"That he might want me to do weird things." Her voice dropped to a whisper. "You know, weird sexual things. Scary things." She swallowed. "You know… autoerotic asphyxiation, or maybe not even scary things, just disgusting things. But he didn't even press sleeping with me." She paused, seeming a little uncomfortable, then went on quietly. "We're not specifically *ordered* to sleep with the clients, but there's an understanding that they get what they want if they're paying the price. And that trickles down to us in money and…in prestige on the runway. It's no secret that Natasha's highest earners get the best gigs. But…this guy, no pressure. I'm babbling. I guess I am still maybe a little nervous."

"Kari, you have my number, right? If not, I'll make sure that you do now."

Kari pulled out her phone and Jasmine quickly gave her the number to her burner phone.

"We're having lunch, right?" Kari asked.

"Lunch, yes, but keep your phone near. If you're afraid at any point, you call me immediately!"

Kari frowned, but then smiled. "You can call me, too, you know, except that… Well! You seem just fine, and I imagine…" She broke off and laughed suddenly, leaning forward. "I might have been willing to pay some big bucks myself for that blue-eyed wonder who chose you."

Jasmine smiled weakly.

"You're okay, right?" Kari asked. "I mean, with him."

"Yes, I'm just fine," Jasmine managed.

"What is he like, that Jacob? Those eyes of his… If he ever looked at me the way he looks at you, wow. I'd be putty."

"Putty," Jasmine repeated. "That's me."

"Girls!" Natasha called. "Time to take your stations. Sasha has called—the services at the grave site are ending. We will be ready, the most gracious of hosts and hostesses."

And so, they were on. They all trailed out of the dressing room.

Natasha was by the balcony door; it was open for them to head down the stairs.

Jasmine smiled as she passed Natasha. Only Kozak was supposed to have a key. But Victor wasn't here. And Ivan was downstairs, setting up the main bar, giving orders to the catering company.

Jasmine hurried downstairs along with the others.

She knew that somehow, she would get that information to Jacob.

Lightning didn't strike twice...

Unless sometimes, it did.

NO BULLETS RANG out at the cemetery.

The priest, resplendent in his robes, carried through the service. Women had been given roses; they walked past the coffin to drop them down upon it.

"I need a moment," Kozak told his companions.

He was at the coffin alone, except for the four cemetery workers who waited discreetly to see that the coffin was lowered six feet under. The hearse was preparing to leave. Antonovich, Suarez and Garibaldi waited while other mourners filed out to their cars.

Donald McPherson Connor was starting to walk away.

Jacob was a distance from Victor Kozak as it was; he wouldn't be any farther from the man if he walked toward Connor. He excused himself to the trio of bodyguards.

"Mr. Connor!" Jacob called out.

The man stopped walking and looked back at him, eyeing him distastefully. Jacob noticed that he was lean but fit.

Probably plenty strong. Certainly strong enough against a slim blonde girl.

Connor was evidently irritated at having been stopped—by Jacob, at any rate. "Yes, Mr. Marensky, what is it?"

"Well, I just wish to apologize, and I hope that we don't keep bad blood between us. I was, in fact, hoping that you found Miss Anderson to be up to your expectations."

"Miss Anderson is a truly lovely woman. I am enjoying her company."

Jacob forced a smile. "Excellent. She is quite beautiful."

"Not as intriguing as Miss Alamein though," Connor said. He was an oddly dignified man—soft-spoken. "So, Mr. Marenksy, what exactly do you do in relation to the Gold Sun Club?"

Then again, Jacob had seen some of the most innocent and soft-spoken men and women possible turn out to be vicious and as cold as ice.

"We have shared business interests. I run an art gallery," Jacob said.

"So I hear," Connor said, his British accent a little clipped.

"I'd welcome you for a visit. See if there's anything that catches your eye. Just what is your enterprise, sir?"

The man's smile tightened. "No enterprise—other than the stock market. Now there, sir, is bloody criminal action from the get-go, and yet quite legal."

"Ah, I believed that you had worked with Josef—and now Victor."

"I simply require a certain kind of companion."

"I see," Jacob said, still smiling. Just what was it that he required? "Well, sir, I shall see you at the club. I just wished to clear the air between us. Please understand, my arrangements had been made first."

"Oh, yes, I understand perfectly, Mr. Marensky." Connor was still looking at him with watery blue hatred.

"Jacob?" Kozak was calling to him.

"Excuse me," Jacob said, spinning around to return to Victor Kozak's side.

"We must be leaving now," Kozak said.

"Yes, of course."

"You and Connor are good then?" Kozak asked him softly.

"Oh, as good as we can be, Victor. As good as we can be."

"Please, then..." Kozak indicated the road through the cemetery; theirs was the only car that remained. "Sasha, you will drive."

"Yes, sir," Antonovich said, sliding into the driver's seat.

Garibaldi took the front seat by him. Kozak slid into the back, between Suarez and Jacob. The car rolled out of the cemetery, onto Southwest Eighth Street and then headed for I-95 and the extension out to South Beach.

The funeral itself had gone off without a hitch. Now, all they had to do was make it through the reception—the celebration of life where the mourners would come together and Smirnoff would receive his last honors.

Smirnoff, Kozak and their peers really were criminals. Jacob had seen one too many a decent person cajoled into and then hooked on drugs. And abusing the trust of hopeful girls was reprehensible. But Jacob wanted Kozak prosecuted and locked away—not on a slab with a bullet in his head.

As the car rolled up to Kozak's special parking place at the back of the property, Jacob felt Kozak's hand wind into a vise on his arm.

The man looked at him, and there was fear in his eyes, quickly masked as Garibaldi came around and opened the door.

Jacob got out.

"My friend, I know you will change things!" Kozak said. He caught Jacob's arm again, turning to show him where they were. "Cops—down there, at the end of the block. That guy with the long hair and the beggar's cup at this end? A cop." He pulled Jacob along to show him the men to whom he was referring.

And then he whispered to Jacob, "Here. This is where they will try to kill me. Somewhere here, at the club."

Chapter Eleven

It always amazed Jasmine to see the people who came out for such an event—the last rites for a man they had to have known conducted criminal activities. She was also certain many people on the guest list had not sat through the long religious ceremony at the church, nor attended the final graveside services.

The club was busy within minutes of the door opening.

Ivan stood at the main doors dressed in his best designer suit. Natasha was at his side tonight, ready to greet everyone as they came in; she had finished her busywork, prepared her various crews and was ready to be the grand hostess.

Jasmine had been given a tray of canapés to carry around, and she did so smoothly and easily. Though maintaining her demeanor as a courteous robot was not as easy as it might have been—Kozak and the goons and Jacob had yet to come into the club.

When they finally did, she breathed an inward sigh of relief.

She tried to maneuver herself around to Jacob's position casually, making it part of her regular sweep of the room. When she made it to an area near the street entrance, he was still standing with Kozak and the body-guards.

"Gentlemen," she said quietly, offering up her tray.

The bodyguards quickly reached for the little quiches. Jacob inclined his head slightly and took a canapé, as well.

Kozak turned to her. "What I need is a drink, Jasmine. Will you get me a vodka? I'm sure that Natasha has seen to it that our hired bartender knows what is my special reserve."

"Yes, of course," Jasmine said.

But Natasha swept by at that moment, giving her a serious frown. "Jasmine, you are to move among our guests."

"Yes, Natasha," she said.

"Natasha," Kozak said softly. "We have many people working the floor. I would like Jasmine to go and get me my drink."

"Victor, I can do that for you," Natasha said.

"You are the hostess. Let Jasmine go," Kozak said. "It's time that I...that I welcome our guests and give my little speech here, eh? But one vodka first!"

Jasmine headed off to the bar. The man there gave her an appreciative look and she smiled in return. "I need a drink for Mr. Kozak—his special reserve. He believes you'll know what it is."

"Yep," the bartender said. "I've been given the bottle and serious instructions. It's a unique vintage from Russia, not sold in the United States." He grinned at her, reaching beneath the bar for the bottle. He got a glass and said, "Just two ice cubes. Rich men and their drinks."

"Thanks," she told him.

"I live to serve. Come see me again!"

She nodded and started to hurry away but turned back. "Did you meet with Mr. Kozak before this event? Did he give you the bottle?" she asked.

He shook his head. "I met with the praying mantis. Oh, sorry—the entire catering company met with Natasha. She gave us strict instructions."

"And the bottle of vodka?"

"No, it was here where she said it would be when I came in. Hey, sorry, I hope she's not a friend of yours—I'm an actor and this catering company keeps me in cash while I'm pounding the pavement. I'm sorry. Please, I didn't mean to be offensive."

"You need to be a lot more careful."

"Please, don't get me fired."

"I won't, but… Never mind. Thank you."

Once again, she turned away, but then something about the situation seemed disturbing. "Would you mind? Give me four more drinks, just like this one but with regular vodka. Something good, just not Kozak's special reserve."

"Anything for you."

She smiled. And prayed that she and Jacob had come to know one another in their undercover roles as well as they had come to know one another personally.

Kozak and Jacob, with Garibaldi, Suarez, and Antonovich behind them, were heading toward the stage. Jasmine took a step back, her heart pounding, wondering if she was wrong and if she might just cause the entire operation to implode—and put them all, including the guests, in serious danger.

But her hunch was strong. She had seen Natasha with the key.

Natasha was definitely sleeping with Kozak—but had she been sleeping with Josef Smirnoff before? Was she part of what came with taking over the business because she wouldn't be ousted herself?

Jasmine walked toward the men.

"Special for Mr. Kozak, and gentlemen, I believe it was a long day for you, as well. I hope I have not displeased you, Mr. Kozak."

She looked at Jacob, just lowering her eyes at the glass he was to take, and gave the barest shake of her head. He shouldn't drink it. He would know—surely, he would know!

Jacob's striking blue eyes fell on hers. Before Kozak could answer, he said, "That was very thoughtful of you."

"Nice, sweet, as always," Antonovich said happily, and he looked at Kozak.

"Definitely. One vodka, boss, eh?" Suarez asked.

"One vodka," Kozak agreed.

Jasmine dared look around as the men took their drinks. An up-and-coming beach politician was entering with a lovely young news reporter on his arm. Natasha was doing her duty and greeting them.

"I must get to the stage," Kozak said.

"I'll get you there swiftly," Jacob assured him.

Jasmine flashed a smile to all of them. "I'd best get to my canapés," she said. She started to walk away.

"A second?" Jacob asked, looking at Kozak for permission, as well.

"Yes, then you will walk with me, stand by me, at my back," Kozak said.

Jacob smiled and stepped away with Jasmine. She had her chance. "Natasha had the key tonight," she said.

"Might be important. Kozak wasn't here. I don't think they plan a shooting."

"Poison in the vodka?"

"I could be wrong."

"Thanks. You gave it to me."

"You knew!"

"I knew," he assured her, and then he squeezed her hand and stepped back.

"To the stage," Kozak said. He seemed very nervous.

As he should be! Jasmine thought.

As he walked away, Kozak took a sip of his vodka. He frowned instantly. The man did know the taste of his special reserve.

And that wasn't his special reserve.

But Jacob guided him toward the stage. Jasmine saw Jacob casually and discreetly set his own glass down on a waiter's tray.

The waiter was Jorge. He looked across the room at her and nodded.

JACOB STOOD JUST behind Victor Kozak as the man took the microphone, thanking everyone for coming, and for honoring Josef Smirnoff. He told a few tales about his friend and talked about the way Smirnoff had loved Miami Beach and how the club had been a dream for him.

"Sparkling like the Miami sun!" Victor said. "He was my business partner. He was my friend. In his honor, we will rename the club—it will be *Josef's* when it opens to the public tomorrow night. While we faced senseless violence and his death here, we are a powerful people. We are South Floridians, whether we were born here or we were lucky enough to enter this country and find this paradise as our home. We are strong. And, in his name, we will prevail!"

As Kozak spoke, Jacob kept his eyes on the room. He also mused that Kozak didn't think that peddling escorts or drug dealing were really bad things to do. Illegal, but not bad.

He saw the police—in uniform, and undercover— and the agents in the room. And he knew each of them was watching for the first sign, so much as a hint, of the barrel of a gun or someone reaching into a pocket.

But he was pretty sure Jasmine was right; guns would not be blazing. A killer must right now be waiting for whatever poison might have been in the special reserve to work.

"Make it quick," Jacob managed to whisper.

Kozak took heed. He quickly asked the crowd to honor Smirnoff's memory and enjoy his dream. Then Jacob took his arm and led him from the stage.

"Tell your men you feel sick," he said. "That I'm going to get you upstairs."

Kozak heeded him once again. "I am unwell! Sasha, you will watch the east stairs. Antonio, you will watch the west. Alejandro, you will take between them. I am... I must sit down. Alone. The day... It has been too long. Mr. Marensky will see me upstairs to my office. Tell Ivan and Natasha they must remain the finest hosts."

"Yes, sir," Garibaldi said quickly.

"Hurry, and stumble as we walk up," Jacob said quietly to Kozak.

Antonovich nodded to the policeman at the base of the stairs; the man noticed Kozak, nodded in return and unlatched the velvet barrier. Jacob set his arm on Kozak's back and they headed up the stairs. Halfway up, Kozak pretended to stumble.

"Good, good, we keep going," Jacob murmured.

They passed the expected security. They made it to the door, and Jacob passed through it quickly. A cop met them in the hall.

"Getting Mr. Kozak to his office," Jacob told him.

The cop nodded.

They opened the door to the office—despite the massive security, Jacob entered first.

The office was empty. He had expected it would be. The killer would be waiting for Kozak to fall downstairs.

And everyone would think the day had been just too difficult for Victor Kozak. The man drank, he liked his cigars, and maybe he liked some of his smuggled product, too. His heart could just give out, after a day like today.

And the poison wouldn't be found during an autopsy, since such substances would not fall into the realm of regular tests.

Kozak sat behind his desk and sighed deeply. "I really could use a drink!"

"I'm sure you keep something in here. Then again, I'm sure there are others who know you keep something in here," Jacob warned him.

"So. I will not drink. What do I do?" Kozak asked.

"We wait here. We see if someone comes. Maybe we call an ambulance. We let the crowd know you're in the emergency room, barely hanging on."

Kozak drummed his fingers on his desk, smiling. He stared at Jacob.

"You are not an art dealer, are you, Mr. Marensky? As a matter of fact, your name isn't even Marensky, is it?"

THE NIGHT SEEMED VERY, very long.

Jasmine moved about the floor as she had been directed, watching the stairs now and then. She saw Jorge with one of the catering crew, an FBI plant, and knew the vodka was probably already on its way to be tested.

But the bartender, she was sure, had just been hired on for the night.

She saw the other girls milling about the room, doing exactly what they had been told to do. They were pretty and silent and moving like robots. She watched the stairs. And to her relief, people began to leave.

While the club had been open and music—soft, somber music, much of it Russian—had played through the night, there was no dancing. After the speech, after the food and free-flowing alcohol, there was little else to do.

People murmured about coming when the club was up and running again. Big names in music had been booked before Smirnoff's death—they were probably still on the agenda.

She was doing her last round with coffees and coffee liqueurs when she saw the man, Donald McPherson Connor, stop Kari Anderson and talk to her. Then he slipped out the door.

A moment later, Kari followed.

Jasmine walked back to the bar quickly, ready to dispose of her tray and head out.

But there was a man at the bar. A little man with big glasses, a nerdy smile and wild bushy hair. "Don't," he said softly, then called to the bartender. "Another, my friend!"

"Pardon?" Jasmine asked, setting her tray down. She didn't care what he was saying; Jacob had Kozak upstairs. Things were coming to a head. And Kari was leaving with a man who just might be a very sick murderer.

"No, we're on it," the little man said. He spoke more loudly. "I mean, man, you're not just a beauty, lady, you are really cool looking. Those eyes of yours—emeralds!" He lowered his voice while pretending to study her eyes. "Special Agent Dean Jenkins, working in association with Wolff. We have a man following Connor and Miss Anderson. Keep your cover."

"That's very nice of you, sir," she said. "I work for the club. We don't date customers."

Garibaldi came up behind her. "Is there a problem?" he asked, glaring at the man who had just identified himself to her as FBI.

Dean Jenkins lifted his hands. "No, sir. No problem. I'm totally a hands-off guy, just complimenting beauty."

"He was very sweet. No problem at all," Jasmine said quickly.

To her relief, Garibaldi ambled away.

Jasmine turned with her tray of coffee cups and coffee drinks.

Natasha was standing there. "All is well?"

"Yes, of course."

"Have you seen Mr. Marensky?" Natasha asked her.

"I believe he went up with Mr. Kozak. He wasn't feeling well."

"They are upstairs? Still?"

Jasmine didn't have to answer. She heard the sound of an ambulance screaming through the night. People began to chatter nervously.

"Oh, my God! Victor!" Natasha cried. She turned and raced for the stairs. She was stopped by Garibaldi, with whom she argued. But this time, Garibaldi had apparently been given strict instructions by Kozak himself.

The wailing sirens stopped.

Natasha kept arguing with Garibaldi. Ivan was coming to join her, a strange look on his face. Was he frowning…or was that a look of satisfaction?

No one was near Jasmine at that moment. She heard a soft whisper at her ear.

Dean Jenkins was standing just behind her. "Jacob is with Kozak. They're heading to the hospital. Word will be out that he collapsed and that they're afraid of a heart attack."

Jasmine let him know she had heard him, nodding slightly, watching along with the others. She moved away from him. As she did so, she felt her phone vibrate in her pocket. She quickly made her way close to the bar, behind a structural beam, and answered it, halfway expecting Jacob.

But it wasn't Jacob.

"Jasmine!"

It was Kari Anderson.

"Jasmine, I need to tell you—"

"Kari, what? Kari?"

Jasmine looked at her phone; the call had ended. The line was dead.

"So, I WILL DIE. Or I will go to prison for the rest of my life," Kozak said, sighing softly. He shrugged. He was lying in the back of an ambulance. Comfortable.

It was a real ambulance. But they weren't real paramedics manning the vehicle, though they would really take Kozak to the hospital, where he would really be admitted.

Jacob had feared that Natasha or Ivan might have made their way upstairs before he'd managed to get Kozak out, but the ambulance had arrived just in time— and Kozak had been shoved right in and the vehicle had taken off into the night. Within moments of closing the ambulance doors, Jacob had revealed to him that he was FBI.

"Victor, the whole operation has to go down," Jacob told him. "I'm sure if you give the district attorney any help you can, he'll make the best arrangements possible."

"I can give you cartels. Names of the men who come and go with drugs and drug money."

"I'm not the DA," Jacob said.

"And I discovered that I do want to live, however long that may be," Kozak told him. He sighed. "My friend, will you do one thing for me?"

"This will be out of my hands now, Victor."

But Victor smiled. "This is a small thing. Before I am locked away, will you see to it that I get just one more…"

"One more what?"

"Shot of my good vodka!"

"I will do my best, Victor. I'm sure you have an attorney, and… I don't know. But for now, your best service is to give us the men who did put those bodies in the oil drums and who left the headless men in the Everglades."

"They want me dead."

"All the more reason we need anything you have to find out just who is calling the shots."

Jacob felt his phone vibrating in his pocket.

Jasmine? She had saved the night, somehow suspecting there might be poison in the vodka. But her cover might be jeopardized...

He answered the phone quickly.

It was Dean Jenkins. "She's gone after Connor, Jacob. Your detective associate."

"What? How? When?"

"The commotion started with the siren. She disappeared. And she saw Kari take off after Connor. We have a man on him, of course, and I'm on my way out, but—"

Jacob leaped up and hurried to the front of the ambulance. "Stop, let me out—quickly!" he said.

"Yes, sir. But—"

"Proceed, get him to a room, guards all around," Jacob said.

"Will do," the driver promised.

The ambulance jerked to a halt. Jacob jumped out and began to run. He had blocks to run, blocks filled with tourists, diners, children...

But at least Connor's apartment was north of the club. At least...

Jasmine was a cop; a good cop. She'd be all right. She'd think it out.

She was also emotional. She was afraid Mary had disappeared because Connor had done something horrible to her. Afraid that same horrible thing might happen to Kari...

"Hey!" a man protested.

Jacob just nudged past him and quickened his pace.

THANKS TO DEAN JENKINS, Jorge and all the other police and agents working the case, Jasmine knew where to go. Connor's room. She knew the street, the hotel complex and the number.

Naturally, it was on a side street—one that was poorly lit, for the beach. One that was a bit austere, where the rich came to stay, unburdened by the noise and ruckus of the average working-man tourist.

She ran up to the building. She could see the lobby through the plate-glass windows that surrounded the handsome interior. It was an old deco place redone—velvet upholstered chairs and a check-in reception that wasn't a counter but a desk. She could see a man with a newspaper in the lobby, watching the door.

FBI. The man watching Donald McPherson Connor? If so, he was nowhere near close enough.

Jasmine hesitated, taking a deep breath. One more time—one more try.

She pulled out her cell and dialed Kari's number. It rang once and went straight to voice mail.

She pocketed her phone and tried for a regal and nonchalant manner. She waited for the clerk to walk back into the office behind the desk.

Then she sashayed through as if she belonged there, despite her elaborate if dignified waitress uniform. She didn't know the man with the newspaper; he didn't know her. She offered him a brilliant smile and sauntered on through to the elevator.

She realized, in the elevator, that Connor had taken the penthouse; a floor all to himself. She was surprised when the elevator let her choose the top floor without any additional security.

The doors opened into a charming vestibule, rather than a hallway. It was as if she had arrived at someone's grand house. Handsome double doors led into the apartment itself.

She tried knocking, her heart beating a thousand drums a second. It would be illegal for her just to enter. She certainly couldn't force it open.

She waited…and no one came. The door might well be unlocked in such a building—in a good neighborhood, with security in the lobby.

And if she said she entered because she thought she heard a cry…

Just as Jasmine reached for the handle, the door opened.

Connor stood there, a gun in his hand.

"Ah, Jasmine," he said. "We've been waiting for you."

As HE RAN, Jacob envisioned every manner of horror. His breath was coming hard; his calves were burning.

He knew he had made the right choice, running. It was the weekend on the beach, cars were bumper-to-bumper. For some reason there was an element of local society who thought it was cool to drive down Collins Avenue and show off their cars, some elegant, some souped-up, some convertibles, and some…just cars. Some with music blaring, and some discreetly quiet.

He was moving far faster than the cars.

And still…

He pictured Jasmine, bursting in on Connor. And Connor, ready for her, shots blazing before she could enter the room; Jasmine shooting back, maybe even taking the man down, as well. Injuring him, maybe killing him, but then lying there in a pool of blood, dark hair streaming through it, almost blue-black in contrast to the color of blood, eyes brilliant emerald as she stared into the night, and yet…sightless.

He had to stop thinking that way. He wasn't prone to panic; he'd have never survived his past.

His phone rang; he answered it anxiously, still running. It was Dean Jenkins.

"Natasha, Ivan and the trio have headed to the hospital. I was just escorted out of the club. It went into lockdown. I found a place behind a dumpster by the cars. They all left together in the limo."

"Thanks. But no one goes in to see Kozak. They can be herded into a waiting room. They can't be near him. They can't know he's not really poisoned."

"We've got a 'doctor' ready to talk to them. As far as they'll know, Kozak is being airlifted to a trauma center where they're fighting to save his life."

"Thanks, Jenkins."

"Anything on your end yet?"

Apparently, Jenkins couldn't hear the way that he was panting. Just one more corner…

"Almost there."

He turned the corner and saw Connor's building, grand touches of Mediterranean-style along with the fine art deco architecture.

He ran through protocol in his mind—there was no right way to burst in on the man. This was a small part of what was going on; they didn't know who had killed Josef, who had tried to kill Kozak. The operation was in a crisis situation at the moment—and he needed to keep his cover.

He ran to the front, stopped briefly for a long breath and to gather his composure. He saw the agent with his newspaper—and the tiny dolphin tie tack that identified him. A clerk in a handsome suit sat at the desk.

There was no time; Jacob entered the lobby, headed over to the man he'd never met, and greeted him. "Henry, how are you doing?"

"Great—fine fishing today. The kids come in tomorrow. We're going to take them over to Key Biscayne to see the lighthouse and then back to the Seaquarium— let them swim with some dolphins."

"Sounds like a plan. I've done the dolphin thing myself…" Jacob watched as the clerk headed to a back room. "How long?"

"Connor—just twenty minutes or so. Kari Anderson— fifteen. And then, another woman, just a matter of minutes."

Minutes…

Jacob headed for the elevator. It only took seconds for a bullet to find its mark. But as he reached the elevator, he realized the other agent had leaped to his feet to join him.

"I'm here now," Jacob said. "If I need backup, you'll know. If I'm not down—"

"Wait, there's just something you need to hear first," the agent said.

CONNOR NEVER HAD a chance to use his weapon.

Jasmine judged her distance—and the awkward way the man was holding the gun. She ducked low and took a flying leap at him, catching his legs, toppling him.

She'd been right; he was no gunslinger himself; he was completely inept. His gun went flying and he let out a yelp that made him sound like a wounded kitten.

She straddled him, pinning him down. "Where's Kari? What have you done with her?"

"What have I done with her?" He seemed stunned.

"You bastard, what have you done with her?"

It would be unethical, but…she was still playing a role. She'd taken him, and she meant to get the truth from him, beat it out of him if she had to. She could get away with this—one high-class escort worried about another, attacking a man…

But just as she was about to deliver a good right to his jaw, she heard her name called.

She looked up.

Kari was standing in the archway to the next room.

At the same time, she felt strong arms wrap around her waist, drawing her off of Connor. She twisted and fought and turned—

Jacob!

Jacob, stopping her, when she had the man down… "Let me go!" she demanded furiously.

"Jasmine, Jasmine, it's all right, you don't understand!" Kari cried. She rushed over to Connor, going down on her knees and trying to help the man up.

Astonished, Jasmine turned to Jacob. "What in God's name is happening?" she demanded, wrenching free from him. "Has everyone gone mad?"

Jacob turned and closed and locked the door and then looked at her.

For one moment, she felt extreme panic. Were they all in on it? Was Jacob a turncoat, had he somehow tricked the federal government, was this all…?

No! She believed in him, she knew him, knew this couldn't be.

"I admit, I don't fully know myself," Jacob said. "But we need to give Mr. Connor a chance to explain."

Connor was up on his feet, standing next to Kari—who was protectively holding his arm. "What is going on?" Connor asked.

"You first," Jacob told him.

"I'm just a citizen," Connor said. "Trying to...do the right thing."

Kari spoke up then, passionately. "Donald's daughter came to Miami Beach and wound up modeling with the group." She let out a long breath. "She was found dead on the beach. Drug overdose."

"I hire them to get them out," Connor whispered.

"But...but..." Jasmine began.

"Nan, my daughter, talked to me. She was frightened. She said that she couldn't forget what she had seen, and she was afraid that someone knew she knew about the cocaine, and...then she was found dead. She wasn't an addict. She didn't do drugs. I called the police—there was an investigation, and it went nowhere. The officers tried, but Nan wasn't found anywhere near the club, she'd been out with friends, she'd said she was leaving, and...they killed her. I know they killed her. And I couldn't get justice, so—"

"Donald made arrangements for me to get away—far away. Hide out, and then start over," Kari said softly. "I wanted to get ahead so badly, be rich and famous... be loved. I did things I'm not proud of. And I couldn't see any way out. But... Donald is a savior!"

"I need some kind of proof," Jacob said. "And if this is all true, Mr. Connor, I am so sorry and, of course, so grateful, and you're a fool, as well. You're risking your own life."

"My life does not matter so much anymore," Connor said flatly. "I have proof—our airline tickets. I was taking Kari to London tonight and then on to Yorkshire, to settle her with my family there."

Jasmine stared at them all, incredulous. And then it hit her. Connor's daughter...dead.

"Mary," she murmured.

"Mary?" Connor said. "Mary Ahearn?"

Jasmine stared at him.

Connor smiled. "Lovely young woman. She tried to help me find out which one of those horrible people was responsible for Nan's death. She tried to find out what was going on."

"So, you gave her a death sentence, too," Jasmine whispered.

He shook his head, looking a bit confused but still smiling. "Mary is alive and well. She's at my estate in Yorkshire, happily working on a play she's been longing to write. Of course, she'd love to be acting, and she's very fond of British theater, so she just might want to stay on. I asked her not to contact anyone from her former life until we were sure she was safe."

Jasmine would have fallen over. She felt Jacob's strength as his arms came around her.

He was staring across the room at Connor. "We will have to verify your information. And I hope you're telling the truth. If so, I swear to you, we will get justice for your daughter. I'm setting you up with an agent to get safely out of the country. I don't think you'll be bothered tonight—there's too much else going on right now."

"Why did you call me? Why did you hang up?" Jasmine demanded of Kari.

"My—my phone died! I figured I'd call you and

let you know I was leaving as soon as possible," Kari said. "And then we were getting my things, and Donald promised he'd come back and get you out, but he thought you were safe, that Jacob might be a criminal, but he'd be watching over you and then somehow, he'd get to you and—I'm so sorry!"

"One thing, please," Connor said.

"What?" Jacob demanded.

"Who the hell are you people?" Connor asked.

Chapter Twelve

It felt odd that it had just been that afternoon that Josef Smirnoff had been lain to rest. The ceremony at the club had taken place, and Jacob had ushered Kozak out in an ambulance, pretending the man was at death's door.

While Jacob and Jasmine were at Connor's suite, Kozak had gone into the hospital—and then out another door. He had immediately been ushered out to a FBI facility out west in Miami, in a little area with scores of ranch houses built in the 1970s, heading west off the canal that bordered the Tamiami Trail all the way across the south end of the peninsula to Naples, Florida.

Agents watching the hospitals—the beach hospital where Kozak had first been taken and the county hospital with the trauma center where he'd supposedly been brought later—had kept up with Jacob; Jasmine had been in touch with the MDPD who had in turn been in touch with the Miami Beach department, and everyone was on alert in case another attempt was made on the life of their new informant.

The entire inner core of Kozak's circle had arrived at the beach hospital, only to be assured that everything was being done, but that no one could see Victor Kozak. They had left together, but now Ivan and Natasha were back at the club with only Antonovich to watch over the doors. Natasha had been a mess, so Jasmine and Jacob were told—and had to be sedated when she was told that Kozak was on the verge of death.

Jacob had received many calls from both Ivan and Natasha, but he had told them both that he also had been kicked out of the hospital for having grown too insistent on seeing a man when an intensive care crew was busy trying to save him.

It was well after midnight by the time Donald McPherson Connor and Kari Anderson had been escorted to the airport—and safely onto their plane. Jasmine had gone from being ready to rip the man's throat out to being his best friend—they'd wound up talking and talking.

Kari had told her she'd wanted to say more, but she couldn't. She'd been afraid of what Jasmine might say or do, not at all certain that Jacob wasn't on the rise through the gang—or that Jasmine wasn't already completely beneath his control.

Connor had spoken about his own grief and then about dealing with it in the most constructive way he could.

"You really took chances," Jacob had told him.

"Not so much. I wasn't in on anything. I was just a client. Not someone making money—I was someone giving them money." He paused and shrugged. "And money is something I have. But it means nothing when you don't have the ones you love to share it with."

Jacob had to admit, he was a bit in awe of the man himself. Grief and loss often destroyed the loving survivors; Connor had channeled his resources and himself into saving others.

Naturally, Jacob hadn't immediately trusted what he heard, but with the information Connor gave him, the FBI offices were able to verify his story. The man did own a huge estate in Yorkshire. In truth, he had a title. He also held dual citizenship and spent as much time in the States—recently in the pursuit of saving the lives of young women—as in Great Britain.

And so it was two in the morning when Jacob and Jasmine returned to her apartment. She didn't seem the least bit tired. She was keyed up and alive, filled with energy.

"She's all right, Jacob! Mary is fine. She's in England… and I've been so, so afraid!"

He was sitting on the sofa, wiped out. She'd been all but flying around the room. In her happiness, that flight took her to fall down on his lap, sweeping her arms around him, her smile bright and her eyes as dazzling an emerald as could ever be imagined.

Her touch removed a great deal of his own exhaustion.

"She's alive, and you have to meet her. Oh, Jacob, to think I wanted to skin that man alive, that I thought he was part of…" Her voice trailed off and she frowned.

"What?" he asked, reaching out to stroke back a long lock of her hair.

"We're no closer to the truth. Nan Connor was afraid because she was a witness to a huge cocaine deal. But we don't know who saw her, and there's no way we can find out. We're pretending that Kozak is dying, but none of the gang has risen up to try to take over."

"Jasmine, as far as I know, they wouldn't dare do so. They don't believe that Kozak is dead as of yet, and they won't dare play their cards until they do."

"Where do we go from here?"

"Everything is in motion. I don't even call the shots from here on out. I'll go out tomorrow to interrogate Kozak, but it's going to be up to men with much higher positions than mine to determine what our next steps are. Kozak was grateful just to be alive." He paused, looking at her. "That was an amazing save tonight—the poison in the vodka. How did you know?"

"When he talked about his special reserve, it occurred to me that he'd be the only one drinking it. I'd hoped I'd find out who had brought the bottle and handed it to the bartender, but the guy was from the catering company and he said the bar had been set up when he got there, with the instructions that the special reserve stuff was for Kozak and Kozak only."

"Impressive." He smiled, watching her eyes. "You are a veritable beast. I thought you were going to rip Connor's head off. We're lucky you didn't shoot. He had a gun, right? You need to slow down—you could have gotten yourself killed."

"I could see he didn't know what he was doing with the gun," Jasmine said. Then she frowned. "How did you know that he wasn't going to kill anyone?"

"The agent watching him, Special Agent Daubs, Miami Criminal Division. He'd overheard Connor and Kari talking. And he watched them. Said he was a pretty good judge of men, and I guess he was."

"I'm glad," Jasmine said softly.

"So now, once again, we wait. Tomorrow, I'll spend some time out with Kozak. And you and Jorge and others will be on the beach, waiting, ready to move if anything does break—play your part. But don't go anywhere near the club."

"I still have my uniform."

"If they call you, let me know right away. And for now—"

"Tonight?" she asked seriously.

"Sleep would be on the agenda."

"Ah, yes, sleep."

"Perhaps some rigorous exercise to speed the process," he suggested.

"We are still playing roles," she murmured.

"Jorge did say we were method actors."

"We can always work on method," she whispered.

Jacob wondered vaguely what it was about a special woman, that her slightest whisper, the nuance in her words, her lightest touch, could awaken everything in a man. There was no one in the world anything like her, he thought.

She stood, reaching for his hand. He rose, smiling. In the bedroom, they both saw to their weapons first. They barely touched, shedding their clothing in a hurry.

He went down on the bed, patting the mattress, and for a moment, she stood, sleek and stunning as a silhouette in the pale light from the hallway. She moved with grace, coming to him, and then she was next to him, in his arms, and if anything, they were more frantic that night to touch and to tease and to taste one another. To make love.

Later, when they should have been drifting off to sleep, she rose up on an elbow, looking at him, empathy in the ever-brilliant sheen of her eyes. "Forgive me, but…"

He knew what she wanted to know. So, he told her about growing up in Miami at first and moving to New

York. Falling in love with Sabrina in high school, college, the service…

"Going off to the Middle East," he said. "She was always so worried about me. And she was vibrant. Full of life. We were happy. I'd done my service and I knew I wanted to head into the FBI Academy. I was certain I'd make it. We never thought… Well, she was diagnosed, and three months later, she was gone."

"I am so, so sorry."

"It was over ten years ago now," he told her, rolling to better see her face, stroke her cheek. "But you… hmm. Can't figure how you manage to be unattached. Of course, Jorge told me that you do have a tendency to shut a guy down before he can ask you out."

"Jorge talks way too much."

He laughed softly and pulled her into his arms. "That's all right," he told her. "I'm not an easy man to shut down."

She grinned, indicating their positions. "I didn't try very hard to shut you down."

He laughed and she was in his arms again.

SHE WAS NO good at waiting. She would never make it full time in undercover work.

Jasmine actually tried to sleep after Jacob left. His phone had rung far too early, letting him know that a car was coming to take him to the safe house where Kozak was being guarded. But sleep was impossible. She made coffee, washed and dried her hair and was tempted to try to do her own nails, since she had a rare moment of downtime. She reminded herself how incredibly happy she was—how grateful.

Mary was fine, alive and well. Kari was fine, too.

They'd met a man who was trying to prevent future wrongs.

Still, someone within the gang was truly cold-blooded. At least eight people were dead because of the person within who considered murder to be a stepping-stone to criminal power.

If only Jacob were there to bounce her theories off of. They worked well together. Even when they were just playing roles. But the roles had become so much more. She'd found someone who seemed to really care about her, who could be with her, for all that she was, for what she did.

These roles would come to an end. That didn't mean they had to stop seeing each other, but her life, her work, was here. And his life and work were in New York.

It was foolish to think about the future. In the middle of this, she couldn't even be certain that either of them had a future. She had faith in herself and faith in him and all their colleagues—but no one entered into law enforcement without recognizing the dangers.

Worrying about the future was not helping her keep from crawling up the walls.

She couldn't call a friend and go out. She was still undercover. And Jacob had told her not to go near the club.

She was on her third cup of coffee when she realized that she could call Jorge. She was so antsy she'd probably annoy him, but Jorge never seemed to mind. As the thought occurred to her, she felt her phone ring.

"Jorge!"

"Hey, gorgeous, whatcha doing?"

"I was about to call you. I'm waiting. Doing what I was told to do. Climbing the walls. Being such a desperate cop I'm ready to watch a marathon of *Desperate Housewives* with you."

"Well, I have a reprieve for you. I'm on my way. All sanctioned. Come out to the corner. I'll be by for you."

"Perfect. Jeans okay?"

"Jeans and sneakers. Great. See you in five minutes."

"This is cleared with Captain Lorenzo—and the FBI?"

"Yeah, we're supposed to be heading to a music venue controlled by the gang. Top groups. Acting like normal people. Waiting like the rest of the folks around us, finding out if Kozak is going to make it. Gauging their reactions."

"Okay!" Jasmine rang off and shoved her phone into her cross-body handbag. She hurried out, carefully locking her apartment, all but running by the bathers out by the pool, aware of the bright sun and the waving palms.

A car pulled over to the curb; it wasn't a car she knew, but an impressive SUV. FBI issue for work down here?

Jorge rolled down the passenger-side window. "Hop in!" he said cheerfully.

"Where did you get the car?" she asked.

"City of Miami Beach," he said. He was smiling broadly, but she frowned. Something about him didn't seem quite right.

But while she and Jorge might never have discussed their personal lives, they were solid working partners. They always had one another's back. He would die for her...

It wasn't until she was inext to the car that she realized Jorge wasn't alone in the car.

There was a man in the back, but Jasmine's focus

went to the fact that he had the business edge of a serious knife against the throat of a woman he'd shoved down in the seat. The young woman was trying desperately hard not to snuffle or cry out, with that blade so close to her artery.

It was Helen Lee, the sweet and lovely young woman with whom she and Kari had shared the runway.

Helen was absolutely terrified.

The man with the knife smiled. She was not entirely surprised to see who it was.

"Welcome, Jasmine. Now, Jorge, drive. And no tricks, no running us off the road. You wouldn't want my hand to slip. You wouldn't want to see this blade slice right through Helen's throat, would you? Jorge— drive. Now. Jasmine, smile. Please. It will keep my hand so much steadier."

Jasmine's gun was in her purse, but she couldn't reach for it then. So was her phone. She believed that the man would slit Helen's throat.

As she slid into the car, she kept her bag clutched tightly in her hands.

FROM THE OUTSIDE, it looked like any other house. It sat off 122nd Avenue and Southwest Eighth Street—the Tamiami Trail there and farther west—or Calle Ocho when you headed way back east toward downtown Miami.

Built in the 1970s, it was a ranch-style home like many of the others surrounding them. It had a large lot, but so did several other houses in the area. This house, however, had a little gazebo out front, covered with vines—a fine place for an agent to keep guard—and a large garage and a few storage sheds out back.

The living room was like any other living room. It had a sofa and some plush chairs and a stereo system and a large-screen TV. The windows were all barred—but then, so were many of the other houses in the area, a deterrent to would-be burglars.

Just like so many other houses, there were signs on the fence that warned Beware of Dogs, and the dogs were the kind for which people should be wary. Signs also warned about the house being protected by a local security company, one used by many of the other residents of the area.

There was a kitchen, usually well stocked. There was a well-appointed gym, but then again, other people had home gyms. A dining room sat between the living room and the kitchen. The house boasted four bedrooms.

One of those bedrooms had no bed.

It had a table and chairs, and it was where guests were often required to engage in conversation with those who had brought them here.

Kozak sat in one chair. Jacob sat in another. Also at the table was Dean Jenkins—the man Josef Smirnoff had first approached in fear for his life.

One other man had joined them, Carl Merrill, a prosecutor from the United States Office of the Attorney General.

"As I told Jacob—before I realized how determined my would-be murderer was—I have never killed anyone," Kozak said.

"Your actions have resulted in the deaths of many," Merrill said.

"I can give you so much," Kozak told him. "But I must have a deal. I must."

"What is that you think you can give me? We've got

you, head of an organized crime gang, and enough evidence of your activities to prosecute," Merrill asked.

"Names. I can give you the names of men who look squeaky-clean, who are working with the cartels out of South America. There are bigger fish than me in Miami."

"Victor," Jacob said, "you can't even give us the name of the man who wants you dead, who wants to take over the Deco Gang. Let's see—he's been working for you. And we know he forced a lethal dose of cocaine into a young woman who was a model for you. And he's likely responsible for at least three corpses in oil drums in Broward County and three headless corpses in the Everglades."

Kozak spun on him. "I don't kill. And I don't order executions!" he said angrily. "If I knew, could a murderer have come so close, would I have been about to drink poison?"

"Deals have yet to be made, Victor. We need help now. Who locked the door to the balcony on the day that Josef Smirnoff was killed?" Jacob asked.

"Josef." Kozak sighed. "I can't go to a federal prison…not in the general population. We had reputations. There are too many men who might think me guilty of crimes I did not commit. A man in my position does not deny violent acts to others of his kind. A reputation is everything. I let mine grow as it would."

Jenkins leaned forward. "Victor, let's start here. Did you know that Smirnoff contacted me?"

"No, I did not."

"Had he been acting nervous in any way?"

Kozak appeared to think about that and slowly shook

his head. His voice was husky when he spoke. "If he was afraid, he would not have shown it anyway."

"Do you believe he suspected you?" Jacob asked.

"If so, he shouldn't have."

"Was he sleeping with Natasha—were they a real couple?"

Kozak hesitated on that one. "Yes, she was…strong. And good."

"So, you inherited Natasha along with the leadership," Jacob said. "She had the key to the balcony yesterday."

"There is only one key. She had it because I would not be present."

"Do you think it is Natasha who might be trying to kill you? Would she be hard enough to have one of her girls killed—and to order the execution of those men?"

Kozak smiled. "Natasha, she is a woman. But in business…this business? Natasha serves," he said softly.

Jacob had to wonder at that.

But Kozak was convinced of the truth of his words. He shook his head. "I don't know, I really don't know. As they say, keep your friends close, but your enemies closer. I have kept my people close. I don't know how they can be hiring these killers, desperate people."

There was a knock at the door. The agent who was the house's "owner" stepped in. "Special Agent Wolff, a word."

"Now?"

"Yes, sir. Now."

Jacob politely excused himself. Outside the room, he realized the agent was anxious.

"It's a call from Captain Lorenzo, sir, MDPD. Our

men on the beach were following a car out of the club, but they lost them on the causeway. I—"

He stopped talking and handed Jacob the phone.

The man on the line quickly, tersely, identified himself as Captain Mac Lorenzo.

"I don't know how she did it, but Jasmine managed to contact this number and leave her phone on. She's in a car—they're headed west somewhere. Jorge is driving, Jasmine is in the front. There's a man in back, and from what I can hear, he's taking them somewhere. It sounds as if they're headed for an execution. We've got men on it, but they keep losing them. I've already asked the Feds to hop on it as quickly as possible, but you were close to that group. I'm hoping you might know where they're being taken."

Jacob froze for a split second; he felt as if the life had been stripped out of him.

"I need the exact location those headless bodies were found," Jacob said. "Speak fast, I'm already moving. And keep the others back. If the killer feels cornered, he'll kill whoever he has close out of spite. Get me backup, but keep the backup back."

Lorenzo kept talking. Before he finished another sentence, Jacob was in a car and heading west down the Tamiami Trail.

"Not so slow that the police notice us. There's no need to risk another of the city's finest."

Hearing the voice of the man in the back, Jorge cast a quick glance toward Jasmine. His eyes were filled with agony. She knew how he felt.

A quick look in back assured her there was already

a fine line of blood creating a jagged necklace along Helen Lee's throat.

Jasmine and Jorge would both fight, play for time, for the life of another, as long as they were both still breathing.

There was no way to let him know she'd gotten her hand into her purse, and that she was pretty sure she'd hit the number one; a priority call that would hit the phone Lorenzo had just for communication with her.

But would Lorenzo know where they were going? How could he know when she didn't know?

West. They were headed west. Jorge was driving as slowly as he could reasonably manage without drawing the man's ire or suspicion. He was in no rush to bring them to their destination. They were off the beach now, across the causeway on a long, long drive that seemed to be taking them out to the Everglades.

It was a land a few of the hardiest knew well, where airboat rides could be found, where the Miccosukee kept a restaurant and reservation lands, where visitors could find out about their lives and their pasts.

A place where, no matter how many hearty souls worked and even lived, there were acres upon acres that was nothing but wetland, part of the great "river of grass," filled with water moccasins and alligators, even pythons and boas.

"To the Everglades," she said aloud, as they whipped past the Miccosukee casino.

She turned around and stared at Ivan Petrov.

"You want to kill Jorge and me. Why?"

He eyed her coldly and then smiled. "I don't believe that Kozak is dead. He's the one who brought Marensky in. You did something with his drink. Marensky called the ambulance, and now…now they do not report that Kozak is dead."

"Whatever your argument with me, why Helen?" she asked.

His smiled deepened. "She happened to be there," he said.

Ivan Petrov. They should have figured; they had looked at Kozak, at Natasha, at the goons… They would have gotten to Ivan. He was never off the list.

"I need some guarantee you're going to keep Helen alive," Jasmine said. "Then Jorge and I will do as you ask."

"You are with the government," Petrov said.

"I swear to you, I am not an FBI agent. Neither is Jorge."

"Then you are trying to take the lead, playing up to Kozak. Well, they have cold feet. The enterprise will never be what it should be under Kozak. He is a weakling—he doesn't know how to remove what festers among us. Drive, Jorge. And turn around, Miss Jasmine."

The casino was behind them. Minutes were counting down. They were coming up to Shark Valley when Petrov told Jorge to slow the car down.

He couldn't be going to Shark Valley! There were trails and bike paths, tourists and rangers all about. Unless he meant to kill anyone in his way.

They didn't turn into Shark Valley. They passed the entrance, and the Miccosukee restaurant to the right on the road.

Then suddenly, Kozak said, "Here."

Here? She knew of no road here…

"Now!" Petrov commanded.

Helen let out a scream as the knife pierced her flesh. Jorge turned.

JACOB WAS MET by Mickey Cypress of the Miccosukee Police. The man was in his early forties, lean, bronze and no-nonsense. He'd been waiting for Jacob right outside the entrance to Shark Valley.

"You don't want to go exactly where the bodies were found," he told Jacob. "The Everglades is literally a river, and the bodies were carried until they were snagged by the mangrove roots." He had a map out on his phone and he pointed to a spot that seemed to be just beyond a canal where they stood.

Jacob glanced at the map. Suddenly, two giant male alligators went into some kind of a battle in the canal.

"Leave them alone, completely alone," Cypress told him. "There's a marshy trail we can take through here, and a small hammock. That's where I think we'll find their killing grounds. There was no road there before, but some fairly solid ground. I think they created their own way."

Cars drove up next to them. Men in suits got out— the backup.

Cypress looked at him. They were probably good agents; they just didn't look ready for a trek into the water and marshy land.

"Special Agent Wolff!" one of them called.

Jacob looked at Cypress.

"I'm with you," Cypress said. "Um, if you're trying for stealth…"

Jacob nodded and headed back to the agent calling to him. He asked him to hold their position and keep a line of contact open. He walked back to Cypress.

The local cop told him, "Trust me, I know how to get there. I was the first on call when the bodies were found. I've been on this."

"I trust you," Jacob assured him. "We need to hurry. I got after them right away, but they still had a head start."

"Then we move."

Cypress started over a small land bridge, just feet from the male alligators defending their turf. Water came cascading over them from a massive flip of a tail.

They kept walking.

IVAN PETROV HAD his knife—and a gun on his belt. He kept the knife at Helen's throat.

Jasmine clung to her purse.

"Drop it!" Petrov commanded. His knife moved ever so slightly.

Helen gulped out a cry. Tears were streaming down her face—silent tears. She tried not to sob and stared at Jasmine—any movement would cause a great chafe of the knife against her throat. Her eyes were both imploring and hopeless.

"Go!" Petrov commanded. Jorge walked ahead; Jasmine behind him. He sheathed the knife and drew his gun.

"I don't understand, Ivan. Who were the people in the oil drums?" Jasmine asked.

"Well, I will tell you," Petrov said. "The first, his name was Terry Meyers. He thought he should manage the club—and the women. That was long ago, when Smirnoff had barely begun to settle into South Florida. Smirnoff was, in fact, surprised when Meyers failed to arrive for a meeting. The second, well, he failed to show with a payment. He made me look bad. You can't deal with people who don't deliver on goods or who don't make their payments. It's bad for business if you don't follow through. Same deal for the third loser."

"The three who weren't in the drums," she said. "They were the ones who killed Josef."

"Yes, actually, they were very good. I was sorry to see them go. But you see, they couldn't live. If they had been apprehended, well… I did hire them personally."

"You admired them so much, you beheaded them," Jasmine murmured.

Jorge glanced back at her; she was doing the right thing, keeping him talking. There were two of them. They could survive this. They had to get Helen in a safe position, and then they could rush Petrov—he couldn't shoot them both at the same time.

But they had to get Helen away from him first.

Jorge suddenly stopped, letting out a shout.

"Move!" Petrov commanded.

"There's a gator ahead in the path," Jorge said, falling back by Jasmine.

"That's fine," Petrov said, dragging Helen around and waving his gun at the small gator on the trail. "We're almost there." He fired the gun toward the gator. The creature moved off into the surrounding bracken.

There was some kind of a structure there, a broken-down shack, a remnant, Jasmine thought, from the time when various Florida hunters had come out and kept little camps.

It was now or never—Petrov had just fired the gun, he was looking away, he was holding Helen, but the gun wasn't directly at her throat.

Jasmine didn't let out a sound; she made a silent leap for the man.

She bore him down to the ground. Helen slipped

free, screaming hysterically. She began to run back in the direction from which they had come, screaming all the while.

Petrov's gun hand was flailing; in a second, the barrel would be aiming at Jasmine's face.

But Jorge was there, stomping on the man's wrist, kicking at the gun. It went flying into a gator hole, filled high with water.

But Petrov wasn't going down easily. He caught Jasmine and flipped her down to the muddy earth.

Jorge kicked his head.

Petrov had the knife on his belt now; Jasmine went for it. Seizing it from Petrov, she sliced his hand. He cried out as blood gushed.

And then, a gunshot fired. They all went still.

The knife still tightly in her grip, Jasmine turned to the sound.

Standing casually now before the rotting wood of the old shack was Natasha. She shook her head.

"Men. They are worthless, eh? They continually think they are in charge, and they have no idea. Ivan! A silly girl and these two. You have a gun, you have a knife, and they best you. What would you have done without me, Ivan?"

She shook her head again at Ivan, but then smiled at Jasmine. "Yes, you are one who knows how to manipulate a man, eh? It's the only way, until you have seized the position of real power. And then they will bow down before you, and they will become your toys, and you will command them. It's a pity you must die. It will be hard for me… Oh, maybe not so hard, because now Ivan and I will have to crawl through this wretched swamp looking for that silly Helen. If she doesn't kill herself first. Maybe it will not be so hard. I will kill your friend first, so you can watch him die, and he will not have to watch you die? How is that?"

"I should have known you were the one with ice-cold blood running in your veins—right from the beginning," Jasmine said.

Natasha shrugged. "Me? I am not so much the killer. I like others to do the killing."

"And then you kill the killers."

Natasha smiled. "Ivan killed the killers. I simply cut off their hands and their heads…and fed them to the swamp. Enough talk." She took aim.

But Natasha couldn't have known what hit her.

He came from behind. His arm came down on hers and Natasha screamed with shock and pain as she lost her grip on the gun, as she was tackled to the ground.

Jasmine stared.

Jacob was there. Impossibly, Jacob was there. He'd slipped around silently from behind the hut, and he was now reading Natasha her rights and handcuffing her, heedless of the fact that he was on her back and pressing her face into the mud.

He looked at Jasmine, his recitation breaking. He nodded toward Petrov, who was trying to turn and escape.

Jasmine turned to Petrov, but another man—never before sensed nor seen—went sliding past her.

"Not to worry. I've got that one."

Jacob yanked Natasha to her feet. He spoke into his phone. Jasmine and Jorge were still just standing there, incredulous to be alive, when men—a little ridiculously dressed in fine blue suits and leather loafers—came running through the brush.

"Got her, sir," one of them said to Jacob, taking Natasha. He was young, younger than Jasmine. A brand-new agent, she thought, but ready to do whatever was asked of him, including running through a swampy, mucky river in his office attire.

He was gone; Natasha was dragged away. And then they heard shouts; Ivan had been apprehended, as well.

"Helen—Helen Lee is running through the swamp," Jasmine called out, her voice echoing through the mangroves and pines.

One of the agents came back. "No, ma'am, we've got her. She's fine. A little scratched up and still hysterical, but…we've got her. She's going to be okay."

"Hey, I'm coming with you," Jorge said. "She knows me. I'll get her calmed down."

And then, for a moment, Jasmine and Jacob were standing there alone. A large white crane swooped in and settled down near them, seeing a fish in the shallow gator holes that surrounded them on the small hammock.

Slowly, Jasmine smiled. "Your timing is impeccable."

He let out a long soft sigh, and then he grinned. "So I've been told."

She raced across the mud and the muck that separated them and threw herself into his arms. And they indulged in one long kiss, both shaking.

"You are kick-ass," he told her.

"But not even a kick-ass can work alone," she whispered. "You saved our lives."

"Only because you were doing a good enough job saving your own life," he assured her. "Lord, help me, this may be ridiculous, but I think I love you."

"This may be more ridiculous," she said.

"What?"

"I know I love you!" she told him.

"Special Agent Wolff? Detective?" They were being summoned.

Hand in hand, they started back along the path. "Paperwork," Jacob murmured.

"And then?" she asked.

He wiped a spot of mud off her face. "Showers," he said. "Definitely showers."

She smiled and he paused just one more minute, turning her to him.

"And then," he said, blue eyes dazzling down on her, "then figuring out our lives. If that's all right with you, of course."

She rose on her toes and lightly kissed his lips.

She could have done much, much more, but others were waiting—and there were some very large predators near them. The human ones might be down, but while she wasn't afraid of the creatures here, she wasn't stupid enough to get in their way either.

She broke the kiss and looked into his clear eyes. "It's all right with me."

Epilogue

The woman hurrying toward him along the long stone path over the castle's moat was truly one of the most stunning creatures Jacob Wolff had ever seen. His initial opinion of Jasmine had never changed.

Her skin was pure bronze, as sleek and as dazzling as the deepest sunray. When she smiled at him, he could see that her eyes were light. Green, he knew, an emerald green, and a sharp contrast to her skin. She had amazing hair, long and so shimmering that it was as close to pure black as it was possible to be; so dark it almost had a glint of violet. She was long-legged, lean and yet exquisitely shaped, even in jeans, sweater, boots and a parka.

She didn't pause when she met him. She threw her arms around him and leaped up so he had to catch her, and laughed as he spun with her in the rising sunlight that did little to dispel the chill of the damp day. No one saw them.

Donald McPherson Connor's "estate" had proved to be a castle. Small, admittedly, but *a bit of an historic home*, as Donald called it, and far out in the countryside of northern England.

"Best vacation ever!" she told him, sliding down to stand.

He looked behind her. They were no longer alone.

He'd headed out for a walk on the grounds right after morning coffee; Jasmine had stayed behind to wait for Mary and Jorge—the two had been in a lengthy discussion of just how cold it might get during the day, and throwing her hands up, Jasmine had indicated he should go ahead.

His hike had been serene. The countryside seemed to stretch endlessly, beautiful rolling land with horses and sheep and cattle.

He'd had vacation time built up—you couldn't just hop off to an amusement park or the mountains or the French Riviera in the middle of work when you were deep in an undercover operation. He felt this time off was well deserved, for himself and for Jasmine. It had been impossible for them to turn down Donald Connor's suggestion that they come to visit Mary.

They had a suite in the tiny castle. No windows facing a beach, but instead an arrow slit that looked out over a stretch of land that was misty and green. They had long nights together and days with amazing friends.

Jorge and Mary caught up with them. "Off to the theater, if you're sure you don't mind the walk," she said.

Mary was as gentle and sweet a woman as Jasmine had said, wide-eyed and kind, with blond hair as long as Jasmine's raven tresses. Mary had cried when she'd come to the airport to meet them; she'd been so sorry to have frightened Jasmine, to have put her in danger. But Donald had explained that he was just an ordinary citizen—he'd needed Mary to not say a word to anyone until she was safely out of the clutches of the Deco Gang. She'd been lucky to have an up-to-date passport.

Mary told them that Natasha had instructed her they had more escort work, and the intended client was a man she had seen come and go with different suitcases. She had suspected the man was part of their drug operation. And by then she knew that the girls weren't really models, that the so-called models were being prostituted, and that she just might not be able to do all of the things expected of her. And that if they suspected that she knew too much—or anything at all—she just might wind up dead.

Jasmine explained to her over and over again that it was all right—they'd put a stop to it all, and possibly saved many more lives.

Natasha had gone through people quickly. In her mind, so it seemed, people were as disposable as silverware or linens that were no longer needed.

There was, of course, a note of sadness to it all. They could do nothing for Donald's daughter; she was gone. But while he couldn't be happy, the man was grateful and satisfied. Her killers would find justice.

"A walk is great," Jacob assured her.

"Okay, so maybe these ugly shoes are good," Jorge said, slipping an arm around Mary's shoulders. The two of them moved slightly ahead. Mary began telling Jorge about the history of the area and how old the theater they were about to attend was.

Jasmine looked up at Jacob and smiled. "It's a children's play we're seeing, you know."

"Mary wrote it—I can't wait to see it. Donald will join us there?"

"Exactly," Jasmine said.

Mary suddenly stopped. She looked back, grinning. "Hey, I was talking to Donald this morning, earlier. He thinks you guys should have your wedding here."

Jasmine stopped dead. "Mary, we're visitors here. And we haven't—" she looked at Jacob, a flush rising to her cheeks "—we haven't even…"

Talked about marriage.

They had talked about everything else. A long-distance relationship seemed like half measures. But then, what to do? Jasmine loved the people with whom she worked, and she loved Miami. Jacob understood. They were looking into a transfer for him to the Miami office.

It had only been a few weeks since they'd survived the murder attempt in the Everglades; they'd been mulling over all possibilities in the meantime. And of course, finishing the endless paperwork, the United States Attorney General, the police, evidence, witnesses and everything else that went with the end of such a complicated case.

Kozak was going into witness protection; both Ivan and Natasha would be prosecuted for the murders they had committed. Victor Kozak had given the authorities all they needed to apprehend a number of the drug smugglers in Miami Beach, and information regarding them that might lead to solving many of the cold cases on file across Greater Miami.

Antonovich, Garibaldi and Suarez had worked for Kozak, and though they had faced stiff interrogations, they hadn't actually been proved guilty of any crimes. Jacob hoped that the three would find better employment.

Petrov still had a problem believing he was going

down—he'd tried to throw everything on Natasha, but in turn, Natasha had tried to throw everything on him.

The man had been a fool, Jacob had told Jasmine, when they had been alone and curled together one night. He'd underestimated the power of a woman. And, smiling, he'd assured her, "That's something I never would do."

Now, Jacob grabbed her hand, forcing her to look at him. "I don't know—the wedding here. What do you think?"

"I…" Jasmine looked at him.

Jorge let out a sound of frustration. "Oh, come on! You know there's going to be a wedding. Seriously, who else could either of you live with forever and ever, huh?"

He was right. You were very, very lucky in life when you found that one person who complemented you in every way.

Jacob looked into her eyes, so strong, so gentle, so giving… Dazzling.

He figured he could answer for both of them. "I don't really care where we get married. As long as we do. And I do need to get you all to New York. I have a friend—I've worked with him and the love of his life, and her family owns an Irish pub on Broadway. Her brother is also an actor and can score all kinds of theater tickets, Mary."

"New York—oh, I would love it! But first—a wedding in a castle. We'll let you do the honeymoon alone, and then an after-honeymoon in New York. Perfect!" Mary caught Jorge's hand and the two walked on ahead.

Jacob caught Jasmine's hand. He went down on a knee. "Detective Adair, will you marry me? In a castle, at the courthouse, Miami, New York…wherever? I cannot begin to imagine my life without you. It can be here, there or anywhere."

Jasmine came down on a knee, as well. "My dearest Special Agent Wolff, yes. Here, there, anywhere," she assured him. "I can't imagine my life ever again without you!"

He leaned forward, and they kissed. And kissed…

Until Jorge called back to them. "Hey! Time for that later. We're going to miss the play."

Laughing, Jasmine rose and pulled him to his feet. "The rest of our lives," she said.

"The rest of our lives," he agreed.

* * * * *

DOUBLE ENTENDRE

Chapter One

He walked quickly down the street, hands in his pockets. Before the house at the curve of the cul-de-sac, he paused. There was a brisk breeze that evening; it lifted a thick thatch of sandy hair from his forehead and sent it sweeping down again. He gave no notice to the breeze or to the cloud-shadowed moon above him. He stared at the house, tense, impatient.

She wasn't home. Her Ferrari was in the driveway, but he knew she wasn't home. A single lamp burned in the living room, casting a muted glow out on the lush, manicured lawn; when she *was* home, lights blazed all over the place.

Bret paused no longer, but hurried up the mosaic walk to the front door. He fumbled in his pockets for his keys, found them and searched through the jumble until he selected a key, then tried it in the lock. He frowned as the lock refused to give. He was puzzled at first; then his resentment and temper flared. Damn her! She'd had the bloody locks changed!

He took a deep breath to still his irritation, hesitated with a grimace, then shrugged and fumbled in his jacket pocket for a file. In a matter of minutes he was stepping inside.

He took a moment to look around the room at the high cathedral ceiling, the beige furniture against the immaculate white throw rugs and the tiled floor, the glass doors that extended the length of the rear wall and led to the two-story domed screen over the tropical pool. If he opened the doors and walked at an angle across the deck, he would come to the master suite which also had sliding glass doors leading to the pool. Separating the living room and the master suite was the kitchen, as light and contemporary as the rest of the house, tiled in beige and light cocoa. It included a breakfast nook that looked out onto a small rose garden, complete with a dazzling little marble fountain.

His perusal was quick; his eyes didn't stray to the fireplace or to the conversation pit before it. He barely glanced at the endless bookshelves or the video and stereo systems.

Her desk was in the sitting room, part of the master suite. He hurried to it by way of the kitchen and arched hallway.

Fifteen minutes later he was still frustrated at his efforts. He'd read her calendar; he'd gone through every note, every letter, every memo, every notation or idea written in her elegant handwriting. But everything he found was ordinary. A meeting with a congressman. An appointment with a nuclear scientist. Another with a beekeeper for a story on the American honey industry. Messages from *The World*, the magazine for which they both worked.

Notes, messages, appointments, but nothing, *nothing*, on Rutger Miller. Of course, he reflected, he hadn't found anything personal, either. No dates were written down, no intimate dinners, no jaunts to the theater.

He paused for a minute, then walked slowly into the bedroom. The drapes were pulled back, and through the glass doors he could see the moon reflecting on the pool, shimmering through the leaves of the palms that were planted at the far side of the water. He could see the deck chairs, the glass-topped table between them, the wet bar built of coral.

Ah, California living! A beautiful night and a beautiful place.

It *was* a beautiful place, he reflected, and then his eyes were drawn back to the bedroom—in particular, to the bed. It was queen-size, covered in blood red with soft white throw pillows to offset the deep color. The drapes were white with a palm design in red; the plush carpet was in shades of red, white and gold. And if he walked through the dressing room to the bath, he knew he would find red, white and black tiles, gold-toned fixtures and a huge sunken marble tub, with more glass that looked out to the enclosed garden.

But he didn't walk through to the bath. He gave himself an impatient shake for gazing at the bed too long, walked briskly to it, took a seat and stared at her answering machine. He turned it on and listened to the recording of her soft, husky voice saying that she wasn't available for the phone, but "thank you so much for calling," etc., etc.

And then he listened to the messages. Nothing much. One of the copy editors from the magazine calling to ask her a question, a girlfriend suggesting lunch—and one long breath before the phone was hung up.

With a sigh he turned the machine on again and tried to think of where else she might keep information. Secret information.

He started suddenly. There was a click as the front door was unlocked, and then he heard the sound of her laughter, a sound that somehow wrapped around his heart and caused his body to go tight with tension. He gave himself an impatient shake and crept silently back through the sitting room to the hallway. From there he could see her, watch her silently and secretively.

She was dressed in white and red that night: a white halter dress with a wide red belt, red shoes and bag and even long red earrings. Her blue-black hair swung in soft waves over the white dress, creating an arresting and stirring contrast. As she turned on the overhead light, the living room seemed to sizzle to life, just as she did. He could see her eyes as she tossed her purse onto the sofa. Her eyes were deep green flecked with sparks of gold. Her features were delicate and heart shaped, and she appeared both very feminine and very determined, very competent. Her confidence showed in her walk, the lift of her slim shoulders, the soft swing of her hips, the easy, floating length of her long-limbed strides.

Now she turned cordially to the man who followed her—like a puppy, Bret thought a bit scornfully. Don't fawn after her, buddy, he wanted to warn the man. It won't get you anywhere. She'll lead you to the gates of heaven, then laugh while you fall into the pits of hell.

Bret leaned back against the doorframe, crossing his arms comfortably over his chest. The glare from the living room now hid him safely in shadow, and his cynical knowledge of her told him that he might well enjoy the scene that was coming. His sardonic smile faded slightly for a minute as he wondered if he might be misjudging the situation, if this man with the fawning, adoring expression just might have come to mean something to her.

Well, it didn't matter, Bret told himself irritably. If things started going in a direction he didn't like, he would quickly see that it changed. Unreasonable? Yes, of course, he knew that logically. But right now reason didn't seem to matter very much, Bret realized grimly.

He moved a little farther back into the shadows. She was speaking softly, sweetly, to the slim young man with her.

"Jerry, thanks so much, it was a lovely evening." She touched Jerry's cheeks, and he caught her palm and kissed it.

"I'm so glad you enjoyed yourself. The play was good," he told her.

She kept smiling and retrieved her hand, then walked toward her kitchen. Bret flattened himself against the wall.

Her smile had faded a bit as she retrieved her hand—graciously, of course. "Jerry, what can I get you? Coffee? Or a drink? I think I've got just about everything."

"Yes, you have, Colleen," Jerry muttered, and though Colleen turned around with a light frown furrowing her brow, Bret knew exactly to what Jerry had been referring. Flush against the wall, Bret felt his temper soar. Unreasonably, of course, and he was irritated, even more so as he felt his muscles constrict uncontrollably.

"What was that, Jerry?" Colleen asked.

"Nothing, nothing," Jerry muttered. "I'd, uh, love a cup of coffee."

Colleen smiled vaguely and moved into the kitchen, filling the drip coffee maker, pulling down a set of mugs.

Jerry watched her from the living room with a silly, love-smitten grin on his face. She smiled at him again. "Let me just open the place up and we can sit on the patio."

She was coming through to open the drapes, Bret realized. He hurried past the sitting room and into the bedroom before her, slipping into the bathroom while she hummed her way in behind him. He heard her sliding the glass doors open, then heard her as she moved back into the living room, sliding those doors open, too.

Good, Bret thought dryly. Silently he left the bathroom behind. Now he could observe her quietly from the comfort of the bed.

Moments later he saw her carry a tray onto the patio, set it on the glass-topped table and sit in one of the deck chairs. Jerry sat beside her, mumbling a thank-you for the coffee as if he'd been offered a cup of diamonds. Of course, all in all, Bret had to admit Jerry didn't look a bad sort. He appeared to be about thirty, the executive sort, neat and well-groomed, cordial and social. Bret even assumed the guy was good-looking in a health club sort of way.

Thinking things like that made his stomach knot all over again, so Bret leaned on one elbow and tried to listen to their conversation. Jerry was commenting on the beauty of the house, the way it all opened to the water and the moon. Bret listened with a curious expectancy to her answer—resenting it more than he should when she replied with an airy, "Yes, the design is nice."

Nice! Bret thought bitterly. Yeah, it's nice all right.

Then Jerry started talking about the play; Colleen complimented his choice of restaurant for dinner. Bret drummed his fingers against the blood-red bedspread, thoroughly bored with the discussion of chicken divan. He yawned, felt that he was growing hot and sat up to strip off his gray pullover. By the look of things, he might as well settle down.

They started talking about dessert.

Bret kicked off his shoes and lay back on the bed, his fingers laced behind his head.

Mousse. Dessert had been chocolate mousse.

Bret became suddenly attentive again. The muscles across his chest and stomach banded together like steel. Jerry was suddenly leaning very close to her, stroking her cheek and telling her how beautiful and fascinating she was, how he'd been longing to touch her all night.

Then Jerry's arms were around her and he was kissing her.

Bret tensed inside and out, gripping the blood-red bed cover, ready to leap like an enraged tiger to the patio. She wouldn't dare, she had better not dare—oh, the nerve of the little witch! She had better not kiss him back!

But right when Bret's tolerance had come to the snapping point, he saw that Colleen was firmly pushing Jerry away.

"Jerry!" she reproached him softly. "Jerry, you promised! You know how I feel about things…at the moment."

"But, Colleen…" Jerry began with a frustrated groan.

"Jerry, I like you. You're a very nice guy. But what I need from you right now, if you're willing to give it, is friendship."

She smiled sweetly. Oh, so sweetly! Bret knew all about that sweet smile.

Jerry sighed and stood. "I guess I should go," he said.

But he didn't move. He looked like a man who wanted an invitation to stay.

He didn't get one. Colleen stood, too. Having kicked off her red-heeled sandals, she seemed smaller, more delightfully like a willowy sylph. It was an illusion, of course. She was five-foot-six in her bare feet. Not a giant, but no pixie.

She turned away from her date for a moment, and Bret felt his heart seem to catch in his throat. Something about her expression was so bleak, so pained. Maybe she does miss me, he thought, just a little, little bit.

Who was he fooling? he taunted himself. She hated him—and maybe, at times, he had even given her ample reason. If she had only understood that he had shouted because he had been afraid of losing her...

If he had only understood it himself at the time.

Ifs were useless things in this world, he reminded himself. And the past was far behind him. Maybe, like sparks and tinder, they had just been fated to come together explosively.

And he was a fool to imagine that he saw anguish on her beautiful features. He had wanted it to be there. She was looking up at old Jerry again, smiling a little uneasily.

"Jerry," she murmured apologetically, slipping her arms about his waist and staring at him sweetly. "It was a lovely evening. Thank you," she told him and, standing on her toes, kissed him quickly, then released him to walk him to the door.

Bret heard the front door close, then heard her slide the bolt. He told himself that it was time to move, to confront her or to leave.

He hesitated, lying back on the bed again, lacing his

fingers behind his head and closing his eyes tightly to think. He should have a few minutes. If she behaved as usual she would go out to the pool and dangle her feet in the water. She'd make tea or take a glass of wine out with her. She'd unwind before coming to bed.

He had no right to be angry, Bret told himself. None at all. So why…?

He started, almost making a noise as something flew in his face. He grasped at it, pulling it from his eyes. He inhaled and the scent of her perfume filled his senses.

He was holding her dress.

She was standing just feet away, between the foot of the bed and the doors to the patio. All the lights except one in the living room had been turned off, and she was staring pensively at the moon's reflection on the pool as she absently stripped. Her shoes were still on the patio; her dress was in his hands, and as he watched, her slip fell to the floor like a white cloud. She was clad only in the palest mauve lace bikini. Her back was to him, but that bare back caused a heated eruption in his system that could have rivaled that of Mount Vesuvius. All his muscles tightened, his stomach knotting, his desire bordering on agony.

Still, just at the sight of her. And after all this time. He'd thought he'd cleansed himself, purged himself, of the longing.

Bret took a deep breath, tossing the fragrant dress aside. It whispered to the floor. He clenched his teeth and laced his fingers behind his head again. It was too late for action of any kind now; he'd have to brazen the situation out. And come to think of it, he did still have a few rights.

She wasn't going to see it that way.

But boldness and confidence were often the key to success. He'd have to count on that now.

She stared at the pool several seconds longer, running her fingers through the midnight length of her hair and sending it cascading down her back again. Then, with a little sigh, she turned. For a second she was caught in the moonlight, just like the water in the pool. Her breasts were caught in that glow, full, high, rounded, bouncing slightly above her ribs, contrasting with the narrowness of her waist. The mauve bikini clung like temptation incarnate about the fascinating flare of her hips.

His breath caught in his throat, and he knotted his fingers so tightly that the bones threatened to break. But still she didn't see him. She was blinking against the darkness of the room after the glow of the moon and the silver light reflected by the water.

He had to speak. As it was, he would probably frighten her half to death. And even if she did deserve to be scared—really scared somewhere along the line so she'd use some caution and wisdom—he didn't want it to be tonight.

She was groping blindly for the covers, her eyes still not adjusted to the change in light. And then, of course, she certainly wasn't expecting to find a man lying in her bed.

Bret pulled the covers back for her. She gasped, stunned. And then she drew her breath in sharply, readying herself for a long, very high and panicked scream.

Bret didn't think the neighbors would hear; the house was too secluded. But he didn't want to take any chances. He reached out, grasping her wrist and speaking quickly with annoyance.

"Shut up, Colleen, it's just me."

She gasped again, shocked. And then she was furious. *"Just you? Just you?"* She tried, with the strength of a regiment, or so it felt, to break his hold. "What are you doing here? Get out of my bed, get out of my house. How dare you— *Let go of me!*"

Bret grinned, maintaining his hold on her while he rolled to catch the switch for the bedside lamp. She screamed out something that would have made a seaman blush as light flooded the room, and he laughed dryly, slowly allowing his eyes to wander insolently over her.

"Bret McAllistair, so help me God, I'll call the police, I'll have you arrested, locked away for life, if you don't let go of me!"

She was screaming, trying to break his hold and grab for the spread to cover herself all at the same time.

He laughed again with less bitterness. Colleen hadn't changed. Not one bit. Her heart might be thudding away a mile a minute, but she was still threatening him. Boldness and bravado and raw courage were not qualities that she lacked. He sobered. Wisdom was a quality that she often did seem to miss. She was clawing at his wrists with her long nails, and she should have known better than to get so physical with him. After all, she knew him and knew his temper. It wasn't wise to push him—especially not after the scene he had just witnessed.

"Bret! Damn it, I mean it."

"Shut up and calm down and I *will* let you go!" he commanded irritably, and then he started to laugh again because she did look more dangerous than he did. With her hair wild now and trailing across her heaving breasts, her eyes like green flames and her brows furrowed in fury, she resembled a primeval warrior queen. "Hey! I mean it. Calm down," Bret ordered. He released her wrist and rolled quickly before she could deliver the blow she intended. Still laughing he leaped to his feet and sauntered across the room, showing her his back and closing his eyes tightly for a second in a bid to find strength. He paused, swallowing sharply, hoping to bury the unbidden pain that had attacked his heart like a vicious hammer blow. He had loved her once.

She was struggling to clothe herself with the too-big bedspread. He turned around to watch her laconically, in control again. He leaned against the glass door to the pool, plunged his hands into his pockets and said dryly, "Aren't you being a little overmodest? I've more than seen everything you've got, you know."

Her eyes fell on him with lethal vehemence. "What are you doing here?" she demanded tensely.

He waved an arm toward the pool. "I was watching that touching scene."

"How dare you!" she cried, stalking toward him, the spread wrapped around her like a toga. It was a beautiful attack: she was proud and enraged and looked just like a queen until she tripped over one corner of the spread and catapulted hard against his naked chest. Bret laughed and tried to straighten her. She made a choking sound as if she were strangling and pushed herself away from him. "I mean it, Bret. I don't know what you're doing here, but I want you out now. Out of my bedroom, out of my house—"

He raised one brow, very politely. "Or you'll call the police?"

She floundered a bit; her lashes, dark and thick and beautifully rich, fell over her cheeks for a brief moment. Then she raised her chin to him. "No. I—I wouldn't want to call the police on you. But," she warned, "I will call Jerry."

"Jerry? Jerry?" Bret queried, and then he doubled over with laughter, looking at her again as he moved to the foot of the bed to sit and hold his stomach. Of course, there really wasn't anything so funny about Jerry. He just couldn't stop himself from seeking some way to ridicule the guy who had just been kissing her. "Jerry?" he asked again, gazing at her incredulously. "That skinny little weasel who just left?" He didn't have a damned thing against Jerry, except that he'd been with *her.*

She stood very tall and very proud despite her absurd costume. "So he doesn't spend his days and nights hacking his macho way across hill and dale. He's still quite a man, I assure you."

He was tempted to laugh again, but God, it would be bitter laughter, defensive laughter. Bret sobered instead and ran his fingers through his tousled hair. He hadn't played fair; he hadn't expected her to catch him in the house. But he *was* here, and naturally the meeting was going badly.

He ran his fingers through his hair again, suddenly very weary. "I wouldn't call Jerry if I were you, Colleen," he said flatly, gazing up at her. "It would be rather foolish, don't you think?"

She pursed her lips stubbornly. A range of emotions passed swiftly through her gold-flecked eyes. What were they? he wondered a little bleakly.

She took a deep breath, and he could see that she was struggling to speak coolly and calmly. Just like Colleen! She was by nature impetuous, passionate, tempestuous, but she always wanted to behave rationally or at least give the illusion that she did. But it seemed that tonight she was expecting trouble. Well, she was going to get it, he decided, whether she was expecting it or not.

"Bret, get out," she said quietly, almost with a whisper of pleading. But that whisper was quickly gone as she continued angrily. "I don't know what you're doing here—the last I heard you were in the Middle East—but I want you out now. Off my bed, out of my room and out of my house."

"Aren't you forgetting something?" he asked her wryly.

"Am I?" she challenged.

"Oh, yes," he told her lightly, uncrossing his arms and starting to saunter casually toward her. "Your house is half my house. Your room, half my room. Even your bed is half my bed."

"No! No more!" she cried furiously. "You wanted out and you left."

"It's still my house—my design, as a matter of fact, which you neglected to tell your friend Jerry." He kept moving toward her; Colleen, clutching the blood-red bedspread about her, began to back up. He smiled as she stepped on a trailing edge of the material again and plummeted backward to the bed. It was an advantage he could ill afford to lose.

Bret quickly scrambled over her, straddling her hips. He saw her eyes narrow and knew he was pushing her to a real battle, but since he was way off base and knew it, he had to attempt the bluff. She was very busy trying to untangle her arms—to strike him, he was certain—

so he quickly caught her shoulders and leaned low to speak brusquely.

"Let's get a few things straight, Mrs. McAllistair. I—"

"I'm not your wife anymore, Bret," Colleen interrupted him heatedly, still struggling with the spread, but getting nowhere with her limbs not only entangled by the material but held beneath the force and weight of his body.

"Yes, you are," Bret corrected lightly, pausing to smile grimly. "Until the twenty-eighth of the month, or so my lawyers tell me. So until that time, don't bring Jerry back into *my* house, huh? I feel sorry for the guy, you know, but somehow I just don't want him around."

"Bret McAllistair, get off me!" Colleen seethed, the gold in her eyes sizzling like sparks. Her hair spilled over the bed like waves of shimmering black silk, and he clenched his jaw, aware that he couldn't stay so close to her long without either killing her or giving in to the temptation to remember just how heated her passion and beauty could be.

"Who do you think you are to come in here like this?" she demanded, fighting his hold and struggling with the spread. Bret realized that he needed little effort to restrain her; the massive spread was doing the job with the efficiency of a straitjacket. He sat back on his haunches, keeping his weight off her as she continued to twist and challenge him. "How dare you tell me what I can or can't do? It's my house because I've lived here—"

"Yes, that's another thing, isn't it?" he asked calmly. "I didn't walk out, Colleen. I went to work, and you chose to end it all."

"Oh! This is a ridiculous conversation! You've finally lost your mind, Bret McAllistair. Totally. Completely. Fine. It's your house! Move—and I'll get out!"

"Not on your life," he told her softly, but there was menace in his tone and a promise or a threat as deep as that menace.

She went still and stared at him with comprehension and suspicion. God, she was beautiful, he thought, staring at her fine, flawless features, the smoothness of her skin, the depths of her eyes. His voice caught in his throat, and for a moment he could barely breathe. Then something in him hardened. She was beautiful and bright. Determined, tenacious and cunning. She could laugh and capture a heart, smile and steal away a man's soul.

But he'd already lost his soul once.

"What are you after, Bret?" she asked flatly.

"The Rutger Miller story," he answered, equally bland.

She laughed suddenly, and the brittle, humorless sound might have been an echo of his own bitterness.

"Ah, yes, a story! What else?" she reflected dryly, sweeping her lashes over her eyes. "That's your life, Bret, isn't it? I get the honor of your presence because of a story! My Lord! This is just like déjà vu! You thrive on excitement and assume that you're the only person capable of handling even the slightest hint of danger. You've done this to me before, Bret." She gave him a small frozen smile. "Not again. No way, Bret McAllistair," she told him coolly. "It's my story."

"No. Not anymore, it's not."

"And why is that?" she challenged.

He moved off the bed, releasing her from the weight of his body and standing idly before her. "Because Rutger Miller's body was found last night—dredged up from the river."

"What?"

She paled so quickly and so completely that Bret was sorry he had spoken so harshly. Inwardly he winced. But it was for the best. She was going to get hurt if she didn't learn to stay away from the danger zones.

"Dead!" she said with a gasp, and he saw that her lips trembled, her fingers clutched convulsively at the spread. His words had hurt her even though she hadn't fully comprehended them. She had cared about Miller. That was obvious. And it was also natural for Colleen. For all her professionalism, she never managed to stay uninvolved emotionally.

"He is dead, Colleen. Rutger Miller is dead." Bret didn't mean to be cruel, but he had to make her understand the implications. "Colleen, I want to see everything you've got on him. I want to hear every tape, and I want to know every little thing he ever said to you in private."

"It's…still my story," she whispered, and he knew that fighting him had become instinct to her because her eyes were glazed; she was still in shock from his words.

"Colleen?" He reached down and touched her cheek gently with his knuckles. For a moment, as she stared up at him, she looked lost and vulnerable, soft and innocent, her eyes wide and luminous and trusting….

Almost as if she needed him.

But then she closed her eyes and twisted from his touch. "Leave me alone, Bret. Rutger was my friend. The story is still mine."

"No, Colleen. And the longer you fight me on this one, the longer you'll be plagued with me in your life.

In *your* house. And who knows, I might even wind up in *your* bed again. So be a good kid, huh? I'll give you a few minutes to get dressed, then you can come out and show me the videos, okay?"

He didn't wait for an answer. He sauntered from the bedroom through the sitting room to the kitchen, where he shrugged, opened the refrigerator and helped himself to a beer.

Bret leaned against the wall, closing his eyes. He knew her. Right now she would still be lying there in turmoil, aching for Rutger Miller and trying to decide whether to attempt to strangle Bret or to graciously pretend that she had decided to be magnanimous and allow him to share her information. He hoped that by now she would have decided that she couldn't get rid of him, and she knew she couldn't strangle him.

Bret sighed, wincing as a little shudder shook him. He was staying. She didn't know yet what she had gotten herself into; she didn't realize the deathly extent of the danger.

Yes, he was staying, no matter what. Because he was still—like it or not—in love with her.

Chapter Two

Colleen stared up at the ceiling, stunned and aching. Her heart and mind were spinning. Rutger was dead. Poor old Rutger, so torn with conscience over the past! That conscience had brought him to her, to the law, and because of it, he had paid with his life.

And she had received the news from Bret.

Bret! What was he doing here? She didn't dare think about it too much. She would either dissolve into ridiculous and futile tears or grow so angry that she would become as combustible as a can of high-octane gas. How could he be so cruel? He had walked out on her without a backward glance and returned with such confidence and audacity that he might never have left.

The story, she told herself dully. Bret was after the story. What was Bret ever after, but the story?

Tears burned in her eyes. She stood quickly, blinking with fury. Not this time, Bret, she promised herself. Not this time. You're so damned sure I'm going to come waltzing through that door and spill my guts to you! Well, it isn't going to happen.

Decisive thought and action—that was what she needed! Colleen quickly tore through her drawers for a pullover and a pair of jeans, slid into them, raced to her closet, and then hobbled around with a total lack of grace as she tried to tie both sneakers without sitting down. A determined look was etched across her features as she did so. *Damn him!* He'd decided that he wanted to be married, and so they had been married. He'd spoken and assumed that his word was law. And when she'd dared just once to try to defy him, he'd turned his back on her as coldly as a winter freeze. Oh, God! What a fool she'd been! She should have known not to marry him. He'd been around; he was experienced. And from the very beginning she'd fought against her sense of insecurity because of it. They could be at a party in London, Madrid, Paris or New York—anywhere in the world—and a svelte beauty would walk in and approach Bret, and Colleen would be left to wonder just what their relationship had been before she and Bret had married.

Or would be again, she thought bitterly.

God! She had never wanted to hurt a man, never wanted to strike out at anyone as she wanted to strike out at him. But then, she'd never been hurt herself as she had been hurt by Bret. And hurting, she had learned to grow a tough shell. Facade though it might be, it had gotten her through.

"Not this time!" she whispered aloud to herself. He was back, but she wasn't handing over her story. She owed more than that to Rutger Miller. Rutger had come to her. And now he was dead. She owed him, and she didn't owe Bret a damned thing.

Colleen tiptoed past the sitting room and stared through the kitchen into the living room. How like him! She could see the back of his tawny head. He was sitting on the sofa, which faced the hearth, his legs comfortably stretched out on the coffee table, sipping a Miller

Lite. Waiting, with his supreme confidence. His shoulders were still bare, broad and bronzed and gleaming in the soft light of the room.

Instantly her heart seemed to stick in her throat. All the heartache and loss she thought she had learned to live with rose to encompass her in a shudder of pain. She longed to reach out, to touch his gleaming tanned flesh, to feel the ripple of muscle there, and the sweet fainting sensation of being held in his arms. Strength and tenderness combining. Soaring passion and electric heat along with laughter and the inner ecstasy of being loved.

Illusion! she reminded herself cruelly. And if she was stupid enough to be his entertainment because he had walked back in to take her story, she deserved whatever heartache came her way.

No, not again.

Colleen swallowed fiercely and silently slipped back to her bedroom. *Her* bedroom. He had walked out. He had no rights.

She paused for a minute, glancing around for her purse. She remembered then with dismay that it was out in the living room, where she had tossed it when she came in. She winced, then shrugged and moved to the nightstand at the left side of the bed. There was only about twenty-five dollars there, but she wouldn't need a fortune to go buy herself a cup of coffee somewhere. She had extra keys to the back of the house—how the hell had he gotten in anyway? she wondered with a shudder of fury—even if she didn't have a set for the Ferrari. All she had to do was leave for a while. Surely he was too busy to sit in the living room forever.

Colleen made one last check on his position. He was

still sitting very comfortably on the couch. Then she went back to her room and reminded herself that she had to move silently. She winced when she tripped as she slid out to the patio. She stood dead still, listening to the pounding of her heart. But she heard nothing else; her awkward movement hadn't been as loud as she thought. Trying very hard not to make any more mistakes, she tiptoed across the patio to the screen door. There was a lock on the handle and another at the top, but neither seemed to make any noise as she lifted them. Then she was out on the grass, shaded by the giant oaks at the back of the yard.

"Up yours, McAllistair!" she whispered, a bit giddy with her victory. He could wait all damned night if he wanted. She wasn't coming out to tell him a thing.

Her lips curled into a little smile, but she found that she was blinking again as she trotted past her Ferrari and out to the gently lit sidewalk. Even as she smiled, she paused, bending over for a moment, fighting a pain in her stomach and an overwhelming dizziness. How could he do this to her? How could he come back into her life when she had just started to learn how to live without him? It hurt, oh, it hurt so badly!

She straightened, gritting her teeth, and hurried along the sidewalk. Most of the houses were dark and silent, she noticed. It was almost midnight. It was, in fact, probably a little dangerous and maybe even stupid for her to be out like this. It wasn't a crime-free neighborhood. No neighborhood was. But the way she was feeling right now, if a mugger were to come after her, he would be damned sorry that he had.

She glanced up as she came to the Lords's house. There was a light on above the porch. Joe and Marge had probably gone to the movies. Colleen narrowed her eyes a little against the muted light. She waved suddenly, seeing that Marge's dad, down from Minnesota for a vacation, was rocking away in the coolness of the night. He waved back to her, then suddenly frowned.

Colleen hadn't heard a thing. All she felt was a sudden rush of wind. Then her feet were off the ground, and the breath was knocked out of her so thoroughly that she could only gasp when she intended to scream. A hand clamped over her mouth as she was lifted and held taut against a naked chest.

She heard Bret's strident whisper. "Fool!"

She pushed against his chest, trying to wrest her mouth free of his hand. "Let me down, Bret!" she managed to grate out. "I'll scream bloody murder, and I mean it." Marge's dad was probably getting to his feet right now. "Mr. Pierson—" She started to shout, but Bret was already spinning around to face the old man. "I tell you, Mr. Pierson, what is a man to do with the modern woman? Colleen just doesn't realize the dangers that stalk the street at night! She never listens to me."

There was a false, plaintive tone to his voice, as if he were begging the more experienced man for advice.

Colleen heard Mr. Pierson chuckling.

"I think you've got the right idea, young man! Take her home, give her a little loving, let her know it's her welfare that concerns you."

"Yes, sir!" Bret responded respectfully.

Colleen had had enough. She caught some of the tawny hair on his chest between her fingers and wrenched it as hard as she could.

"Ouch!"

She tried to sink her teeth into his flesh. He was still

smiling at Mr. Pierson, but he gave a low groan through that smile as he pretended to bow tenderly toward her for the sake of his audience.

"You've had it!" he growled very low, for her ears alone. But there was no loss of malice in those words because of their quietness. He tightened his arms around hers. Her knees were forced almost to her nose, and suddenly his fingers were streaking far less than gently into her hair and her head was being arched back, her eyes forced to his. And then he was lowering his lips to hers, hovering just above them to whisper, "You are an honest-to-God idiot, Colleen. Haven't you understood anything? Your life could be in danger!"

"Yours is going to be in danger if you don't let me down!" Colleen whispered furiously in return. She didn't dare shout; his grip on her hair was too painful. Tears were already burning in her eyes, and she'd be damned to a thousand hells before she ever cried in front of him.

"Always full of threats!" he responded. And then his lips crushed down on hers. They tasted like Miller Lite and like him. Even as she pressed furiously against his chest and tried to twist from the calculated assault, she felt an inward melting. Warmth and persuasion and whirlwind command were blended uniquely in his touch; he was angry, and she knew it by the force of his lips. But it was as if he had found something unexpected and shattering—just as she had when his mouth descended to hers. The movement of his lips, the provocative velvet thrust of his tongue, tantalized her flesh, along her teeth, finding warm interior crevices that sent erotic sensations all through her body. Maybe it was just memory, memory of all that had once been, and maybe her traitorous flesh recalled all too easily that he was a man as unique as his kiss.

For a moment she went slack in his arms, savoring his taste and scent, the hard, breathtaking pressure of his lips. And then something inside her seemed to erupt with both pleasure and pain. She loved him, God, how she had loved him. She had felt completely destroyed when he had left her. And now…to appear the concerned and outraged husband before a neighbor… He was using her again! While she went hot and pliant with love and desire, he was merely honing his seductive skills!

She started to growl deep in her throat, fighting him again. The pity of it was that it made little difference. He moved his hand against her hair, as if to caress her.

He pressed her face back to his chest as he broke the kiss. "By George, Mr. Pierson, I think I've got it!" he called out cheerfully. "Good night!"

Colleen knew he couldn't make out her words as she cursed him furiously. The sandy hairs on his chest were tickling her nose; she felt the ripple of his muscles as he hurried back down the street with her in his arms like a wayward colt.

At last she managed to twist her head and lambaste him in a fashion that allowed him to clearly comprehend her every word. But it was too late by then; they were reentering the house through the front door. Her epithets were failing to disturb him. Colleen thought angrily and a little desperately, "You are incredible. Your ego, your manners. You haven't got a shred of common decency in your body. You'd sell your mother for a story—"

She broke off because she was suddenly falling

through the air and landing hard and breathlessly on the sofa where he had so recently been sipping his beer. She drew a deep breath, ready to attack again, but he was suddenly leaning over her, not touching her, but locking her between the parallel bars of his arms and staring at her with features drawn taut and grim. "Colleen, shut up."

She swallowed, trying to find the courage to hold fast to her righteous rebellion.

"And if I don't, McAllistair?"

"I think you will," he said quietly, and although there was no threat at all in his words, there was in his voice. And she had run out of things to call him anyway, although a few might well bear repeating, she thought.

He waited. She chose not to say any more, but stared at him with fires sizzling in the gold centers of her eyes.

He sighed and moved. Wasn't that movement worth a moment's silence? she asked herself. She couldn't bear for him to be so close. She didn't dare take a chance of forgetting what he had done to her because, no matter how she might ridicule herself for it, the attraction was still there, made more powerful by absence and longing. She had learned when he left that no other man was like him, that all men would fall short in comparison.

She hadn't known that just seeing him could fill her with such painful longing. Dear God, she was a bright and intelligent woman. She knew that only fools clung to a relationship that could give nothing in return!

For a long while his eyes held hers; then he sighed, rubbed the back of his neck and wandered toward the patio. "Colleen, you really don't understand the importance of what has happened or the danger."

Was he talking about the story or himself?

"And you don't understand that you've been out of my life for a long time! I didn't even know that you were back in the country, much less the state or city! And even if you legally own half of this house, you had no right to break into it or into my life!" she stormed in reply, jumping off the couch to follow him halfway across the room. "That was assault out there on the sidewalk! I should call the police! Maybe Mr. Pierson doesn't know that our divorce is pending, but Marge certainly does, and—and you can't just run around doing things like this, Bret!"

He turned to face her, mockingly arching a tawny, well-defined brow to hide the bitterness in his heart. He'd been back for a month. He'd tried to keep his distance until he'd been called about Rutger and heard that Colleen was involved. Then he'd known he had to see her because, no matter what her feelings were, he couldn't bear the thought of her in danger.

"You ran out on me," he said pointedly.

"*I* ran out on *you*!"

"You were supposed to come to the living room."

"Oh… Lord!" Colleen threw up her hands in exasperation. "I didn't make any deals with you, Bret McAllistair. You broke into the house, you invaded—"

"Why did you change the locks?"

"Because I didn't want you back in here!"

"It is half my house."

"Oh, God, this is getting us nowhere!"

"How true," he replied dryly. "Sit, Colleen, and start talking."

"I have nothing to say to you."

He laughed with no amusement. "Now that, my dear

Mrs. McAllistair, I don't believe. You've always had plenty to say, whether I wanted to hear it or not."

"You're mistaken. You're the one who always had things to say."

Bret opened his mouth as if to argue with her, then shut it with what seemed to be an audible snap of the jaw. He walked across the room and took her by the shoulders with such conviction that she didn't think to shake his hands away.

"Colleen, this thing is serious. Can't you ever trust me? I'm not here to take anything away from you."

She moved back, hands on her hips, her head cocked slightly as she looked at him. "Then just what are you doing, Bret? And for God's sake, why on earth should I trust you?"

He gave her an exasperated and disgusted sigh. He wandered back to the sofa and sank down to the cushions, then picked up his can of beer. A moment later he let out something like a snort and snapped the can of beer down on the coffee table. "Damned thing's warm!" he muttered, and even that seemed to be Colleen's fault.

"Want another?" she drawled sweetly and kept smiling as he twisted around on the sofa to stare back at her.

"You're being rather courteous. Funny thing, I never quite trust you when you are."

"I'm always polite to my guests."

"I'm not exactly a guest, am I?"

"Then get your own beer."

"I knew not to trust you," he said dryly and rose. But he paused before walking past her. "I'm glad that we've both established the fact that I'm not a guest in my own house."

He started whistling. Colleen froze for a moment

with a frown furrowing her brow; then she raced after him, stopping to clutch the wall at the entryway to the kitchen. "Bret!"

He was digging behind the yogurt cartons on the bottom shelf to get to the beer. He cast her a quick, irritated glance. "What?"

"You're *not* thinking about staying here, are you?"

He stood, closed the refrigerator door and leisurely pulled the tab on the beer can, watching her all the while. "Colleen, it *is* my house. I've given you peaceful residence in it for almost a year."

"Only eight months, Bret, and—"

"As a matter of fact, Colleen, yes. I'll be staying here for a few days."

"You will not!"

"Colleen, be reasonable. I never caused you a bit of trouble. I stayed away all that time. I built the damned place! It was my property, my design."

"Yours, yes! It never was *ours*, was it, Bret?"

"Colleen, get off it! Obviously I considered it yours, too. I'm the one who's been without a home, right?"

She raised a brow. "You left, remember?"

"Correction. I went on assignment."

"*My* assignment!"

He emitted an impatient sound and stalked past her on his way out of the kitchen. Frustrated, Colleen stared after him. If only she could grow to colossal size for just five minutes! Long enough to pick him up and toss him out on the sidewalk!

She was definitely still too shaky from the physical encounters she had already endured to even think about trying to throw him out. And if she called the police, well, it *was* his house, and she hadn't thought to have any legal provisions made. They'd be legally divorced in less than a month, and the lawyers would settle all that.

She crossed her arms over her chest and walked into the kitchen herself, calling to him over her shoulder. "Bret, if you're staying, I'm leaving." She kept talking as she walked through the sitting room and into the bedroom, reaching into the closet for her overnight bag. "I'm not going to run out the back door again. I'm going to pack my suitcase, grab my purse and keys and—"

She dropped her suitcase on the bed and then stopped short; he was in the doorway again, leaning comfortably, one hand on his hip, the other about his beer. His silver-gray eyes were on hers, narrowed just slightly, but beyond that he appeared completely relaxed and very much at home.

"You're not going anywhere, Colleen."

"Oh, come on, Bret! You can't stop me. This is the twentieth century, remember? Or," she added softly and very sweetly, "perhaps they neglected to tell you that in the first place!" Still smiling over clenched teeth, Colleen went to the closet again and grabbed two hangers, suddenly so tense that she wasn't even sure what kind of clothing she had grabbed.

She turned around again to hurry back to her suitcase, but crashed into his still-naked chest instead.

"Bret! Will you please get out of my way? And would you put your shirt back on! I'm starting to feel like I'm being stalked by Johnny Weissmuller!"

She stared up at him and caught a glitter of laughter in the hard silver of his eyes. "Can't take the heat, huh, Colleen?"

"Would you move, please? I'm not asking you to leave anymore; I'm volunteering to do it myself!"

He shook his head; the laughter was gone from his eyes, and his features seemed taut and maybe even a little sad.

"Colleen, you're not leaving. You're going to come out to the living room and sit down and tell me everything you know about Rutger Miller."

She took a deep breath and closed her eyes, but it didn't help. All that happened was that she inhaled the rich scent of his chest, soap—Irish Spring, she was certain—and something vaguely musky, powerfully masculine and, like his kiss, totally unique to him, subtle, and sensual on a primitive level.

He would use her again. Make a fool of her, then leave her. Unless she could be harder than he was.

"Bret, there is no reason in the world anymore that I should do what you say. I don't even owe you the courtesy of listening. There is nothing between us anymore. You're a rival journalist, nothing more. There's no reason—"

"Colleen…"

She started violently when his arms slipped around her again, his hands locking at the base of her spine so that her hips were pressed to his. His voice was rough, his eyes so hardened that they looked almost black. She stiffened and forced herself to return his stare, allowing herself to shiver only inwardly. Bret could be very dangerous when he chose; a number of people had learned that when they had thought to stand in his way. But he would never hurt her, not physically, at any rate.

"Colleen, you are going to listen to me. Because, believe it or not, you beautiful bitch, I'd just as soon not see you dead."

"Bret—"

"I mean it, Colleen."

"There's not a damned thing you can do!" she shrieked at last in utter frustration and more than a little fear. She raised her arms against his chest, grunting as she tried to break his hold.

"Colleen, don't kid yourself. I'm getting tired of this. Really tired. Pay attention to reason."

"Reason! What is reason? Bret says jump, and Colleen asks just how high?"

Something in his face hardened. "That's about right, for the time being."

"Like hell—"

"Colleen," he said very quietly and with an irritatingly calm assurance, "I'm *asking* you as nicely as I can not to give me any more trouble. Because if you do…"

"What?" she challenged.

He shrugged. "I'd have to come up with some type of persuasion you simply couldn't resist."

She stared at him for a minute, then burst into laughter.

"Ah…you don't think I'm serious."

"No."

"Want to keep testing me?"

He asked her in such a way that she wasn't sure that she did. But she lifted one delicate brow, trying subtly to break his hold about her waist.

He pulled her closer. She was disturbingly aware of the rock hardness of his stomach muscles, his hips and his long legs, of his naked chest pressed against her sweater, against her breasts. She knew that he was aware that she wore no bra, that her breasts were crushed to him, that her nipples were grazing his flesh through the soft cashmere of the sweater.

And that she was beginning to flush because of their intimate contact, though she was also aching to escape him.

"Bret…" She lowered her head.

"You think I'm kidding, Colleen. I'm not. I'd take some fairly drastic measures right now. Trust me. It would be easiest to sit down like a good girl, with a glass of wine, and talk."

Her eyes met his, and she found an amused glimmer of silver laughter in them again. As well there might be, she thought acidly. He knew damned well that, after one glass of wine, she talked a blue streak. "Trust you?"

"Seems the intelligent move to make when you have little choice, doesn't it?"

"I'll make coffee, Bret."

He shrugged, releasing her. "Suit yourself."

Only then did she realize her mistake. She had just agreed to talk.

"Where are your interview tapes?" he demanded.

She smiled very sweetly. "Sorry, Bret. They're not here. They're at the office."

Undaunted, he gave her a grim smile. "Then let's sit down and talk, okay? Come on, get your sweet derriere moving. Unless you want me to move it for you?" he asked politely.

She cast him a warning gaze and sailed on past him. In the kitchen she stopped at the stove, ready to reheat the leftover coffee. Her hands were shaking when she picked up the pot.

From behind, Bret reached for it and set it back down. He gave her a little shove toward the living room.

"You need the wine," he told her, and she decided not to protest.

She felt the need for a whole carafe full of the stuff. Anything to blot out the fact that he had come back into her life like a bolt of lightning out of the blue.

She walked into the living room and pulled off her sneakers, tossing them into the center of the room in an act of defiance. Fat lot of good it would do her, she reflected, but it made her feel a little better to take her aggravation out on her sneakers. Then she sat on the couch, curling her feet beneath her. She could hear Bret in the kitchen opening the wine. She thought a little sourly that Bret never had trouble with a cork; the man had never to her knowledge crumbled a wine cork into a zillion pieces. Bret just did things; he never had problems.

Colleen leaned back and closed her eyes.

Like the time they met. A whole bunch of reporters had been on location in Central America. They'd all been shaking like fools because a band of guerrillas toting machetes had been on their tails. Bret had been the last to board the plane. He'd barely looked ruffled. A machete had split the air over his head, and he'd merely looked annoyed when he turned to take a right jab and flatten his attacker to the country's sad excuse for a runway....

"Here."

She opened her eyes and accepted the wine from him. He didn't try to sit near her. He sat at the end of the couch cross-legged, his bare feet also curled beneath him. She glanced at his toes, thinking how they had once spent an evening laughing at them. Just like the thick tawny mat on his chest his toes had little clumps of chestnut and golden hair. Every single toe. When he wasn't paying attention and she was in a mischievous mood, she always attacked his toes until he *was* paying attention.

"Colleen?"

She lifted her shoulders in a shrug of resignation. She might as well tell him the innocuous stuff.

"Rutger Miller called me at the magazine about three months ago." She shrugged. "I didn't even know who he was at first. I know I'd heard something about the Helmond diamonds disappearing during the war, but it's such an old mystery.... Anyway, something he said triggered my memory, and I knew he was important. As soon as I hung up that first time, I hit the computers and dug up all the old newspaper and magazine stories on the scandal that I could find."

"Go on."

She stared at him a little bitterly. "You would have known who he was right away, wouldn't you?"

He didn't look condescending; he just shrugged lightly. "I was always big on reading about the war. That particular story intrigued me from the first. Something seems to be missing besides the diamonds. But believe me, Colleen, I'd be willing to bet that the majority of the world has forgotten all about the scandal and Rutger Miller." He paused for a second, and his voice changed slightly. "Go on."

She took a long sip of her wine. It was a German white, one that he had introduced her to.

"He said that he liked my style, that he believed I cared about people." Bret made an unflattering sound. She cast him a sizzling stare.

"Sorry," he said dryly. "Do go on."

"The first time I met him was about two weeks later. No notes, no recorders. He asked to just meet me and have lunch. I agreed. I was too fascinated by the opportunity to press my luck."

"What did you talk about?"

Colleen forgot for a moment that she hated Bret and loved him. She took another sip of her wine, reflecting on the day she had first seen Rutger Miller. He'd reached the restaurant before her, but when she had approached the table, he had stood. He'd been very tall and very slim, and as straight and dignified as a statue. His hair had been white, his eyes crystal blue. His face had been worn, lined and weathered. His handshake had been firm and warm. And as they had begun to talk, she had come to realize that the crystal glaze in his eyes was one of acute pain.

"We, ah, talked about normal things at first," Colleen said at last. "He mentioned his grandchildren in Germany and asked if I had any kids. He—"

"Did you tell him you were too busy?" Bret interrupted dryly.

Startled, she stared at him. He had been the one…

"Sorry, never mind. Go on."

Hurt and suddenly very nervous, Colleen stared down at her glass.

"Colleen, I said I'm sorry."

Be flippant, she warned herself. It was the only way to handle him. "For what?" she asked airily and didn't wait for a reply. "Then we started talking about the war. But only in general that day. And that—that was when I started to like him. He—oh, never mind. You'll think I'm silly. Or unprofessional."

Bret shook his head impatiently. "You can't accuse me of ever thinking anything like that, Colleen. Tell me what you were thinking."

In that moment she felt an acute sense of nostalgia so strong it was painful. No, there were some things of which he could not be accused. How many times had they sat, just as they were, discussing their assignments with one another? Seeking approval, giving support.

Or maybe not, she thought dryly. She had needed the approval; he had given the support. She wasn't terribly sure that Bret McAllistair had ever needed anything or anyone.

When he wanted things, he took them. Wasn't he giving her further proof of that right now?

It didn't matter. Suddenly she wanted to tell him her impression of the man because it was just possible he might understand.

"Bret, he was just like what I always thought a man like Lincoln or Robert E. Lee might have been like. I mean, involved in terrible things, watching war, watching battle. Watching death and dying a little all the time along with his men. When he talked about certain things—Normandy, for one—he almost flinched. He could still see the pictures in his mind, Bret. Of all the fallen men, the Allies as well as the Germans. He thought it was all such a waste! And he managed to explain to me how the German people had felt, how they had believed the Third Reich would give them new self-respect when they had been so horribly humbled at the end of the First World War."

He smiled. For a second she thought he wanted to reach across the couch and touch her cheek, not in passion or anger, but in tenderness. "I don't think you're silly, Colleen. I understand." He frowned, leaning his head back and rubbing his temple. "It's making the picture clearer, too."

"What picture?" Colleen asked.

"His murder," Bret murmured. "What else did he talk about?"

"Just the war—that day."

"When did he start talking about the Helmond diamonds?" Bret demanded.

She hesitated only briefly, then realized that she could talk and still preserve the information she wanted to preserve. After all, several of the discussions she'd had with Rutger about the diamond heist were on tape, public property or at least that of the magazine. Bret had access to them.

"The first time we talked about the diamonds was at the first taping. I guess he had decided that he trusted me by then, or else he was simply ready to confess all he knew."

"Which was...?" He waited, but she took her time, and finally he spoke again. "Colleen, in the Brainevrault battle, hundreds of soldiers were massacred. Allies and Germans. History proved that it was unnecessary. Two commanders were supposed to have called a halt to it, but they were too busy stealing hidden French diamonds to care what was going on."

"That's the part that isn't true!" Colleen cried out. "Rutger wasn't involved—not that way. He was only the second in command, and he had been ordered to stand still at the entrance to the tunnel. Just the same as Captain Sam Tyrell."

"Oh, yeah, right!" Bret protested. "That's why Sam Tyrell was court-martialed and shot for treason!"

"He took the rap, Bret. That's what Rutger was trying to tell the world. The real culprits were the generals, MacHowell and the German, Rudy Holfer."

Bret watched her, taking a casual sip of his beer. "So where are the diamonds?" he finally asked her.

"I don't know."

"You never were a good liar, Colleen."

"Damn you!" she charged, her temper soaring. "I'm not lying, Bret! Use some sense! If Rutger had given me the diamonds, the world would have known it! So why murder Rutger Miller, then?"

"Why, indeed?" Bret asked, smiling. Then he uncoiled himself with the silent grace and beauty of a panther and plucked her wineglass from her hands. "It's empty."

"Leave it that way," she said sourly. He grinned, returned to the kitchen and came back with more wine. She took the glass from him, smiled sweetly and consumed the wine in one long sip that left her stomach—and every other organ—burning like a brushfire. Then she laughed because his expression was so disapproving.

"Your idea, McAllistair. Aren't I falling right in line with the grand design? Souse her up and strip her mind?"

"Cute, Colleen."

"And true," she said demurely.

"It isn't going to get you out of anything."

She smiled and yawned. "Of course not. Who does survive an evening with the grand inquisitor of all time?"

"I'm not an inquisitor," he growled gruffly. "I'm trying to help you."

"Ummm," she murmured noncommittally. Oh, God! What had she thought she would prove? Her head was suddenly spinning like a tornado straight out of *The Wizard of Oz*.

"Dummy!" he muttered irritably, and she was vaguely aware that he was still standing in front of her. Her lips curled slightly because she wanted to believe that the insult had been voiced with the slightest inflection of affection. Then he was leaning over her, very close, and she thought again that, as well as having one of the greatest sets of shoulders a woman could ever hope to see, his scent was arresting, so muted and fresh and yet entirely sensual.

She winced, closing her eyes tightly. *The better to crush you with, my dear,* the Big Bad Wolf had said. And that, too, was Bret McAllistair. Perhaps she had been the only woman he had ever called his wife, but what had that been in the end? Nothing to hold on to in the night. Nothing to love. Nothing that could hold him to her.

Fight him, always fight him, she warned herself. Don't get hurt again....

"Colleen!" He was talking to her again. She opened her eyes and longed to laugh; he looked so fuzzy.

"Colleen, what have you got in there to eat besides yogurt? You've got to get something into you."

"Why don't you just try sodium pentothal?" she suggested bitterly, then laughed.

"Don't push me," he warned her dryly. "I'm trying to save that for my last resort."

She lifted a hand vaguely. "There's all sorts of stuff. Crackers. Cheese. Sandwich meat. Help yourself. You're going to anyway."

"So are you!" he asserted impatiently.

She knew he had gone because she didn't feel warm anymore, because his unique aroma was gone from the air, because she felt absurdly empty.

Very absurd. He hadn't been hers since he had chosen to walk out the door, and she had accepted that. When she'd cried her eyes out and lost twenty pounds, she had convinced herself she hated him.

A shaky little sob escaped her, and she stiffened. He was only here now because of her story. Nothing more. She couldn't relax her guard for a single second, and she had to stop remembering all that had been good and wonderful about him, about them together....

She opened her eyes, then closed them. The room kept spinning whether her lids were up or down. She leaned her head back against the sofa, and her body started to slide of its own accord. It felt so comfortable to stretch out, so very good to put her pounding head down on the soft cushion. When she did that, a gray darkness came to blot out the spinning tornado in her mind. She was so tired. She'd been tired before she'd gone out to eat with Jerry and exhausted when she'd gotten ready for bed, only to find that her almost exhusband was in it and determined to make her insane.

Oh, bless that gray darkness! Silver gray, but sometimes black like a storm cloud, just like his eyes...

Five minutes later Bret walked back out of the kitchen with a plate full of crackers, and chunks of ham and sharp cheddar cheese. "Colleen..." he began, ready to explode when he didn't see her sleek black hair rising above the back of the sofa. Then he frowned and walked around to the front.

She was on her stomach, one hand beneath her head, the other beneath her chin. She was breathing with deep regularity; her hair was a fan of wild and provocative disorder all about her face and shoulders. Her feet, slim and small for her height, were hanging off the end of the sofa.

As he watched her, she made a soft sighing sound and curled a little more tightly into herself.

For a minute he was angry, knowing damned well she had downed the wine in one gulp on purpose. Then he smiled because nothing was going to get her out of this one.

He put the tray down on the coffee table and knelt beside her. "Colleen?" he touched her cheek and got no response.

He stood, then bent down to lift her. She was light, no more than a hundred and five pounds that were just all in the right places. Her head lolled back when he lifted her, and he knew that she was really and truly out.

He carried her into the bedroom, paused to nudge the mussed spread out of the way and set her down. He stood, ready to cover her, then paused again. Her jeans were going to be miserable to sleep in.

"Colleen." He leaned next to her again, speaking into her ear. "I'm not attacking you. I just think the jeans should go."

She mumbled something.

He reached for the snap and undid it, pulled at her zipper and then wished that he'd decided to leave her sleeping in misery. After all, she probably deserved it, and he *didn't* deserve what touching her this way was doing to him. It was all too easy to recall the times he had performed a similar task with her awake, very aware and watching him with her green eyes full of sultry tenderness.

And love?

Had she ever loved him?

He compressed his lips and tugged at her jeans. They surrendered to him at last. He stood back, tossing the jeans on the floor. But he couldn't quite turn away. She had beautiful legs. Very long, and with just enough muscle to make her look…perfect. He really didn't know what he was going to do until he reached out to gently stroke her thigh. She gave another soft little sigh, and he pulled back, laughing though there was a definite edge to the sound.

"Rat!" he accused her.

Of course she didn't respond, but he smiled slightly. And he kept watching her, his brow furrowing a little with remembrance. He moved a lock of her hair, and his lip twisted a bit; he couldn't seem to leave her, couldn't seem to command himself to really draw away.

He knelt at her side, safe for the moment. It was safe to watch her and not care about the ravages that might be betrayed by the naked emotion on his face.

"God, I loved you, babe," he whispered. And then he admitted the truth aloud. "Love you. Miss you…."

He smiled again ruefully as he lightly grazed her cheek with his knuckles. He could remember so many good times. If they were still married in the ways that mattered, the emotional ways, he could have awakened her. Crawled in beside her, tickled her toes, stroked the curving line of her spine slowly, patiently, until she began to stir and then turned to him, wakening slowly at first, then suddenly aware, wide-eyed, breathless and filled with laughter that she could be halfway seduced before she knew it. She'd always been so beautiful. And yet it wasn't really her beauty that had enthralled him. Beauty did not make a marriage. It had been the laughter, the life, the warmth, the vibrancy, the interaction….

He gripped his hands together, closing his eyes.

No. It must have been an illusion.

Because they weren't still married. Not really. All that was left was a piece of paper, and even that would be void soon. He had to keep remembering that. She had to keep on believing that he was made of stone. He couldn't let himself get too close, couldn't let her know that there was no stone in him where she was concerned; she could crush him in her delicate, little hand like an eggshell any time she chose.

But it would be so easy just to lie beside her, he thought wistfully.

He clenched his teeth.

"I've got to get out of here," he told himself out loud. But she was mumbling something, and he went down on his knees again, close to her mouth, trying to hear her.

"What?"

"Hot," she muttered. "Sweater's...hot."

"So am I!" he groaned as his whole body shuddered with the ideas that her comment brought to mind. He reached for the hem of her sweater with both hands, then tugged it upward and over her shoulders and head. Her eyes opened blurrily, and she smiled at him. But then her eyes closed, and she turned her head against the pillow.

He stood again, and again he paused, unconsciously clenching and unclenching his hands at his sides. He swallowed fiercely. She was so vulnerable, so erotic, so sensual. Her breasts were bathed in light and heaving slightly with each breath, the nipples as inviting as twin roses. Below them, her ribs, the lines of each barely visible. Her waist, very trim. Then the lace panties that still seemed more invitation than cover... He forced his eyes upward again. Her hair, deep dark velvet, in disarray over the pillow, was curling, waving, haunting him so that his fingers ached to reach out....

"I should curl up beside you!" he snapped out harshly. "Damn you, Colleen, I really should. It would be just as much your fault as mine!"

She gave no response at all.

"Would you snore or something!" he whispered a little desperately. "Could you do some damned thing to be just a little less appealing?"

She moaned some small sound and curled onto her side. With a sharp expletive he grabbed the spread and tossed it over her.

His hands were so tense and shaking when he turned off the lamp that he almost knocked it off the table.

Then, muttering something beneath his breath, he turned sharply on his bare heels and slammed his way into the bathroom.

It was, he reasoned, still his shower, too.

And his cold water.

Chapter Three

The phone was ringing. It sounded as if a million sirens were shrieking.

Colleen tugged her pillow over her head and tried to still the sound. In a second the answering machine should pick up. But she didn't know who would be so merciless as to call her so early on a Saturday morning.

Go away, go away, she willed the sound.

Then she stiffened as memory sent chills racing along her spine. Bret! He had been here, and it was likely that he was still here somewhere. And if the machine answered the phone, he would hear whatever message came over.

She bolted up, marveling at how quickly panic could wake her from such a stupor. But when she blinked the sleep from her eyes and groped for the phone, she encountered flesh instead. His hand was already reaching for the receiver. He had apparently just sat down on the side of the bed. His hair was wet; he was wearing only jeans again, and a towel was slung around his shoulders.

"Will you let me answer my own phone?" Colleen snapped.

He shook off her hand and raised the phone to his ear.

"Bret, it's for me!"

He smiled pleasantly, his silver eyes alight with amusement. "Your sheet is slipping."

"What? Oh!"

Color suffused her breasts, throat and cheeks as she realized that she was sitting half naked in bed with the man who had walked out on her. She grasped the sheet and spread furiously, then made another lunge for the phone.

Too late. He was already issuing a low-toned, "Hello?"

And then a frown furrowed his brow. "Who is this? Wait a minute, please. Wait a minute. This is Bret McAllistair, her husband. If you'll just—"

He broke off, stared at the receiver, then turned slowly to Colleen as he pensively hung up the phone.

"Who was it?" Colleen demanded.

"I'm not sure."

"What do you mean you're not sure? Damn it, Bret, I told you not to answer my phone."

He stood up, too distracted to pay much attention to her harangue. "Colleen, the phone is still listed in my name. I checked on that," he added dryly.

"But—"

"Stop the nagging, Colleen! She'll call back."

"She?"

"Yes, it was a woman. By the way, where are my clothes?"

She felt a little dazed by the abrupt change of subject and the tone of his words. "Your clothes?"

"Yes, clothes, you know, the things made out of cotton, wool, linen and whatnot that we use to cover our bodies. It seems my side of the closet has been restocked in silk."

Colleen sighed and began backing up, the sheet still

clutched against her as she watched him warily. "Your stuff didn't fit me, Bret. The colors were all wrong for my complexion."

"Witty, Colleen, but I'm not in the mood. Where's my stuff?"

"Try the Salvation Army."

"The Salvation Army?" He repeated the words with such shock and hurt and disbelief that she felt a momentary softening.

"Bret…"

"You gave away my navy pea jacket?" Now he was beginning to sound angry.

"You mean the ancient green thing with all the holes?"

"You did! You gave away my pea jacket!"

Irritably, but without taking her eyes off him, Colleen fumbled around on her dresser for her cigarettes, found the pack and lit one, denying to herself that he was making her nervous. She inhaled and exhaled quickly, leaning back against the bureau for support.

"Bret, I'm sorry. If I had known you wanted me to keep all your things so you could drop by one night before the divorce, I would have! If I had known, Bret, I would gladly have stared at all your clothes every morning, day after day, knowing that you didn't live here anymore." Her voice was rich with sarcasm, but light. Good. She was managing much more savoir faire than she would have expected.

But he didn't even seem to notice. He sank back on the foot of the bed and stared at her with a startling reproach.

"You really gave away my pea jacket?"

"Bret! It had a thousand holes in it. It was ten years old!"

He sighed, shaking his head, and stood again. He started walking around the bed, and she froze, not at all confident anymore. He could be nerve-racking when he chose.

She exhaled a little shakily. He wasn't coming near her at all. He was just looking around on the floor for the shirt he had apparently dumped the night before. It turned out to be a pullover sweater. He found it and slipped it over his head, then looked at her strangely, almost as a child who has learned that his parents have given away his cocker spaniel in his absence. A double betrayal because of who had done it.

The hurt look faded quickly; he was all business again. "Up, Mrs. McAllistair. We're going to start where we left off last night."

"Bret..."

"I've made coffee. I'll be on the patio, watching all exits. You've got five minutes to be outside with me, or I'll be inside with you."

Colleen ground her teeth together, drew on her cigarette once again and wondered desperately if there weren't some way to get away from him as she stared rebelliously into his implacable eyes. But then she started wondering just where they had left off last night and how she had gotten into bed—naked.

And if she had slept there alone.

Her lashes fell as she fumbled slightly for the ashtray at her side and crushed out her cigarette. "I'll be out in five minutes," she told him icily.

"Good."

He turned toward the door, and suddenly, although she didn't understand why at all, she wanted to call him back.

"Bret?"

"What?" He turned back to her, his tanned fingers curled around the doorframe.

"I, uh, didn't get rid of everything. There's a box of your stuff in the attic. The pea jacket might be in it."

He looked at her for a moment, his silver-gray gaze unfathomable. "Thanks," he said briefly, then turned to leave again. But he didn't close the door behind him. She saw him pass through the sitting room, the hallway and into the kitchen. And she could still see his broad back and tawny head as he reached for a cup and poured himself some coffee.

For a moment Colleen sat there, chewing miserably on her lower lip. It just wasn't right, and more than that, it wasn't *fair*! How could he be doing this to her? It hurt so much to have him back here, and yet it was all so ridiculously natural. He had walked back in just as if he belonged. As if he had never left. He was completely at home in the kitchen—and in the bedroom. And as she watched him, she longed for it to be right. Her heart seemed to twist and turn with delicious and agonizing nostalgia. She wanted to jump out of bed, race into the kitchen and slip her arms around him, then hold him tight and pretend that nothing had ever been wrong between them.

God! That was the worst of it all. That she could be such a pathetic fool. He had used her with no compunction, then calmly walked out the door. How could she ever, for even a minute, allow herself to forget that fact? Where on earth was her self-respect?

She winced. Her self-respect was sadly lacking, at least where Bret McAllistair was concerned. But not this time. *Not this time!* She didn't care if he thought she was the most wicked witch in the world; she would fight him at every turn.

Colleen didn't know quite what he'd meant by his threat, but she didn't feel like taking any chances at letting him get too close. She made sure his back was to her and hopped out of bed. First she raced to close the door; then she dug in a drawer for shorts and a T-shirt before hurrying into the bathroom. She closed the door, then stared around herself, freshly irritated. *He* had just been in here. The mirrors were steamed, and he had used her razor.

She blinked, feeling the ridiculous urge to cry.

"Couldn't you have used the other bathroom?" she whispered aloud. But then she dropped her clothing on the floor and turned on the shower spray hard and cold. She wanted to be wide-awake and alert, and her head was still buzzing from having downed so much wine so quickly.

As the water beat forcefully against her, she began to wonder again about the phone call. "Damn!" she told the water. "Damn, damn, *damn*!" He'd walked back into her life, and already she was forgetting about business.

She closed her eyes, wishing it had all been a nightmare. Rutger Miller...dead. She shivered. Maybe it wasn't such a bad thing after all to talk to Bret, at least a little bit. He did know what he was doing, and he had an uncanny ability to get to the facts. If Rutger were dead, then someone was after something.

The diamonds. It had to be the diamonds.

Colleen turned off the water, hurriedly dried herself and dressed. When she left the bathroom, she saw that the house had been opened up again. The drapes were drifting in the breeze and seemed to flow out to the patio. The sun was high, higher than she'd expected, and glittering down on the pool.

And Bret was sitting at the table on the patio. A tray with two cups and the whole pot of coffee was on the table as well as a stack of toast.

Colleen walked out and sat down, staring at the pool rather than at Bret. But she could smell the coffee, and she needed it badly so she turned at last to pick up her cup and found his eyes on her.

"Come on, Colleen," he said, and she could have sworn he had learned that hint of a growl from a Doberman.

"I don't remember where I left off!" she snapped reproachfully.

To her horror, he laughed. "You were begging me to take off your sweater," he told her.

"I was not," she protested heatedly.

"The diamonds," Bret said, smiling.

Colleen sipped her coffee, watching him over the cup. "Are you after the diamonds for yourself, Bret?"

He made an impatient sound. "The diamonds are the key to the murder, Colleen. You said so yourself last night. If you did care about Rutger Miller, you should be anxious to see his murderer brought to justice. And you should be smart enough not to sneak around trying to do it yourself."

"I don't know what you're talking about."

"You can't play investigative reporter on this, Colleen. You could wind up getting hurt."

"I see," she said slowly. "I can't, but you can."

"Get off it, Colleen."

She turned away from him, staring out at the water, blinking. It had happened before so why not now? An assignment that he considered too dangerous for her seemed just perfect for him. Perfect enough for him to walk out on their life together.

She took a deep breath. "Bret, I'm not stupid."

"I never said you were, Colleen. But you're very impetuous, and when your eye is on a story, you don't watch the other things that are going on around you."

She didn't want to look at him right then. She knew what she would see. He would be sitting back in his chair, idly sipping his coffee. But though he would appear negligently comfortable, almost lazy, his eyes half closed, he would be acutely aware of everything going on. With his sandy hair, bronze tan and silver eyes, he almost had the look of a California beach boy except that his features were too rugged and hard, and his shoulders were touched here and there with faded scars earned during years of rough living. When he smiled, he looked no more than his thirty-three years, but when his mouth was cast in a grim line, it was easier to place him nearer forty. But now… Right now, she knew, he would be staring at her intently with a look that would both sear her soul and caress it. She had lost her heart, soul and self to that stare once and learned the hell of being his.

She played for a little time, refilling her coffee cup, then decided again that she might as well talk to him.

"On tape Rutger went into depth about the day of the battle. Apparently there was a member of the French underground who had been caught spying and who was about to be executed. He didn't want to die. He sent a message to Holfer, and Holfer decided that maybe the man might have something worthwhile to say. Anyway, the French partisan told Holfer that there were enough diamonds buried in the tunnel to let them all live anywhere they wanted all their lives in the height of splendor. In the meantime Holfer had agreed to meet with the Allied commanders before the battle started over some kind of an agreement that the town be spared no matter what the outcome. He and MacHowell had never met before, but it seemed they had both come to the same private opinion on warfare: they had all been programmed as killing machines and nothing more. They were sick of the war. In a matter of hours, though they didn't exactly become friends, the four of them—Rutger and Tyrell were there, too—recognized that same weariness and disgust in one another. Rutger said he thought Holfer must have decided then that the Germans might come to a draw, but that they wouldn't win. So he allied himself with MacHowell, who had rank over Tyrell. They all agreed to steal the diamonds, with MacHowell and Holfer being the real power behind the decision. You see, though they did mean to be thieves, they didn't mean to be traitors."

"Or so Rutger claimed," Bret interjected.

"I believed him," Colleen said. "I told you, I liked him. Back to the story. Things started going wrong. A brigade of marines came in long before the original troops had expected any relief. The field was strewn with the dead, and our culprits were busy stealing the French diamonds and trying to hide them for themselves. The four of them split up in the midst of absolute confusion. Rutger and General Holfer—who was about to be transferred to the SS, by the way—escaped the country and were supposed to have gone to South America. MacHowell claimed total innocence and pinned it all on the Germans and Sam Tyrell. Sam was executed, and MacHowell went free. But before the war was over, MacHowell had disappeared, too."

Bret absently tapped his cup. "Tyrell dies and everyone disappears. The diamonds never reappear. Then, forty-odd years after the fact, Rutger Miller calls a journalist and suddenly he's murdered. None of it makes sense."

"Yes, Bret, it does, in a way. Rutger was getting old. I think it was weighing terribly on his conscience. He needed to get it all out. He was a good man, Bret. He was just fighting on the wrong side—in the Allied opinion. He cared very much for his men. And I think it bothered him horribly all those years that Tyrell wound up court-martialed and executed."

"So why was he killed…?" Bret mused, rubbing his temples in a manner that seemed way too familiar to Colleen. Then he ceased his action and stared directly at her. "Who had the diamonds?"

Colleen hesitated. So far, everything she had told him was already on tape. It was information he could have gotten anyway. If she went any further, she would be getting into a world of secrets.

Her cup jiggled dangerously as he moved suddenly, wrapping his fingers around her wrist. She stared down at his fingers, long and tight and fitting easily around her own flesh and slim bones. She looked into his eyes and saw that they were a smoldering gray with a sharp, glinting shimmer. It was a warning gaze; he was losing his patience. She hadn't spent two years living with him without learning every nuance of his body language. Not that his rather lethal grip about her wrist could be called subtle.

"Tyrell has the diamonds," she said.

He frowned, releasing her wrist and leaning back again. "Tyrell has been dead for over forty years."

"That's right. And it makes sense, Bret. Ever since, everyone has wanted to know what happened to the diamonds. Tyrell must have had them and then stashed them somewhere. Didn't you read all the clippings? Tyrell refused to say anything except that he was innocent of the charges of treason. MacHowell somehow managed to get out of the entire thing, and both Rutger Miller and General Holfer disappeared. Tyrell must have been very bitter. He absolutely refused to talk about the diamonds. But Rutger claimed that Sam was the last to actually have the diamonds. And it's true, Bret. They never reappeared. They were never seen on the black market, never discovered in a cache. There was never a sudden hike in black-market diamonds to indicate that they might have been cut and sold that way. They just disappeared. It makes sense that Sam Tyrell hid them and went to his death at least knowing that the men who had betrayed him wouldn't receive the rewards of their labors! Sam Tyrell must have stashed them away."

Bret shrugged and poured himself more coffee. "The diamonds still might have been split, or recut, or even reset before he hid them. They could be almost anywhere. But if Rutger really didn't have them, why would someone want to murder him?"

Colleen lifted her hands. "I don't know." She put her cup down and padded barefoot to the pool, sitting at the shallow end and slipping her feet into the water. It was already warm from the sun overhead. What time was it? she wondered. She must have slept as if she were half dead. The evening was a blank. She had known damned well that he had been determined to loosen her tongue, and she had been equally, stupidly, determined to foil him for the night.

"Well," she said, staring at the water, "you've heard all I know, Bret. Why don't you crawl up into the attic, find your pea jacket and leave me in peace again?"

"Not on your life, sweetheart."

She spun around, lifting her feet so suddenly that she sprayed him with water. He started, but merely put down the now-sodden piece of toast he had picked up.

"Bret, I told you what I know! You're the expert. If you want more, go out and find it. With Rutger dead, I really have no more reason to go on with the story."

Bret shook his head, grimacing. "Colleen, I wish I could believe that, but it wouldn't matter anyway. None of your interviews has been published yet, but too many people know about the work that you did with Rutger Miller. There have been hints about the 'mystery about to come to light' in all the major newspapers, in this country and others. Let's go under an intelligent assumption: Rutger was murdered because of the diamonds. And if they weren't found, whoever went to such drastic lengths will be ready to do so again."

Colleen shivered, but she didn't want him to notice so she made an elaborate pretext of shaking off her feet, then stood. "This place is wired for security."

"So well that I broke in with a file with no difficulty at all."

"I could buy a couple of attack dogs...."

"No good, Colleen. Whether it makes you happy or not, you've got a husband in the house again until this thing reaches some conclusion."

"This isn't fair!" she snapped, her heart sinking

steadily as she thought of having him constantly around, constantly playing on her nerves and emotions.

"Whoever said life was fair?" His tone was light.

"How did you get involved in this to begin with?" she asked belligerently.

Bret stood, stretching. He walked around to one of the small ferns along the side of the house and frowned as he twisted off a dying frond.

"Bret?"

He squinted his eyes against the sun and stared up at the high screen and the brilliant blue day above it. "I was called in when they found the body. The homicide detective in charge of the case is a friend of mine. Carly was glad to send me. Seems the police want some good coverage on it to prevent anything else happening."

Carly—Carlton Fuller—was the managing editor for *The World*, the magazine for which they both worked. Colleen, however, tended to be assigned the tamer articles; what Bret handled were labeled Specials. Colleen knew that Bret was held in awe, maybe a little too much so: he always got to do any story he wanted to do.

But Carly... Carly was supposedly a friend of both of theirs. Colleen was hurt that she hadn't been informed that Bret had been called in or even that he was back in the U.S.

"I thought you were still in the Middle East," Colleen almost whispered.

He shrugged, watching her with his head slightly angled, as if he had asked a question. "I've been back almost a month."

"Where?" she persisted, and he had the good grace to hesitate for a minute.

"At Carly's."

Colleen turned around blindly and started walking toward the house.

"Colleen, wait a minute!"

She barely heard him, but even if his words had registered, she wouldn't have stopped. It felt as if the two men had been conspiring against her, and she couldn't lay the feeling down to paranoia. It had happened before.

"Colleen!"

He caught her shoulders and spun her back around to face him. His features were tautly drawn in a grim mask, but she didn't care; resentment was seething in her so fully. She stared at the hands on her shoulders, but he didn't take the hint and release her so she met his smoke-and-silver gaze with her chin raised high.

"Carly didn't want you seeing Rutger's body."

She blinked, but then demanded, "Why?"

"Because you cared about him."

"I'm a big girl, Bret. I've been at this kind of thing for a long time now."

"Listen to me, Colleen. You were involved. You cared. And he—he wasn't taken gently from this life. Someone tried real hard to convince him to give away any secrets before he died."

She lowered her eyes at last. "All right," she whispered. "Maybe I wouldn't have wanted to…see him." Then she raised her head again, and her eyes blazed into his. "But Carly might have had the decency to warn me that you could be running around picking my locks!"

"My locks," Bret flared back, eyes narrowing.

"You can take your damned locks and—"

"Watch it, Colleen. I'm too tired for your kind of sparring match."

"I don't care what you have to say, Bret McAllistair; you were wrong and you know it. You had no right breaking in here when you had been gone all that time. When our divorce will be final in less than a month. Common decency should have kept you out of the bedroom. Among other things, you might have given me a heart attack—"

"Colleen," Bret interrupted dryly, "I have a great deal of faith in your powers of survival. And I didn't mean to scare you half to death. I was just…stuck. And I asked Carly not to tell you I was around. Remember the last time? You asked to see me. So sweetly. You were all smiles and pleasantry just so you could tell me about the divorce. Don't you remember that? Well, I sure as hell do. It didn't seem to make a lot of sense to go through the whole thing again!"

"You left," she reminded him icily.

"I went to work," he retorted briefly.

"Could you get your hands off my shoulders, please?" she asked him pleasantly, without blinking.

He closed his eyes, and his fingers seemed to twitch for a second. Then he emitted an impatient grunt and released her, though he continued to survey her with his eyes.

He took a deep breath as if straining for the ultimate patience needed to deal with a child. "All right, Colleen, I know that this isn't making you particularly happy. But we've got to try to proceed with a mature approach. You're involved, I'm involved. I'm going to be your ghost, your shadow, your second skin, until this thing is solved. For two reasons. First, you may be a bitch, but I grant that you're a damned good-looking one, and when I dredge my memory long enough, I can come up with some soft and good qualities. I'm not anxious to be called in to take a look at your body if they pull it out of the river."

"Thanks. It's nice to know you're concerned," Colleen snapped back with acid gratitude.

"And secondly," he continued as if she hadn't spoken, "I don't trust you any farther than a foot away."

"Ah…you wouldn't want to lose the story, right, Bret?"

"Colleen, I'm trying to be reasonable."

"Reasonable? And complimentary, right?"

"We can try to get along. Help each other. I can stay out of your way as much as possible. And I'll even promise that if you'll try to be decent, as soon as this is over, I'll do everything in my capacity to stay out of your sight forever. I won't contest a thing in court, and you'll be free as the breeze."

She smiled slowly and reached up to smooth a lock of his hair back over his forehead. "Really, Bret?"

His eyes narrowed slightly, but he answered her pleasantly. "Really."

Her hand fell to his chest, and her fingernails played lightly over the soft material of his pullover. She took a step toward him, and he stepped backward to accommodate her.

"All I have to do is accept the situation, right?"

Her eyes were so bright staring up into his, and fringed by thick lashes as inky dark as her silken hair. Her lips were twisted into a smile that appeared almost elfin and very wistful.

"Right," he whispered. God, why did she always have this effect on him? She could make his temper go off like a rocket blast, but she could also make his insides ignite with the same terrible heat. She could make him shake and shiver so badly inside that he sometimes felt as if he were a teenager out on his first date.

"Right," he managed to respond again. She was leaning against him. She was light, but the pressure of her splayed fingers, the hint of her soft breasts, sent him stepping backward again.

"It could almost be like old times, right, Bret?" she queried with a husky breath. "Talking it all out...ordering pizzas and Chinese food in the middle of the night...sipping brandy before the fire, even in the middle of summer..."

"Uh...yeah," he responded a little shakily. And then he grinned with a hint of mischief. "And when you wind up a little too out on that wine, I can tuck you into bed. Just like before."

She halted, paling a little. But her smile was still in place. "Bret, where did you sleep last night?"

The shudder that tore through his body as he remembered putting her to bed left his muscles weak. But he could never show her his vulnerability, especially when she seemed to be calling the shots. Was it real? Was she softening? He knew her. He should be doubting it. But she was touching him, and talking to him with that wistful tone in her voice.

He arched one brow and allowed his grin to twist devilishly. "I'll never tell. Don't you know?"

She wasn't pale any longer; her cheeks were the color of a summer rose. "No, I don't know," she murmured, and now there was an edge to her words.

He smiled broadly. "You really don't remember *begging* me to get rid of your sweater? You were so...very...hot."

She kept smiling but her fingers went still against

his chest. Her eyes sizzled like the noon sun into his. "Are you feeling the heat at all, Bret?" she asked silkily.

"I never denied the heat," he responded, ready to crush her soft and sinuous form into his arms and prove that words and anger had little effect on the simple beauty of chemistry and nature.

But that was when she made her move. Her fingers tightened, and she shoved against his chest with all her strength. Suddenly he was off balance and falling... until he crashed backward into the shattering coolness of the pool.

Dimly he could hear her shout furiously, "Well, then, cool off!"

Anger sent him jackknifing quickly and cleanly back to the surface. Anger at her and at himself for having been such an idiot again. The little witch! If she had any sense at all, she wouldn't wait to see him right now. She would be racing into the house to lock herself in the bathroom until he could really cool off.

But she hadn't run. She was standing near the edge of the pool, her hands on her hips, fury still flaming brightly in the sun-gold depths of her eyes.

"You want a deal, Bret? You've got it! But you'd better try to stay out of my way! I'm not a toy; I never was and I refuse to be treated like one again! I've told you..."

She hesitated, backing away a bit as one firm stroke brought him to the edge of the pool. His eyes didn't look at all like silver. They were as black as the smoldering soot rising above a volcano, as threatening as an explosion about to occur.

"Bret..."

Then they both froze, he with his arms pushing

against the tiled border of the pool to propel himself out, she in the process of backing farther away.

The phone had begun to ring again.

The answering machine would get it, Colleen knew. She should be worried about self-preservation, not about who was calling. She'd known he would be furious, though not quite as angry as he looked. But she didn't want the machine getting the phone. She was sure it was the woman who had called earlier, and she had a slight suspicion of who it might be. She wanted to take the call, and she *didn't* want Bret hearing it.

Another second and another ring passed as she stared at him, a little bit stricken. Then she raced from the patio into her bedroom, diving across the bed to catch the phone.

"Hello!" she gasped out, just in time. One more ring and the machine would have clicked on, recording all their words and amplifying them for anyone within hearing distance to catch.

"Mrs. McAllistair?" It was a woman's voice. Soft and melodic, young and hesitant.

"Yes, yes, this is Colleen McAllistair."

"This is Sandy Tyrell. I—I believe that Rutger Miller mentioned me to you."

"Yes, yes," Colleen murmured. "Sandy, I want to see you. I want to help in any way that I—" She stopped abruptly. Bret, totally indifferent to the water that was dripping all over the carpet, was standing there, watching her.

"Sandy!" she said cheerfully, as if she were talking to a friend. "How about lunch?"

"Lunch?" Sandy Tyrell murmured.

Then, as Colleen watched helplessly, Bret bent down

to flick the switch that would turn the answering machine into a speaker. When Sandy Tyrell spoke again, Bret could hear every word she was saying.

"I—I guess that would be all right, but I—I was thinking it should be more private. Haven't you heard, Mrs. McAllistair? Rutger was killed. According to the paper it must have been horrible. I'm so frightened…."

Colleen grated her teeth and shot Bret a glance that could kill. He seemed not to notice; he was staring at her as if his hands itched to turn her black and blue. He didn't need to speak to tell her that he thought she was the worst liar in history.

"Sandy, please. Calm down. I'm sure no one knows you have any connection—"

"Anyone could find out about my connection!" Sandy's voice rose. "I've never denied it. My mother spent half her life trying to clear my grandfather! I saw Rutger countless times. We had become good friends and, Mrs. McAllistair…" She paused as if she was looking around to make sure no one was there to hear her. "I have one of the puzzle pieces. Just like you have."

Colleen felt her breath catch in her throat. Bret's eyes were on her like silver fire. He took a step toward her, and she had to fight to keep from rolling away in panic; there seemed to be so much menace in that single step.

"Sandy. I think we should talk about this in private. Perhaps you do need police protection."

"Can I come there?"

"I—"

Bret's eyes narrowed warningly. Colleen tried to think quickly; with him staring at her, water still soaking his hair and clothing and delineating every tight muscle in his body, she could hardly think at all.

He nodded. Colleen felt her throat go so dry she was afraid she wouldn't be able to talk at all. She swallowed and wet her lips. "Yes, Sandy, come here."

"We'll be alone?"

"Yes, Sandy, we'll be alone."

"Are you sure?" Sandy asked anxiously. "I won't come if anyone else is there. I tried to call you earlier, and a man answered."

"He's gone," Colleen lied swiftly, then reiterated. "We'll be alone, Sandy. I promise." Despite the fact that she was quaking inside, she tried to outstare Bret.

"All right. An hour?"

"An hour. I'll be waiting."

"Thank you!" Sandy Tyrell whispered a little desperately, and then the dull buzz of the line going dead filled the room.

Colleen continued to stare at Bret warily, her fingers in a death grip around the receiver. Slowly, purposefully, he snapped the button to silence the recorder. Then, with the same slow determination, he wrenched the receiver out of her hand and replaced it.

Colleen thought of him then just as she would a deadly snake. She would have to deal with him the same way: move slowly; make no sudden gestures. Her own gaze locked with his; she tried to smile and slowly slid off the bed.

It was no good. Like a streak of lightning he was on her, ignoring her dismayed gasp, pinning her wrists and pressing her body flat with the entire soaked length of his own.

"Bret, you're hurting me!" she cried out. "You're ruining the bed, you're—"

"The one thing I am," he interrupted raggedly, "is not moving until you decide to do some real talking."

She closed her eyes. But she couldn't shut out the image of his implacable features or the feel of his body against hers. Hard and vital. Warm…despite the cool water that had soaked through her clothing now, too, destroying all the civilized barriers between them. Oh, could she feel him! The crush of his hips, the muscled tension of his thighs, the security that his arms gave her, no matter how false.

A finger brushed her cheek. She opened her eyes and met his relentless gaze.

"Colleen," he said hoarsely, "you've got to tell me everything that's going on."

"All right!" she said with a gasp. Then she added brokenly, "Please, Bret. You're heavy. You're wet, and it's hot, and you're steaming everything in the room."

"Can't take the heat, huh?" he asked, but he moved, and she was suddenly both grateful and disconcerted. She planned to answer anything that he had to say at the moment very politely.

"What? The heat? Yes, it's very hot—oh!"

He had taken his weight off her, but she found herself leaving the bed along with him. Nor did he carry her nicely; it was no *Gone With the Wind*, up-the-staircase scene. She was hanging over his shoulder, feeling terribly unbalanced, and she was cursing him for being insane while her nose crashed into his back.

"Bret McAllistair, what—"

His footsteps were sure and swift. The next thing she knew she was flying, then slicing cleanly through the water of the pool.

Sputtering and gasping for breath, she came to the

surface, fully ready to revile him with every word she knew, along with whatever she could make up. But he was waiting, one foot on the diving board, an elbow casually resting on his knee.

"Well, now we should both be nice and cool, right? Come on out, Mrs. McAllistair. The way I see it, we've got a lot of talking to do in a very short span of time."

Colleen clamped her lips tightly together and swam for the stairs in the shallow end. He was there before her, stretching out a hand to help her. She ignored it, but he caught her hand anyway.

"We're in this together, Colleen. I've told you that. and I want to hear about these puzzle pieces—*now.*"

Chapter Four

Sputtering as she stared up at him, Colleen felt her anger suddenly fizzle, then fall flat. They both looked ridiculous—two adults dripping wet and behaving like a pair of thwarted kids.

She started to laugh.

Bret stared at her warily, not trusting her amusement when he had expected her to come out swinging.

"We *are* going to talk," he warned her.

"Oh, I suppose we are," she said casually, lowering her lashes and thinking quickly. This one was her story; she intended to keep it. But it appeared that she wasn't going to gain anything by fighting him nor was she going to be able to get rid of him, at least not by asking him nicely to go. She was going to have to be agreeable and lull his suspicions until she figured out what she was going to do.

For a moment an ache filled her heart as she allowed herself to dream the same old dreams. Working together... At one time the idea had been so appealing. They *had* worked together in a sense. They had talked everything out. Bret had given her his opinions; she had given him hers. And when things had gotten too frustrating or confusing, he'd always been able to make her forget about them. "The hell with it, for now!" he'd tell her. "I've got this great idea. Let's have hot dogs and wine in the whirlpool!" Or else he'd suddenly started building a fire in the middle of the summer, and they'd sit before it, naked and giggling, sipping hot chocolate and feeding one another grapes....

For a moment her heart seemed to constrict and burn; she caught her breath at the pain of it. What had happened to them? How had something so good become so bitter?

Humbly she reminded herself that he had walked out on her, taking one of her assignments in the process. The story had been more important than their marriage, than her.

Harden, O heart! she commanded herself with a touch of pain, and even a touch of whimsy. It would be so easy to allow the fantasy to happen. So very easy...

And so devastating on the day when it was over and they walked into a courtroom for that last, legal goodbye.

He was back because of another story.

Well, knowing him, she knew that he would stick to her like glue. Her only recourse was to play along. And what would it really matter, anyway? He'd already heard what Sandy had to say; she might as well tell him the rest.

"Colleen..."

His voice seemed to carry a low, warning purr. She smiled, noticed that his gaze was growing warier. "Help me out," she invited with a slightly weary sigh. "I'll tell you the rest of what I know if you promise to get out of here so that Sandy can come over."

"I'll be back, you know," he told her softly, not accepting her hand until the deal was made.

"I assumed you would," she returned blandly.

He bent down and the spirit of mischief seized her again. She longed to pull him back in.

But he was ready this time; he felt the pressure of her hand and looked warningly at her. "Not this time, sweet thing," he said in a wonderful Bogart parody.

Colleen found a toehold against the side of the pool; a second later his other hand was about her waist and she was out of the water, her body sliding slowly down along the length of his. For a second their eyes caught, and all she could seem to feel was that the water that drenched them both was becoming a hazy steam. He was so warmly solid, so vibrant; his touch seemed to promise so many things, things that were exciting and secure and beautiful. And his eyes at that moment were warm as a mist of tenderness that both embraced and sizzled, as if he had also been seized by an unbearable nostalgia, leaving her naked and aching.

Her feet hit the ground. He released her, and the look was gone. His hands were on his hips. "Puzzle pieces," he reminded her.

"Mind if I change first?" she asked acidly.

"Yes, I do. Because you're stalling."

"I'm not!"

"All right, change first. But if you want me out of here when Sandy Tyrell shows up, you'd better hurry."

"Make more coffee, will you?" she pleaded sweetly. Dripping, she hurried to her bedroom and rinsed the chlorine quickly from her body, thinking all the while.

She was a fool. She couldn't be near him, not even for an hour. The chemistry, or whatever the hell it was, was just too strong. And she'd never stopped loving him, never stopped the aching, the longing....

She dressed again, very quickly, in jeans and a T-shirt. Then she rummaged hurriedly in the back of the closet. Somewhere she had a bag with a few of his cutoffs and polo shirts. Not that she meant to be magnanimous or kind; she just didn't want him to stay wet. His clothes conformed too nicely to his body, and his body kept drawing her eyes, and…

He was in the kitchen, pouring fresh coffee, just as she had asked. She placed the bag of his clothes on the counter as offhandedly as she could.

"I remembered where I'd stuffed a few things," she murmured, clutching her coffee cup and quickly sipping some of the hot liquid. "You won't have to slosh around until you leave."

"Thanks." He disappeared into the bedroom with the bag; Colleen continued to sip her coffee, feeling a little numb. He reappeared moments later. His hair was still wet and sleek against his forehead. His knit shirt was bright red; the cutoffs were black. The color combination had always been exceptionally good on him.

Colleen turned away and decided to speak before he could start to ask questions. "Sam Tyrell drew up some kind of a puzzle thing with four parts to it. One was sent to Rutger, one to MacHowell and one to Holfer. The fourth was his, and, according to rumor, it was buried with him."

"But it wasn't buried with him, right? That's the one that Sandy has, I take it."

Colleen nodded and moved out into the living room. There was more space there, so she could keep her distance from him.

Bret followed her. She couldn't escape him. She sat on the couch, and he stood very near.

"So you have a piece of this puzzle. And Sandy has a piece. Supposedly MacHowell and Holfer have the other two."

"That's about it," Colleen said cheerfully.

"That's not about it!" Bret said. He set his coffee cup down, sat beside her and gripped her shoulders hard. She shrieked as her coffee threatened to spill. Bret impatiently took the cup from her hands and set it on the table. "Colleen, that's *not* it, you little fool! Whoever murdered Rutger was most assuredly after that section of the stupid puzzle. Damn it, Colleen, you're in serious danger!"

She wanted to shout at him to please let go of her, to stop looking at her like that. She wanted to curl against his chest and tell him that she was frightened, that she needed him....

But she didn't want his concern or his pity. She wanted to be loved completely, and she couldn't settle for less. Anything except love would eat her up slowly until there was nothing left except pity and bitterness.

She shook off his hold and widened her eyes caustically. "I really don't see why you're so concerned. Just think of the story you'll have if the murderer finds me. What human interest! It will be a Pulitzer prize winner, I'm sure."

He took a long time answering. A long time in which she came to regret her acidic outburst. "That was unworthy of both of us, Colleen," he said softly.

She rose and walked to the back of the room to stare out at the pool, which looked absurdly peaceful. "I know," she said, her voice equally soft. "I'm sorry."

Something seemed to be in the air between them, despite the distance she had intentionally created. It was as if a silver mist escaped him and touched her, embraced her. As if she could turn around and run to him and say that she was sorry, so sorry, and couldn't they just forget it all and send out for pizza to eat in bed, or better yet, call the airport and make reservations for some secluded island where there would be nothing but the two of them and time to love and heal and lick their wounds and get on with their life and love....

Colleen sighed deeply, closing her eyes. Once she had done a long and involved story on battered wives. It had been heartbreaking to talk to her subjects, women with black eyes and broken bones. "You've got to leave him," Colleen would say, referring to their husbands, and they would shake their heads very sadly, as if they knew something that she didn't. They stayed in such horrendous situations; they risked their lives and their souls just to be loved. Bret would never hurt her physically, never in a thousand years. And yet when he had first left, she had felt much the same way as those poor women. No matter what he did to her, she loved him. It was so crazy; she knew better, yet there seemed to be nothing she could do.

She had also done interviews with singles groups and seen women ripped to shreds inside because they couldn't find a man willing to make a commitment, and they went back time after time to men who blatantly used them. Cringing, crying, they were ready to take any little scraps that they could get from men who didn't even pretend to love them. How she had pitied those poor women! She had promised herself that she would always be strong, that she would never cling to a man who didn't really love her.

She turned around at last, grimacing slightly. "Do

you know what I don't understand, Bret?" She was very proud of herself; her voice was calm and rational, her tone conversational. No more tantrums, no more fighting, no more touching. She was going to be pleasant and professional and remote.

He turned to face her and gave her a questioning look.

"Why all this time?" she said.

He knew what she was talking about immediately. He shrugged. "You mean, why all this time with none of the survivors trying to get together and find the diamonds?"

Colleen nodded.

"For one thing, MacHowell and Holfer might very well be dead. Both of them must be in their seventies now."

"Rutger didn't think they were dead. He thought he would have heard…somehow."

Again Bret shrugged. "No one knows for certain where Holfer and MacHowell are now. Some say South America, some say North Africa. It's possible that after the war they fled so secretly that they had no way to find each other. Holfer had just been transferred to the SS. Maybe he was afraid of being pulled into the Nuremberg trials. Who knows?" He rose and walked over to her. He didn't touch her, he just stood before her for a minute.

"Colleen, I—" He broke off, a rueful smile on his face. Then he lifted the back of his hand to her cheek briefly. "I'm going to call a friend of mine on the police force, okay?"

"Why?"

"Because it's the only way I'll leave the house."

"But if Sandy sees anyone…"

"Hey! Have some faith in our law enforcement agencies, okay?"

Colleen bit her lip lightly, then nodded. She didn't know if it was because she was a little bit frightened, or because she knew he wouldn't leave unless she let him make whatever arrangements he wanted.

Bret went to the kitchen phone, and she heard him speaking briefly, casually. When he hung up and returned to her, he seemed relieved.

"There will be a plainclothes cop wandering around the neighborhood."

"Good," Colleen said lightly. She hesitated. "You, uh, didn't bring your car?"

"Carly has it. His is in the shop."

"Want to take the Ferrari?"

A slow grin touched his mouth. "You're being awfully generous. Want me gone that much, huh?"

"Yes, and quickly," she returned. But she smiled; they seemed to be bantering a little, and it was nice. "Sandy should be here any minute now," she added.

He nodded. "I need the keys."

Colleen gave him her car keys, then walked him to the door. He hesitated there for a minute, looking at her. "Don't open the door to anyone but Sandy. Not until I get back."

It was her turn to nod. He reached out and caught a straying tendril of her drying hair. He smoothed it slowly across her cheek; his thumb brushed her lips, and involuntarily she trembled. There was that wistful look about him again, something dry and rueful in his eyes. She knew she should push him away, but she just stood there, as if time and the past and everything that stood between them ceased to matter. As if he were nothing other than the man she loved....

"Take care, kiddo, I'll be back soon," he told her softly.

And then he was gone. Colleen slowly closed the door, then she hurried back to the couch because her knees were about to buckle beneath her.

CARLTON "CARLY" FULLER, was grumbling over a pan of bacon when Bret walked back into his town house. He was still in his bathrobe, a worn terry thing of an indeterminate dark color. His gold-rimmed spectacles were falling low on his nose, and his remaining side tufts of gray hair were fluffed out. He looked like a mad scientist, Bret thought, or at least he did until he looked up expectantly at Bret. Carly had young eyes; they were a deep, sparkling blue. They held intelligence, wit and a deep fascination with and caring for the things that went on around him.

As a boss he was a whip-cracker. He didn't care much for excuses. Bret felt as if he'd never really been a journalist until he'd started working for Carly. Through Carly he'd learned to ferret out the truth, to look beyond the obvious and see a situation from every possible point of view.

Bret had also discovered that there was no one alive more dependable than Carly. In a pinch he was there. He made no promises that he didn't keep. As a friend he was A1. He was no flatterer, and he judged most things that were said to him long and hard. But he had a habit of making you think, and Bret knew that anything Carly did decide to say might be blunt, but it would also be the truth.

He was more than twenty years older than Bret and Colleen and they were both crazy about him.

Yet Carly had said nothing when they decided to marry, and nothing when they "decided" to divorce.

"I never did get the hang of frying bacon," Carly grumbled finally.

Bret laughed. "It's too late to be cooking bacon, anyway. It's lunchtime."

Carly didn't respond. He shook his head, and his glasses slipped farther down his nose. "That wife of yours can cook bacon. Perfectly. No burnt spots, no soggy fat. Just a nice, crisp, perfect piece of bacon." He looked up again at last. "So how is Colleen this morning? She must have taken your appearance more kindly than you expected since you didn't show up here last night."

Bret grimaced. He walked into the kitchen beside Carly, took the fork from the other man's hand and began to unwind the mess of tangled bacon that Carly had somehow created.

"She wasn't thrilled to see me," Bret said.

"Oh," was Carly's simple reply. "Want some coffee?"

"No, thanks. I've had enough coffee to stay wired for a week."

"Oh," Carly said again. "How about some Scotch? I've got some well-aged Johnnie Walker."

"Yeah," Bret said. "Yeah, I could use a good Scotch."

"Come to think of it, so could I," Carly said.

"Scotch and bacon?" Bret asked.

"They're great together."

And they were, Bret mused a few minutes later as he helped Carly pick at the bacon while sipping his Scotch. And man, the Scotch did taste good. Damned soothing after the night and morning he'd spent.

"So is she upset with me?" Carly asked casually.

"No," Bret replied a little bitterly. "All her venom is for me, Carly."

Carly was silent for a minute. "But you stayed."

"She drank herself into a mild stupor rather than talk to me."

Carly smiled a little. "But you got the story from her, I take it?"

"Yeah."

"And?"

Bret proceeded to fill Carly in on what he had learned, then told him that Sandy Tyrell was at the house now. He finished his Scotch in the process. Carly refilled Bret's glass, shrugged and threw another dollop into his own.

"She's not happy. Not happy at all. But I really can't let her handle this one on her own." Bret sobered for a minute. "Not after I saw what they did to Rutger, I can't."

"You asking me or telling me?" Carly quizzed him.

Bret looked at his friend, hurt. "Carly! There's a rather grisly murderer running around. You don't think I should leave it be, do you?"

"Let's turn on the ball game," Carly suggested.

Texas was playing L.A. It was a good game, good enough that each man occasionally interrupted the conversation to yell something at the television set. By halftime they were halfway through the Johnnie Walker.

Even though Bret's outward attention was on the game, his mind remained on Colleen. He had stepped in on one of her stories once before and had been served divorce papers for his efforts.

Bret lifted his glass and stared blankly at the amber

liquid. Her eyes were sometimes the color of Scotch. Dazzling, pure, with a touch of gold.

But he'd been right! The situation had been horrible; she would have been in constant danger. She could so easily have been hurt…even killed.

Why couldn't she understand? He had stepped in because he valued her life above his own. He'd been right, too. Americans had been being killed right and left by the guerrillas. People had just happened to get caught in the cross fire. Civilians…journalists. And now…now Rutger Miller had been murdered, and she was blind to the chilling danger.

"Bret, you just watched a touchdown without a change of expression," Carly commented.

"What? They made a touchdown? Oh. Great!"

Carly was quiet for a minute. "You're still in love with her, aren't you? Colleen, that is?"

Bret hesitated. Carly knew him well. Too well. "I don't know. Yeah, I suppose so," he admitted grudgingly.

"You missed her, huh?"

A little tremor seized him. Oh, yes, he had missed her.…

"She's a beautiful woman," Carly commented conversationally. "Sexy. You sure it isn't lust?"

"Lust? Hell, no!"

"You don't feel any lust?" Carly smiled. "Well, hell, son, I've been keeping you in the jungles too long."

"What the—" Bret began, but Carly laughed.

"Have another Scotch, Bret. Let's see if we can't figure this thing out."

"Figure it out?" Bret asked. He wasn't so sure he wanted to figure it out. He was acquiring a nice buzz from the Scotch, a sense of well-being. It was a false sense of well-being, of course, but it was damned nice.

Carly was going on anyway. "This whole thing started last winter. She was supposed to have that Middle East assignment, but you came to me and told me you didn't want her going—you'd do it. I agreed with you because the situation didn't look too safe, and because you have a habit of landing on your feet, no matter what."

"That's the story," Bret said dryly, staring at his Scotch with fascination again. Someone on the television made a touchdown; he didn't even notice which team had scored.

"Colleen was angry."

Bret snorted. "She was a virago. The guerrillas were safer to be around at the time."

"Because she thought you purposely and willfully stole her best story," Carly continued as if Bret hadn't spoken.

"Right on," Bret mused.

"Well, I don't believe it."

"Believe it!" Bret said bitterly. "She told me that if I went, it was over. And then, when I flew back in with the first story, she called me just as pleasantly and sweetly as she could. She showed up at the magazine looking like any man's dream of paradise just to tell me I didn't need to worry about anything, she'd done all the filing and necessary paperwork for the divorce."

"Oh, I knew she filed the papers," Carly said. "She told me right away. She said I had a right to know."

"Yeah, she told you before she told me." Bret leaned back on the sofa, casting an arm over his eyes. Even with his eyes closed, the world was spinning slightly. He smiled a little ridiculously.

"See, I have this feeling," Carly was saying, "that you didn't manage to explain the situation very well. You probably got mad and walked out on her when she was still trying to talk—"

"Scream," Bret interjected.

"I beg your pardon."

"She was screaming."

"Yes, well, women do, now and then. So do men, for that matter. Bret, did it ever occur to you that she might have had a right to feel a little insecure because of what you were doing?"

"Insecure?" Bret snorted. "Over what? She's bright and beautiful and holds the world in the palm of her hand."

"She doesn't want the world. She wants you. And you've got to admit, Bret, you have a hell of a reputation preceding you."

"What...?"

"Business. You're the top of the line. A hard act to follow. Not that she needs to—you're different people, different writers. She wanted to be in your league, to be worthy of you, and you weren't letting her. And on a personal level, she may know how to behave like the frost queen, but she's a sweet innocent. You're the first man she's ever really loved. You had a string of lovelies stretching down a dozen coastlines—"

"I do not!" Bret protested, the loudness of his own voice making him wince.

"I didn't say that you *do*. I said you *had*. Big difference, my boy, but hard on a woman."

"Well, she's not insecure..." Bret protested, and then

his voice faded, and he was smiling again. He could remember when they'd first met. It had been Colleen's first tight spot, and she had been frightened to death, but she hadn't shown it. Not Colleen. Her face had been a little white, but she hadn't said a word, not a single word, to show her fear.

Their first date had been two weeks later. He'd already heard that she never, never dated coworkers, but she had agreed to see him.

It had been one of the best nights of his life. She'd cooked dinner; he'd brought the champagne. They'd gone to a movie and stayed up till dawn discussing the film, the situation they'd left behind them, the moon, everything and anything.

Two weeks after that they'd made love for the first time. As long as he lived, he'd never forget that night. Everything had been slow and easy. As much as he'd wanted her, he'd heard his own voice say that he didn't want to rush her. But she'd been the one to shed her clothing in the dimly lit doorway, with an odd and beautiful little smile on her lips. And then she'd whispered that he had to do the leading because she wanted to follow....

After that everything had seemed to burst around him like colorful fireworks. It had been like the first time for him, too, because she'd been so exquisite. He'd never forget the sight of her, touching her, the wonderful, awed feeling that she was his and his by choice. He'd been her first lover—by her choice. There had been nothing since to compare with that feeling of lying beside her afterward, holding her. They'd been so close in every way. In time they'd grown completely uninhibited with each other; they'd learned to laugh, to play, to be so damned good together....

You don't own her, friend, he reminded himself.

No, but he wanted her, wanted things to be the way they had been. And then he started wondering again just what really had gone wrong. If it had been so good, how had it fallen apart so completely, so fast?

"One more Scotch, Carly," he said.

"Is that a good idea?"

"Probably not, but I'll have one anyway."

SOMEHOW SHE HAD fallen into a doze.

Colleen had cleaned up quickly, paced the living room, then sat down on the couch to wait for Sandy. She'd lit a cigarette, but smashed it out immediately. Then she'd grabbed one of the throw pillows, clutched it to her and stared at the cold fireplace.

She pictured it with a fire burning, and then in her imagination, she began to see other things. A smile actually curved her lips when she leaned her head back to close her eyes.

She could remember that day so clearly....

Bret had jumped into the chopper right behind her. There had been others there, but there had been an empty seat beside her. He'd looked out the window, watching the ground diminish beneath them. Then he'd turned and looked at her, and she'd heard his breath catch.

"Are you all right?" she'd asked anxiously.

"I've never been better," he'd replied, smiling slowly. She'd liked his eyes, the warm, haunting gray. She'd liked his grin, slow and crooked. "I've never been better than at this moment."

Something touched her. His hand. On hers. She stretched out her fingers, and his curled around them, squeezing a little, strong and reassuring. She'd looked into his eyes again, and although she'd never been closer to death in her life, she felt the most marvelous, warm and exciting sensation sweeping over her. She'd seen him before, of course. She knew who he was. She knew she should have stayed a million miles away.

She could hear the frantic whirl of the chopper blades, thundering no faster than the beat of her heart.

She squeezed his hand back and smiled....

A FRANTIC POUNDING on the door brought her wide-awake. Colleen leaped to her feet and flew to the door, throwing it open without a thought of danger.

And there was no danger, at least not a visible one. The woman standing there was about five-foot-six, but very slim and delicate. Even for this private meeting, Sandy Tyrell was...elegant. She wore a navy sundress with a skirt that emphasized her long legs. A floppy navy hat fell over her huge and haunted deep-brown eyes. Her makeup was perfect, as perfect as her intriguing features.

"Mrs. McAllistair?" she asked in a husky rush.

"Yes, yes, Sandy. Come in."

As soon as the younger woman was in the house, Colleen carefully closed and locked the door, then turned around to Sandy Tyrell. Sandy was nervously playing with the strand of pearls about her neck. She stared back at Colleen.

"I've been so terribly frightened!" she said.

"Would you like a drink?" Colleen suggested.

"No. Oh, yes! Yes, I would. Thank you."

Colleen tried to put her at ease. She spoke lightly as she fixed Sandy a vodka and tonic. Sandy prowled the living room and finally commented on the beauty of the house. Colleen thanked her, then managed to get her to sit on the couch without flying off it every second with nervous energy.

"Poor Rutger!" Sandy said after Colleen suggested she just say what came into her mind in whatever order it appeared. "He looked me up, you know. He'd been in hiding for so long, but his conscience was plaguing him so. He said he'd just had to find me to try, to try to ease my mind about my grandfather. But I already knew! My grandfather was no traitor! He might have been conned into the diamond thing with the others, but he would never, *never* have purposely betrayed his men!"

"I'm sure he wouldn't have done so on purpose, Sandy," Colleen soothed her. Then she paused for a second, trying to phrase her words very tactfully. "Sandy, forgive me for asking, if this is a personal question, but on the phone you said that your mother spent her life trying to clear your grandfather. If you're Sam Tyrell's granddaughter through your mother…"

"Why is my name Tyrell?" Sandy finished for her a little bitterly.

"Yes," Colleen said softly.

"Because my father didn't marry my mother, Mrs. McAllistair. He found out that she was the daughter of a 'traitor' and walked out long before I was born. I don't even know who he is."

"I'm sorry," Colleen said.

"Oh, don't be. It doesn't matter to me anymore," Sandy said with a nonchalance that touched Colleen's heart; she could see that her father's desertion still hurt the woman.

Sandy was off the couch again, walking around, sipping the drink she held in one hand, playing with her pearls with the other. "We became good friends, Rutger and I," she said softly, sadly. For a moment Colleen thought Sandy would burst into incoherent tears, but she didn't, and Colleen breathed a sigh of relief. "We talked about the diamonds. Rutger said he never wanted them found, that he never wanted to see or hear about them again. Then one day he told me that he'd called you, that he wanted to set the story straight even if it were forty years too late. He wanted to see Sam cleared, and then…and then he was dead!"

Colleen waited, and finally Sandy went on. "Mrs. McAllistair…"

"Sandy, please call me Colleen. I think it will make you feel a little more comfortable."

Sandy flashed her a smile. A beautiful smile. Colleen thought she should have gotten rich modeling for *Vogue*.

"Colleen," Sandy murmured, and she came and sat down on the couch again. "Colleen, I told Rutger I was holding the fourth piece to the puzzle. He told me that he'd already given you his. But I'm convinced he was murdered for that puzzle piece."

Colleen carefully placed her own drink on the table. "You think that either Holfer or MacHowell is here, and killed Rutger?"

Sandy was up again. "No, no. I think they had someone kill him. You know, a, uh, a…"

"Contract?"

"Yes, something like that."

"Why do you think that?" Colleen asked.

Sandy's lower lip appeared to be quivering a little. "Because," she said a little breathlessly, then found her voice, "because Rutger had been putting out feelers to try to find the others. He'd made a Moroccan contact, a man who could tell him exactly where MacHowell was and who hinted that Holfer was in the vicinity, too."

Colleen gasped out loud; her nerves seemed to be tingling. If she could just find one of the others...

She was crazy. Getting into things she really shouldn't, or so Bret would surely say. But then, if it had been Bret sitting here, he would already be making his reservations to go to Morocco.

She tried to remain entirely nonchalant. "Sandy, can you give me the name of this man?"

"What? Oh, yes, his name is Eli Alibani."

Colleen moistened her lips. "And do you know how Rutger contacted him?"

"Yes, there's a hotel. In Marrakech. Rutger would go through the proprietor and leave messages. Eli Alibani would get back to him."

"Sandy, do you know the name of the hotel?"

"The Bête Noire."

Black Beast in French. Just the name of the place gave her the creeps.

But she knew she was going there.

"DAMN! IT'S SIX o'clock!" Bret said, wincing as he heard his words slur. He hadn't drunk that much Scotch, had he?

Carly was up, staring at the clock. "You'd better get back."

Bret rose with a groan as everything spun around him. "Drunk, Carly!" he muttered, swaying a little. He clutched his head between his hands, hoping to still the swaying sensation. "What a time to go on a binge!" he groaned.

Carly was laughing, and the sound hurt Bret's head. "Oh, I wouldn't worry about it. Didn't she conk out on you last night?"

"Hasss nothing to do with conking out," Bret said indignantly. "I'm...protecting her."

"Oh, yes, that's right. You've grown purer than lust."

Bret replied with an oath that clearly told Carly what to do with himself.

Carly laughed again. "Don't worry about it. I'll call the police station and see that someone watches the house. They owe us both some favors."

"Oh, God!" Bret moaned. "I already arranged for someone. Now I have to meet a cop like this!"

"No, you don't. I'll put you in a taxi, and when you get there, you can just walk right up to the door. You'll never have to see the cop. Just concentrate on walking. You'll make it. I've seen you fake being sober before."

Carly was already calling the taxi. "She'll think I wrecked her car," Bret said bleakly.

"She'll know why you're not driving," Carly assured him. "And I'll give her a call, just to be sure."

Bret was on his feet. He gave Carly a friendly thump on the back that almost sent the older man flying.

"I gave her that car, you know, Carly. She tried to give it back."

Carly saw the hurt in his eyes; maybe he'd go home and talk to Colleen the same way. And maybe, just maybe, she'd see his eyes the way Carly was seeing them now, and she'd realize how much Bret loved her.

"Yeah, she tried to give it back. I had to tell her that

I didn't want used things. That she could shove it into a canal for all I cared."

"Let's get you down to that cab," Carly said.

Bret stiffened his shoulders. "I can walk!"

"Sure you can."

Bret paused at the door again. Carly decided to walk down to the street with him. The cab was already there. Bret started to crawl into it, then turned back.

"Why the hell did you ever have to hire that woman, Carly?"

"'Cause she's a good journalist. And a sweet kid. And I might have hired her, Bret, but you're the one who married her."

"Yeah, I did, didn't I?" Bret said. His jaw twisted, and he gave himself a little shake. It really did seem that he was capable of shaking off the effects of the Scotch purely by using his willpower.

He smiled up at Carly. "And I'm still married to her, Carly—for about a month, at least!"

Chapter Five

Colleen sat by the pool, her jeans rolled up, her toe drawing circles in the water, her fingers curled around a large cup of tea.

Sandy Tyrell had been gone for about an hour. Bret wasn't back, and Colleen didn't know whether to be annoyed or relieved.

She sighed, nibbling lightly at her lower lip and thinking about Sandy Tyrell. The woman had been very frightened. Colleen had told Sandy that she was welcome to stay, but Sandy had said it was unnecessary. The police had quizzed her after Rutger's death, and they were keeping an eye on her town house.

"But I didn't tell them about the puzzle!" Sandy said. "I was afraid to. I suppose that anyone could know it existed, but you're the only one who knows I have my grandfather's piece. Of course, you'll have it now."

And just like that Sandy had turned over her piece of the puzzle. The two of them had studied it. Colleen's piece had a drawing of a mountain and the French motto *N'Oubliez Pas*. Do Not Forget.

Sandy's piece showed a ski lift, and the legend was English: Earth Is the Mother.

They had mused over the fragments for a long time,

and all they'd been able to come up with was that the diamonds were buried in a not-forgotten place in the earth, somewhere near a ski lift.

"I want it to be your problem, not mine!" Sandy had said with her lips trembling. And then she had looked at Colleen. "I suppose you'll try to find Rutger's Moroccan contact."

"Yes, and I'll find out what happened. You'll be okay, Sandy, really you will," Colleen had assured her with more confidence than she really felt.

It was then that Sandy had gone off on a tangent. "I hate to ask you personal questions," she said at last, "but that man who answered the phone this morning, was it your husband? Bret McAllistair?"

Colleen had felt a moment's hesitation. Sandy had given her a lot of trust; it seemed important that she respond in kind. "Yes," she said.

"He's involved, isn't he?"

"Not completely."

Sandy just nodded. She picked up a little porcelain piece, a Lladro maiden, from the coffee table.

"He's a very attractive man," she said lightly. "I've, uh, seen his picture. And he's been on the news a few times."

"Yes, he has a habit of doing that," Colleen had murmured.

Sandy had turned to her then, not looking quite so nervous. "He's just marvelous. If he's in on it, I really won't mind."

"Thanks."

"I'd heard you were getting a divorce."

"Yes."

"Oh?" One of her beautifully plucked brows had

arched; then she'd blushed prettily. "I'm sorry, I didn't mean to pry."

"Oh, for heaven's sake, Sandy, don't worry about it!" Colleen had snapped. She immediately regretted the words, Sandy had appeared so crushed. She'd apologized and assured Sandy again that she intended to do everything in the world to see Sam Tyrell's name cleared. She didn't add that most of the world had probably already forgotten the man.

When Sandy left, Colleen had been absurdly relieved because, no matter how determined she was not to lose her battered heart to her husband again, she was certainly in no mood to watch another woman simper over him.

Where the hell was he?

Her brooding gaze lifted to the bedroom. All the sliding glass doors were open; she could see her bed and the drapes, drifting a bit in the breeze. She closed her eyes.

That was where it had all ended.

Bret had come back from a two-week assignment in London. She had been given a chance at the Middle East story in his absence, and when he'd come in, she'd been packing.

She'd run to embrace him, but he'd been as stiff as a poker. And when she tried to tell him about the Middle East, he'd interrupted her curtly.

"I'm going."

"What? You mean we're going together?"

"No. I mean *I'm* going. *You're* staying here. I've already been through the whole thing with Carly. I'm going, you're staying."

For long moments she'd been dead silent, stunned. "Why?"

"My God, Colleen, sometimes you act as if you haven't got a brain in your head! It's dangerous over there!"

"You seem to forget, McAllistair, that I met you in the midst of some very real danger. I'm not an idiot. I don't fly off the handle. I don't panic and I don't scream!"

"You're screaming right now."

"I don't believe this! You're stealing *my* story!"

The gaze of contempt he gave her was horrifying. "Right, Colleen, right. I'm stealing your story. I'm doing any damned thing you think I'm doing, but you're not going."

She hadn't been able to believe it: the shattering silver ice in his eyes, the total lack of regard for her feelings. And then all the other little fears that she could generally tell herself were ridiculous had come crowding in on her. He'd just come back from London. Not long before they'd met, he'd been seeing an English-woman. Lady something or other. Colleen had met her once at a dazzling reception she and Bret had been invited to in Washington. She was lovely, tiny, delicate— and the height of sophistication.

There was really no reason to suspect anything. No reason except for her own loneliness when he was away and her own fears that she couldn't really keep a man like Bret.

She added that he had been away, that they were about to be parted again, and he'd barely touched her. He'd just hopped on the story like a jackrabbit, ignoring her and coolly and calmly beginning to pack.

"If you walk out of this house now, Bret," she'd said,

trying to be as remote as he was and not pitch into a real crying jag, "it's over. I mean it."

He hadn't even glanced her way. He'd continued dumping his London clothes in the hamper before taking out clean things. The only response he'd made to her comment had been a tightening of his jaw, an action she'd long ago learned meant that he was determined in whatever course he'd chosen.

"Bret! I mean it and you're not even listening to me."

"Colleen, you're acting like an emotional child."

"You stole my story. It's more important to you than I am!"

"What's happening over there right now is more important than your petty feelings of jealousy, yes."

"Petty feelings of jealousy! I'm not jealous, I'm furious!"

He'd given her one of those exasperated sighs that could drive her up the wall. "Colleen, we'll talk it all out when I get back."

"If you walk out, there won't be anything to talk about."

"If I don't walk out, you might not be around to talk."

"Oh, Bret! That is—"

"Shut up, Colleen."

"Bret! Damn it, if you don't stop and listen to me, I'll—"

"Listen, Colleen. You just do whatever you feel you have to do, okay?"

And that had been that. He hadn't tried to touch her; he'd just gone. When the door had closed, she'd burst into tears.

Two weeks later she'd filed for divorce. In the days

and weeks that had followed, she'd finally quit crying herself to sleep every night.

But in all that time she still hadn't really learned to sleep without him, to live without him. And now he was back.

A little sob escaped her, and she gave herself a furious shake. He'd been back, but he hadn't tried to call her or see her.

Not until Rutger had died. Not until there had been a story to steal. Nothing had changed. Nothing.

Especially not the attraction he held for her.

Colleen started suddenly. The phone was ringing. It rang so long that the machine picked it up. She listened to her own voice, and then her boss's.

"Colleen, it's Carly. Pick up. C'mon, Colleen, pick up the damned phone, will you?"

By that time she had reached the extension. "Hello, Carly. What's up?"

"How'd things go?"

"Fine."

"Learn anything?"

Colleen hesitated. She hated to lie to Carly, but she wasn't going to wind up cooling her heels at home. Not this time.

"Not really. Not yet. Only that Sandy Tyrell is scared silly. I'm hoping I'll get somewhere soon." She hesitated for a second. "Where's Bret?"

"On his way home. That's what I really called to tell you." Now Carly was the one hesitating. "Colleen, be decent to him tonight, will you? We, uh, got a little carried away watching the game."

"What are you talking about, Carly?"

"You'll see. Oh, and listen, don't worry about anything else. I want the two of you to keep your noses to the grindstone, all right? You've got carte blanche on expenses, so run with it. We're way ahead of the pack. Hell, we might even beat the daily papers on it!"

"Thanks," she murmured, the wheels of her mind churning swiftly. "You say that Bret's on his way back?"

"Yeah."

She exchanged a few more pleasantries with him before she hung up. Then she quickly dialed the airlines and booked herself through to Marrakech, first class. She didn't get carte blanche on expenses that often.

For a few minutes she chewed the eraser on the end of her pencil, wondering how to elude Bret in the morning. She'd have to get to the office to run off a copy of her puzzle piece, and then to the airport. Somehow she was going to have to leave him sleeping and trustful. She was going to have to do it, she assured herself, no matter what the cost.

"Oh, you fool!" she whispered dismally. She wanted an excuse to be with him....

"Don't think!" she told herself, and with a sudden spurt of energy, she raced into the kitchen and dug into the freezer. She found some steaks and slammed them into the microwave to defrost them. She dug into the closet for some wine, set a bottle in the refrigerator to chill, then pulled the steaks out of the microwave and poured a little of the wine over them, shrugged and added the rest of the bottle.

Someone was pounding on the door again. Not frantically as Sandy had. Determinedly, almost like the Big Bad Wolf. If she didn't answer the door soon, it was likely to be pounded in.

Colleen hesitated for a second longer, reminding herself that she was going to be charming all evening. Then she hurried to the door. "Bret?"

He had told her not to answer it unless she was sure. "Yes!"

She opened the door. He just stood there, grinning crookedly and swaying a little. She frowned, but then he walked by her and sank into the sofa, lacing his fingers behind his head and stretching his legs out on the coffee table. "Okay, how'd it go?"

She stared at him, still frowning. He was pronouncing his words very carefully and still grinning.

"It went well."

Colleen walked nearer to him and caught a whiff of the Scotch. "You've been drinking," she commented dryly.

"Yeah, a little. Let me hear about Sandy Tyrell."

Colleen perched on the edge of the coffee table, watching him, the wheels of her mind spinning once again. It was perfect! If she could just get him to drink a little more, he'd sleep like a log!

Be sweet, be sweet! she cautioned herself.

"Sandy Tyrell is a very frightened lady. That's about all I learned. Oh! Poor thing, she's pretty bitter. Her name is Tyrell because her father never married her mother. He heard about the scandal and dumped her flat. She gave me her puzzle piece."

"She did?"

"Umm. I'll get it."

He stared at her, surprised. She smiled and hurried to get the sheet of vellum paper. He was still staring at her when she returned, and she kept smiling, partially with real amusement. His hair was mussed over his brow, and his eyes were that gleaming silver, but they were also slightly red.

And somehow he looked all the more appealing to her.

"You look a little beat," she said. "Want a pillow?"

He wasn't that drunk; his eyes narrowed like a hawk's. Colleen decided she was pushing her luck, but his gaze fell from her to the paper she was holding. "No, I don't want a pillow."

"Earth Is the Mother," he muttered, staring at the paper she'd handed him. "Great, the diamonds are buried in the earth." His gaze was suddenly sharp. "What does your piece say?"

"*N'Oubliez Pas* and it shows a mountain, like this one shows a ski lift. Doesn't tell you much, does it?" she asked pleasantly.

Once again he was carefully studying her. She started talking again, a little too fast. "Oh! Bret, we can see her again, together. She knows about you, and she doesn't mind your being involved."

He smiled at her with a total lack of humor. "Okay, Colleen, what aren't you telling me?"

"Nothing!" Nervously she started to rise from the coffee table, where she had resumed her seat.

"Colleen!"

He certainly hadn't been drinking enough. He rose, an arm outstretched to stop her. With a quick gasp she eluded him, wondering dismally what good it would do. He'd catch her in two steps.

Except that he didn't. He tripped over the coffee table and hit the floor with a dull thud. Stunned, Colleen turned back.

"Ohhh," he murmured painfully, stretched out on the floor and rubbing his temple.

She tried not to laugh, not even to smile. She even knelt beside him and touched his cheek in a gesture of concern. "Bret! Are you all right?"

He stared up at the ceiling. "Just great."

"You liar!" she charged him. "You and Carly were drinking all afternoon. And I'll bet you didn't eat a thing!"

"Bacon," he murmured.

"Bacon and Scotch?" she asked incredulously.

"Yeah. It's really not half bad."

"Dummies!" she teased. "Come on, let me help you up. Did you really hurt your head? I'll get you some ice for it."

She grated her teeth as he leaned against her. He didn't look it, but he weighed a ton. And even with the scent of Scotch about him, he smelled delicious, and touching him sent little shivers racing through her system. Shivers that became a trembling of memory she could not deny.

"You're drunk as a skunk, McAllistair," she told him. She started to laugh, really enjoying the situation. Bret never got drunk. He never even got tipsy. "Oh, I love it!" she taunted him aloud, her eyes sparkling like gold dust.

Well, he wasn't really falling down drunk. He found his own balance and sat on the couch again, eyeing her dryly. "Just like a woman. She loves suffering."

"Oh, you're not suffering. Let me see your head."

He caught her shoulders when she leaned over him, and her eyes met his suspicious gaze. "You're being awfully nice. I don't trust you when you're nice, Colleen."

She pulled away, ostensibly hurt. "Really, Bret…"

"Well, then, why this sudden solicitude?"

"I'm trying to be pleasant, for old times' sake. I'll get some ice."

"Colleen, it isn't that bad."

But she got him some ice anyway. Then she slipped off his sneakers and tucked one of the throw pillows behind him. Afterward she quickly broiled the steaks that had been marinating in the wine. She served him on the couch, and he watched her with greater and greater suspicion, yet he seemed too bemused to protest.

Colleen just kept smiling.

He finally did protest when she opened a bottle of wine. "I don't need another drink."

"This isn't a drink, Bret. It's wine, for dinner."

"I don't want any."

"All right," she said stiffly, and painstakingly began to pour her own back into the bottle.

"What are you doing?"

"I'm certainly not going to drink alone."

"Ah, hell, Colleen…"

"Well, how was I supposed to know when I spent all day fooling with these steaks that you were going to spend all day playing macho man over at Carly's and—"

"Okay, okay! I'll have a glass of wine!" He was too pleasantly lethargic to fight her. His head was spinning too much. He knew he still shouldn't trust her and, for that matter, he didn't. But it was pleasant. Whatever she was up to, it was irresistibly pleasant.

"You really don't have to, Bret."

"Pour the damned wine! You're giving me a headache!"

Smiling sweetly, Colleen poured the wine. Bret accepted his glass. "I want you to call Sandy Tyrell first thing in the morning and arrange a meeting for the three of us," he said in a warning tone.

"Of course, Bret!"

The food was delicious. The wine, which went with it perfectly, was smooth and dry. Bret continued to watch her warily, but as she chatted idly about Sandy, he began to relax. She really seemed to be out to please tonight. Maybe she really was offering the olive branch of peace, at least for the time being.

He set his plate down and winced a little at the crick in his neck. She was up immediately, standing behind him, massaging his shoulders. The pressure of her fingers sent little waves of hot electricity through him. Her touch was a butterfly caress at first; then it turned firm and soothing....

Or it would have been soothing if it hadn't created such tension in his body. He was aware of nothing but the desperate longing to turn around and pull her onto his lap.

He didn't move. This was her game. He had to see how far she was going to take it. And there was something more.... Whatever it was, he didn't quite have the will to stop it. There had been too many times when he'd longed just to see her face, to feel her touch, to hear her whisper. He didn't want to break the spell.

"You know," he murmured, allowing his words a hint of fuzziness, "you didn't plan this grand hostess routine quite perfectly."

"I didn't?"

He rolled his silver gaze to hers. "You should have been wearing something soft...slinky."

She chuckled huskily. "I can fix that."

She turned to leave, but he caught her hand. "Why don't we fix it…together."

Wariness crept into her eyes. "Bret, let's not rush things here." She tugged lightly on her hand, but he pretended to ignore her attempt to escape.

"I was thinking of the, uh, the whirlpool."

"The whirlpool!" For a moment her tender facade dropped, but she quickly retrieved it. "Bret, I'm trying to be decent," she said quietly. "To be friends…"

He opened his eyes wide with affronted innocence. "I've got shorts on. You own bathing suits."

"Oh," she murmured, and he watched with a secret smile as she dropped her lashes quickly. "I'm not so sure you can make the whirlpool," she told him, but he could see the wheels in her mind clicking away. Whirlpool…warm, soothing, relaxing. She was trying to put him out for the night, and she was doing a damned good job of it. Why?

He lifted one hand helplessly. "You could assist me."

She smiled and allowed her fingers to play lightly over his cheek. "All right, Bret. Just let me get it going and…change into something more appropriate."

He closed his eyes and smiled while she walked out. It was just like old times, even if for a devious purpose. The sound of her voice was as throaty as a caress; it seemed to remain in the air like a haunting perfume. And if they were talking and laughing…and if her touch was igniting a sweet sizzle in his bloodstream…then surely she could not remain immune to memory herself.

He opened his eyes. She was back, wearing a white bikini. It was wonderful. Her flesh was golden against it, her hair the color of midnight. Her legs were long and slim and wicked, and her breasts were full and provocative against the white bra, mounding above it so that his fingers itched to reach out, his palms to caress.

He took a deep breath and gave her a lopsided grin. "Are we all set?" he asked her lazily.

"Hmm."

"Give me a hand."

She did so. He was careful to lean heavily against her. He rested his head against her shoulder and inhaled deeply the fresh scent of her hair.

"Careful, watch your step!" she warned him.

He smiled again, his gaze hidden by the silken web of her hair. "Oh, I'm watching it."

He felt a tremor from her and was amused and fascinated. What was she doing? It didn't really matter, he decided.

Seconds later they reached the bathroom. The water was swirling away, steam rising, creating something like a tropical mist, hazing the glass and hiding the foliage beyond. Bret stepped into the tub and landed with a splash. He caught Colleen's eyes in a naked moment. They were torn, as if she were beginning to worry that she was taking things too far....

She caught him watching her and quickly smiled. "Nice?"

He leaned back, closing his eyes. "Perfect. Relaxing...." He felt anything but relaxed. The warm, swirling water pounded around him, a good feeling, but like something that promised more. Much more.

He opened an eye. "Aren't you coming in?"

"Sure."

"Don't forget the wine."

"Oh, I won't."

And then she was sitting across from him, their

kneecaps grazing. Bret pushed himself up again, startling her as he laced an arm through hers and sipped his wine. Her face was just inches away. He reached out to touch her lip, his fingers moist and warm.

"Remember how we used to do it?"

"What?" She gasped a little as she spoke.

He smiled. "Drink wine. Out of each other's glasses...."

"Oh." She returned his smile and sipped from his glass, and suddenly they were so close he could barely stand it. He lowered his glass and his elbow grazed against her breast, and he remembered again its fullness, so soft when crushed against him....

Careful! he warned himself, and he leaned back lazily, allowing his lids to fall halfway over his eyes. "Makes you so sleepy, in here."

He watched her. Oh, God! How he loved to watch her. The beautiful length of her throat, the rise of her breasts, the dancing gold and amber of her eyes. She looked a little nervous, yet there was that odd little smile curving her lips, as if she'd been captured by memory herself. A memory that haunted the present with warmth and tension and a growing excitement. He stretched a leg and ran his toe lightly over her thigh.

"Remember our honeymoon?" he asked her lightly.

"Yes. You carried me over the threshold and slammed your foot into the dresser. You broke three toes, at a ski lodge."

"Ah, but I'd never intended to do much skiing anyway."

"We never left the room."

"Great, wasn't it?"

"You've got quite an ego."

"You were super, Colleen. You fretted over my every

movement. You brought me breakfast in bed, you gave me the most incredible massages."

"Maybe you should have married Florence Nightingale."

He leaned close again, very slowly, until he was just inches away from her once more, surrounded by the roar of the pool, by the mist, by her sweet fragrance. He kept watching her eyes and moving forward until his lips touched hers, tasted wine and felt them trembling.

He moved away. "You were always beautiful, Colleen."

He fell back against the tub. "Wow…the warmth. The wine, the woman, the song… I'm half…half asleep in here."

"Are you?" She sounded a little anxious, a little relieved and a little triumphant.

"Ummm." He closed his eyes completely and let his head roll back. "Ummm…"

"Bret. Bret!" Now she sounded like a sober person, carefully dealing with a drunk. "Bret!" Was she really alarmed that he might drown? "Bret, come on, I've got to get you out of here. We've got to get you into bed before you're out completely. Come on, Bret! I can't carry you."

She was already outside the tub, turning off the motor, clutching a towel and tugging at his arm. "Come on, Bret!"

He staggered out of the tub, leaning on her heavily. "Ummm. You're a good woman, Colleen."

"Sure," she humored him. "That's your real opinion, right, Bret?"

He paused, pulling away from her. "Colleen! I'm shattered. I'm stunned that you could say—"

"You're drunk, you letch. Come on."

He let her lead him again. Two feet away from the bed he balked and began tugging at his cutoffs.

"Bret!"

"Can't sleep in these things. They're soaked."

Was it the heat of the water? Or was it her nearness to him? He didn't know, but the ache inside of him was terrible as her body took on a beautiful blush. She wasn't quite as assured as she tried to act. She was nervous; she was trembling....

He dropped his wet clothing in the middle of the floor and climbed compliantly into the bed. "Exhausted," he murmured.

"Of course you are," she said soothingly. She was very near, stretching over him to pull up the sheet.

It was time for him to make his move. The perfect time. The raging of his blood, the pulsing of his heart, told him so. He was at the mercy of his yearning, the ache he felt, the unconquerable beat of desire flaring and swelling in his loins, in the tempest to hold her close, crush her near, bring the taste and feel and scent of memory forcefully into the present. It was in his head, in his heart, in his body, like the driving rush of the water, like a beckoning melody on the wind.

He couldn't let her go.

He slipped his arms around her, capturing her when she would have risen. "A good-night kiss, Colleen, for old times' sake..."

Did she know exactly what she was doing at that moment? Colleen would wonder about it later. Or was she still living a pretense? Had it ever been pretense?

She should never have kissed him, but it seemed so innocent. And he seemed so...disarmed. But she was a fool all the while because she hungered for more of him each time she touched him, heard his voice, felt the heat of his body near her own. It seemed like an eternity since she'd held him, an eternity since she'd known the dizzying, blinding joy of loving him. He'd been gone so long…and there had been no one like him, no one she wanted to touch, to know.…

"A little kiss…"

"A little kiss," she told him, and in that moment her fate was sealed. His mouth touched hers with tender warmth and then with a searing hunger. He tasted delicious. She reveled in the firm pressure of his mouth against hers, the heated velvet of his tongue moistening her lips, playing so provocatively against her teeth. She felt the wonder of his arms, heard the beat of her own heart. He touches me and I am electrified, she thought.

His weight shifted suddenly, and his fingers danced a shivery trail over her arm. They stroked her naked flesh, both lulling and fascinating. They caressed her shoulder, grazing her spine.…

And suddenly she was both gasping with astonishment and shuddering with a hot liquid sensation of delight as a tug of his fingers stripped her of the bikini top, and his hand wrapped her breast, cherishing its weight.

No! Oh, no! He could seduce her so easily, mind and body and soul.…

"Bret!" Breathlessly she broke the kiss, planting her palms against his chest. Above her she saw the smoke-and-silver intrigue of his eyes, and she shook her head a little desperately.

"A kiss, Bret!" she choked out. "I didn't intend… this!" she whispered softly.

"Didn't you?" he asked her. Was there a note of

mockery in his tone? She refused to hear it. She wanted to believe his eyes, the tenderness in them, and the longing....

"No," she mouthed, but the strength ran out of her as she spoke.

"For old times' sake," he whispered. His fingers met hers where they pressed against his chest, and he pulled them away, his eyes holding her spellbound. Helplessly she watched her fingers curl convulsively around his. His mouth moved to hers again, searching and coercive and powerful. His body moved against hers, long and hard and strong, warm and vibrant. A naked body with naked flesh that touched hers in a thousand wonderful ways. So good, melding to her, yet beautiful all alone. She felt the sinews of his body, the fascinating, supple flow of muscle. She inhaled his male scent, so mysterious and yet so familiar, so sweet. It called to her on a level older than time....

She returned his kiss, seeking out his tongue, loving it with her own. The world seemed to spin, silver like his eyes, as the rush of a crystal-studded wind. Desire flooded her, mercurial and hot like her blood.

His lips broke from hers and pressed against her throat, against her collarbone. For a moment she stared up at the ceiling, and with a brief flash of sanity she wondered, Why? Why had she loved him so much, needed him so much...clung to him so desperately and lost him? Had she felt so alone when her parents died that she had held too tightly to the man she'd learned to love, known too great a fear that he, too, would leave her? Had that caused him to turn away, to turn his back on her?

And here she was again, loving him, touching him, wanting him, when it was so wrong....

His mouth closed around her breast, suckling at the peak, sending a sharp throb of splendor throughout her body. She gasped. Her fingers were no longer at her sides; they threaded into his hair, clasping his head as her body thrilled to his touch. His palm coursed over her belly and caressed her hip, and his fingers slipped beneath the edge of her bikini bottom, deftly undoing the buttons at the side. His knuckles brushed the flesh of her inner thigh slowly, softly stroking her skin until her limbs were quivering and afire. Then suddenly he was inside her, and she cried out and writhed as everything within her seemed to melt like lava....

His lips moved back to hers, and his tongue dueled with hers as she kneaded the muscles of his shoulders, raking her nails lightly over his back, twisting, turning beneath him.

She thought, with just a touch of the sweetest pain she had ever known, that it couldn't really be wrong. He was the only man she had ever loved; she still loved him, would always love him. And even if this could only be for the moment, she was his wife. She wanted this. Wanted him, to have, to hold, to love...for just this night.

Thoughts whirled from her mind in the form of a tempest of desire. His hands swept along her body, caressing intimate, secret places. His tongue continued its deep, thrusting invasions, and she seemed capable of only one thought.

He touches me, and I am electrified....

He wondered if she saw that he was trembling, that his hands shook with longing when they moved over her, that his whole body shuddered when he entered her warmth and found her embrace. Again and again, with each stroke, ecstasy seized him, sweeping over his frame, easing the burning longing in his loins, creating the hunger all over again. Why was she so different? Was it love that could hurt so badly, then bring pleasure so great? As he lifted his head and moved above her in a rhythm that rose like the pitch of a wild wind, he watched her face, and he thought he knew what it was that got to him so badly. It was something in her eyes, so dazed with her desire, in the delicate beauty of her face, in her lips, dry now from the ragged depths of her erratic breathing.

Loving her, he dipped to moisten her lips with the tip of his tongue. And in the thunder of his thrust, they locked in another kiss, then rolled without breaking rhythm as he caught her hips to stroke ever more deeply into her. Tonight. He had tonight. He didn't have the right words; he only had his love. Tonight he sought to cement himself within her memory, this man who loved her, could love her, like no other.

It was beautiful. The feeling peaked, held, then soared again, until the moment when they both knew it must crest and explode like tiny fragments of silver falling around them. Breathless, drenched and still, they lay wrapped in something intangible but unique between them.

She knew she cried his name, her voice husky and filled with all the things she could not say. He fell from her yet remained entangled with her, his thigh against hers, his hand on her breast. And the words he had whispered remained with her: "Colleen. Always so beautiful, so special, so… Colleen. Mine…my wife…for now."

She turned against him, words suddenly bubbling on her lips. She wanted to know why. Why he had walked out on her. How he could love her so tenderly and passionately and well and walk out on her so easily.

For a story.

She felt cold suddenly. Horribly cold except where his body still touched hers. A whisper rose to her lips. "Bret?" It was a half sob, filled with heartache. It was the question of what could possibly have gone so wrong.

"Bret?"

He didn't answer her. She frowned, pushed his hand away and rose on one elbow and stared at his handsome face, gleaming now with the sheen of their passion. His hair was tousled arrestingly, an engaging smile in place at the corner of his mouth.

His eyes were closed.

"Bret!"

Colleen poked his shoulders, but he didn't move. Then a sigh escaped him, and his head rolled to one side. "Bret!" She picked up his hand and dropped it. It fell limply to the bed.

"Bret McAllistair, damn you!" she sputtered.

Still he didn't move. And then she began to cry. She had finally accomplished her goal. Oh, yes! she mocked herself. She'd gotten exactly what she wanted. He was out like a light.

It was just that it was too late.

Way too late for her.

Chapter Six

Colleen's alarm rang at a quarter to five. For a split second she cringed at the nerve-racking sound, then she leaned over to hit the button and shut it off. Nervously she turned back to look at Bret, then sighed with relief. He was still sleeping soundly.

Very soundly and very comfortably. His legs were stretched out over the bed, and his arms were also flung wide. He was tan against the sheets, and his hair, mussed over his brow, toned down the rugged planes of his features. He looked as vulnerable as a teenager, except that teenagers didn't have shoulders as broad as his or a thick mat of sandy curls on their chests, his muscle tone or...

"Damn you!" Colleen whispered, suddenly feeling angry. She threw the covers over him in a flurry, forgetting in that heated second that, above all, she didn't want him to awaken. She caught her breath, realizing what she had done, then expelled it slowly. He really was out like a light. Still, there was no sense in taking chances.

She climbed out of bed and discovered that she was a little sore from the night's passion, and that got her angry all over again. She stared venomously at his sleeping form and silently told him exactly what she thought of him while she quietly packed. With that task completed she grabbed her clothing and hurried into the bathroom, closing the door carefully behind her.

A shower helped. At least it made her feel wide-awake and less temperamental. And clothing made her feel a lot safer around Bret, even if he was dead to the world.

She was ready quickly. Dressed in a tailored blouse, nylons, heels and a fitted skirt, she crept back out and tiptoed to the bed. It was only five-thirty. With any luck he'd sleep at least until noon.

She meant just to look at him and then rush away, but she paused, her breath catching with sudden pain. He looked so appealing, sprawled out on the bed, tumbled and disheveled. When they had been married, she'd always loved it when she had awakened first, though it hadn't happened often because he tended to wake at the slightest sound. Such occasions were all the more special because they were rare. At those times she had been able to lie beside him and watch him, savoring all the little things about him. And then, of course, when she grew restless, she could edge against him, run her fingers along his chest, do all sorts of little things until she would realize that one smoky eye was half open, and that he was just waiting for her to realize that he was awake before wrapping his arms around her. He'd be smiling....

Smiling complacently, just as he was now. Oh, his eyes weren't open now, but he still had that half grin, that smug and amused and male triumphant grin lifting the corners of his lips.

"You son of a bitch," she swore in a whisper. If she weren't leaving, she'd be tempted to throw a bucket of cold water in his face. He'd played her along all night; he'd never been as soused as he had pretended. He'd seduced her without the least bit of effort, and she'd helped him all the way.

"Damn you!" She didn't dare kick him so she kicked the bed.

And then she went very still, admitting that she'd had no desire to fight him, that she'd even been about to tell him that she loved him with all her heart, that she hadn't wanted to file the papers but had been convinced that she had to after the way he left her.

Thank God she hadn't been able to tell him. By the light of day it was a little easier to be strong, to remember that he had walked out on her for a story—and that he had only walked back into her life because of another story.

For a second she felt a little guilty. She did believe that he was concerned for her safety. But she could handle herself, and she intended to do just that.

She gave herself a little shake. He was going to be furious, but he deserved exactly what he was getting. It was what he had done to her. And, she reminded herself resentfully, at least he had gotten a royal goodbye. He'd barely spared a wave for her.

Thus determined, Colleen made herself turn away from him, though her heart was aching. It would have been so much easier to crawl back in beside him, hold him, fall into the fantasy again. But that was just the point, wasn't it? she asked herself. Love was the fantasy. Her fantasy. And if she weren't so tired, she wouldn't be so frightened that she would burst into hurt and bitter tears.

She hurried out of the house, then stood dead still in the drive, her temper rising again. Her car wasn't there.

"That damned drunken letch!" she swore. "He didn't even bring my car home!"

For several seconds she stood in front of the house, swearing. Then she kicked the door and hurt her toe. With another spate of oaths she unlocked the door and hurried to the kitchen phone to call a cab. She kept her voice low, starting to grow nervous at the first hitch in her plan. As she spoke, she kept glancing toward the bedroom, but she didn't see or hear anything, and the dispatcher promised to send a cab right out.

Colleen hung up the phone carefully, then wondered why she was so worried. It wasn't even six o'clock. There was no reason for him to awaken. He hadn't awakened at the alarm, and he hadn't made a single movement while she'd stared at him, cursed him and loved him.

Even so she chewed her lower lip nervously, hoping that the cab really would come soon. She'd heard about Bret long before she'd met him. How he had an uncanny ability to sense things. To know where there might be danger. To awaken at the whisper of a breeze when something was afoot....

But not, she told herself, when he had consumed large quantities of alcohol the day before, even going beyond his chosen cutoff point to humor her and cause her scheme to backfire against her rather dramatically.

Still, she tiptoed to the bedroom door. His arm was cast over his face now as if he were protecting his eyes from daylight.

Colleen grabbed her purse and bag again and silently hurried to the front door. She didn't want to take a chance on the taxi beeping. Out on the walk she began to pace, glancing at her watch every other second. Come on, come on, come on.

"Colleen?"

She heard him bellow just as the cab rounded the corner and slowed down in front of the house. She picked up her travel bag and dashed down the walk.

"Let me put that in the trunk—" the young cabbie began pleasantly, hopping from the driver's seat.

"No!" Colleen almost shrieked. "I'll, uh, just hold it. Please, hurry!"

"To where?"

She gave him the address of the magazine. He closed her door and walked around to his own. Colleen stared back at the house just in time to see the door open. Bret was there, a sheet wrapped around his hips, looking like thunder.

The cab pulled away from the curb. Colleen screwed her face into the semblance of a smile and waved. Bret started to tear down the walk, but stopped short, tripping over the sheet and almost losing it. Her smile became real as she saw him redden, apparently only just becoming aware that he was wearing nothing but a sheet in public.

Then she caught the look on his face just before the cab rounded the corner and headed toward the city. Dark and tense and furious, his temper probably compounded by a bit of a hangover.

She turned around in her seat and stared straight ahead, wishing her lower lip would quit trembling. All he wanted was the story, and this time he wasn't going to get it. After she stopped by the office and got on the plane, she would have hours and hours in the air to sleep, to heal her pain, to force herself to quit dreaming about the night and Bret McAllistair.

"What you got in the case, lady? Diamonds?"

Colleen's eyes met those of the cabdriver in the rearview mirror. He looked a little green.

"What?"

"This isn't some kind of jewel heist or something, is it?"

"Good heavens, no!" Colleen exploded.

The cabbie fell silent for a second. "You running away from something?" When she didn't respond, he cleared his throat. "If that man attacked you or—" Now the young man was beet red. "I mean, if you're a victim of rape, you should report it."

It was too much. Colleen burst into laughter, and then she apologized, sobering, because the cabbie seemed to be one of the rare individuals in the world who was still sincere in caring about others.

"I'm sorry," she said. "He didn't rape me." No, she added silently, he seduced me, damn him! "Uh, he's my husband," she told the cabbie. It *was* still true, after all. "We're just having a bit of a business tiff, that's all."

"Oh." He sounded relieved. Then he sighed. "Boy, that's a real problem these days, huh? I mean, women want to feel like women, and men want to feel like men. And then there's all this equality stuff. Sure hard today, isn't it?"

"Hmmm. But…" Curious, Colleen leaned over the seat. "Don't you believe in equality? I mean, if a woman can do a job, shouldn't she be allowed to?"

"I suppose. I don't know. I think I'd have a real hard time handling it if my wife was making more money than me."

Colleen leaned back against the seat, grimacing dryly. "Well, he can't be suffering on that score. He makes more money."

The cabbie met her eyes in the mirror again and shrugged. "Hope it works out, lady."

"Thanks."

Colleen got the cabbie to wait in front of the magazine offices, while she ran in. She was the only one in the building; the eerie night-lights were still on. She shivered a little, then quickly made photocopies of both puzzle pieces and locked the originals in the bottom drawer of her desk.

Just as she was running past the switchboard, the phone began to ring. There was a dull buzzing sound, and a little red light kept appearing on the board. It was Bret; she knew that it was Bret. The buzzing seemed to echo painfully in her head, just as the red light seemed to be a reflection of the stabbing pain in her heart. Was she wrong? Was she walking out on what could have been a chance to salvage her marriage, her life with Bret, all the best things in existence?

She wound her fingers together in a tight fist before her, closing her eyes and suddenly gasping for breath. He had only come back for the story. There was nothing to salvage. And she wasn't going to be robbed of her own work again. If she could just move her feet, she could get into the cab and then into the plane, and with each mile she traveled she would get a steadier grip on her emotions.

If she could just move. If she could just take the first few steps.

The switchboard kept buzzing. Colleen took another breath and then another. And then she turned, stepped out the door and carefully relocked it. Mechanically she returned to the cab, and forty minutes later she was in the air. Five hours to the East Coast, another six hours to Madrid, and then one more short flight to Marrakech. With the time change and layovers she would arrive to see another dawn, a full day in which to find the Moroccan.

Leaving her time to forget Bret. To forget the longing. To forget the horrible aching in her heart.

BRET SWORE SOFTLY when he caught the sheet in the door as he entered the house. His head was pounding with the most god-awful hangover he'd had in years. It wasn't the Scotch, most assuredly not the Scotch. It was the wine. The wine with which she'd plied him, tricked him. The wine that he had drunk like an idiot, so enamored of the moment that he would have sold his own soul to hang on to…

His own soul. Not hers. What the hell was she doing?

Bret groaned as his head continued to throb. Where was she going? Didn't she realize that this thing had gotten out of hand?

He grabbed his clothing and stumbled into his pants, then picked up the phone. He dialed Carly's number. When his friend and employer answered with a groggy and annoyed voice, Bret realized that it was still short of 6:00 A.M.

"Carly, it's me. Bret. Sorry, but I've got to know. Did you talk to Colleen last night?"

"Yes, yes. I called her."

"Well?"

"Well, what? I told her you were on your way back,

and I suggested she go gently with you. Why? Did you have a row?"

"No," Bret said dryly. "She was as gentle as a lamb."

"So what's your problem?"

"She's gone. Did you say anything to her? Tell her to do anything? Give her any messages?"

"No...oh, yes, I did. I said you should both keep your noses to the grindstone and that she had carte blanche on expenses. Why?"

"She's gone."

"Maybe she just went out shopping."

"At this hour she couldn't have." Bret slammed his palm against the wall in a new burst of panic. If his head hadn't been pounding so fiercely, he would have panicked earlier. "Carly, she left here with a suitcase. Where could she have gone?"

"Maybe just to a hotel."

"No, she's too devious just to be heading to a hotel. Oh, hell, I could wring her neck!" He paused, trying to think. Remembering the night. The fantasy he had been too willing to believe, the sweet ecstasy and the fireworks and the ridiculous pleasure he had felt at turning the tables when he had known she was up to something. "Sandy Tyrell," he said suddenly.

"What?" Carly demanded.

"Find out where she lives for me, will you, Carly? Sandy Tyrell must know where Colleen is. I'm going to call the office, just in case."

"I'll get back in touch with you soon," Carly promised.

Bret tried the magazine offices, but the phone rang and rang. At last he slammed the receiver down, realizing with a sick feeling that even if she were there, she wouldn't pick up the phone. Not when she had left with a suitcase.

He moved into the kitchen and put on a pot of coffee. It would help, he hoped. While the coffee brewed, he wandered into the bedroom and sank to the bed. He could still see the impression of her body in the mattress.

"Colleen, you fool," he murmured aloud, a pain constricting his stomach. God, what kind of a price had they both paid for their night together?

He ran his fingers through his hair, then clutched his head dismally between his palms. This room...they'd been in it together so many times, good times and bad.

He winced, suddenly remembering one of their arguments. Bret closed his eyes tightly against the memory that came to him so strongly. He could see it clearly, down to the details. They'd been dressing for a political banquet, he in a tux, she in a silver gown with black thread running through it. It had been backless, and the material had clung to her. With her midnight hair she'd been spellbinding. It had begun so simply. There had been a full moon; he could remember the way it had gleamed into the bedroom to dazzle off the small diamond pendant she had asked him to secure about her throat.

"Who are we sitting with?" she'd asked. Such innocent words.

"Senator Baker."

"Oh, Lord! We're in for another night of private questions. Senator Baker can't understand why we haven't produced a score of children yet."

He could remember his fingers stiffening, the way he had suddenly felt so cold. "Well, what's the problem?" His voice had come out reflecting that sudden chill. "We'll just tell him that Ms. Journalist of the decade is way too busy."

He could remember her spinning away from his touch, but it had been all right. He hadn't wanted to touch her at the time.

"Why don't we just tell him that your career is valuable and mine isn't?"

"What the hell is the matter with you?"

"With me? I think you're the one with the problems."

"Really?"

Retrospect always seemed like such a painful thing, Bret thought. He could picture himself that night so clearly now, in a way he never could have seen back then. Little words, so easily said, so casually spoken. If he could only go back, he would have slowed down. He could have said, "Wait a minute. What are we talking about here?" And the outcome might have been different. Not that that night had been the end. But after seeing the look in her eyes the other day and after his rather sodden outbursts to Carly and Carly's replies, he could see that he had been at least partly at fault.

He had coolly adjusted his tie and given her an offhand glance. "I haven't got a problem in the world. Neither have you. Full speed ahead, all guns on deck. Ms. Colleen McAllistair will investigate and report from here to eternity. If I should ever come up with any rampant paternal urgings, I'll just have to look up the maternal type for the next go round. I'd just as soon not see my children raised by a typewriter, should I get the urge for procreation."

"Bret, you are one son of a—"

"Save it for later, can you? We're late."

"Damn you!"

"All right. Take your own car."

He moaned aloud. God, he'd been awful. Just because she'd stunned him with her words, thrown a ridiculous scare into him. It had always been a vague idea to him, having a family. But he wanted one. It had never occurred to him that she didn't someday want the same thing. Why was it that when people were hurt, they struck out so blindly?

By the next day they'd been speaking again. And a week later it had seemed that the whole thing had blown over.

But it probably hadn't. Not really. Though their marriage had seemed to break up when he had stepped in to cover her story, he felt that time and a solid look at the truth were teaching him otherwise. Their marriage had not broken up because of a single incident. It had been a result of little incidents, incidents that might have been correctable—if only one of them had forced the issue and really spoken.

Bret rubbed his temple miserably. He didn't really know what to think anymore. For many long months he had told himself that she had never really loved him. If she had, she would never have been able to file the divorce papers. Papers to end it all. Because there had been so many good times, wonderful times, close times, to outweigh the bad.

Maybe, he reflected, it did appear that he had stepped back into her life to take something from it again. And maybe, as Carly had suggested, he hadn't really given her much to offset any doubts she might have had about his love. Oh, he'd never been unfaithful. In a thousand years he didn't think he would ever have the desire to be so. No one could offer him what she did. But didn't everyone need assurance now and again? Especially someone like Colleen. Someone who didn't talk too much, but had learned the devastation of loving and then finding herself totally alone. She'd been so close to her parents and so young when they had been killed together in an accident. And maybe, just maybe, she wasn't as strong or independent or capable as she had always appeared to be....

No, he reminded himself dryly. She was capable. Very capable, and too damned devious. And none of it mattered now. None of it could be allowed to matter. Even if she never spoke to him again in all the years to come, he had to find her. He had to be a part of this thing—and he had to make sure she survived it.

"Damn it!" he swore aloud, angry again. What the hell was she doing?

He forced himself to go back to the kitchen. Coffee would help his hangover if nothing else. He entered the room just as the phone began to ring again. He clutched the receiver quickly, his heart thudding. Maybe she had just gone out. Maybe she was calling to tell him where she was....

"Colleen?"

"Sorry, it's Carly. I've got Sandy Tyrell's address for you. I'd go straight over if I were you, while it's still early. Want me to come? I can pick you up in, say, ten minutes in the Ferrari and bring your clothes at the same time. I take it you'll be staying at the house."

"Yeah. Yeah, thanks, Carly."

Ten minutes. Enough time to duck his head under a ton of cold water and consume a lot of coffee. Perfect.

Carly was outside in exactly ten minutes. He slid

out of the driver's seat and let Bret take the wheel. In another fifteen minutes they were in front of Sandy Tyrell's attractive town house.

"This really is early for a call," Carly muttered as they left the Ferrari.

Bret shrugged. "Unless Colleen was lying, Miss Tyrell shouldn't be too shocked to see me. According to Colleen, Sandy said that it was okay for me to be involved. But then," he added with a grimace, "Colleen also said she was going to get the three of us together today."

Carly rang the doorbell. They waited patiently for several moments, and then Bret became defiantly impatient. He pounded on the door.

"Hey!" Carly warned. "She's going to think she has a mad attacker out here."

"She will have one in a few minutes," Bret muttered. But just then they heard a soft, frightened female voice. "Who's there?"

"Miss Tyrell? It's Bret McAllistair. Colleen's husband." Nothing. "Listen, I know it's really early, but I need to talk to you. I'm worried about Colleen."

They heard the rattle of a lock; then the door eased open. Sandy Tyrell stepped back. She stared at Bret with huge, wary eyes, clutching some kind of chiffon wrapper to her. He was almost tempted to whistle. She was a stunning woman, tousled from sleep, but somehow totally elegant nevertheless.

"Oh! Who...who's that?" she asked, indicating Carly.

"Carly—Carlton Fuller—our publisher, Miss Tyrell. He's quite safe, I promise you."

"Come in." Her fingers fluttered to her throat and then down. "Would you like some coffee?"

"Sure," Carly said with a reassuring smile. Bret shot him a quick glance, and Carly inclined his head with a slight warning. If they were going to get anything out of Sandy Tyrell, they couldn't press her into a more nervous state.

"Yeah, coffee sounds great," Bret murmured.

But he hated to wait. He apologized again for the early hour as she moved from the hallway to the kitchen, and he gazed casually about her place. It was all done in chrome and glass and white: immaculate white carpet, white plush sofa and deck chairs, and white walls offset with magnificent oils to provide color.

He leaned over the counter that connected the living room and kitchen and, with a friendly grin, complimented her on the town house. She responded with a quick warm smile, and he took a breath before he started to question her.

"Sandy, Colleen disappeared early this morning. I'm—"

"Earlier than this?" she interrupted.

"Very early. Listen. I can't tell you how worried I am. Colleen is a bright lady, but I think she's in over her head. I know about the puzzle pieces, but is there anything you know that I don't? Any lead, any clue? Any idea of where she might have gone?"

Sandy Tyrell lowered her head, and her hair fell in delicate feminine profusion about her fine features. Bret thought she paled slightly.

"Do you take sugar, Mr. McAllistair?"

"No, thanks. Sandy…"

Her hands were trembling as she poured the coffee. Carly stepped around and gently took the pot away from her. "Miss Tyrell, please. You've got to help us. Colleen could be in desperate danger."

She remained silent.

"Please!" Bret grated out hoarsely.

She looked up at him. "I think she's headed for Morocco."

"Morocco!" Bret and Carly chimed in stunned unison.

Sandy nodded unhappily. "I, uh, I didn't think she'd do anything right away." Her face was almost as white as her carpet; her eyes were enormous and filling with tears. "I'm so frightened."

"Miss Tyrell!" Carly said softly, but with a stern force. "The only way you'll ever live without fear is to get to the bottom of things. Bret and Colleen can make that happen, but right now Bret needs all the help you can give him!"

"Marrakech," Sandy murmured. "I think she's gone to Marrakech. To the hotel Bête Noire. To find a man named Eli Alibani. He's the man Rutger had been in touch with to find Generals MacHowell and Holfer."

"Oh, God!" Bret groaned. She would probably be there hours and hours ahead of him. In Marrakech. A foreign place where she didn't have friends or even acquaintances on the police force.

"May I use your phone, Miss Tyrell?" Carly asked.

Sandy nodded. Bret realized that even Carly was ahead of him, already calling the airlines, identifying himself and checking to see if Colleen had made reservations. Bret watched as Carly nodded slowly, hung up the phone and dialed again, calling the magazine's travel agent for urgent bookings to Marrakech.

Sandy cleared her throat while Carly was talking.

"Uh, make that reservations for two, please. I'd like to accompany Mr. McAllistair."

Carly covered the phone's mouthpiece with his hand.

"Sandy," Bret said, stunned, "that isn't necessary."

"If you have problems, finding this man Eli or getting him to find you, I might be decent bait." Her lower lip was trembling.

"You don't have to do this," Bret began.

"No," she admitted nervously, her words very soft. "But I might have sent Colleen into something awful. If anything happens to her, I wouldn't be able to live with it…and besides, Carly is right. If I don't go out and get to the bottom of things, I'll never be able to live without fear again."

Carly looked at Bret, who nodded slowly.

"Oh, hell! I'm going on this one, too," Carly said a little gruffly. He pulled his hand away from the receiver and made reservations for three. He hung up and looked at the other two. "We've only got an hour and a half to get to the airport," he warned them.

"I only need a few minutes," Sandy said, calmer than she had been since they'd arrived. "Honest. Five minutes to pack, and five to make a phone call to cancel things. You know. I swear, just a few minutes."

"You can have at least fifteen," Carly teased gently. She offered him a faint smile and disappeared into her room.

"Marrakech!" Bret exploded. "Carly, when I get my hands on her, I'm going to—" Frustration and fury and his present inability to reach her made him break off with a growl.

"Tie her to a stake?" Carly queried lightly, reaching for his coffee cup and taking a long sip. "Actually,

I suppose I'd rather like to see her lovely hide at the moment myself."

Bret groaned. "Carly..."

"Bret," Carly said with a long sigh, "you might as well get a grip on your emotions. We've got a long flight ahead of us. And there's not a damned thing in the world you can do until we get there."

Carly was right. It was going to be a long, long time till they just got there. They were going halfway around the world.

And there wasn't a damned thing he could do for all that time. Not a damned thing except torture himself with worry and pray that she would be safe.

Chapter Seven

Marrakech at last!

It was beautiful; it was exciting. It was a blend of color, of voices, of accents and languages. It was European businessmen walking the streets in three-piece suits; it was women heavily veiled and cloaked, hiding all but their eyes according to ancient Islamic custom. There were old clay buildings, and narrow, barely passable streets; there were scattered skyscrapers, and above all, there were the mosques. So many of them! It was known as the "city of mosques," and Colleen could easily see why. Their enchantment and grandeur were all about her, their minarets touching the sky with constant fantasy and magic.

She was here at long last. And the excitement of the city was like a potent tonic after the endless hours in flight. Hours in which she had barely slept, thinking about the past, thinking about Bret. And even when she had managed to sleep, she had dreamed about him. Sweet dreams, dreams that recalled little snatches of their life together. Their wedding night. Staring at the mirror above their bed in the Poconos, looking at one another and bursting into laughter as soon as the bell-boy had gone. They could be so alike, their thoughts traveling like a warm rush of waves, their laughter fading as they touched, and their kisses fusing with wonder and hunger....

The scene faded, to be followed by another moment, captured in her heart, and then another. The moments were so lovely...even the night before, when she had intended to lure him to sleep and had instead become prey to his touch, to the warmth of his lips, to the longing for it all to be a real marriage, solid and secure.

Dreams could fade to nightmares, and she began to envision scenes that caused her to whimper in her sleep, to shift and cringe in her first-class seat. She could see his face, deadly handsome, deadly cold, matching his words. He could look so impassive, as if she didn't matter at all, as if their time together was but an interlude.

In the mists of sleep she could even relive that political dinner with the senator and her own thoughts at the time. She had watched Bret with a young, lovely and rich widow and wondered if perhaps he weren't thinking that she'd create beautiful children, that she'd be a perfect mother....

Colleen had awoken more exhausted than when the champagne served to the passengers in first class had finally let her sleep. She'd been determined to remain angry, rather than become teary eyed at all she had lost. Damn it! She had been right to file for a divorce from him. He had almost literally asked her to by walking out without a care in the world. Flying off to cover *her* assignment, and returning only because of another assignment, then taking advantage of her for old times' sake.

She hadn't dared to sleep again, so all those long hours had been spent in horrible conflict. She loved Bret so much; it had taken forever for her to believe that he had really left her. She had learned to live without him. Then he had walked back in, and in a single night she had discovered ecstasy all over again—and agony. They'd spoken; they'd made love. And yet nothing had changed. He'd never said that he didn't want the divorce, that he wanted to talk, that there was a chance for them to make their marriage work. And no matter how bitter the acceptance, even she realized that making love did not make a marriage. In reality they had probably never really understood one another. From the West Coast to the East she had fought tears; from New York to Madrid she'd found anger. And from Madrid to Morocco she had sunk into absolute misery once again. She couldn't think about Rutger; she could barely remember why she was on the plane. Now that she had landed, she could change that. She could force herself to change that because she had cared for Rutger, because of Sandy and because she was a journalist, and a damned good one at that.

She had to cling to her work; it was her only defense against a shattered heart for the second time.

She could let the absolute fascination of the place seep through her, soothe her. She was a reporter; she was young and alive and working, and in her bones she knew that this could be the best work of her career if she could only discover the elusive truth. She could sense the culture in the air, the scent of broiling lamb from the street vendors, the jangle of donkey bells, the high rolling pitch of the criers, or muezzins, calling the faithful Muslims to prayer from the balconies of the countless minarets.

There were people and animals everywhere. Goats and chickens and sheep. Buses passed overloaded with humanity, men, women and children clinging to windows and doors.

Her cabdriver, a young man named Ben Arafa, spoke relatively fluent English, and he'd appointed himself her tour guide. She had introduced herself to him, and he addressed her every other second as Ms. Colleen McAllistair until she begged him to stop, wondering how she had managed to wind up on a first-name basis with a cabdriver in such a short time. But he was such an eager and charming young soul that she shrugged and accepted the obvious. This was Marrakech, after all.

"Marrakech is but one of our capitals," he told her. "There are also Rabat, Fez and Meknes. The king must spend time in all the capitals. Most of the government offices are in Rabat. It is considered the main capital. But Morocco is a country of diversified people and landscape, and also tradition dies hard. So we keep our four capitals. But I think Marrakech is the most beautiful."

Colleen looked out the window at the fine Moorish arch they were passing under. They had gone from the modern to the old again. A group of men walked the street in what Ben called *kumsan*, long tunics that fell to their ankles.

"Casablanca is fun, too," Ben said, ignoring the fact that he was driving to turn around and stare at her. "You know, *Casablanca*. Humphrey Bogart. It's a smashing movie."

She smiled at him a little distractedly. "Watch the road! Yes, yes, I know *Casablanca*." Ben's usage of the language was very strange, with Americanisms and Anglicisms meshed together.

He turned around again. "I've been to America. You know—"

"Ben! You're going to hit that goat!"

The taxi veered and swooped. The road was narrow; with the archways it seemed dark even though it was early morning. Clay buildings crowded on top of one another, and women ducked into doorways when the cab passed, balancing laundry baskets on their heads.

The cab jerked to a sudden halt.

"We're here?" Colleen asked.

"No," Ben said, fuming. "There is a donkey cart in the way!"

He stepped out of the cab and started shouting in Arabic. Someone shouted back. Suddenly it seemed as if the whole street was shouting.

The donkey sat down.

"Stupid, stupid, stupid!" Ben muttered in English, and Colleen leaned through the window to look out. Her eyes widened with alarm; a tall man with a dark, weathered and nastily scowling face was edging around the cart on a horse. There was a sword with a long blade attached to the belt he had wrapped around his *kamis*.

He was railing at the situation so emotionally that he pulled out his sword and waved it in the air.

"Ben, maybe we could just wait a little," Colleen suggested.

"Berbers!" Ben announced with irritation. "Horsemen, in town to sell their livestock. They should stay in the desert!"

The angry man on the prancing horse was coming toward them. "Get back in this cab!" Colleen pleaded.

Ben said something in Arabic, much more softly and pleasantly. The Berber swung down from the horse and looked into the cab. Ben kept talking. Colleen felt herself being raked by dark, inquisitive and lascivious eyes. She felt her face burn a little. It seemed that the street was suddenly filled with men, all watching her and smiling with great interest. She tilted her chin and tried to outstare them with silent dignity.

The horseman laughed again and said something to Ben, who answered politely.

"What's going on?" Colleen whispered uneasily.

"He thinks you're beautiful," Ben responded. "He asked if you were an American, and I told him yes."

"Oh. And what else?" she asked, noticing that he was hesitating.

"He, uh…"

"What?"

"He says he'd give me a whole flock of sheep and three gold chains just to see you naked and are you interested?"

"What?" The word came out in a breathless shriek. The Berber kept smiling. Colleen smiled, too, and convinced herself that the offer wasn't as frightening as it sounded; surely the man would take no for an answer and go away, as long as she wasn't insulting.

"Tell him…tell him that I have a husband."

Ben said something, and the Berber shook his head regretfully. Then he spoke to Ben again before bowing low and remounting his horse. He waved his hand and started yelling, and the stubborn donkey was forced to its feet.

Colleen leaned back against the cushions with a sigh of relief.

Ben turned around and smiled at her. "He said that your husband is a fool. You should not be let loose on the streets. If he were your husband, he would veil you from head to toe and never let you out of your tent."

"Well," Colleen said lightly, "then I'm certainly glad that he isn't my husband."

Ben kept staring at her speculatively, his gaze musing and fascinated. "Have you really got one?"

"One what?"

"Husband!"

"Oh, ah, yes, I do."

"And he let you come here—alone?"

"Ben, I don't mean to be rude, but would you please drive the cab?"

He shrugged, turned around and restarted the engine. But then he let the engine die, turned around to lean on the headrest once again and spoke to her passionately.

"No! I cannot take you to this place, the Bête Noire. It is a very bad place. The man—the Berber on the horse—he was not a bad man. He was a herdsman, offering you a payment, if you understand. At the Bête Noire…there are men who are not so good. There are men who smuggle and men who sell drugs. And men who make prostitutes of little children. We have laws, we have police, but you must understand, very bad things can happen."

Colleen was first surprised and then touched by the young man's concern. In her heart she suddenly felt that he was right. If she walked right into the heart of a caldron, she could expect to be burned. She had been a fool to come here alone. But she had come; she was here. And it seemed that the answers to the diamond heist, to the forty-year mystery, to Rutger's death, were all within her grasp.

Except that she didn't dare move.

It was daylight. Broad daylight. Ben had just assured her that there were police and law-abiding citizens and…

"Why are you here?" Ben interrupted her thoughts with a tone of desperation in his voice.

"I, um, I'm looking for a man."

"Your husband? He left you? He is doing something illegal? Is he in the drug trade and hiding out in Marrakech?"

"No!"

"He murdered someone!"

"No, no, no! Ben!" She sighed with exasperation, not sure whether to laugh or cry with exhaustion and confusion.

"I can help you," Ben told her, his tone beginning to sound excited. "I told you, I know about Americans. I have a cousin in New York. I have been there. I learned my English there, and it is very good, don't you think? And I can speak French and Spanish and—"

"Ben, whoa, wait! I'm sure that you do know all about Americans." Didn't everyone have a cousin in New York? she reflected with some amusement. "But I'm sorry, I don't want anyone else to get involved."

"You're a reporter!"

She hesitated. "What makes you think so?"

He laughed, his dark eyes sparkling. "Because only a woman reporter would be…"

"Would be what?" Colleen persisted with a warning in her voice. But apparently she didn't sound very vicious.

Ben hesitated only a second longer. "Stupid enough to come here!" he finished.

She was too tired to be really angry. And he was

probably right. She had been so determined to outdistance Bret that she was rushing toward a precipice.

"Thanks a lot," she said dryly.

Ben was silent for a second. "Let me take you to a good hotel. A decent hotel. And if you wish to find a man, I can make inquiries for you."

"Oh, God! Let's just get out of this alley for starters, shall we?"

"You'll buy me a drink at least?"

Colleen laughed. "I don't know. How old are you?"

He grinned, his smile wide and attractive. "Not so young. I'm twenty. How old are you?"

"Really! That's not a question you ask a lady."

"You asked me!"

"Fair enough," Colleen chuckled. She liked Ben. She liked his enthusiasm, and she liked his concern. She watched him drive through the narrow street and back to what passed for a major road. "I'm twenty-six."

"See, very young, too."

Colleen threaded her fingers through her hair, sweeping it back from her face. "I've put on a lot of mileage in those years," she said lightly.

"Your husband does not take care of you."

"He's not supposed to take care of me."

"Certainly he is! Just as you are supposed to take care of him!"

"You're a brat, Ben. Surely you don't speak to all your paying customers this way."

"Only the beautiful women."

"Umm," Colleen murmured wryly. "Oh, what the hell. I don't know what I'm doing anymore, anyway. Take me to a nice, decent, safe place and I'll buy you your drink while I decide what to do."

Thirty minutes later she had checked into a beautiful, modern hotel that was owned by an American corporation and called, rather appropriately, The Marrakech. She showered quickly and changed into a pair of black jeans and a shirt, then rejoined Ben in one of the plant-laden bars. The clientele was intriguing: there were a number of Americans, a group of German businessmen and dozens of Spaniards on holiday. French wafted melodiously from the bar to Colleen's table. The bartender was Moroccan, dressed in the traditional *kamits* and wearing a tarboosh, the tall red brimless hat that was common in the area.

Ben seemed to watch the people with a fascination equal to her own. He spoke casually about Moroccan customs for a while, telling her that the old way of describing the country in Arabic, *Maghrib Al-Aksa*, meant farthest west. Then he began to plague her with questions again, which was probably for the best since she had begun to feel numb.

"Where is your husband?"

"At home." I hope, she added to herself. Would he still be there? Or would he already have figured out how to trail her? Knowing Bret, he would have tracked down Sandy Tyrell's address and gone after her as soon as he decently could. And Sandy…would Sandy have told him everything?

Maybe it would be for the best if she had, Colleen thought morosely. Maybe it would be best if Bret did take over. He wouldn't be afraid to go to the Bête Noire, nor would he have to worry about turning down offers of sheep from eager horsemen!

Ben leaned across the table and lowered his voice. "There is no reason for you to fear me. I am a Moroccan. I know how to move about the city, I know how to say the right things and how to keep away from danger. I could be a messenger. I can find this man for you."

"I don't think so...."

"Colleen McAllistair," he said sincerely, "I have been on my own since I was a boy. I have been a beggar and a thief. I swear that I can do this for you."

Colleen hesitated. "Why should you?"

"Because I like you. And you will pay me, right?"

Colleen started to laugh. "Sure. Right."

"And you will trust me because you've been on your own, too, right?"

She narrowed her eyes slightly, surprised by his comment. "What makes you say that?"

He grinned. "You have the look."

Colleen sipped her drink, a Coke. Anything stronger and she might have crashed onto the table. "I've never been a beggar or a thief," she told him with a smile.

"But you've been on your own. Survivors have the look."

She shrugged. "I guess. Although I don't know if I'd really call myself a survivor. My life has been blessedly comfortable compared to many I've seen."

Ben shrugged. "My father died when his horse trampled him. He was drunk. Three months later my mother died having a child that never breathed. I was twelve." He spoke flatly. "Yours?"

"My parents?" Colleen hesitated, feeling the familiar jolt of pain. She had learned that time healed all wounds, but never completely. "They were killed together in an accident. There was an earthquake—just a minor tremor—but apparently it cracked a faulty beam and our roof fell in." She shrugged. "I'd gone out to get the mail."

"I'm very sorry. How old were you?"

"Seventeen. Not as young as you. Well," she said briskly, "what next?" She didn't want to sit there getting maudlin with a young man she still barely knew, even if he was eager to help.

"The Bête Noire. You tell me what you wish. I will go there."

"I can't. I just can't be responsible—"

"I told you! I have been in that district. I was a very good thief before I went…straight."

If she weren't so tired, she could probably think a little more clearly. Ben sounded so outraged and certain. And maybe he was right. He was a man; he was a Moroccan. He could probably throw out a feeler for her and come to no harm. If he had told her the truth, he had been surviving on some pretty rough streets for a long time.

"All right, all right, Ben!" she said. What else could she do? Just sit in Marrakech? "I'm trying to find a man named MacHowell. There's supposed to be another man, who can be reached through the proprietor of the Bête Noire, who can contact him. The contact's name is Eli Alibani. Just see what you can find out. Don't— please, I mean this—don't put yourself in any danger." She hesitated. "Ben, the man who was trying to reach him first was murdered in the States. This could be a very bad situation."

"Murdered?" Ben's eyes widened. "And you are here alone—after him?"

"Let's not go through this again. Involving you is definitely a mistake. Let's just forget it."

"I'll need some money. This Eli will surely want

to be paid for information in advance. One hundred American dollars."

"Ben…"

He stood up, grinning. "I'll be fine. I am a man, a thief of Marrakech." He grinned. "Humphrey Bogart."

"No, no, no. This isn't *Casablanca*."

He chuckled. "No, the plot is different. I am going now. I will go home first. I will wear my baggy trousers, my *saraweel*, and my full hooded cloak, my *jallabiya*. I will blend right in. And I will come back to the lobby and call your room. You must slip me the money now, before I go."

Slip him the money! He'd probably run away with it. He had just told her that he was a thief.

She was too tired to care. If he stole the money and deserted her, she'd either have to give up or pray that some sleep gave her a few answers.

She was careful to give him the money casually. "Be careful," she warned him.

He touched his fingers to his forehead, then bowed. As soon as he left, Colleen decided that she'd made a grave mistake. But it was too late to do anything. She paid the check and felt her exhaustion cover her like a blanket as she made her way to the elevator. Upstairs she locked her door, felt the cool breeze from the humming air conditioner and pitched onto the bed fully clothed.

She didn't have any dreams about Bret. She was asleep as soon as her head touched the pillow.

The phone must have rung at least ten times before it penetrated the depths of her sleep. But when it did, Colleen's eyes flew wide open, her body tensed, and she jumped like a rabbit to catch it.

"Hello?"

"I found him!" Ben's voice was both triumphant and a little amazed, as if he hadn't really believed he could do it himself.

"MacHowell?" Colleen said.

"No, no. Eli. But I've made arrangements for you to see MacHowell. And I did it very well!" Ben said proudly. "I said it must be in the open, that people must be all around."

"Good, good," Colleen murmured. "When do I get to see him?"

"At dusk, at the souk in the East Medina."

"The souk in the East Medina?"

He laughed with nervous excitement. "Medinas are Moorish-Arabian sections of the city. And the souk is an open-air market. Like a bazaar. It is fun; it is crowded. There are people everywhere. You cannot be hurt there, Colleen. I will be with you. I will protect you—with my life, if need be!"

Colleen was touched by his gallant, if dramatic, concern. "I hope that won't be necessary, but thanks," she murmured. "Okay, I'll be right down."

She hurried into the bathroom to wash her face, adrenaline rushing through her system from both fear and excitement. She was about to see MacHowell. She was almost three-quarters of the way through a four-part mystery. And MacHowell might well know where Holfer was.

She paused at her door, suddenly shaking. What was the matter with her? She was forgetting that someone had viciously murdered Rutger. And that his death had almost undoubtedly come at the command of one of the very people she was seeking.

Holfer or MacHowell.

Her fingers were trembling as she wrapped them around her shoulder bag. She was crazy to be doing this.

She swallowed, feeling a little dizzy. She couldn't turn back; she was so close. And thanks to Ben, no danger could come to her. She was to meet the man in public. As long as she acted with good sense she would be all right. She would be careful to stay in full view of dozens of people at all times.

She squared her shoulders, then smiled slowly because excitement was rushing through her again. The forty-year-old mystery had intrigued the world, but she had the chance to come up with the solution, to find the truth.

Colleen paused just outside her room and rested her head against the door as she locked it. Wasn't it also true that she was trying to prove something else? To Carly, yes, but mostly to Bret. She needed to prove that she was totally competent, that Bret had no right to question her ability to do her job. But wasn't she also trying to prove it to herself?

She'd never questioned her life so deeply until now. Until the last few days. Bret had walked out after she'd warned him that their marriage would be over if he did. He had never protested, never tried to see her, because it hadn't mattered to him. He was cold about his objectives. He would step on anyone, even her, to reach them.

Then what had the other night been? She swallowed, bitterly deciding that he was a healthy, virile man who had never pretended to be a saint. They had been together…so why not? He'd been involved with other women before their marriage; he'd probably been involved with others since they'd split. But she had walked straight into his arms, and he wasn't the type of man to turn down an open invitation. He'd never been adverse to a little episode of romance before he moved on to the next adventure.

There was a burning warmth against her eyelids, and she slammed a sneakered toe against the door while she whispered, "Damn him!" Then she spun around, determined to be competent, just like Bret. Wary, eyes open and always competent.

Ben was waiting for her at the bar. His dark eyes were bright with excitement as he sipped Turkish coffee. He stood when he saw her, almost knocking over the pretty little whitewashed cocktail table. "I'm going with you, yes?" he asked her.

Colleen smiled as she sank into the chair across from him. "Yes, I suppose. I don't even know where I'm going without you."

He sat down, too, drawing a finger around the rim of his cup. "You will like the souk. All visitors like the souk." He stared at her, still excited. "What is this? What is going on here? When you write your story, will you mention my name?"

Colleen laughed. "If I get this thing solved, I'll mention your name all you like!" He was still looking at her eagerly. She ordered American coffee, and when it arrived, told him a bit of the story.

"Diamonds!" he said eagerly.

"Yes, it's all over diamonds."

"Well, this MacHowell will certainly not hand you a load of diamonds."

"I'm not expecting him to, nor would the diamonds

be mine if he did. They would be returned to the French government."

Ben shook his head, a little bewildered. "All those diamonds… You could be rich. You could be set for life."

She lowered her head, hiding her smile. "I have nothing against money, Ben. But I like to work." She glanced at her watch. It was almost seven. "Shouldn't we get going?"

"Darkness will come between eight and nine. Yes, we might as well head for the souk."

A twenty-minute drive in Ben's cab brought them to the souk. As Ben had promised, she loved it. Tables and counters were spread along the edges of the narrow streets, flanking clay and adobe shops. The evening sky had turned a beautiful pink and crimson; men shouted out their wares and chanted in alluring singsong tones. Chickens squawked and squabbled, and there was the occasional bleat of a lamb. Craftsmen carved beautiful designs on natural leather; smiths tinkered with copper and silver, and ivory workers carved delicate figures from tusks that had been brought north from southern Africa. Incense hung in the air. Candles and lamps were for sale, along with washbasins and intricately woven prayer rugs. People watched Colleen; the shopkeepers gave her flashing white smiles, and she knew that they saw her as an American, a lady with money, one to charm.

"Blouses, miss! The finest silk!"

"Great bargains on copper!"

Ben stood at her side like a friendly watchdog, and she admitted that she was very glad of his presence. Although the customers in the souk were often French, Spanish, Europeans of other sorts, and even Americans, she granted that this was a largely Arabian and Islamic country, and women had been given a place in the background. Their purpose here was to do laundry, cook, have babies and entertain the men.

They passed beneath an enchanting Moorish archway. The sun was setting, casting glorious beams of light against a tinker's assortment of copper. For a moment pain stabbed her heart. Once it would have been so much fun to be here with Bret. They would have enjoyed it together, felt the magic like one, the fascination....

But would any of it have been real?

"Down this street," Ben said.

They passed under another arch. There was no traffic here and fewer hawkers. It was a long adobe hallway, filled with beautiful arches and tile mosaics and shadows.

"Here?" Colleen asked a little uneasily.

Ben pointed to an old man selling prayer rugs. "Yes, he is Mohammed Kenezer. I was told that we should come here."

It was all right, Colleen decided. The hallway was an overhang flanking a mosque. And the street was just beyond it. A street with a slow but steady flow of traffic.

The only bad point was the lingering shadows beneath the arches. Yet even as Colleen warily eyed the pillars that cast the shadows, a man stepped from behind one of them.

He looked typically Moroccan. He wore the red brimless hat, the tarboosh that she had seen so frequently. He was very dark—swarthy, she decided. Dark eyes, dark hair, a thin and narrow face, just as in all the mummy movies, she thought. There was a strange gleam in his eyes; he might have been an attractive man, except that he seemed...evil.

Nonsense, she assured herself. You couldn't tell whether someone was evil, not at first glance, anyway. It was just the incense and the aura of the setting sun, the arches and the shadows....

"That's him," Ben whispered tensely. "Eli."

"I thought I was to meet MacHowell," Colleen said irritably.

"I thought so, too."

The Moroccan approached them. He was very tall and slim.

"Where is General MacHowell?" Colleen asked sharply.

The Moroccan bowed to her and gave her a full flashing white smile. "Surely, miss, you will see him. But the general has been leading a quiet life for many years now. You will understand if I ask your business first."

"I will tell you," Colleen hedged, as wary of Eli as he seemed to be of her, "that I have no intention of harming the general. I must speak with him about the past. It could concern his life."

"Please!" The Moroccan lowered his head with a pained expression, then glanced at Ben. "We will discuss this alone!"

"I *won't* leave her alone!" Ben insisted like a young tiger.

Eli smiled condescendingly. "I understand. We will just step a few feet away. We will stand by the arch and go no farther."

Ben looked at Colleen. She nodded. They wouldn't be more than twenty feet away from one another.

Eli grabbed her arm and led her to the archway. "You must understand that the general is frightened," he told her.

Colleen realized that she was standing in shadow. "If he is frightened, then he must help me."

"How can I be assured you have no wish to hurt him?"

Some instinct of danger began to alert her. Colleen glanced over at Ben. He wasn't far away, but a silversmith had pushed a cart between them. Uneasily she started to turn back to Eli. "All I can give you is my sincere promise that—"

She broke off, inhaling to scream. The pleasant smile was gone from his swarthy face, and his hand, covered in a soaking wet rag, was nearing her mouth from the rear.

She never had a chance to scream; instead of air she inhaled a sickly-sweet odor that seemed to instantly paralyze her limbs. Vaguely she felt his arms, strong and wiry, as he caught her falling form. She saw a huge blanket, clutched in his other hand, bringing darkness over her.

As the world faded she caught one last glimpse of Ben. The silversmith's cart had turned over. Things were rolling everywhere, and Ben was caught in the midst of the confusion.

She saw his eyes briefly, but she could not tell if he stared at her with horror or satisfaction. Had she been set up?

She was swept off her feet and carried along the hallway. The last sound she heard was a car's motor, and she smelled exhaust mingled with incense.

Her last thought was of Bret.

Bret. Oh, God. Even if he didn't really love her, he would never have let her come to this.

Her senses dimmed; her mind went totally black. She swirled into a vortex of darkness....

BRET DIDN'T WASTE any time when they reached Marrakech; he, Carly and Sandy Tyrell headed straight for the Bête Noire. He didn't notice the streets; he didn't notice anything. All he wanted to do was reach the damned place—and Colleen. His nerves were so jangled that he thought he would explode if he didn't see her soon. The god-awful long trip hadn't helped much, either; Sandy Tyrell was very beautiful and very sweet, but she was like a clinging vine. She was terrified of flying, terrified of what they would find, terrified of every stranger that passed by, even thousands of feet up in the air. He'd been obliged to spend hours telling her soothing things, assuring her that the pilot knew his business, that the stewardesses were smiling because they were happy, that they actually loved to fly. Sandy had described the puzzle pieces to a T for him; she had talked about the past, about her mother—with a bitter poignancy—about the misery of living down her grandfather's reputation. He'd learned things, a number of things, and yet none of them had seemed to matter much. Not when he was on fire with worry over Colleen. It would have been better if he'd been able to enjoy a few drinks and knock himself out a little.

Like Carly. Damn Carly. He'd managed to sleep for the majority of the trip. "Ici—voilà," the cabbie said. He didn't speak English, but he did speak French, and he'd been the first available driver.

"Oh, my God! We're getting out here?" Sandy

moaned. Her long-nailed, elegant fingers wound around his arm.

"I can have the driver take you on to a good hotel…" Bret began.

"No, no! I don't want to be alone!" Bret took a deep breath. He owed her his patience. Without her, he wouldn't even have begun to know where to look for Colleen.

"We'll both be with you," Carly said reassuringly.

Bret took her hand and squeezed it. "We'll get the driver to wait," he told her and quickly made the arrangements in his adequate, if not entirely fluent, French.

"Come on," he told the others.

"What do you think you're going to be able to do in there?" Carly asked him.

"Well, I'll ask some questions. And if I don't get any answers, I'll try shouting and stirring up some trouble."

"Wonderful plan," Carly muttered.

And then they were standing before the Bête Noire. It was an ancient building, made of clay, with an arched facade covered in chipping, faded paint. There was no door, just a short flight of steps to some kind of public room.

It looked like a den of thieves. There were no women inside, only groups of men, drinking at scattered tables. Sandy hung behind with Carly. Bret approached the long serving bar. The place was very dark and filled with smoke.

Bret set his hands on the bar. A thin man with rotting teeth eyed him warily as he dried a glass with a filthy rag.

"I'm looking for a man," Bret said in English.

The barkeep shrugged. "There are many men here. Look."

Bret's fingers itched to grip the bartender's neck. He smiled. "You have beer?"

The man served him a warm brown beer. Bret wondered what disease he would get from it. It seemed that all the conversation from the men sitting at the tables had ceased. Shivers tracked along his spine; he didn't like having his back to the others.

"This man I'm looking for is called Eli," Bret said loudly, turning around to survey the room. "He knows an Englishman named MacHowell—"

He broke off, ready to reach for the small pistol concealed beneath his jacket, when Sandy gave him a forceful, warning jab in the ribs. But there was no one touching her; she was just staring into the shadows at the back of the room.

And then Bret realized why. There was an old man coming toward him, an old man with snow-white hair and a drawn and weathered face. He wore a European business suit, and his eyes were as green as a summer field.

"I'm MacHowell," he said simply. "What do you want with me?"

Bret didn't get to speak because suddenly there was a scream followed by a streak of movement. A Moroccan youth came hurtling up from a table, flying at MacHowell like a flash of lightning.

"Where is she?" the youth shrieked.

"What the devil?" MacHowell began.

Stunned, Bret flung himself between the two. He caught the young Moroccan before the boy could hit MacHowell; it took all his strength to subdue the man.

"He took her! He took Ms. McAllistair!" the youth cried out. "She was to meet him at the souk. Eli was there instead. He's done something with her."

"What…?" Bret began.

"Young man, I haven't the faintest idea what you're talking about!" MacHowell said in confusion. "I haven't seen Eli in weeks, and he's a scurvy sort at best. I never trusted the man. He'd do anything for a few pounds."

"Eli took her where?" Bret thundered out.

Before the old man could answer, there was another commotion, this time near the door. Another man had risen from a table to run for the arched doorway. He crashed into Sandy, who screamed. The man pushed her aside and kept running.

"Get him!" MacHowell shouted. "He's one of Eli's friends!"

Bret didn't need to hear more. He forgot all about being exhausted and tore after the man, pausing at the entranceway only to get his bearings. He heard the sound of sandals flopping against the dirt and started to run again. He turned down an alley, and the man was right in front of him.

A flying leap brought him down on the frightened Moroccan, who immediately began to writhe and moan in Arabic.

"Where is she? Where is my wife?" Bret demanded. The man kept moaning in Arabic. Straddled over him, Bret caught his shoulders and began to shake him. "My wife. Where is she?"

He didn't hear the footsteps behind him, but Mac-Howell's words finally registered in his mind. "He doesn't speak a word of English, young man. Let me."

Bret clenched his teeth and swallowed miserably, releasing his hold on the culprit. MacHowell knelt down beside the man with an agility that was surprising in a man so old.

He began to ask questions in Arabic. The sullen Moroccan didn't answer. Bret, incensed, raised a fist. The Moroccan threw out his hands in protest and began to jabber away.

At last MacHowell turned to Bret. "We must let him go."

"Let him go?" Bret repeated incredulously.

"Hmm. Yes. If you want your wife back, we've got to start moving quickly."

"Where is she?"

MacHowell hesitated, then spoke quickly. "If we're lucky, she's still in a little village on the side of the mountains in the custody of a petty emir, the local dirty old man."

"Oh, God!" Bret both swore and moaned.

"It gets worse," MacHowell warned him.

Bret's eyes shot to MacHowell.

"This man, Hassan, is known to offer creature comforts for business deals. When he is finished with a new…" MacHowell hesitated, then shrugged "…conquest, he keeps the woman a prisoner. And offers her to his associates."

Bret was on his feet, swearing in panic. "Where is this village?"

The young Moroccan who had almost attacked MacHowell was right behind them. "I know where it is, and I've got my taxi right here," he said. "Dear Allah, let's go!"

In seconds they were all in the taxi: Bret, MacHowell, Carly, Sandy and Ben. Bret's fingers dug into the dashboard, and his heart hammered in his throat. His temples pounded. Somewhere in the back Sandy was sniffing in fear. Not even Carly seemed to have anything to say.

But Bret finally thought of something. He turned to the Moroccan youth who was driving and demanded, "Who the hell are you?"

Ben began to explain. When he had finished, Bret began to quiz MacHowell.

There was nothing else to do. Ben had explained that it was going to be at least a three-hour drive, and Bret knew he had to try to remain sane somehow.

Chapter Eight

Colleen didn't know exactly when she began to return to consciousness. She didn't just open her eyes, but became aware of little things very slowly. Her fingertips first... They felt ridiculously sensitive. They were touching something cool and silky. She wasn't even really aware of danger; she felt as if she were wrapped in a fog that was soft and gentle and swirling. She felt her body with incredible keenness, yet it was almost as if she were outside herself, aware of things only from some higher, more celestial, plain. Everything was gray, soft, soothing, floating...and her eyelids were heavy. So heavy. It was the greatest effort to tug them open, and even when she did, it seemed that the world was still gray. Then a sharp, pungent odor suddenly streamed into her nostrils, and she dragged a hand up to try to force it away. The gray paled a bit, and she saw a silhouette. In another moment she saw the grinning, masklike face of the dark man in the tarboosh. Eli. Except that his mask was no longer a convivial one; it was amused and pleased—and cruel.

Eli was not making arrangements for her to meet MacHowell. Even in her daze she realized that. She had been betrayed, set up. By Ben? She remembered his eyes, large and dark, just as her vision had faded along with consciousness. Or had General James Mac-Howell planned all this himself? Had he heard that she was in Marrakech and immediately made plans for her disposal?

"Wh-what…?" The single word was difficult to say. The face became a hazy blob before her, then came into focus once again.

"Mrs. McAllistair, you are with us. In spirit, at least. Welcome to the humble abode of Hassan Ydh Rabak. I will be leaving you now. Hassan has been expecting you. He has been quite anxious, as a matter of fact."

He was smiling pleasantly, so pleasantly that she felt a terrible fear penetrating the fog that swirled within her mind. Somewhere inside herself she began to realize that she was in real danger, that she was far away from law and order and anyone who might be able to help her.

"Who…are…you working for?" Her voice was so distant, so strained. She sounded like the hookah-smoking caterpillar in *Alice's Adventures in Wonderland*. Wonderland. Oh, yes! She had stepped into a Moroccan bazaar, met this man and fallen into a dark tunnel from which she could not seem to escape. It was not real. She had to fight the fog and find reality. If only she could talk! "General MacHowell…?"

"I'm so sorry. You won't be seeing MacHowell, Mrs. McAllistair. I'm afraid I'm just one of the things you can purchase here. A go-between, an emissary. I'm hired by the job, you might say." Something blurred before her eyes; it was his hand. Distantly she felt his fingers against her cheek, stroking lightly. She struggled desperately for the strength to fight him. He laughed, his hand returned to his lap. "Ah, yes, you would have been fascinating. But the arrangements have all been made, I'm afraid. You see…" He shifted slightly, and Colleen realized that she was in some sort of sunken bed. His hand waved, and she saw another man standing behind him. A tall man in loose trousers and a billowing shirt, with a sharp nose and a wide, toothless grin. He appeared to be built like a sumo wrestler. Colleen narrowed her eyes to focus better, but the cloud in her mind returned.

"I hope you will be very happy with Hassan. I'm afraid he doesn't speak a word of English, so you won't be able to complain. And I've told him a bit of a white lie so he won't even understand your actions."

"White lie?" None of this was making sense. She was a lost Alice; surely she would eventually awake from the nightmare.

"Anything can be for sale, Mrs. McAllistair. Even American reporters. Hassan, however, believes you're in business for yourself. He also believes that you consider American men to be soft. We've anticipated you having a disagreement with our arrangements, you see. He's promised to be very—what is the word?—macho! Oh, yes, that's it. Macho with you! When you scream and fight, he will think you're loving every minute with him."

She had to fight the numbing fog that continued to strip her of the ability to resist. Her mind was becoming sharper; but her limbs still felt like lead. She was beginning to understand her position all too clearly. She had been so easily tricked! Like a rank amateur. Easily and completely tricked and taken. She had been chloroformed and sold to a toothless old letch.

"But I'd be nice to Hassan if I were you, Mrs. McAllistair." Eli was shaking his head. "Someone dislikes you very much. In fact, I'd say someone hates you. But you'll understand that later. For now…" He shrugged. "Your life, if not your virtue, is safe as long as you are with him."

"What…?"

He moved away. Gray streamed and swarmed around her again, deepening and deepening until there was nothing but black.

Minutes later—or was it hours? She had no way of knowing—she became aware again. It was different this time. She was aware of things in a very real way. She remembered the conversation with Eli; she knew instantly that she was in a horrendous situation. Panic washed over her; before she dared open her eyes, she clenched her teeth so that she would not scream until she had seen her position, if she were alone, how she could escape.

She raised her lashes just a fraction of an inch and carefully looked out at the world. The room was very dark; there were candles burning on low tiled tables arranged around the foot of the sunken bed. It must have been night outside, but there was a pleasant breeze. There were gossamer drapes floating at Moorish arched windows. They appeared to be a soft dazzle of pastel colors, caught by the flutter of candlelight.

Slowly she shifted her gaze. There really was a gray fog in the room. Incense was burning in small pots on the low tiled tables, filling the air with the scents of jasmine and sweet spice. The walls were shell-pink clay, the floors strewn with elegant rugs.

She twisted slightly, and her eyes flew fully open as

a gasp of shock and horror escaped her despite her determination to remain calm.

The toothless Hassan was perched on the edge of the bed, grinning happily.

Colleen discovered that she could move and move quite well. In a flash she was on her knees, scooting as far away from the man as she could. He laughed delightedly with a vast pleasure that made his massive frame rise and fall. He clapped his hands with a child's joy and said something to her in Arabic.

Colleen shook her head, clutching at a silken pillow for some sort of protection. She was panicking again, she realized, but why not? She had no idea where she was, and this roly-poly titan thought she'd gleefully hired herself out for the evening. She was going to start screaming in pure, desperate hysteria at any second.

She couldn't! If Eli had told her any form of truth, Hassan would think it was all part of the game. She had to stay calm. She had to convince him that she was a victim. Oh, God! Why the hell had she ever run off without Bret? Bitterly she realized that Bret would never have gotten himself into a position like this. He would have been suspicious. He would never have walked blindly into danger.

Hassan said something, then laughed again. He reached out to her, and it was all that Colleen could do to keep from slapping his hand away. She rolled quickly, finding her footing on the left side of the bed, near the windows.

"Hassan," she said firmly, planting her hands on her hips and attempting to look outraged and dignified. It wasn't easy. She was missing one shoe, and her hair kept falling into her face. "Hassan, listen to me. This

is all a big mistake. A tremendous mistake. I'm a reporter. An American reporter. I am not a call girl. Not
for hire. Do you understand?"

He was watching her with his wide grin still in place.
Colleen realized that he wasn't getting her point at all.
Nervously she pushed her hair back. There was a door
about twenty feet from the bed. What would happen if
she reached it? Was the house full of servants? What if
she raced to the windows and screamed for help? Would
anyone hear her? She had no idea where she was. Would
anyone care? Would anyone think a thing of a woman
screaming in the night?

Hassan was rising, albeit slowly. He had a lot of
weight to shift around. Colleen stifled a gasp and
backed toward the window, putting a hand out in front
of her to ward him off even as he neared her. "Hassan!
Listen. Pay attention. You could be in serious trouble.
You could wind up arrested. In jail for years. Oh, God!
Why don't I speak Arabic? *Parlez-vous français?*"

Apparently Hassan did not speak any French. He just
kept grinning—and coming closer.

Colleen gave up and rushed to the window. "Help!
Help! Someone, help me!"

She gazed out at the night. It seemed that the nearest
building was half a mile away. There was no one out
on the streets. She was screaming to an empty sky, and
the ground was two stories below her. She spun around,
leaning against the clay frame of the window. Hassan
had almost reached her. His fingers, heavily laden with
rings, were stretching toward her.

Colleen slipped beneath his outstretched arms and
raced to the door. He chuckled with good-natured
humor. She cast him a quick glare, then reached for

the curved brass handle on the door and wrenched at it. The door flew open only to leave her face-to-face with two swarthy men. Startled, Colleen stared at the pair. She tried to smile. "If you don't mind, I'll just be leaving now."

Her sentence ended with a shrill shriek as something closed around her waist. Hands. Hassan's hands. She was lifted straight off the floor and treated to another of his enthusiastic, deep-chested chuckles.

Colleen clawed at his fingers, but he barely noticed her efforts. She kicked out at him with fury. The hell with reason. Panic had taken over, and instinct was all she had left.

The doors closed. Hassan carried her across the room, and she found herself flying face first back to the sunken bed. Her breath was knocked from her, and she gasped for air as she fought to rise from the pillows. She rolled quickly, desperate to see where the overgrown Arab was.

She breathed a little easier. He was standing by the bed, his arms crossed over his chest. Smiling.

Stay calm, she told herself again. Rational. Reasonable. If Eli had spoken the truth, Hassan was no cutthroat out to hurt her. He simply thought he had purchased an evening's entertainment.

"Oh, Hassan! Please? Can't you understand me? Please try! Eli is a bad man. This isn't real—"

She broke off because he was talking. She couldn't understand a single word. Suddenly he reached down for her hand.

"No..."

Desperately she shook her head. Wasn't that the same

in any language. "*Se habla español,* Hassan? Oh, come on! How about Italian. No, *non, nyet.*"

She gasped, finding herself on her feet and horribly close to him. He was still grinning. She tugged at her hand to no avail. He led her to the far corner of the room, where the shadows hid a screen, a big brass bathtub and a silken caftan.

"Oh, no!" Colleen shrieked. "No, no, no, *no!*"

He nodded, very pleased with himself.

"No!" He wasn't getting her message. Colleen gave a mighty twist of her wrist and kicked him with all her strength.

Hassan grunted and paled with the sudden pain, then stared at her with new respect, though his smile faded at last. It was replaced by an annoyed scowl. Again he came toward her. Retreat seemed the better part of valor, and once again she was backing away.

"When I say no, I mean no!" she said warningly, almost tripping as she backed into the bed. Frantic, she steadied herself and warily skirted it until she reached the other side.

Hassan followed. She noticed that his feet were bare, and his toes, too, were ringed with gems.

"Hassan!" She made a mad dash for the window again. For all his weight, Hassan could move quickly when he chose. His fingers closed around the waistband of her jeans, and she found herself in the air again, struggling like a kitten whose mother has clutched it by the scruff of the neck. In seconds she was making another nosedive into the pillows.

Hassan was definitely annoyed. When she rolled over this time, he was standing above her with his hands on his hips and railing at her in no uncertain terms, even if she didn't understand a word. He stamped a bare foot against one of the elegant throw rugs and pointed at the screen and bathtub. To further emphasize his monologue, he strode like a titan to retrieve the caftan and throw it over her. She still couldn't understand him, but it was becoming obvious that Hassan hated jeans.

Desperately thinking, and terrified that it was going to be all over any second, Colleen just stared at him. He rattled on and on, waving his arms. Then suddenly he pointed at the screen again, spat out one more sentence and turned to stride toward the door, swinging it open so furiously that she was sure the hinges would snap.

But they didn't. Hassan disappeared, and the door swung shut with a bang.

For a moment all Colleen could do was stare at the door. Then she realized that she had miraculously received a reprieve. Hassan wanted her to get bathed and dressed first.

"Oh!" A frantic little sob escaped her, and she flew off the bed again. The door, she realized, staring desperately around for another miracle, would do her little good. The swarthy bodyguards were beyond it.

She raced to the window, and for a moment her heart took flight. There were vines growing all over the shell-pink clay walls. Perhaps she could grasp one and crawl down.

Nervously Colleen reached out to test one of the vines, reminding herself that she had wondered while watching Tarzan films in her youth how it was that he never happened to pick a weak vine, and how the damned things had never once broken while he swung through the jungle.

She tugged at the vine and was horrified when it instantly broke off in her hand.

"Damn!" she swore.

There had to be a way out!

Sheets! She ran to the bed and tried to strip it. The sheets were silk; they were slippery even to the touch. But it wasn't until they were in her hands and she was back at the window that she realized there was absolutely nothing to tie them to. Tears started to fill her eyes and slide silently down her cheeks. Bret would never be able to save her now. He'd never know where she was. Why had she been so foolish, so determined to handle things on her own? He wouldn't have let this happen. He wouldn't have been trapped.

Suddenly, standing there with the breeze flowing over her, the sheets clutched ridiculously in her hands, she wanted him more than ever. His cool thinking, his assured silver gaze, his broad shoulder to lean against. She even longed for the brunt of his temper, the lash of his tongue, the chilly distance he could put between them when he chose.

Distance! She had to quit standing there crying. Bret was far away. He wasn't with her, wasn't there to help. She had to pull herself together and do something.

Getting mad at Bret seemed to be the easiest thing to do, she thought suddenly. It was all his fault. If he hadn't stolen her story the first time, she wouldn't be here now. She would never have felt that she had to prove something to herself. She would never have been alone, prime pickings for a toothless, beringed sausage!

Colleen dropped the sheet and looked around the room. She bit her lip and hurried over to the screen and the tub. There was a vase full of some kind of oil there.

A heavy vase. If she could hide herself somehow and get the guards to rush in, she could try to crack them over the head and run out.

Them. How was she going to get two of them? It was impossible.

It couldn't be impossible. It was her only chance.

In desperation she came up with a plan. After setting one of the sheets and the vase by the door, she took the second sheet and two of the candles over by the screen. Praying that she wouldn't asphyxiate herself, Colleen patiently dangled the sheet over the candle until it caught fire. Then she set the sheet next to the screen.

The fire burned itself out almost instantly. Tears flecked her lashes as she tried a second time, swearing a thousand oaths against Bret as she did so. Then she quit swearing to pray silently with her breath held so that the sheet would catch fire this time.

Eventually it did. When her eyes watered again, it was because of the smoke. She waited until the fire had really taken hold, then she screamed and raced back to grab the vase and the sheet.

A second later the door burst open. The two guards rushed in, yelling in Arabic. Colleen waited until they were past her, coughing at the smoke. Then she leaped forward, tossing the sheet over them and bringing the vase down with all her strength on what she thought was a head.

It *was* a head. She heard a startled groan and then a thud as a body crashed to the floor. The second man was still struggling with the sheet. Colleen hesitated, trying to decide whether to run or to crack him with the remnants of the vase. She heard footsteps pounding from somewhere and furious shouts. If she didn't get out quickly, someone else would come.

As a compromise she pushed the struggling form, sending it falling to the floor. But when she regained her own balance, ready to run, it was to discover that Hassan, huffing and puffing, was running into the room. The whole screen was blazing now, and smoke was everywhere.

Hassan looked ready to kill. Colleen turned and ran across the bed. Hassan followed her, staggering this time. If she could run quickly…

She started to run toward the door, hope soaring in her heart. But even as she ran, she screamed. Something flew hard against her. Something warm and breathing and living that seemed to have flown straight through the window.…

She winced with pain, tears flooding her eyes as she hit the floor. Dazed, she realized that it couldn't be Hassan. Hassan was on the bed. The thing was gone from her—and it wasn't a thing. It was a body, a man. That man was standing on the bed over Hassan, shouting furiously, ready to pounce like a tiger.

Colleen gasped, astonished. "Bret!"

Someone raced into the room, a young man. Stunned, Colleen gasped out his name. "Ben!"

Colleen struggled to her knees. Bret was still swearing at Hassan, trying to drag him up by the back of his shirt.

"Stop!" Ben pleaded with him. "The fire. We've got to get out of here!"

Hassan said something, and the young man answered him. Then he spoke to Bret. "Mr. McAllistair, leave him! Let's get out of here! This man is not at fault. He purchased her through an arrangement. Dear Allah, let's go before his friends arrive!"

Bret was staring at Hassan again with fury and the lust for vengeance in his eyes. Colleen was still on her knees, stunned and amazed. Bret was here, in Morocco. And Ben was with him.

"Mr. McAllistair!" the young man pleaded.

For another long moment Bret held Hassan in a death grip. Then he dropped both the shirt and the man and leaped from the bed to Colleen, reaching down to drag her to her feet. Dimly she saw Hassan getting up, and she heard more footsteps.

"Let's go!" Ben pleaded.

He led the way. Bret followed, pulling Colleen. Outside the door they passed a number of heavily veiled women racing along with buckets of water and blankets.

They ignored the fire brigade and pelted down a stairway. The house was a blur to Colleen. She saw a courtyard and another door, and then she was out in the night, her wrist still clutched in Bret's hand. They ran out to a clay wall, and then they were running down the empty street. Far ahead Colleen could see a large black automobile. Its engine was suddenly gunned.

She could barely breathe; her side ached f ning, and tears stung her eyes. Bre and she was free of

was here; she was

from run-

Hassan. Ben hadn't set

met Bret and brought him to

was so relieved and grateful.

idiot!" Bret rasped out at her as

"God Almighty, woman, I don't

ounce of sense in your entire frilly

dain of his words sent gratitude falling from her like a discarded coat. She stiffened, feeling his hand at the small of her back as he opened the rear car door. Ben was racing around to the front.

"Idiot!" Colleen swung around, pushing Bret's hand away. "And I suppose you think you're some damned kind of Errol Flynn? I was out of there before you ever made your appearance, Mr. Wonderful."

His voice dropped to a low and furious pitch. In the moonlight his eyes glittered like silver knives, narrowing in on her. "You ungrateful little bitch! Next time you're determined to kill yourself, I'll be damned if I'll stop you."

"Please!" Ben called. "Get in the car."

Both of them had the good sense to look back. It seemed that a flock of black crows was flying after them; a score of servants had rushed from Hassan's clay manor.

Colleen felt herself shoved into the car next to another body. She issued a long exclamation of shock when she recognized Sandy Tyrell, and then saw that an old man—looking dignified, even in the darkness—sat on Sandy's other side.

"Sandy!"

"⸺ you all right? I had to come after I realized the ⸺ ⸺ you into!" Sandy said earnestly.

⸺ a shrieking tailspin, and they ⸺ behind them.

⸺ h, fine."

⸺ the front seat.

"Are you ⸺
danger I had sent yo⸺
Ben jerked the taxi into⸺
sent dust flying onto the horde⸺
Colleen gripped the seat. "⸺
"You shouldn't be!" Bret s⸺
"Oh, honestly!"
"Bret, please," someone⸺
someone with a familiar ⸺eat,
"Carly!"

"Hi, sweetie," Carly said pleasantly. He twisted around to grimace. "Couldn't miss out on this one."

She thought she heard a low growl rumble from Bret's throat. He sounded like an enraged Doberman held in control by an invisible leash.

Colleen ignored him and looked past Sandy to the old man, a forced smile on her lips. "How do you do? And if you don't mind my asking, who are you?"

He chuckled softly. "General James MacHowell."

"MacHowell!" Colleen echoed. The same awful fear she'd experienced earlier seemed to crash over her like a waterfall. She was ready to jump over Sandy and throttle the old man, but she didn't. She screamed at him instead, her voice shaking. "You bastard! You set me up! What the hell are you doing here?"

"Colleen!" Bret snapped. "If it weren't for the general, we might never have found you."

"It's true, my dear," Carly told her.

"But Eli was the contact! *Your* contact!"

MacHowell was shaking his head sadly. "Eli is a free agent. It's true he knew where to find me. But Eli has a tendency to work for the highest bidder."

"And you, Colleen, have a tendency to be an idiot," Bret said dryly.

Colleen's eyes jerked from MacHowell to Bret. It was very dark as they moved along the rutted dirt road; she could see only the shadow of his profile, but it was enough to tell her that his jaw was set at a furious angle. God! She'd wanted to see him so badly; she'd longed for him; she'd been so sorry for all that she had done.

And now here he was, behaving like a whip-cracking staff sergeant. Her eyes seemed to burn with sudden moisture, and she stiffened with furious resolve. "Bret,

I repeat, I was doing fine without you. With or without your dramatic entrance, I was on my way out."

He turned in his seat so abruptly that he startled Ben, who was left to struggle with the veering car as he jerked the wheel. Sandy gasped, but Bret didn't seem to notice.

"On your way out! To where? How far would you have gotten before Hassan's people came after you? And, Mrs. McAllistair, Hassan was nothing more than a minor torment. A night's discomfort. You would have survived Hassan."

She didn't understand the look on his face or the way his fingers seemed to tremble, as if more than anger were goading him.

Suddenly she remembered Eli's words to her. "Someone dislikes you very much."

She swallowed, trembling with a cold fear that coursed along her spine. Her mouth felt dry. "I—I don't know what you're getting at."

"You were about to become a star in the East, Colleen. Hassan…has uses for women in his business deals."

"What? You're crazy! He thought I was a prostitute, or so Eli warned me. He would have—"

Bret turned around, effectively ending the conversation. General MacHowell spoke much more gently than Bret would have. "He would have turned you over to one or more of his partners, Mrs. McAllistair. I'm afraid such things are reality here. Women have few rights. You would have disappeared, American or no. And as long as you were appealing and useful, you would have survived. As soon as you caused too much trouble, you probably would have fallen into a canal or something of the sort."

"Oh, God!" she said, gasping. She swallowed hard, afraid that she was going to get sick or faint.

Sandy suddenly clutched her hand, trying to offer some kind of support, but Bret didn't turn around. It was silent in the car. Then she turned to search out Mac-Howell's eyes again.

"I don't understand this! If you didn't set me up, who did?"

He shook his head. "I don't know."

Bret gave a snort. "There's only one party left who it could be."

"Holfer? Rudy Holfer?" Colleen whispered.

"MacHowell thinks he's here, too," Bret said stiffly. "He's never seen him, but he believes it."

Again Colleen started to shiver. What kind of a human being could so coldly and calculatedly have set up the entire thing? Her kidnapping and sale—through a third party—to men capable of thinking of her only as a commodity, to be disposed of when they were through!

The same person who had ordered Rutger's death.

And the only suspect left was Rudy Holfer, the German who had been transferred to the elite SS corps of the Third Reich just before he had disappeared.

"Oh, God!" she whispered again.

Bret seemed to suddenly explode from the front seat. "Idiotic...brat!"

"Children, children, please!" Carly interrupted pleasantly. "Bret, I really think we've had enough excitement for the night without causing poor Ben to drive off the road. You're wrecking his nerves. We have a long drive ahead of us."

"And you'll all come back to my place, of course, where we can sort this bloody thing out," MacHowell said easily. Colleen could have sworn that he winked at her. "In warfare, my dear, you learn that the most frightening battle, once it's over, must be considered a battle won. And then, of course, it is time to go on to the next." He smiled. "You do realize that we now have three pieces of the puzzle. And each other. We'll get some sleep and look at everything afresh in the morning."

In the morning…

It was almost morning, Colleen realized. Her second morning in Morocco. And Bret was here.

And they were already three-quarters of the way through the puzzle.

THE SKY WAS pink when they reached Marrakech. Mac-Howell's place was actually on the outskirts of the city, but Colleen's luggage had to be retrieved from her hotel. She and Bret were careful not to speak to each other except in necessary monosyllables; they were both tired and furious yet determined not to explode again in front of the others.

After picking up Colleen's luggage Ben began driving to MacHowell's residence. He seemed depressed until MacHowell casually invited him to stay, too. "You might as well, dear boy. You've been in on things this far!"

It was about seven o'clock when they drove through a set of immense wrought-iron gates and approached a marvelous, two-storied estate in the native shell pink. It had romantic Moorish archways and endless balconies and towers; the arches were framed with dazzling tiles, and the entryway was an elegant study in marble. Surveying the place, Colleen found herself surreptitiously watching MacHowell and wondering if he hadn't found the diamonds years ago. Surely this mansion had cost an arm and a leg, even on the outskirts of Marrakech.

He must have noticed her gaze because she found him watching her with a sad, little smile as they crawled out of the car.

"Family money, my dear. After the war I sold all my holdings in England. There was nothing left for me there except guilt. I came to Morocco and bought a tile factory."

She nodded, lowering her head, not sure if she believed him or not.

A slim woman in a caftan and a man clad in a robe hurried down the steps. MacHowell said something in Arabic; the two nodded and hurried back up to the house.

"Fatima and Abhad will have rooms ready for you in a few minutes. We'll have coffee in the courtyard."

Seconds later they were all in the courtyard, gazing about with fascination. There was a fountain in the center, tinkling melodiously and catching the reflection of the rising sun. Massive stairways leading to the living quarters flanked the tiled courtyard. Carly commented idly that someone could do a story on MacHowell's estate alone.

MacHowell served them all coffee in delicate china cups. Ben leaned back against a pillar and stared about him. Carly wandered around, and Sandy and MacHowell sat across from one another at a little table and began to speak in quiet tones, MacHowell telling her all the good things he could think of about her grandfather.

Colleen tried to keep her distance from Bret. His eyes were red rimmed from lack of sleep, his hair was disheveled and his chin sported a night's growth of tawny beard. She wasn't ready to offer her gratitude to him yet. She was still too stunned by recent events, both threatened and real, and too hurt by his anger and total lack of tenderness. And too tired. She was afraid that if they tangled now, it would be a cat fight. They both needed sleep.

MacHowell's houseman, Abhad, returned quickly to say that their rooms were ready. Colleen was relieved. She felt a bit like falling apart and was praying that she wouldn't until she was alone. She murmured a thank-you to MacHowell along with the others and nodded when they all agreed to adjourn at three o'clock in the courtyard.

But as soon as they reached the top of the stairway, she knew she was in trouble. Abhad pushed open the door to a huge, breezy room with a view of the distant mountains and indicated that it was to be Bret's.

Bret gripped her wrist. "Thanks, Abhad. My wife and I will be very comfortable here."

Colleen stiffened, too nervous and tired for one of his private tirades. She was also keenly aware of the others around them and of the warning silver sizzle in his eyes.

She smiled. "Bret, we're both so exhausted…" Her voice trailed away with the silent reminder: and everyone here knows that we're in the process of a divorce!

His smile was even more pleasant than hers. His voice might have been the most congenial purr. "Sweetheart, I wouldn't dream of letting you out of my sight again."

A slight push against her back sent her stumbling unprepared into the room. Bret told the others quietly, "Good night. 3:00 P.M."

Then he closed the door, turned around and leaned against it—and stared at her like the cat who had just cornered the canary.

Chapter Nine

"Bret, I am not sleeping in this room with you!"

"Why not? You didn't have any problems the other night."

"I didn't intend—"

"Oh, I know you didn't. You intended to charm me into a stupor and nothing more. But…" He lifted his arms in a helpless gesture. "'The best laid plans of mice and men oft go astray.' Robert Burns wrote that, I believe." He sounded polite. Very cordial.

Nerve-rackingly cordial. And he was smiling now, leaning against the door. "And your plans did go slightly astray, didn't they?"

"My plans?" She reiterated sweetly. "I really don't know what you're talking about. You're the one who sat over at Carly's swilling Scotch all day. I didn't have a damned thing to do with it."

"Ah. I see. The dinner, the whirlpool, the wine… that was all just because you're really sweet and giving at heart, right?"

"Why not?" Colleen returned with nervous bravado. Damn him. He looked good. He was standing there goading her, and he looked good. Disheveled, bearded, bleary-eyed and all, he looked wonderful to her. And all in all, whatever his motive, he *had* come flying through a window, ready to do battle for her. Besides, he was right. How far would she have gotten? She swallowed, chilled at the thought of having been caught. Returned to Hassan, then passed on when he was through with her.

If only he hadn't yelled at her with such furious hostility. If only…

If only what? she wondered bleakly. They were constantly at odds. Constantly going in different directions. Constantly fighting.

And he had a tendency to win. He would win tonight. But she wasn't going down without a fight. Not when this little interlude of his was going to cost her all over again in heartbreak.

His lashes lowered; then he rubbed his stubbly chin with his palm and grimaced. "I see. You were all charm, Colleen. It was sheer accident that you forgot to warn me that you intended to run out in the morning. To Marrakech, of all places. One man has already been murdered, but you blithely run off to Marrakech. A slip and nothing more."

Colleen turned around to walk over to the window. Beyond her lay a fertile oasis of palms and brush, and behind that, far away, rose the mountains, gold and mellow with the morning. The floor beneath her was fabulously tiled and scattered with rich Persian rugs. The bed was massive, larger than king-size, and covered with a handwoven brocade spread. The dressers and wardrobes and end tables were low and Moorish and beautifully carved. She could see the open door to the bath, done all in white, with curved windows and a massive, round, claw-foot tub that seemed to beckon.

Two people. This was a perfect place for two.

She closed her eyes. She was crazy. She had been crazy to get so close to him again, crazy to make love with him. Crazy to risk an involvement that could only end in pain. That would end completely in divorce court, not even a month from now.

She turned around. He was still leaning against the door, watching her lazily. Like a smug cat again, pawing away at the canary playfully—before the kill.

"Really, Bret, think about the situation. It would be best if we didn't sleep together."

"You're welcome to the floor."

"What?"

"I'm not going to drag you into bed against your will, Colleen, even if you do deserve a little dose of your own medicine. A little good old-fashioned treachery. But I'm too damned tired to play games. I'm not going to attack you, seduce you or touch you. But neither do I intend to let you out of my sight again."

Colleen clutched her fingers together, not sure if she was relieved, insulted or heartbroken. She *was* tired, though, and dangerously close to tears. She'd wanted to be competent, but now, more than anything, she wanted to be held and cherished and assured that everything was going to be all right. Even if it were a fantasy.

But he didn't want her.

"Well?" he inquired lightly.

"Well?" she whispered.

He lifted his hands. "What's it to be? A truce for the time being? I'd dearly love to take a bath and relax, but if you won't give me your word to sit still…"

The words fell warningly on the air.

She leaned against the window, and a cool, mocking smile curved her lips. "Let me hear this one. If I don't, what?"

He seemed to muse over the question carefully, walking farther into the room as he pulled his shirt over his head. Despite herself she watched him, her heart catching a little, her abdomen warming and quivering inside at the bronzed muscles of his shoulders, the tightly sinewed display of his broad back and narrow waist, the temptation of the curly blond hair that feathered his chest.

"Hmmmm…" he murmured, tossing his shirt on the foot of the bed and planting his hands on his hips. He angled his head slightly, surveying her as he might a computer program. Then he shrugged, and she realized that his temper had faded somewhat, that the silver glitter in his eyes now was one of amusement.

"If you won't be a good kid—and heaven knows, shame at the hassle you created should cause you to be so—I'll have to forsake that nice, calming, soothing idea of a long hot bath. And we'll have to stretch out together just as we are now. Since it would be rather crude, not to mention archaic, to shackle you to the bed, I'd have to sleep with my arms around you to see that you didn't disappear again."

"Oh, really? I thought you weren't going to touch me."

"Only if you insist. I would, however, take your word for your good behavior. Damned if I know why, but I would."

"You're always so complimentary, Bret. How did I ever survive without your honey-sweet tongue?"

He grinned suddenly. "You like my tongue, huh?"

"Oh, go to hell, will you!" Colleen snapped. He

chuckled, and she was determined not to lose her cool again.

He was walking toward her, and the quivering sensation began all over again. That feeling of melting inside and becoming electric at the same time.

She lowered her eyes and quickly walked past him to perch on the foot of the bed. "I'll give you my word that I'll stay, Bret. But you can take the floor."

"Not on your life, my love. I'm exhausted. Ah, come on, Colleen! I saved your damned life! I saved you from the arms of a fat pervert—"

"Maybe I like fat perverts!" Colleen interrupted. Damn, she'd been wrong! She'd made a mistake. She could have been killed.

She needed nice words. Gentle words. Not his flippancy and erratic temper.

"Colleen…"

"Oh, go take your bath! Drown in it, for all I care! I won't leave!"

"Do you mean that?" he asked her softly.

She stared down at her hands. "Yes."

She heard him turn. A minute later she heard the sound of rushing water.

She fell back on the bed, casting her arm over her eyes with a sigh that threatened to turn into a sob. Things had gotten so out of hand. The story, her life. Bret was there, not thirty feet away. She loved him so much, but there was nothing she could do. She was so tired, yet on edge. If only she could forget everything else and go to him, maybe, just maybe, he would forget that he was furious, that she had tricked him, that…

That they were getting a divorce he obviously wanted.

And maybe *she* could forget that loving him with all

her heart could not make their marriage work, could not make him love her, really love her, more than journalism, more than a story.

BRET SANK INTO the tub, instantly glad of its warmth. Maybe it would make him stop shaking. Maybe it would give him more control over himself. He'd never been so scared in his life. Terrified. In his line of work he'd seen so many horrors, so much death and pain and despair. He'd always been touched by it, but he'd learned that no man could cure the despair of the world. He had helped when he could;

he'd learned to be distant when he could not. Yet the thought of Colleen, of something horrible happening to her, had shattered everything inside him. Even when things had been all right, when she had been safe with him again at last, all he had been able to do was yell and scream.

She had been stupid, he reminded himself.

Not really. She just wasn't equipped to deal with ruthless and desperate people.

Still, he'd wanted to hold her, clutch her to him, touch her everywhere and assure himself that not an inch of her flesh had been harmed. But he hadn't been able to do that, only shake and yell and scream and play out his fear in fury. Somehow he always did that. He wanted her so badly, yet she might have been a crystal glass, something he was terrified to hold because he would be too clumsy. He would touch her, and everything would shatter all around him.

He sank farther into the tub, closing his eyes and splashing warm water over his face. This thing had to end. Quickly. Because he couldn't stand this kind of fear. He couldn't go on worrying that someone might be after her for what she knew.

Worrying…when he couldn't be with her. When he couldn't hold her, touch her, love her, have her at his side always. He opened his eyes, reaching for the soap.

And that was when he saw her.

She was standing in the doorway, a massive towel wrapped around her. It was white. Her hair curled over it like black waves. One shoulder leaned against the doorframe, and her head rested against it, too. She was watching him with her eyes wide, her lips twisted into a wistful little smile that tore at his heart.

"I thought I could use a bath, too," she told him quietly. "Would you mind?"

He leaned back and smiled at her slowly, then lifted his hands from the rim of the tub, indicating the size of it. "It's a big tub," he told her.

She started to walk toward him, then hesitated. Bret lifted a hand to her. She came nearer and knelt down by the tub. He reached out, lacing his fingers through the hair at her nape, his hand gently cupping her skull as he pulled her to him. "Come here, babe," he said softly and she did.

His lips touched hers and parted them, and he felt all the fiery warmth of her kiss. She dropped the towel as her arms moved around him. Her nails raked through his hair, ruffling it, and then her fingers were on his shoulders. Everything was moist and warm, the water, the steam around them, the salt taste of her tears as they slid down her cheeks.

Bret stood, feeling the sleekness of her body next to his, the welcoming softness of her breasts. He swept her into his arms, then slowly sat again, cradling her on his lap in the bath. His whispers touched her throat; his fingers rippled over her belly and then hugged her close against him, her back to his chest, her buttocks on his thighs. "Don't you know…don't you know?" he whispered hoarsely. "I almost went out of my mind. Colleen, please, for the love of God, don't do anything like this to me again."

She twisted around, slipping an arm around his neck and laying her head against his chest. "I'm sorry, Bret. I'm really sorry. I was so terrified. Hold me, Bret…."

He did. He held her tightly against him, and he moved his hand gently along her arm. It was comfortable. Natural, as it had been to be naked together when they were truly married. Just to be together, knowing each other so well, was a delight.

And it was also sexy. Exciting, just as it always had been. Her breast seemed to move into his palm, and it was natural for him to caress it, tease and taunt the nipple, then grow hard and hot himself as the bud crested at his touch. Natural for him to moan softly, to duck and touch it with his tongue, and then taste its fullness in his mouth. Natural for them both to spiral ever closer to a fever of desire as she moaned and arched against him.

"Do you know what you're doing to me?" he asked her breathlessly. Her eyes seemed completely golden now, still brilliant with the mist of tears, yet heavy lidded like those of a hunting tigress.

"I think you're doing it to me," she corrected him, and she moved slightly, sinuously, against him, using her body to sensuously stroke the heart and heat of his desire.

"Witch!" he accused her, growling slightly, and he cast back his head to better search out her eyes. "If we share the bath, we'll share the bed," he warned her, and as he spoke, he brought his hand questing intimately between her thighs.

He heard the sharp intake of her breath and shuddered, then watched with fascination as she moistened her lips with the tip of her tongue and smiled slowly, wickedly, invitingly....

"Must I wait for the bed?"

Her fingers, delicate, elegant and masterfully exciting, closed around him. His heart gave a little thud, and a jet-speed thrill of heat coursed through him. He could have sworn he ceased to breathe.

He watched her as she gracefully moved over him, the sleek tenderness of her thighs wrapping around his hips. And he lifted his hands from the tub again as he smiled at her.

"Like I said, it's a damned big tub."

His hands spanned her waist, helping her, guiding her, touching her, finding the fevered rhythm of their need. He caressed her buttocks, stroked her back, touched her breasts and loved the beauty of her face. Wild feathers of raven-black hair curled around her shoulders, as wanton as the reckless passion that flamed between them. Sweet and urgent, increasing with every gasp for breath, each rampant beat of their hearts, each driving thrust and stroke that melded them ever closer together. So good...

Until the crest, the pinnacle. The wondrous moment when the sheen of their bodies matched the glitter of the water, when they gasped out their pleasure, when she fell against him, moaning with a strangled little cry and shuddering with the shattering impact of the climax that had burst upon them.

She closed her eyes, savoring the feeling. The

warmth of the water around her, the warmth that seeped through her, his warmth, filled her body with ecstasy, touching her like a tangible eulogy for the love that might have been.

He held her and tenderly nibbled at the lobe of her ear. "This doesn't mean that you get out of sharing the bed," he said hoarsely.

"You're greedy," she mumbled lazily.

"You're right," he whispered.

She didn't mind. Finally he stirred, telling her that the water was growing cold. Then they both started laughing because neither of them had realized that they had soaked the floor with wild sprays of water overflowing from the tub.

"We need to soak it up..." Colleen began.

"It will wait," he assured her. Bret was already out of the tub, sweeping up the huge towel she had discarded earlier. "Stand up, Venus," he teased. "I'm still in my Errol Flynn mood."

"What...?"

He was grinning; she was laughing. He caught her hands and pulled her to her feet.

"I'm going to slip and break my neck," she said.

"Oh, quit bitching and live recklessly," he countered, then wrapped the towel around her and lifted her extravagantly into his arms.

"All right, *you're* going to slip in the puddle and kill us both!" she accused him, giggling into his chest.

"Don't you ever shut up?"

She did a second later when she descended on the bed and he took a flying leap to land beside her, instantly attacking her with kisses on her throat, her breasts, her cheeks.

She laughed and caught her breath. He teased and fondled and suckled her breast and began to whisper, "I love…"

Another kiss followed, and she almost cried out, Say it, say it, oh, please say it.

"I love…to make love to you."

Tears came like fire to her eyes. Those were not the words she craved, yet they were enough. She had warned herself that this could not last forever. And she would not deny what was between them now.

She caught his cheeks between her hands and stared hungrily into the silver depths of his eyes. She kissed him with passion and greed and tenderness and told him that she loved to make love to him. It was enough.

"WHAT WE DID was wrong. That cannot be contested," James MacHowell said to Colleen.

They were alone in the courtyard; Colleen had awakened before Bret and came restlessly down to the courtyard to find something to eat. MacHowell had been there when she'd skipped down the last of the stairs, giving instructions to his houseman. Seeing her, he ordered a typical English tea, with scones, pastries and meat pies. The tea was Earl Grey; the meat pastries had an exotic taste. They were lamb, MacHowell told her, and though the recipe was English, the flavor was all Moroccan.

Colleen didn't really care what they were; she was starving. So hungry, in fact, that she ate several before sighing softly and leaning back with her tea. That was when MacHowell had begun to reminisce.

His green eyes were cloudy, as if he were seeing another time, actually going back. As if he had done so many times before. "Yes, it was wrong. Very wrong, and we all knew it. But…" He paused, shrugging. "It was not quite so wrong as it appears today. We did not know how many would die; we had no idea…" Again he shrugged, and the movement seemed to be filled with his pain. "It was near the end of the war, you see. We were all so tired. Before France, I had been in Italy. One day we would take a town. The next day the Germans would take it back. We never knew, we just never knew. Then, in France, it was worse. You would think you were safe, you would think you could sleep for the night in a deserted barn, and you would lie down and find that the hay had been mined. I started in the ranks, but I worked my way up during the war to become a general. I never wanted to be one. I wanted to go home. I was sick of watching young men die, watching them smile one minute, then seeing them blown into pieces the next."

He took a sip of his tea, sighed and shuddered. "The whole thing came about because Holfer and I were trying to avoid the battle. History has taught us that the war ended in '45. We did not know how close it was then. Holfer was, I believe, more tired than I. He had just come from the Russian front, where he had watched his men starve and freeze. Again history has taught the world that the Germans were the villains of the Second World War. That Hitler was a lunatic. Holfer did not know that then. He led troops of boys, foot soldiers, common fighting men. They knew only battle and death. Nothing of politics, death camps or that their great 'Fatherland' had been doomed from the start. That's always the pity of war, my girl. Innocent boys and young men go out to fight it, while politicians direct it from their desks. Poof! A squadron is wiped out.

They remove a little pin from a map. That is all. They do not see the blood and the death…but forgive me. I am not asking that you excuse any of us. I am not giving excuses for Holfer, or Rutger Miller—or even Sam Tyrell. We were all in on it. This French partisan told us that he knew where the Helmond diamonds were hidden. Fabulous, fabulous diamonds, once owned by an aristocratic Franco-Deutsche family, now the property of the French government. A man could escape the war with those diamonds. He could live for an eternity with another name, another identity. In fact, many men could escape the war with them…."

His voice trailed away. He drained his tea, then lit a cigar with shaking fingers. "Well, you know the rest. All hell broke loose while we were stealing the diamonds. Thousands died—while the generals were stealing diamonds. Thousands."

Watching MacHowell, Colleen could not help but feel sympathy. Though he had not been executed as Sam Tyrell had, that might have been the more merciful punishment. The ravages of guilt on the man's face told Colleen that he had paid with every moment of his life since the slaughter. Yet she didn't know what to say; she couldn't assure him that it was all right. It hadn't been. It wasn't.

She moistened her lips with a sip of tea. "General, what happened…after? I spoke to Rutger, you know. He told me that he and Rudy Holfer escaped through Switzerland to Austria straight after the battle. What happened to you?"

He smiled with bitter ruefulness. "I ran into the field. When I heard the noise of battle, I knew something had gone horribly wrong. I ran straight into the field. It wasn't from bravery, though. It was pure horror. I was desperate to try to do something. Instead, I didn't do a damned thing. I got shrapnel in my shoulder. I thought I was dead for sure. But I didn't die. I woke up in a hospital, clear of any thought of a court-martial. I was suddenly a downed hero."

"So why did Sam…?"

MacHowell shook his snow-white head miserably. "Sam was probably the most innocent of the lot of us. But he ran, you see, with the diamonds. And the Americans, well, it was a time when patriotic feeling was running very high. Americans did not betray other Americans or their allies. Sam was a scapegoat for every other man who made a wrong move, who went AWOL, who picked up a bottle of French wine or plundered delicacies from a shop window. He was judged guilty before he was even tried."

MacHowell picked up a small ivory cigarette box from the table and passed it to Colleen. She accepted and lit one with a quick thanks, then leaned back, exhaling, to study MacHowell again. She did feel sorry for him, terribly sorry. A moment's greed had in a very real sense cost him his life. He had lived in his own hell ever since.

"General, why didn't you ever try to find the diamonds? Why did you come here and disappear?"

"I didn't want the diamonds after I saw what happened because of them. And I came here because I couldn't endure being back in England, knowing what I had done to so many of my countrymen." He smiled, puffing on his cigar, watching the smoke drift from it. "I know where the diamonds are—or at least what country they're in," he said flatly.

"You do?" Colleen said, stunned.

He reached into his breast pocket and produced a sheet of paper, old, brittle and worn at the edges. Colleen recognized it instantly; she had already seen two such pages.

Rutger's and Sandy's parts of the puzzle were both locked safely in her office, yet both had been perfectly reproduced and hidden upstairs in her luggage. She felt a stirring of excitement; the puzzle was so close to being solved! And once it was solved, she would be safe again. Sandy Tyrell would be safe again.

"Can—can I see it?" Colleen asked a little breathlessly.

"Of course."

He opened the paper and smoothed it out on the table. Colleen stared at it. There were no words in any language on MacHowell's paper. There was simply a shield with a beautiful medieval coat of arms.

She stared at MacHowell, baffled. "What is it?"

"A coat of arms."

"Yes, yes, I know. Of what?"

"Vienna."

"Vienna! The diamonds are in Vienna?"

MacHowell shook his head. "No. At least I don't think so. Tyrell resented me the most. I was the other Ally, and I became a bit of a hero, while he was to lose his life. He sent me this, I believe, because it's really the most obvious. He was finally caught and arrested by the MPs in Austria. It stands to reason that the diamonds would be there."

"Perhaps. General…" The words came from over Colleen's shoulder, and she quickly turned around. Bret was leaning against the wall at the foot of the stairway, watching them both coolly, and she wondered how long he had been there. He started toward them as he continued. "When you see the pieces of the puzzle that we have, they will make more sense to you than they do to us."

He dropped the copies of the pieces Colleen had carried in her luggage on the table. Colleen stared at them, then looked furiously up into his eyes. In her absence he must have thoroughly rummaged through her things.

MacHowell didn't seem to notice the renewal of the hostilities between them. He spread out the other sheets. "The mountains, yes. A ski lift. Earth Is the Mother. Yes, this all makes sense. They are buried somewhere in the Austrian mountains near a ski lift. Most probably near Salzburg, I would say. *N'Oubliez Pas*. This means nothing to me. Do Not Forget? No, no, I do not know what this means."

He looked up at Bret. "Sorry. I can tell you no more than that. And again, I am sorry. I do not care if the diamonds are ever found or not. They are nothing but misery. They are best forgotten."

"General," Bret hunched down by the table, his tone quiet and persuasive, "they cannot be forgotten. This is no longer a mystery from forty years ago; it's a mystery of the present. A man was murdered—cruelly, viciously murdered—not forty years ago, but now. And it was assuredly over those diamonds. Others are in danger because of them. Tyrell's granddaughter. Colleen. Myself. Even you, General MacHowell."

MacHowell carefully trimmed the ash off his cigar, staring down at his shaking fingers all the while. "I'm an old man, McAllistair. I cannot matter much."

"All life matters," Bret said simply. "Rudy Holfer must also be an old man, yet not so old that he cannot kill or hire killers. He has to be alive and looking for the diamonds. We have to find either him or the diamonds,

MacHowell. We owe it to Rutger and we owe it to Tyrell. To ourselves, to our own lives. There is no going back."

MacHowell looked up at Bret, his green eyes troubled. He sighed. "Yes, yes. I suppose. So what do we do now?"

"Two things," Bret said.

"And what, pray tell, are they?" Colleen asked a bit caustically.

Bret shot her a dry glance, pulled up a chair and straddled it backward. He spoke to MacHowell. "I think Ben and I should take a look around this evening for our friend Eli and try to find who hired him. Rudy Holfer is obviously somewhere in the vicinity. If we fail to find him, we head for Austria."

"If we head for Austria," Colleen snapped, "we're leading Holfer straight to the diamonds."

"No, I don't think so," Bret returned, pouring himself a cup of tea and taking a huge bite out of one of the pies. "How can we lead him there when we don't really know where we're going? And we'll split up. I know a guy with the U.S. Embassy in Vienna. Bill Dwyer. I think I'll contact him first, then make travel arrangements. You, Carly and I will go somewhere in Lower Austria. MacHowell and Sandy can start off in the Tirol region. Dwyer can see that they're protected."

"And what about us?" Colleen demanded.

"Oh, us, too, of course."

Colleen threw up her hands. "And what is all this going to prove?"

"I'm not sure," Bret admitted. "But Holfer can't follow both parties. We'll travel separately and spend a few days apart, then meet somewhere outside of Salzburg."

"And?"

"And hope that something brilliant comes to one of us."

Colleen didn't get a chance to reply. Carly spoke up from the bottom of the stairway. "What's this? Where are we going?"

He approached the table, and Bret began to show him the maps and explain. Colleen noticed that Sandy, still pale and wan, was also in the courtyard, and that Ben, yawning away, had followed Carly down the stairs. Bret backed away from the table to explain it to them.

Ben cleared his throat. "Where am I going?"

"What?" Bret muttered, a little surprised. "Ben, you've been great. But you're not involved in this."

Ben sat down stubbornly and buttered a pastry. "You will need me to help find Eli, yes? I have a passport. I have travel papers. I have been in this!" He raised his dark eyes to Bret. "Mr. McAllistair, please! I can be your driver. I am the best driver in the world! I can speak a little of almost everything. I can—"

"He can come with us!"

Everyone turned, startled, as Sandy spoke up at last. She looked at Bret accusingly. "If we're going to split up, Ben can come with us. That way there will be three of us, too." She paused, swallowing. "I never thought that we would split up. Please, let Ben come. The general is old. I'm terrified."

Bret threw up his hands. "You're in, Ben." Then his eyes narrowed, and he wagged a playful finger. "So eat quickly, will you? I want to take a trek back into town to visit the police and find out what we can about our friend Eli's acquaintances."

Smiling happily, Ben dug into his food. Colleen moved away from the table to give the others room.

Still thoroughly irritated that Bret had gone through her things without a word to her, she asked him coldly, "How soon are we leaving?"

He arched a brow at her tone. "For where?"

"For the police station, to find Eli."

"You're not going."

"But I—"

"For once in your life, Colleen, make things easy! Please stay here."

"I'm the one—"

"Who's in the greatest danger. If we're worried to death about you every second, how the hell are we going to find Eli?"

She opened her mouth to argue that since she was the one who had been attacked, she had more right than anyone to be involved, but before she could speak, she felt a gentle hand on her shoulder. It was Carly.

"He's right, Colleen."

Colleen closed her mouth and nodded, inwardly admitting that she was ready simply to fight Bret on anything because he'd searched her luggage. But that was a private issue; she could bring it up later—and she would. It seemed that every time she came close to him, she paid dearly.

She stared down at her feet while Carly gave her a paternal hug. As she stared at the ground, she began to frown. Sandy's delicate beige sandals were damp and gritty.

She looked up at the woman and interrupted someone's conversation. "Sandy, your feet are all wet."

Sandy flushed. Colleen thought she looked exceptionally beautiful. Tired and wan seemed to become elegant and feminine on her. "I wanted to see the mountains," she told Colleen. "I needed some air. But," she shrugged miserably, "I walked outside and…panicked. I came back in. I would love to walk and look around…."

Bret laughed pleasantly. He strode over to Sandy and took her hand with a little squeeze. "I can remedy that. Come on, I'll take you for a walk while Carly and Ben finish eating."

Sandy looked at Bret with gratitude and something like awe and rapture. The two of them walked away.

Colleen sat at the table again, smiled radiantly at the general and lit a cigarette, thinking that the flame she produced with the lighter was no hotter than the one shooting through her. She was jealous, damn it.

She wanted to scratch Bret's eyes out and throw Sandy in the dirt and roll her around.

How could she be so insane? she asked herself bleakly. She kept needing him, wanting him, loving him and he was a free agent in every way that mattered. Hadn't she been the one to file the divorce papers?

"There's one thing that bothers me."

"Pardon?" Colleen realized that she hadn't been paying any attention to James MacHowell, though he had assumed that she was.

"Holfer," he murmured.

"What about Holfer?" Carly asked, pulling up the chair across from Colleen and helping himself to tea.

MacHowell shook his head sadly. "I just wouldn't have thought it of him. Killing Rutger like that…"

"I don't think Rudy Holfer killed Rutger in person. I think he paid for the assassination," Colleen said. Really, what was the matter with her? This was serious, sad, vital, and all she could seem to think about was Bret. With anger, with jealousy, with the heartache that constantly reminded her that she had never stopped loving him.

"I still don't see it." The general struck a match and held it to his cigar. "It's been over forty years since I've seen him, but…"

"He had just been switched to the SS," Carly reminded MacHowell.

"But he didn't want it. Don't you see? That's one of the reasons he was ready to go for the diamonds. When we went into the basement of that church in France to get them, he told me quite disdainfully that he considered the so-called glorious corps to which he was being transferred to be nothing more than a group of cowardly vultures. He was a fighting man, a soldier of the field. Not a murderer."

"But really, MacHowell, you barely knew him," Carly said.

MacHowell shrugged. "That's true. Still…" He shrugged again. "I suppose that none of us ever knows the other fellow completely, do we?"

He sipped his tea as the group fell silent. Carly and Ben ate quietly, leaving MacHowell and Colleen to their own thoughts.

No, we never really know one another, do we? Colleen mused sadly. For all that she had loved Bret, loved him and lived with him, he was constantly surprising her. Hurting her, angering her and then touching her again. Never letting her forget that she did love him. Even if she didn't know him completely, didn't fully understand him.

And then there was Sandy.

Oh, damn them both! she decided in anguish. Then she

tried to convince herself that she was being ridiculous, that the two of them had done nothing but go for a walk.

She sighed softly and decided on more tea. She was going to try very hard to act as if she hadn't noticed. To tell him he had no right to go through her luggage, but nothing more. She was not going to act jealous, since it would only amuse him.

She wasn't going to have a damned bit of control over what she said to him in the long run, she admitted sheepishly. And she was going to be nervous and miserable until she did get a chance to be alone with him and tell him exactly how she felt.

"Do you?"

"I'm sorry. Do I what?"

"Play chess?" MacHowell asked her.

"Oh, yes."

"Good! We'll have something to keep our minds occupied."

Nothing will occupy my mind but Bret, Colleen thought.

Yet something else did come to her while she sat across the chessboard from MacHowell.

His place really was magnificent. Fabulous in every way, very, very expensive. What if he was right about Holfer? If Holfer could not be a murderer? What if General James MacHowell was capable of incredible deception?

Then it was quite likely that they were being hosted by the murderer himself.

And that was not a comfortable thought at all.

Chapter Ten

Bret must have come in very late. Colleen had fallen asleep waiting for him, and she hadn't even awakened when he'd entered the room and crawled in beside her. But as she lazily opened her eyes, aware that it was sometime around dawn, she knew that she was curled with her back to his side. A little startled, she swung around to look at him.

He was awake, wide-awake, his fingers laced behind his head, his gray gaze staring ahead at nothing. He didn't look at Colleen; he just spoke. "Eli is dead."

Colleen gasped. "Dead!"

"The police found him at about midnight, at the bottom of a well."

"How?" Colleen whispered.

"Throat slit."

"Oh…" she murmured, feeling ill and clutching the sheets around her.

Bret swung his legs off the bed, ran his fingers through his hair, then shot her an assessing glance. "Don't, Colleen. Don't waste any sympathy on him. He would have sold his own kids for a profit. You live like that, you're bound to get caught."

Colleen nodded. It wasn't that she was feeling sym-

pathetic; the man had been willing to sell *her* to certain
death. It was just so frightening. Rutger and now Eli.
Someone was playing for very high stakes. But weren't
the diamonds just that?

"You okay?" he asked her.

"Yes."

"Good." He rose and reached to the floor for his
jeans. He'd been sleeping in his white shorts; for some
reason she smiled a little, remembering that he hated
fancy-colored underwear. She'd once bought him a
pair with little hearts on them for Valentine's Day; he'd
stared at them and laughed and sworn he'd never wear
them. He never had.

"I'm going to go down and get some coffee. Do you
want me to bring you some?"

"Please."

He disappeared out the door. Colleen crawled grog-
gily out of bed and hurriedly shed the oversize T-shirt
she'd slept in. She dressed in slacks and a cotton shirt
and waited. He'd seemed distant. Cordial, but distant.
She felt a little numb herself.

Half an hour later Bret still hadn't returned to the
room. She'd straightened the bed and the bath, then
cleared a little table by the window so they could sit
there and drink their coffee. Still he didn't arrive. She
was about to go downstairs herself when the door
opened at last and Bret, barefoot and bare chested, re-
entered the room carrying a silver tray holding a coffeepot and delicate cups.

He must have realized how long he had been by the
expression on her face. "Sorry," he told her. "Sandy was
downstairs, and she needed a little soothing."

"Sandy needed soothing?" Colleen echoed sweetly. "And of course you were right there."

She collected the tray from him and set it on the table, poured herself a cup, then took a sip while she casually pulled out a chair and sat down.

Bret hadn't moved. He watched her, then came slowly across the room, poured his own coffee and took a seat across from her. Colleen pretended to study the sun rising over the mountains outside the window. He lit a cigarette and asked with a mixture of curiosity and amusement, "Do I detect a faint note of sarcasm?"

"Sarcasm?" She stared straight at him, eyes innocently wide. "Certainly not. Poor Sandy. We must take care of her at all times, above all else."

Bret leaned closer to her, a little annoyed. "She didn't have to come here, you know. She came because she was horrified that she might have been the cause of some injury to you."

"Ummm," Colleen murmured noncommittally.

Bret began to laugh. "You're jealous, aren't you?"

"Certainly not," she said pleasantly. "Why on earth would I be?" She pushed back her chair and stood to stare out the window from closer range. "Why should Sandy bother me? I have no idea where you've been for months—or who you've been with."

"And that doesn't bother you?" Bret asked quietly.

She searched desperately for an answer, then started with a gasp when his arms suddenly came around her and he whispered in her ear, "Does it?"

For a moment she was tempted to clutch the arms that held her, to tell him yes, it bothered her terribly. That she had lain awake for nights, eaten alive inside while

she tortured herself with visions of him with someone else.

She didn't say any of it. She spun away from him
and returned to the table, where she refilled her coffee cup. "Bret, a few weeks from now you'll be legally
free as a bird. You'll be able to pursue whatever female takes your fancy, though God alone knows who
that might be!"

"Oh? I thought I had rather decent taste in women."
He was behind her again, ruffling her hair so provocatively that she was certain he was going to remind her
that he had married her.

He didn't. He took his seat in front of her again and
smiled pleasantly. "Sandy is beautiful."

"Yes, I suppose she is. Except, of course, that you
have to be into the nervous, skinny, cringing type."

Bret laughed. "Ummm. And I suppose Jerry is God's
gift to single women?"

Colleen ignored the taunt and shook her head sadly.
"I really don't see her for you. No hips. She just doesn't
look like the Earth Mother type."

"Oh, I don't know. I've seen marvelously thin women
with hordes of children."

"You're having a horde?"

"One or two. Possibly three."

"At once? That's a litter."

"You *are* jealous."

"I'm not!"

He raised an eyebrow and coolly lit another cigarette,
a smile tugging at his lips. "Ah, well, I'll have my litter.
And what will you do? Call Rent a Grandchild when
you're finally too old to go story hopping?"

She returned his cool smile. "No, I'll invent them.

I'll tap them out on the word processor from my wheel-chair."

His smile faded suddenly. "It's a pity, Colleen, that you won't let anyone get close to you. I think it was your parents. They died and left you when you were young and vulnerable. Maybe it's not a conscious thing, but I think you live with this fear that if you really care about someone, they'll go away, and you'll be devastated. You'd rather throw them out first yourself. Throw away everything."

She tried to maintain her own smile. "You're wrong, Bret. I'm very interested in loving someone. Someone who isn't more interested in the world at large than his own home. I never threw a thing away. You did."

"You little bitch!" he exploded suddenly, slamming down his coffee cup so hard that the liquid spilled onto the table. He reached out to touch her, but didn't. "Oh, the hell with it! What difference does it make? This argument is useless."

"It is, isn't it?" Colleen said, trying to keep the terrible depression from her voice. "We just don't seem to want the same things, do we?"

"Maybe not," Bret murmured. He hesitated. "Sorry, Colleen. I didn't mean to yell."

She laughed a little wistfully. "You're a yeller, Bret. It's okay. I just wish that—that we didn't fight so easily," she murmured a little lamely.

He pushed his chair away from the table and paced to the door, his hands in his pockets. In a moment he stepped up behind her, gently teasing her cheek with his knuckles. "So do I," he said at last. "So do I."

Colleen caught his hand and kissed the palm, dangerously close to tears. "It's kind of nice, though," she said a little breathlessly, "to have this time together, isn't it?"

His arms locked around her, and he rested his chin on the top of her head. "You don't mind? You had a fit about staying in this room with me at first. Remember?"

"Yes, I remember. But…"

"But what?"

She didn't dare look at him. There was only so much that she could take a chance on giving away. "To say that I don't care for you, that I don't want you physically, would be rather ludicrous. I thought I could deny it. But I can't. That proved rather obvious when we were back home."

"Did you want me?" His chin gently nuzzled her hair. "I wasn't quite sure if you wanted me or simply wanted me dead to the world."

"Plans backfire."

Bret was silent for several moments. "That they do," he said at last. Then he stood, releasing her and starting for the door. "Get your things together, Colleen. With Eli among the departed, we've got no way to trace the man who hired him to dispose of you. And if it was Holfer, we've got no way to search for him. We might as well split up and head to Austria today."

Colleen nodded as Bret set his hand on the doorknob. "Oh!" she said suddenly, stopping him. "Who has the puzzle pieces?"

She saw his lashes lower and his jaw tighten. "I do. Why?"

Colleen stiffened. "I just wanted to know where they were. And by the way, I don't mind being together for this last lovely fling, but I do mind my belongings being riffled!"

He sighed with condescending patience. "Colleen, you walked out while I was still asleep. We needed them. I found them. If you had been a proper sleeping companion and remained by my exhausted side, I could just have asked you for them. As it was, I woke up wondering if you were still in the same country as I was."

"Bret…"

"Don't worry, I won't riffle your luggage again." He grinned suddenly. "I'd much rather riffle your body."

Then he was gone, the door closing behind him. Colleen sat for a long time, drawing patterns on the table. At least they had managed to be a bit mature about the situation. The attraction was still there between them, achingly strong. And they had more or less agreed to stay together for the time being because they wanted one another so badly.

But why, if they wanted one another now, couldn't they make it last for a lifetime? she wondered. Why couldn't they make their marriage work?

If she didn't get up, she would start crying. She planted her hands against the table and stood, then found herself looking around the room instead of packing.

It was a beautiful room. It had been the setting for some beautiful moments between them. She would never forget it.

IT WAS AT the airport that she first saw the tall blond man.

Bret, Carly and MacHowell were at the ticket counter, straightening out their various reservations. Ben was attempting to entertain Sandy with monologues on Moroccan life-styles. Colleen had tried to feign an interest in his words, but it just wasn't there. She felt too disheartened. Despite Bret's plans she felt that the story was about to reach a tragic dead end. Just as their marriage was.

She ambled off a bit from the other two and stared out a plate-glass window. She saw him then, reflected in the glass. He was as tall as Bret, with closely cropped hair so light it was almost platinum. Even in the reflection she could see that startling coloring, his pale, pale hair and startling blue eyes. His eyes were deep and bright and penetrating. He was in a European suit, broad shouldered, slim, very much like a Nordic athlete. She stared at him in the glass, intrigued and unaware for several seconds that he was staring at her, too, that those curious blue eyes were locked with hers.

She spun around. He didn't leave. Instead he approached her.

"Frau McAllistair," he said simply. There was something in his hand, a long white envelope.

"Who…?"

He stuffed the envelope into her purse. "I will talk to you when I may." He inclined his head toward the others. "You should trust no one. I will find you when the time is right. When we can speak. Alone."

He turned crisply on his heel and walked away. For a long moment Colleen was too amazed to run after him, and his steps were so long and determined that he had almost disappeared when she finally did, her heart pounding. Who the hell was he? Not Holfer. He couldn't be Holfer because Rudy Holfer had to be in his seventies, at the very least. This man was young, somewhere between thirty and forty. Bret's age.

Colleen searched through the crowd at the airport, running, pausing, running again. She thought she had caught a glimpse of his platinum head when a hand landed on her shoulder.

"Colleen! Damn it, what the hell are you doing? I can't leave you for a second! You don't have the sense of an untrained chimp! Where were you going?"

She clamped her teeth tightly together and turned around with a fierce effort to control her temper. Bret's eyes were dark with exasperation; his hair had that disheveled look it took on when he had been running his fingers through it with worry. He'd been concerned, she'd grant him that. She was about to shout out that he had made her lose the mysterious blond man when she realized that the others were running up behind him.

She lowered her head quickly, hiding her eyes and struggling for an innocent facade. She didn't know why she felt such a tingling of alarm, but she suddenly decided to keep her secret to herself, at least until she was alone with Bret and Carly.

She raised her head, smiling sweetly. "I'm sorry. I was, uh, just looking for the ladies' room."

Bret looked totally irritated, as if he couldn't believe such stupidity. He made a sound in his throat that was a portent of a lecture to come, but he didn't get a chance to speak because Sandy broke in pleasantly.

"Oh, good! We can go together." Then she turned her lovely eyes on Bret. "That would be all right, wouldn't it?"

He muttered something and threw up his hands. "Let's all head for the ladies' room."

The men waited outside. "I'm sure he doesn't mean to be so brusque," Sandy told Colleen softly when they were alone. "He just worries about you. And not without cause, not here. You were kidnapped, remember."

Colleen smiled. "Thanks, Sandy," she said briefly.

The other woman was trying to be decent, but she wasn't in the mood to hear any suggestions regarding Bret. She knew him too well to want to hear about his motives from another woman, no matter how nicely the advice was intended. As soon as she had the thought, she felt awful; it was true that Sandy didn't have to be here. She was terrified every moment, she had come only to help Colleen and Bret.

"Don't worry," she assured Sandy with a much nicer smile. "I'm accustomed to him. He doesn't bother me." She linked arms with Sandy, and they rejoined the men together.

Bret had a slip of paper for Sandy and some gentle words. "You're going to be fine. This is the name of a friend, Bill Dwyer. He's with the American Embassy. I met him last year when there was a problem with some Austrian wines. He's going to meet you all in Tirol, make some police connections and the like. You feel okay about everything?"

Sandy nodded. It was time for them to part. She gave Bret a fierce hug, then did the same to Colleen and Carly. Ben hugged Colleen and then James MacHowell did, too. "It's been such a pleasure, dear. You've done so much for me."

"General!" she protested. "We'll be back together in a week."

He smiled at her, and she felt a little tremor. Then their flight to Rome, where they could transfer for a flight to Vienna, was called, and she was running with Carly and Bret to make it.

Bret was curt and distant when they boarded the plane. "Don't run off alone again!" he warned her bluntly, then turned his attention to the window.

"What you did was very dangerous," Carly warned her more softly, yet she knew he agreed with Bret that she had behaved foolishly.

Colleen stared down at a magazine without seeing it, impatiently waiting for the jet to become airborne. The hell with you both! she fumed inwardly.

As soon as they had left the ground, Colleen politely excused herself to Carly.

Bret turned around with annoyance. "Again? You just went!"

A flush touched her cheeks. "Bret, really! You can't control everything, you know!"

She swept by Carly and hurried to a rest room. Alone at last, she pulled the envelope from her purse and quickly scanned the note inside.

Dear Mrs. McAllistair:

I am not the villain you think me. I have heard of Rutger's death; I was not the cause. Someone else must wish to claim the diamonds. I do not know who; I do not understand. I will help you all that I can, yet I or my son, Wilhelm, must see you alone since, as I have said, I do not know who may be dangerous. Please believe that I am not a murderer, only a victim of greed.

Sincerely,
Rudolph Holfer

Colleen started trembling; her heart seemed to pound ridiculously loudly in the tiny cubicle. She fumbled with the lock on the door with fingers that shook so badly she could barely budge it. Then she ran down the aisle of the plane and practically leaped over Carly's lap.

"Colleen!"

Both men looked at her with incredulity and annoyance, then curiosity. Her eyes were as bright as new pennies. She was still shivering with excitement. "Look!"

Bret took the note first, then turned to her sharply. "Where did you get this? When?"

"What is it?" Carly demanded, reaching for the paper.

"At the airport. I was trying to chase him—"

"Chase who?" Carly interrupted.

"You were trying to chase Holfer?" Bret grated, staring at her pointedly. "What kind of a fool are you?"

"Holfer?" Carly said.

"Not Rudy Holfer. It was his son, Wilhelm."

"And you were trying to chase him! Good God, Colleen, when the hell will you ever learn? You would have gotten outside and been whisked away again!"

Colleen grabbed his arm in exasperation. "Damn you, didn't you read the note? He isn't guilty! It's someone else!"

"Oh, Colleen!"

"Well, it could be! Bret, I am so tired of your giving absolutely no credence to my words."

Carly cleared his throat loudly. Their flight attendant was in front of them, trying to maintain her antiseptic smile and serve them lunch while pretending she didn't notice the argument.

"Lovely day, isn't it?" Carly said.

Bret and Colleen curved their mouths into plastic smiles. The stewardess set trays before Carly and Colleen, smiled at Bret when he turned down the offer of a meal, then made a hasty retreat. "Bret, Holfer could be innocent!" Colleen insisted in a vehement whisper. She swallowed, realizing what her words could mean. She had liked James MacHowell very much, but she couldn't clear him any more than she could Holfer. He could have staged everything that had gone on. He could have been sympathetic and giving, coming to her rescue with Bret just to get more information on the diamonds, or what they knew. "Bret, MacHowell has that huge estate. Even in Marrakech it must have cost a small fortune."

"But if he has all that money, why would he want the diamonds?" Carly asked her.

"All right, maybe he already found the diamonds years ago. Maybe…"

Bret exhaled loudly. "If he already has the diamonds, why kill Rutger?"

"I don't know," Colleen admitted. "Vengeance? Maybe he thought everything that happened was Rutger's fault…." Her voice trailed away. She felt Bret's eyes on her with condescending patience. "I don't think it's Holfer!" she snapped. "And, as I said before, I am extremely weary of your behaving as if I haven't got a mind!"

"You've got a mind. You just don't know how to use it," Bret responded. "Fact, Mrs. McAllistair: we don't know who *is* guilty and who *isn't*. Therefore, it was foolish for you to have gone running off after anyone alone!"

"It was a crowded airport!" Colleen replied with such vigor that she turned on him and, in doing so, managed to upset her lunch tray onto his lap.

Bret yelped as hot coffee spilled on his leg, and he

jumped up in his seat. His head crashed into the light panel overhead, and he began to swear furiously under his breath.

"Bret! I'm sorry," Colleen said contritely. She tried to pick pieces of lamb off his clothing. "I'm really sorry."

The wary stewardess came rushing back with napkins. Bret accepted her assistance with his teeth clenched, assuring her that he was all right. Again the woman appeared quite relieved to leave them.

"Oh, Lord," Carly groaned. "You two are embarrassing."

"I didn't do it on purpose!" Colleen protested.

"You couldn't have aimed better if you'd tried," Bret muttered. "Just because you're not interested in my future fatherhood…"

"Bret, I said I'm sorry!"

"Not as sorry as I am," he snapped. "Excuse me." He crawled over them both. "I think I'll go to the back of the plane for a cigarette."

Colleen closed her eyes with a sigh as he left. She opened them to discover Carly watching her, barely suppressing his laughter. "It was rather funny," he admitted, and Colleen couldn't help but laugh, too.

Then her laughter faded, and she looked at him bleakly and moaned. "Oh, Carly! Why are we always at each other's throats? I can't make a move without his coming on like a four-star general."

"Maybe he loves you," Carly suggested.

Colleen gazed out the window at the white clouds slipping by them. "Do you know, Carly, that's the funniest thing about it. I believe that he does care. Just not enough."

Carly sighed. "Enough for what, Colleen? Enough to be concerned with the things you do?"

"That's not it, Carly, and you know it. His career is always uppermost in his mind. No, not even his career, really. The lure of excitement or something. Carly, admit it. He walked out on me. And the only reason he's back now—"

"Do you honestly think it's the story, Colleen? You two are like tinder and a match when you get together, and I'm not talking about tempers."

"Carly, it's nice to be together. I admit it. But I'm not naive enough to believe that a few nice nights together can put this Humpty-Dumpty shell of a marriage back together. If he did want a marriage—a real, committed kind of a marriage—he wouldn't always be yelling at me!"

Carly laughed. "Okay, he shouldn't yell. But maybe if you talked…"

"We argue."

"Can I take the window, Colleen?" Carly suddenly asked, moving past her at her nod. He sat down, then winced. "There's still coffee on the seat," he told her. "This is wonderful. I'm the managing editor of one of the most prestigious newsmagazines in the country, and I'm going to running around all day like a kid with toilet-training problems!"

Colleen started to laugh again. "I really am sorry."

He nudged her elbow. "Don't tell me. Tell him."

Colleen glanced up quickly. Bret was back. Carly tactfully turned his attention to the window.

To her surprise Bret slid beside her, put his arm around her shoulders and pulled her head close so he could whisper to her.

"I'm sorry."

She jerked back, staring at him suspiciously. He didn't really look all that sorry. But there was a nice warm sizzle in his eyes, and he was grinning crookedly.

"I didn't mean to jump all over you." He leaned closer and stroked her cheek intimately. "Really."

She trembled a little, touched as always by his nearness, by the gentle tone of his voice.

"Are you, uh, okay?" she asked him, and to her surprise she found she was blushing. "I mean, I didn't cause any real harm, did I?"

"Well, you did wound me."

"I am sorry."

"That's okay. You can kiss it and make it all better."

"Bret!"

"Not now, Colleen. This is definitely a public place!"

She started to laugh, and when he ruffled her hair, she was happy to lean against his shoulder. His scent was so pleasant; he felt strong and warm and wonderful, and she savored his slightest movement. If only they could make it last.

THEY ARRIVED IN Vienna at 8:30 P.M. local time and checked into the Hotel Socher, where Bret had told the others they would be. It was a wonderful place, Colleen thought. There was an old-world beauty about the place with well-polished wood, chandeliers and European charm.

They ate at a sidewalk restaurant, starting with a wonderful Austrian wine that added to the feeling that this was a night of rest. They passed everything around the table: cabbage, potato salad, sausages, rich brown bread, schnitzel and delicious skewered beef. When they had thoroughly stuffed themselves, they sat back with coffee *mit Sahne*, with whipped cream piled high. They discussed everything: the puzzle pieces, MacHowell and the strange appearance of Wilhelm Holfer at the airport.

They didn't come up with anything, but somehow Colleen felt happier. They'd discussed the situation rationally, politely, and Bret had listened intently to everything she'd had to say.

At eleven he said that they needed to go to their rooms, he was expecting to hear from Bill Dwyer by eleven-thirty.

"Just who is Dwyer?" Colleen asked, yawning as she and Bret stepped into their room.

Bret shrugged. "He's an attaché with the diplomatic force here. I only met him briefly, but he was very cordial, and he helped me when I was covering that problem with the wine. He seemed grateful that I kept it from panicking vacationing Americans." Bret paused, then shrugged again. "All I really asked him to do was get some police protection for Sandy and MacHowell. But he was eager to get involved, probably because there really isn't that much for him to do here."

He threw himself onto the bed, next to the phone, laced his fingers behind his head and smiled at her. There was a definite silver glitter in his eyes. "Why don't you take your shower while I wait for my call?"

"I suppose I could," Colleen murmured.

She showered with high excitement already coursing through her body. She combed her hair until it gleamed and touched her body with scented talc and a spray of perfume. Then she wrapped herself in one of the oversize towels and opened the door, ready to be ravished.

But Bret was on the phone. He glanced at her, gave her a remote smile, then stared at the pencil he was idly tapping against the bedside table. Curious, Colleen moved into the room and perched beside him. As she listened to his conversation, she realized that he was talking to Sandy.

Which was fine, really. Except that he talked and talked, soft words, soothing words, encouraging words. Things were going to be all right. Yes, they'd all be together soon. Yes, he missed her, too.

"What?" Colleen asked without thinking.

Bret waved her question impatiently aside and kept talking. She walked angrily back into the bathroom, then returned to stand in front of him. At last he hung up the receiver, looked up and smiled at her.

"That was touching," Colleen said sweetly.

He grimaced. "She needs a lot of reassurance."

"Ummm."

"But she's feeling better now. Dwyer is there, and apparently she likes him."

"How nice."

"Are you ready to make up for your brutalization of my poor body on the plane?" he teased, reaching for her.

Colleen took a small step backward, eluding him. "I certainly am," she promised sweetly. "They say that the very best thing for burns is cold water," she told him, and as she spoke, she doused him with a bucket of ice water that she'd been hiding behind her back.

"Colleen!" He jumped to his feet, this time reaching for her with such swiftness that she couldn't elude his arms. She was pulled against his body, trembling at the strength of his muscles beneath his damp clothes.

She lifted her chin to him, still smiling. "Sandy

doesn't need to get that much assurance on my time," she said pointedly. He still felt rigid and tense, and the eyes that surveyed her shot silver sparks.

"I'm ready, I'm ready!" she protested, and she let her towel fall as she pressed ever closer to him.

His arms tightened around her. She could feel the heat of his arousal through his clothing. He nipped lightly at her earlobe and whispered, "You're going to make it all better?"

She nodded, a little breathless when she finally discovered that she could speak.

"Ummm. I'm going to kiss you…all over."

"Promise?" His hands smoothed down her spine and caressed her buttocks, lifting her to the length of his frame.

In seconds she was lying on the bed, and he was beside her. She began working at the buttons on his shirt, then touched her lips to the pulse at his throat before pausing momentarily to stare into his eyes.

"All over," she said solemnly. "I promise…."

And then she fell silent because she meant to keep that promise.

Chapter Eleven

First thing in the morning Bret called the police in the States. He had expected them to have discovered something about Rutger's death, but he was disappointed. They hadn't found a clue to the murderer. It had all been very neat: no fingerprints, no weapon, nothing at all to help them.

Except, perhaps, the secrets of his past.

Carly made a perfunctory long-distance check with the office; then they started west along the autobahn in a rented VW. At noon they took the turnoff at Melk, drove by the huge and forbidding monastery and in another thirty minutes reached Dernstein, where the main attraction was the ruin of the castle where Richard Lion-Heart had been held in captivity by Leopold V of Austria.

It was a beautiful place, built along the Danube. Tourists were everywhere, but they managed to secure a table at a restaurant right on the water. The Danube, gray that day rather than a poetic blue, ran by them in glorious splendor, and high above the ruins stood sentinel.

They ordered beer and sauerbraten and idly discussed the story layout, should they have a story. It was somewhere during the cover-art conversation that Bret turned rather impatiently to Colleen. "What is your problem? You keep sighing, and you have all the enthusiasm of a wet blanket."

Colleen took a sip of her beer, coughing a little when it seemed to go down the wrong channel. "I just don't think I really understand what we're doing. I mean, this is lovely. Absolutely beautiful. I'd love to be here on vacation, staring at the Danube all day. But we're not on vacation, and I just don't see that any of this is doing any good. Do you really think that anyone who is after us is going to believe that we're dawdling along like tourists?"

Bret shrugged. "Maybe not. I just don't have any better ideas at the moment. Do you? We can hardly tear apart every mountain. They stretch forever once you reach the western border. Who the hell knows, maybe they aren't even near the western border. We're searching for a needle in who knows how many haystacks."

"If we had Holfer's piece of the puzzle," Colleen commented, "we might know."

"It's my fault that we don't, right, because I stopped you from chasing your beautiful blonde?"

"Possibly," Colleen retorted. What had she said to him about Wilhelm Holfer? She lowered her eyes, trying to remember. Yes, she had eventually described him as a striking man, handsome, with beautiful blond hair. Was Bret jealous? How nice, for a change. She couldn't help but be grateful that, for the moment at least, the fragile and elegant Miss Tyrell was no longer with them.

"And that's another thing!" she announced before Bret could respond. "I don't understand anything about this friend of yours, Bill Dwyer. He must have been in Vienna, but rather than waiting for you and Carly and me, he flew out to meet Sandy and MacHowell. Wouldn't it have made more sense for him to talk to us first?"

"First of all," Bret said, "he's an acquaintance, not a friend. We're lucky to get any help from him at all. Second, he probably thinks MacHowell is more important than either of us. And then…" He paused, grinning as he mused.

"Then what?"

"Maybe he's heard about Sandy Tyrell. She is a rather gorgeous creature, you know. Bill is young and single. Maybe he wanted to give her a shoulder to lean on."

"Jealous?" Colleen inquired sweetly.

"Would you two *please* go for a walk," Carly suggested. "Wear off some combat energy. It's not far to the top of the ruins. There's a beautiful view. Just beautiful. You'll be too breathless to argue on the way, and you'll give my tender ears a break!"

Colleen sat back in her chair with a sigh and stared across the table at Bret. His eyes seemed to match the color of the Danube, gray and churning. They had been heading toward another of their whiplash disagreements, and she knew she was as much to blame as he was. She didn't have any answers; she just felt restless and discouraged. She turned her eyes to him, smiling.

"We might as well. Objectively, if we're getting a bit of a vacation out of this, we might as well use it. Carly, sure you don't want to come?"

"Heavens no, I did it before. Back in '65, when I was stationed at Garmisch-Partenkirchen. I'll wait here. Besides, our friends in the Tirol might give us a call, and this way I can let the hotel know where to find me if they do."

Colleen and Bret walked through the narrow winding streets, alive with shops and flowers, that led to the upward trail to the ruins. They found a sign in several languages warning that it was a twenty-minute walk up. "Sure you're up for this?" Bret queried Colleen, glancing down at her shoes. They were sandals with little heels.

"Of course," she returned.

For fifteen minutes she preceded him. In places there were steps, in other places just dirt and pebbles. It began to feel as if she were walking straight up. She was breathing raggedly and grabbing onto an occasional bush to keep her footing long before the first ten minutes were up. She finally paused several feet ahead of Bret, gasping and trying to slow her heartbeat before he caught up to her.

The view was already breathtaking. She could look down and see the town, the spires and the roofs, and the Danube, shimmering beneath the sun. Clouds were beginning to roll in, casting a mist over the mountain.

Bret was panting behind her. She clicked her tongue in disapproval. "You smoke too much," she told him with a saccharine note of concern.

He shot her a dry glance. "And you don't?"

"No, not really." She patted his cheek and started on ahead of him again, calling over her shoulder, "I'm far more moderate. In everything, don't you think?"

"No," he said flatly, and a second later he passed her.

They walked for several more minutes before they passed a couple heading downhill, who gave them a cheerful greeting in German. They both responded, glad of the chance to stop again for a breather. Colleen moved to the outside of the path to allow the others room and was surprised when Bret suddenly gripped her arm.

"What's the matter?" she asked him, startled, as he pulled her back into the center of the trail.

"This isn't the Empire State Building, you know. No guardrails, nothing. You've got to watch your step, especially in those stupid heels."

He released her before she could reply and started up the trail again. "I think twenty minutes must have a different meaning to Austrians, even when it's written in English!" he muttered.

Silently Colleen agreed. It was a beautiful walk, but it was long.

"Ah!" Bret exclaimed. She almost crashed into his back. They had reached a plateau and a section of the wall.

"We're here!" Colleen said joyfully.

Bret shook his head, grimacing. "No, that's where we're supposed to be." He pointed upward, where there were the remains of more walls, arched doorways, parapets, and even a complete chamber. He set his hands on her shoulders and pulled her back against his chest. "But we're close!"

Slabs of rock set in the loose dirt formed the only road up. Bret took Colleen's hand, and she was glad. A fall wouldn't have sent her plummeting down the mountain, but it would have caused her some nasty scratches.

A few minutes later they reached the top, and Colleen was glad that they had come. The breeze was just perfect, cool and inviting. The ruins were intriguing. It was fascinating to wonder about the people who had once walked there, the knights and the ladies, rulers and serfs. The Danube seemed to be a silver ribbon far below them.

Colleen paused in front of a wall with a complete Norman arched window. Bret climbed higher, through another archway to what must have been a parapet.

He breathed deeply, enjoying the view. Then suddenly, and quite inexplicably, he felt as if the hair were rising on the back of his neck, and a chill shook him.

He closed his eyes and listened. Then he heard it, a shifting of stone and dirt, as if there were someone there with them.

But there wasn't. They hadn't passed another person since they had seen the German tourists going down.

He opened his eyes again. It was far from nightfall, but a coming storm had darkened the sky all around them. It seemed that he could touch the dark, brooding clouds, and the wind was whipping all around them. Far below the Danube churned a deeper and deeper indigo gray.

He heard it again: the scattering of pebbles. He remembered his words of warning to Colleen. There were no guardrails here. A step in the wrong direction and... nothing. Nothing but jagged spears of rock for hundreds and hundreds of feet.

He turned around in something approaching panic; he couldn't see her. "Colleen!"

The wind seemed to tear his voice away. Suddenly he heard the fall of something heavy, not a pebble, but a good-size rock.

"Colleen!" Half stumbling, he hurried back to the archway where he had left her, his heart pounding wildly. There were dozens of places here where someone could hide. Behind a wall, in the brush…

"Colleen!" He stopped twenty feet away from her, breathing more easily. She was fine. The wind was whipping her hair about her fine features like a velvet cloak. Her eyes were very wide and brilliant, catching the last of the sun.

"Bret! You should have seen it! It scared the life out of me. That boulder just came—"

He had her hand by then and was pulling her back. "Come on. We're going down."

"Bret, I…"

They both heard it that time: another shifting of dirt and rock. Bret stared at her for one second. She looked so small and slim in her light cotton sundress. Fresh and feminine and fragile—and totally vulnerable.

"Let's go!" he told her and dragged her behind him.

He had been wrong. Night was coming, and quickly now. Bracken and trees seemed to reach out for them; the stone steps were slick and damp, and the dirt seemed to provide no traction. They passed the first stretch of wall and kept going. Halfway down the path seemed to broaden again. For a while it was a simple walk; the lights of the town below were coming closer. Then the path veered, and the steps gave way to rock. Colleen gasped, spinning and tripping. He turned to pull her up, and his eyes caught sight of something on the trail behind them. Something dark moved quickly and disappeared into the brush.

"Come on!" he implored her. Gasping, she fell again. Two steps to the left and she would have been hanging by a fingerhold. Hanging over the cliff, with nothing below.

"A house!" Colleen said with a gasp a few minutes later, and Bret was grateful to see it. It meant that they were almost back to the street. Almost back to people, in full view, where an "accident" could not occur.

"Hurry!" he muttered. The sound behind them was suddenly no longer furtive; they could hear footsteps hurrying in their wake.

Bret pushed Colleen ahead of him. "Run!" he told her, and then he turned, ready to face the attacker and buy her time.

But even as he spun, knees slightly bent, arms braced to lunge, his eyes widened in amazement. His body went lax, and he began to laugh. A second later Colleen was beside him, wrapping her arm around his waist as they panted and laughed together.

Their "attacker" was in full view now. He couldn't have been more than ten years old, and he was looking at them both as if they were definitely crazy. He passed them with a pleasant *Guten Tag*.

Bret and Colleen grimaced at one another. He slipped an arm around her shoulders, and they started to follow the boy at a leisurely pace.

"This is getting to me," Bret groaned.

"You! My dress is ripped, my legs are scratched to ribbons and I don't think my heart will ever beat normally again!"

"Does it beat normally?"

"What?"

"Your heart. I think it's rather frosty, myself."

"Hey, you're the one who's made of stone."

"Am I?" He paused. "I was thinking of you up there. That it would be nice to lock you away in a high tower, where you couldn't get into any trouble."

"Ummm, where I'd be in a place where you could float in and see me and then forget that I exist while you wander around the globe at your convenience."

"You really don't trust anyone. You can't talk without getting nasty, can you? Your parents died, Colleen. They didn't leave you. And you—"

"Talk?" she protested, swinging at him. He saw that she was on the verge of tears, and he wanted to put his arms around her again, yet he feared that she wouldn't let him.

"You're the one who can never—" She broke off suddenly, staring past him.

"What is it?" Bret demanded tensely.

"Carly. He's sitting in that little cemetery at the start of the path."

Bret followed her gaze; she was right.

"What do you suppose he's doing?" she murmured curiously.

"Well, he's not praying over departed strangers," Bret muttered in reply. "He's waiting for us. Something must be up. Come on, let's hurry."

The ground was level enough for them to run, and they did. Carly must have heard their approach because he stood and came around the iron gate to meet them on the path.

"What's wrong?" Bret demanded. Not only Carly's presence but the dark tension in his features warned them there was something very wrong indeed.

Carly hesitated for a second, gazing into Colleen's anxious eyes.

Colleen's mind, riddled with guilt over her dislike of Sandy, instantly moved in the other woman's direction. "Oh, no! It's Sandy!" she whispered. "Something's happened to Sandy."

"No, no. Sandy is fine. Healthy, I mean. It's, uh…" He paused, sighing unhappily. "It's MacHowell."

"MacHowell?" Bret echoed.

"He's dead," Carly said.

"How? What? When?"

Carly shook his head. "I spoke to Bill Dwyer briefly. He said he'll give us all the details when he sees us. Sandy was with him, and Dwyer had to get a sedative for her. We've got to leave right now. We've got to meet them at the Château Moreau outside Salzburg tonight."

Colleen closed her eyes for a minute; the ground seemed to be spinning beneath her feet, and she was afraid that she was going to pass out.

MacHowell! She remembered his face when they had parted, his words. Despite that, she had at least partially suspected him—and now he was dead.

Which left only one more suspect. Rudy Holfer. And she had been ready to run trustingly after his son.

"Colleen, are you all right?"

Bret's arms were around her, holding her, warm and strong and supportive. She nodded. Bret. He was always there for her. And maybe she was wrong. Maybe she *had* been afraid to really love, to hold on with her whole heart. If she could just break past the wall, perhaps she could trust herself to believe the words he might say if she gave him the chance to say them.

"We've got to go," he told her softly.

She nodded. Somewhere there might be time to work on their own lives. But not now. MacHowell was dead. She couldn't believe it; she couldn't accept it. It seemed like empty words.

IT WAS LATE when they reached the outskirts of Salzburg, sometime after midnight. Colleen had been cramped in the back seat of the VW, brooding and wallowing in a certain amount of guilt. She just had a sense about Holfer, no matter how guilty he looked, and that had seemed to leave MacHowell as the villain. By the same token, General James MacHowell had been a nice man. She kept remembering his face and his words.

And now he, too, was dead. So much for her sixth sense. Holfer had to be pulling the strings.

"We're here."

Carly tapped her shoulder. She hadn't even realized the car had stopped. Colleen straightened, stiff and weary. Carly helped her out of the car; Bret was already on his way up the steps to the Château Moreau.

Colleen massaged her neck and stared up at the place; it looked like a miniature fairy-tale castle. The grounds were very green, but the air was cold and crisp. Wide stone steps led to the lobby, and through the plate-glass windows Colleen could see one of the lounges. There was a huge fire burning in a corner; skis were racked along a wall, and couples in sweaters and parkas were drinking steaming concoctions at the warm wooden tables ranged around the fire. Colleen could even hear their laughter.

"A ski lodge?" she murmured to Carly.

"We're looking for a ski lift, remember?"

"Of course," she murmured. She turned around and narrowed her eyes. Moonlight played on the mountains that flanked the château. They were beautiful. It was summer, but they were capped with glistening snow.

Bret came back down the stairs with a uniformed bellboy behind him. "Emil will see to the luggage," he told Colleen and Carly. "Sandy, Ben and Dwyer are here already. They're waiting for us in a little room off the lounge."

Colleen said hello to Emil, then followed Bret as he led the way back up the steps. They turned left before reaching the reception desk, and Colleen discovered that the lounge was down a hallway lined with banners and medieval arms. They passed through the laughing crowd by the fire and into a smaller room off to the side. There was a fireplace there, too, Colleen noticed gratefully. Sandy, Ben and a man who had to be Bill Dwyer were already sitting in front of it at a round wooden table, sipping steaming drinks.

Sandy saw them first. "Oh, you're here!" She leaped to her feet and ran straight into Bret's arms. "I'm so glad to see you, so very, very glad."

Ben smiled a little weakly at Colleen and Carly. Bill Dwyer stepped forward and introduced himself quietly. "I'm sorry that we have to meet under such strained circumstances," he told them. He was a little shorter than Bret, with a medium build, pleasant hazel eyes and light-brown hair. The all-around American, Colleen found herself thinking. He had the perfect voice and manner for his position; he was grave without being morose and appeared both assured and comfortable with his responsibilities. "I took care of things the best I could from here," he went on. "I managed to locate a distant cousin in Yorkshire and arranged to have the body sent back for interment in the family vault."

Carly said something appropriate. Colleen suddenly felt like crying. She wasn't so sure that General Mac-Howell would have wanted to be shipped back to a family vault. He had made his home in Morocco for so long.

"Shall we sit?" Bill Dwyer asked. He gazed at Colleen thoughtfully. "Have you eaten? You look as if you could do with a warm drink. These things are marvelous. Château specials. Coffee with blackberry schnapps and cream. Shall I order for you?"

Colleen gave him a grateful smile and sank down into a chair beside Ben. He looked so depressed that she gave his hand a squeeze. "What happened?" she asked as Carly sat down next to her.

Sandy was still hanging onto Bret's shoulder, murmuring something in his ear.

Ben shook his head bleakly. "I don't know. We wound up parted, but only for a minute. He wanted to see the view. Mr. Dwyer was with us. We thought we would be safe."

"Yes, but—"

She broke off because a smiling waiter was coming in. Bill Dwyer spoke with him in fluent German, then explained in English that he had ordered food, too, because it had probably been hours since they had eaten. Conversation waned as the meal was set up at the table: cold salads with vegetables, steaming hot brown farmer's bread and sautéed veal. Their drinks had come, too, and Colleen discovered that she wanted the hot, spiked coffee more than the food. By the time everything was ready Sandy seemed much calmer. She was seated at Bret's side, a mug in her hand, and when he pressured her gently, she started to talk about what had happened.

"I don't know what to think. The scenery was beautiful, as you can imagine. The mountains were full of color. So many flowers... General MacHowell wanted to be out in the air; he said that he hadn't felt so good in ages. We took the car up to a lookout point and..."

She paused, shaking her head and breathing deeply, as if she were fighting tears. "Bill and I—" she shot the diplomat a shy glance "—were discussing the puzzle pieces. He knows this area, you see, so I was trying to tell him everything. We had wandered off a bit. Then, quite suddenly we realized that he was gone. We called. We looked everywhere…."

"He was at the bottom of the cliff," Bill Dwyer said.

Bret stared pointedly at Ben. "Where were you?"

Ben started. "I was setting the emergency brake on the car! I'd never left it. You must ask Sandy or Mr. Dwyer. I had to move it after I had let them all out."

"I was thinking…" Sandy began, forestalling any reply that Bret might have made. She swallowed nervously and looked up, and her voice seemed tight. "There wasn't anyone else up there. No one but us. He seemed so very strange all day. Quiet, sad."

Bill Dwyer cleared his throat. "What I believe Sandy is trying to say, Bret, is that she thinks the general might have done it on purpose."

"Suicide!" Colleen said with a gasp.

Sandy looked at her with wide eyes and nodded slowly.

"I—I don't believe it!" Colleen protested. "He was so eager to help us. He said that he hadn't felt better in years."

There was silence at the table; then Carly's sigh could be heard plainly by them all. He placed his hand gently over hers where it lay on the table. "Colleen, who of us can really understand what went on in his heart and mind? He seemed to be a very fine man, but he had lived all those years with the guilt of having seen his men slaughtered before him."

Sandy inhaled shakily. "Once he told me that—that I shouldn't feel too bad for Rutger Miller. He said that Rutger was better out of it, where God could be the final judge and perhaps grant him the forgiveness he could not find on earth."

Colleen lowered her head. Perhaps they were right. Perhaps she hadn't really known the man at all. None of them could really have known him; they'd barely met him.

But something inside her was rebelling. He had been so willing to look for the answers with them, as if finding the truth—and Rutger's murderer—might be a form of atonement.

"What do we do now?" Ben asked bleakly.

Colleen looked up, as curious as Ben to hear Bret's answer.

He shrugged, leaned back and lit a cigarette and pushed his finished plate of food away. "We're at the main center of the ski slopes. I guess we get a good night's sleep and see if we can't come up with something in the morning."

"Ski slopes!" Sandy muttered. "There are ski slopes everywhere. *N'Oubliez Pas* and Earth Is the Mother! Where can that get us?" she demanded passionately.

Bret looked at Bill Dwyer. "You know the area, Bill. Have you got any ideas?"

Bill shook his head apologetically. "I'm afraid I don't. But we could make some discreet local inquiries. See if the words mean anything to anyone around here."

Bret nodded, and Ben yawned. Colleen looked at him quickly. His dark, handsome features were sallow; there were deep, circular grooves beneath his eyes. "Ben," she said softly, "you could go home, you know."

He quickly sat up very straight. "No, no! I will see this to the end with you. I wish to be here. Please don't send me back."

"No one is going to send you back, son," Carly assured him. "But I think we should send you to bed for the night. And I think I'll go up myself. I do have an idea for tomorrow, though."

They all looked at him. He smiled at their hopeful faces. "I think we should go skiing. Ask the people using the slopes if they know anything about a 'not forgotten' run. What do you say?"

Bret chuckled. "Carly, I'd say it's the best damned idea I've heard in years. We'll meet about ten?"

"Ten, in the breakfast room upstairs. Ben, go to bed."

Ben rose and obediently followed Carly out. Colleen realized then that, no matter how badly she felt about James MacHowell, she could barely keep her eyes open. "I think I'm about ready for bed, too," she said, looking across the table at Bret.

"I don't think I can sleep. Not yet," Sandy said.

"It is getting very late," Bill Dwyer murmured apologetically, as if he should offer to stay up, but just didn't think he could do so.

"Don't worry, Sandy," Bret told her, and his voice had a husky quality that seemed to rake along Colleen's spine. "We won't all desert you. I'll stay down here for a while. These coffee things are good." He gazed over at Colleen and smiled politely. "But you go up, Colleen. You look like you need the rest."

Jealousy, Colleen decided, was really an ugly emotion. She should have been so grieved over the general that she was able to think of nothing else. And she *was* grieved. She hadn't been able to help respecting his honesty and involvement, although he knew full well that one of his strange brotherhood had been brutally murdered.

But she was jealous, too. Lovely Sandy, gentle Sandy, clinging Sandy, feminine Sandy, wanted Bret.

And she was apparently getting him.

Colleen stood and managed a smile. "Well, I think I will go to bed. Good night, Sandy. Bret. Mr. Dwyer."

"Bill," Dwyer corrected her with a crooked smile, standing, too. "And I'll walk you up to your room and make sure you're locked in safe and sound."

"How nice," Colleen said sweetly. She couldn't help but send Bret a quick glance to make sure he was aware that someone was concerned with *her* safety since he was determined to expend his protective efforts in another direction.

Bret didn't even glance at her as he mumbled, "Good night."

She felt like yelling at him, but she managed not to by warning herself that she was overtired and feeling bitchy.

Bill Dwyer whistled softly as he escorted her to the elevator. Colleen gazed at him curiously. "This is really nice of you, you know," she told him. "I'm sure your duties don't require you to go to such extremes to assist reporters."

He laughed pleasantly. "Actually, my duties tend to be rather boring. U.S. relations with Austria are comfortable. I get a few lost tourists, a kid on dope now and then and that's it. I'm awfully sorry about that nice old man, MacHowell, but other than that, it's rather exciting to be involved with you all."

The elevator arrived. While they took it to the second floor, where their rooms were, Bill entertained her with a story about the chalet. "The builder wanted it to be the next best thing to a real castle, and you'll note that most of it is very atmospheric. But then he turned around and planned to turn the breakfast room into a disco at night, and, well, wait until you see it! Contemporary tacky is the best description I can give."

Colleen was still smiling when she let herself into the room she was to share with Bret. She locked the door since Bret had his own key.

"See you at ten," Dwyer called to her.

"At ten," Colleen agreed.

She listened to his footsteps as they moved down the hall. Then she sighed as she looked around the room. It was pleasant, but nothing terribly special. Clean, neat, pleasant.

She was exhausted, but suddenly not sleepy. The puzzle pieces were spinning through her head, and she kept seeing James MacHowell's face.

She also kept remembering that Bret was downstairs with Sandy, giving her his shoulder to lean on.

"What's the matter with Bill Dwyer's shoulder?" she muttered out loud.

She went ahead and took a long hot shower, then donned one of her more feminine nightgowns, trying to assure herself that she wasn't competing with Sandy.

Bret still wasn't back. She crawled into the double bed with its fresh sheets and feather comforter and tried to sleep. She couldn't. Her eyes wouldn't close. She just kept staring at the little wooden clock on the bedstead.

And staring…and staring. She watched the minute hand wind around and around. Her heart and mind became a miserable tumult. She wanted to tear him to ribbons, yet she knew full well that their divorce would be final in a matter of weeks.

Her eyes were still on the clock when the door opened. It was almost five o'clock. She closed her eyes before he could see that they were open.

She heard him shed his clothing, go into the bathroom, shower and brush his teeth.

Tears hovered like hot needles behind her eyes. Was he trying to wash away Sandy's scent before coming to bed?

A moment later she heard the bed creak beside her and felt his hand touch her shoulder. His palm was warm, slightly calloused, his fingers long. She knew his touch so well.

With all her energy she steeled herself against it.

"Colleen?"

"Bret, leave me alone. I'm sleeping."

"You're not. I want to talk to you. I want to explain—"

"Damn it, Bret. There's nothing to understand. You're a free agent, free to do whatever you want. You don't owe me an explanation, and I don't want one. In less than a month our marriage will be all over. We'll go our own ways. We'll live our separate lives, Bret. I'm exhausted. Please leave me alone!"

He did. He rolled onto his back, but she knew that he was awake, staring up at the ceiling.

She pressed her face against her pillow, praying for sleep to come, more miserable than she had ever imagined it was possible for her to be. Sleep seemed to elude her as they lay together, stiff and rigid and more distant than they had ever been.

Chapter Twelve

She finally fell asleep, and when she awoke, she couldn't figure out why she had done so. It was growing light beyond the drapes, yet it was quiet, and beneath the feather comforter it was warm and comfortable.

She turned. Bret was still sleeping, his back turned toward her, only the top of his head visible above the comforter.

She tried to close her eyes and go back to sleep, but she couldn't. At last she rose, quietly showered, then dressed. She brushed her hair and dabbed on makeup, shaking her head at the face that returned her stare from the mirror. She had smudges beneath her eyes, and she looked pale. Certainly not a picture of energy or fragile beauty.

Brooding over her appearance wasn't going to help her any, she decided. Coffee might improve her mental state.

Bret was still sleeping when she quietly let herself out of the bedroom. It was barely eight-fifteen. She could go up to the breakfast room, order coffee and try to sort through all the things in her mind before she was forced to see anyone else.

The breakfast room was on the third floor; as Bill had warned, it was a horror of naked neon lights and black veneer tables. As she stood in line waiting to be seated, she realized that Emil, their bellhop of the previous night, was acting as host. He smiled when he saw her.

"Guten Tag." He grinned, lowering his voice conspiratorially. "It is ugly, is it not? By the harsh light of day?"

She laughed. "I'm afraid I have to agree."

He grimaced good-naturedly. "It is not so bad outside. Would you like to sit on the terrace? You can see the real castle from there."

"Lovely," Colleen said, thanking him. She followed him between the tables to an open glass doorway that led to the terrace. In contrast to the inside, the outside was beautiful and gracious. The tables were covered with white cloths. Flowers filled the balcony trellises. And on one of the distant snowcapped mountains there was, indeed, a real castle.

"Is it a real castle?" she asked Emil as he served her coffee.

"Ja."

"Is it open to the public?"

"Nein. It belongs to an old man, if our local gossip is good. An old German man. No one ever sees him, though. There are high gates and many dogs. He is an eccentric. A recluse. But the castle—our schloss— makes a beautiful view, doesn't it?"

"Yes, yes, it does," Colleen agreed.

"I must go back to the door. Would you like your waitress yet?"

"I think I'll wait a bit to eat, if that's all right. I don't suppose I can tie up the table...?"

"Nein, nein! Sit as long as you like," Emil told her, then left.

For a while Colleen just sipped her coffee and stared

up at the schloss. It really was beautiful, high and yet embraced by the mountains. Clouds surrounded it, and even in summer it sat on a crystal blanket of snow.

At length, though, she pulled a pen from her purse and began to draw on her napkin. She definitely wasn't an artist, she decided; her mountain looked like an upside-down U, and her ski lift wasn't much better. But no matter what she drew, she couldn't get anywhere. Earth Is the Mother meant nothing more than what it said. And *N'Oubliez Pas…*

That meant even less than nothing to her. Austria might be a small country, but not when you were looking for buried diamonds. It was ridiculous to keep trying to make sense of it all.

But when she didn't, her thoughts reverted to Bret. And she would find herself growing angry and aching terribly. She had to learn to stay away from him. Had to! She couldn't keep going through this.…

A paper suddenly landed on the table. Startled, Colleen looked up.

There was a man standing in front of her. Tall, blue-eyed and shockingly blond, with handsome, well-defined features.

She gasped. He smiled, drawing his gloves from his hands and taking the seat opposite her.

"Hello, Frau McAllistair. I told you that I would find you."

She couldn't move; for a moment she panicked. Rutger was dead. And Eli. And James MacHowell. And this man, the son of Rudolph Holfer, had very calmly and righteously sat down beside her, almost touching her.

When she could move, she looked around in desperation. He lifted a hand scornfully. "What is it that you are thinking? That I shall reach across the table to strangle you in full view of so many others? Perhaps then I shall leap down three floors to escape?"

"I—I don't suppose you would," she managed to say.

He leaned closer to her, still smiling a little grimly. "I have no wish to harm anyone. Neither has my father. I know you cannot accept that, yet I must persist. You have come to our front door as it is."

"Your front door?" Colleen repeated, dazed.

He pointed to the schloss far up on the mountain. "It is my father's home. He seldom sees anyone. He seldom goes anywhere. He entombed himself many years ago. But he would like to see you."

This was it! Colleen thought excitedly. He was here, right in front of her.

"That's wonderful," she told him. "We're all going to meet up here at ten. We'll be happy to meet your father."

"Nein, nein!" Wilhelm Holfer said impatiently. "Don't you understand? No one can be trusted!"

Colleen sighed. "Mr. Holfer, I'd be an idiot, under the circumstances, to go running off with you alone."

He stood, reaching for his gloves. "Then I have done what I can for you. I shall persist, yet I must wait until you trust me, yes? For now, we have given what we can. *Guten Tag,* Frau McAllistair."

"Wait…"

She tried to call him back, but he was already gone, not over the balcony, but into the breakfast room. Colleen stared after him in turmoil; then her eyes fell to the paper he had dropped, and she gasped out loud.

It was the fourth piece of the puzzle. Worn, yellowed and frayed, but in her trembling hands.

She spread the page out. The drawing seemed to be

of a box with a roughly drawn figure inside it. Above
the box was a desk, with another stick man sitting at
it. Colleen strained to make out more, and she realized
that a swastika had been drawn on the shirt of the figure at the desk.

"Would you like more coffee?"

"What?" Colleen almost screamed the word, she was
so startled. She looked up to find Emil standing over
her with a coffeepot.

"I beg your pardon. I just wanted—"

"Oh, yes, Emil. I'm sorry. You, ah, startled me."

"Did I? I'm sorry."

"I'd love more coffee, Emil. Thank you."

The Austrian filled her cup, gazing idly at her drawing. "Where did you get that? It looks like a bunker."

"Bunker?"

"*Ja,* bunker. What is another word? You know, offices, rooms, dug into the earth." She must have gazed
at him blankly because he continued with a little exasperation. "You know, such as Hitler had in Berlin."

She felt a streak of excitement rip through her, as
if she were on to something, if she could just reach it.
"Emil, are there any bunkers around here?"

"Oh, no," Emil said, and her heart seemed to drop.
But then he paused. "Well, yes, maybe."

She tried not to scream again. "Emil, what do you
mean, maybe?"

"There is the oubliette. But that was sealed before
the war was over." He laughed. "Oubliette! How perfect. Everyone has forgotten it."

Colleen caught his hand and dragged him down into
the chair next to her. "Emil, what is the oubliette?"

He stared at her as if she were mad, then shrugged

as if all mad female Americans should be humored. "I remember it only from school, really. And, of course, because I grew up here. It was a cabinet room, you understand? A place for high-ranking German officials. But many Austrians were working with an—an underground, you understand?"

"Working for the Allies? Like partisans?"

"More like spies, yes?" Emil said. "They would be taken for interrogation. And if they did not answer, they went to the oubliette."

"Which was?"

Emil pointed at the paper. "Like this. A small square room. Very deep. There would be only a hatch door, high above. If they answered, they might be brought up. If not…" He shrugged. "Most talked after endless days without water. They would be brought up, interrogated again, then probably shot."

Colleen gasped for breath. The sense of excitement, of discovery, was with her so strongly that she was shaking. "Emil, where is this place? Can it be found?"

"Certainly. Well, I think, anyway. The entrance was boarded up long, long ago. And the lift closed."

"The lift?"

"*Ja*. The mountain itself used to be a wonderful ski slope. But then…" He shrugged. "More lodges were built, slopes were refined and the lift was outdated. It closed down. Look." He took her napkin and began to draw on it. "This is Esk. It is a tiny village along the road. From Esk there is another road. You cannot miss the old ski lift. The oubliette is somewhere nearby."

Colleen leaned across the table and kissed him. "Bless you, Emil. Bless you!"

She dug quickly through her purse and found a note

for a thousand schillings and stuck it in his hand. He looked at the bill, then at her. "What...?"

"You're a doll!" she told him.

She tore through the ugly breakfast room and didn't bother with the elevator, just raced down the stairs. She almost ripped the handle off the door to her room in her excitement, but despite her fervor and wild energy, the door remained locked. "Damn it," she muttered and pounded on it. Bret didn't answer. Impatiently she looked at her watch. It was almost ten! Bret couldn't still be asleep.

"Bret! Open the door."

He didn't. Muttering oaths against him, she found her key, opened the door, then stopped dead still. The bed had been made; Bret wasn't in it.

"Bret!" She rushed into the bathroom and even checked in the closet. He wasn't there.

"What's the matter?"

Colleen spun around to see Bill Dwyer smiling at her from the doorway.

"I seem to have lost my husband," Colleen said dryly.

Bill lowered his head. "What is it?" Colleen asked sharply.

"Well, uh, actually, I was on my way upstairs to find you. Your husband is out."

"Out? We were all supposed to meet at ten."

"Yes, I know. But your boss had to run over to another hotel. The phones went out here right after someone tried to reach him from the States. There was a bit of a storm here this morning." Bill spoke apologetically, as if it were his fault.

Colleen shook her head. "So where is Bret?"

Again he looked embarrassed. "Miss Tyrell was still

very upset this morning. Your husband decided that since the ski trip had to be delayed, he would take her with him to check with the local police. They should be back by this afternoon."

Colleen sank down on the foot of the bed, almost blinded by the moisture that swam into her eyes. How could he? She had been trying so hard to convince herself that it was ridiculous to worry about Sandy, but now it seemed that she'd been right all along. Bret was so concerned with Sandy that he couldn't even bother to tell Colleen anything himself.

"Can I help you?" Bill asked anxiously.

Colleen laughed. "I think I've just solved the whole damned thing, and no one is even around!"

"What?"

"It's a long story. I think I at least know where to look for the diamonds."

Bill moved into the room, his eyes shining with excitement, like a little boy's.

"Well…" He caught his breath, sitting down beside her. "Why don't we go look?"

Colleen caught something of his childlike thrill. Her blood seemed to race. She should go without Bret. He had gone without her. She shook her head. "Bill, thanks, but so much has happened…."

He sighed, apparently hurt. "I may not look like Ali or Frazier, but I'm not all that incompetent! Besides, I've got a gun I can bring."

"A gun?"

"Licensed!" he assured her. "And I'm a top marksman. Colleen, who knows when they'll all be back? Just think! We could do it. We could do it ourselves! They could come back, and we could be sitting here, sipping Scotch on the rocks, a solved mystery right before us!"

He kept talking. It didn't really matter. She had already made her decision. She cut across him. "I'll just see if I can't find Ben."

"Ben went with your boss. I'll leave a note on Sandy's door. They'll probably go back to her room first."

Probably go back to her room. Did everyone know something that Colleen didn't?

"I'll be right back. And I'll have that gun, just in case Holfer tries anything."

"Holfer?" Colleen murmured.

"Yes, Holfer. He has to be the murderer, doesn't he?"

She shook her head. "It's thanks to Holfer that I know where the diamonds are. Or at least, I think I know where they are. His son gave me the last of the puzzle pieces."

Dwyer hesitated. "That doesn't mean anything except that he wants you to lead him to the diamonds. After all, his piece alone wouldn't mean much. I'll be right back."

Colleen nodded. Her excitement was fading, though, just as the sun faded at twilight. She wasn't so sure she cared about the diamonds anymore. They were rocks. Someone else's rocks. They were only important because they could lead to the finale of a human drama.

But that would mean another finale. Hers and Bret's.

Still, she thought miserably, maybe the finale had been happening all along. Maybe she just hadn't wanted to see it.

"Let's go!"

Bill was at the door again, his eyes sparkling with energy and enthusiasm. She smiled, stuffed some money and her room key into her pocket and followed him. In thirty minutes they reached Esk. In another fifteen minutes they were halfway up the snowcapped mountain. In another five they saw the deserted ski lift.

Bill started to laugh as they tramped through the snow toward it. "I know this place! I came up here a couple of years ago. There were some complaints about the lift. People were afraid that someone would try to ride it. The cables are ready to snap, but the controls still work. They still haven't demolished it or fenced it off."

Colleen gazed at the ski lift and shivered. It was old and built like a rusty cage. Bill was right; it was a hazard. The controls were right beside it. If some crazy kid took a ride on a dare, it could be a disaster. The cables were visibly frayed to almost nothing. At first it moved out not far above the snow, but then there was a drop to the valley far below, where the village of Esk huddled.

"You should work on that," she told Bill.

"I will," he said determinedly.

They kept tramping through the snow, several feet of it, white and pretty, but deep. Colleen wished she'd worn more than a sweater. The sun was bright, but the air was crisp and clean and cold, and her breath steamed in the chilly air.

"What are we looking for?" Bill asked politely.

"Boards. There is supposedly an entrance to a bunker here. It was called the oubliette because prisoners were—"

"I can imagine what they were," Bill interrupted her. He was huffing, too; they had left the car far behind. "It must have been boarded up a long time ago."

"Before the end of the war," Colleen agreed. They were up against the mountain and a wall of snow.

"That would explain why I've never heard of it," Bill

murmured. "I think we're going to have to start dusting the whole mountain to get beneath the snow."

Colleen grimaced. "I guess so." She didn't even have gloves with her. She started pushing at the snow anyway; her hands burned with the cold, and she kept having to stop. "I think I'm going to wind up with frostbite," she moaned.

"You watch. I'll dig," Bill said cheerfully. He grinned at her. "No one was following us here. I kept an eye out. But I don't suppose it would be a bad idea to have a lookout anyway, do you?"

She shook her head. "You've got your gun."

"Oh, yes! I have it. But keep your eyes on the road, okay?"

Colleen nodded. She watched the road, and she started thinking about Bret again. If only he were here. If only they were in on this together. If only she had the nerve—yes, the nerve!—to corner him and tell him that she loved him and demand to know why on earth he couldn't love her, too, when they could be so good together if they only tried. Damn him! What was this thing he had going with Sandy?

BRET HIMSELF DIDN'T quite know what it was. She had been at his door, frightened and beautiful, when he'd barely stepped out of the shower. And he'd wondered why he was the one she had decided to put all her trust and faith in.

There was something funny somewhere. Something that he was just missing. Something not quite right. She wanted to be with him, but not so much to talk as to hear him talk. And she was just as avid when they were alone as when they were with the others.

Was she enjoying it all? he wondered. The excitement of it? Or what…?

He couldn't explain it, but Bret was convinced that if he remained around her long enough, she would say something that would clarify the vague feeling he had, the uneasiness. It had something to do with MacHowell. There was a clue there; someone just wasn't saying the right word.

He glanced her way as he drove the VW back toward the Château Moreau. The police hadn't been much help. They had seemed to think it was mad to believe in treasure maps. The Second World War was history; Austria looked to the future because the past was painful.

No matter how useless the quest, Bret was glad they had at least been to the local authorities. And Sandy had been pleasant and calm. Right now she had her window open, and her hair was blowing in the cool breeze.

She gazed at him and smiled, relaxed. "I have complete faith, you know," she told him huskily.

"In what?"

"In your ability to find the diamonds."

"Do you?"

"Yes."

"And the murderer?"

She looked at him again wide-eyed. "Of course."

Bret smiled pleasantly and returned his attention to the road. "Tell me about MacHowell again, Sandy."

Her lower lip trembled. "I've told you everything, over and over again."

"Have you? How far did you and Bill wander away from him? Were you with Bill all the time?"

"I think so—oh, please!" She covered her face with her hands. "Don't make me go on and on with this…."

Bret sighed. He didn't really understand what he was feeling, what his intuition was all about. Everything rested with Sandy.

He shook his head. Another dead end. What had he been expecting her to say?

"Well, here we are," he murmured as they reached the château. "Let's see if we can find the others. Maybe we've got time left today to reach the slopes, if Carly and Ben have made it back."

They parked the car, walked through the lobby and found the elevator on the ground floor, as if it were awaiting them. The door closed, and Bret found Sandy's eyes on him. She smiled slowly. "It's really a pity..." Her voice trailed away huskily.

It's really a pity what? he wondered. Egotistically, it would be nice to assume she meant that it was a pity he was married, except that she knew that he and Colleen were in the process of a divorce. Maybe she thought they were back together.

But his gut reaction told him that something was out of key. Sandy was out of key.

"I'll see if Colleen's in our room," he muttered as the elevator door opened.

"Bret, walk me to my room first, please?" she asked, the fearful little tremor back in her voice.

He obliged so he was with her when she found the note that had been slipped under her door.

"Oh! It's a map to where they've gone!" Sandy cried ecstatically.

"Who?"

"Bill and your wife! They're on to something, and we're supposed to follow them. Let's go!"

Bret felt his heart begin to beat a little too quickly. He

didn't like the idea of Colleen going anywhere without him. Why had she run off? He mentally berated himself for not taking the time to find her earlier. She had been so damned cold and distant last night, not even giving him a chance to try to describe the uneasiness he'd been feeling.

"Let's go," he said, agreeing with Sandy. His palms were wet, his knees shaking. Something was wrong; he just wasn't sure what. "Uh, I'm just going to grab a sweater, okay?"

He left her in the hallway. She didn't seem frightened anymore.

Bret wrote a hasty note. He wanted to slip it beneath Carly's door, but instinct warned him not to let Sandy see him.

Ben's door was closer to his own. He managed to get the note beneath it, wondering if it would matter anyway. He had to be wrong; Holfer had to be the bad guy in this thing.

Didn't he?

Bret and Sandy hurried back down to the car. She was tense and silent as they drove to the village of Esk. Maybe it was her silence that finally caused the suspicion that lurked in the back of his mind to jell, but he felt he had the key.

Sandy.

He shook his head. He was wrong. He had to be wrong. But it was there: the innocence, the loveliness, the sweetness, the tremors and the fear. They were just too perfect to be real. Sandy had been in touch with Rutger Miller. She was bitter about her past. Almost since he had met her, he had felt compelled to watch her closely.

Bret should have kept going up the mountain, but he didn't. He stopped at the side of the road instead and stared at Sandy. She returned his stare with a frown.

"Bret…?"

"What I want to know, Sandy, is how you managed to kill James MacHowell with Bill Dwyer beside you."

He half expected a vehement denial. He didn't get one. She shrugged and whatever vestige of the fragile femme fatale she had still maintained seemed to slip off her shoulders like a cloak. "You haven't guessed. Bill is in on it."

That one definitely took Bret by surprise. "Wait a minute! *I* called Bill."

"If you hadn't, I would have," she said demurely. She smiled sweetly and lifted her purse off her lap to display the small pistol she was carrying beneath it. "Drive, Bret. I think it's actually your lovely wife who's proving to be the better investigator."

"Sandy, you're not going to…?"

She shook her head. "Bret, don't tell me I won't use the gun. You know better than that."

He turned the key in the ignition. "You don't need the display of force, Sandy. I'd be driving anyway. I want to find my wife, remember?"

"Well, then, I hope we do find her. Alive, of course, for the time being. I'm sure you two will want a few last words."

"I'VE FOUND IT!"

Bill Dwyer's voice was high with enthusiasm. Colleen rushed over to him. He had found some kind of entryway that seemed to go straight into the mountain. It was covered with boards.

"You did find it! But what about the boards?"

"I've got a knife here," Bill muttered. "And the boards are rotting. If I can just—" He broke off, fitting the blade of the knife between the boards. Sweat was beaded heavily on his brow despite the cool air.

Colleen heard a faint creaking in the wood. "You've got it! Just a bit farther..."

There was a loud crack. An entire length of wood split in two. Bill slipped his hand through it and felt around. "A bolt! I've got it!"

There was another screeching sound that seemed to echo all around them—the old wooden door howling out a protest at being disturbed.

"This is it!" he exclaimed, and he bowed elaborately before her, indicating that she should precede him.

Colleen chuckled jubilantly. "No, Mr. Dwyer, you removed the boards. You go first."

He shrugged, clutched her hand, and she followed immediately behind him. For long moments they blinked, and then they sneezed. Dust and cobwebs were everywhere, and the daylight barely filtered in through the door. But then it seemed that the dust began to settle, and a little cry escaped Colleen.

It was the place, the exact place in the last puzzle piece. Twenty feet in from the entry there was an old desk. Charts and papers, yellowed and decayed with age, were strewn over it. Ten feet back from the desk was a hatch.

"The oubliette," Bill muttered. "Are the diamonds down there, do you think? I don't see anything that looks like a safe."

Colleen paused for a minute, then sneezed. She could see, but dust particles still filled the air. "I don't think so…" she murmured. "You see, the picture has the desk in it. I wonder…"

They gazed at one another, then rushed together to the desk. They went through all the drawers and found nothing but more old paper. Frustrated, they stared at one another again. The same idea must have hit them both at once because they started plowing through the drawers again.

Colleen gave out a victorious little cry. There was a lever in the back of a drawer; she pulled it out and found that it gave. And behind the metal wall that held the lever she found a casket. Her hands closed around it as she pulled it out. It was about the size of a short loaf of bread, metal encased with leather.

"Oh, Bill, I think…"

"Let me." He grabbed the casket. There was a lock on it. He slammed the lock against the desk, and the rusted thing gave instantly. Bill set the casket on the desk and threw the top open.

They gasped simultaneously. The glow of the diamonds streaked across the room, red, blue, gold and every color in between. They gave off a fantastic light. Beautiful. Incredible. Diamonds set in the midst of emeralds. Diamonds set with sapphires. All kinds of diamonds, in all manner of jewelry.

"They're fantastic!" Colleen breathed. She had to touch them. She picked up an elegant diamond earring and held it up to the light, barely aware that Bill had moved away from her.

"Put it back, please, Mrs. McAllistair, will you."

She looked up, startled.

Bill Dwyer was behind the desk, one hand on the

desktop, the other closed around a gun. A long gun with a fat nose.

"You've been after the diamonds?" she asked him in slow and stunned disbelief.

"I'm afraid so. And I've spent a number of years in the doldrums of their pursuit."

She felt too numb, too distant, to really believe him. He looked like the nice guy next door. He couldn't be leveling a gun at her. But he was.

She shook her head. Her voice didn't sound at all like her own when she spoke. "You can't kill me. My husband will come after you. He'll find you."

"Oh, I don't think so." He paused, tilting his head toward the door. "I think he's already here."

Colleen's eyes were riveted on the entryway. He was right; Bret was there. Ducking to get in, then standing straight and blinking. He seemed to fill the small bunker with his presence, and in that moment she thought again how very much she loved him.

He saw Dwyer; then his eyes caught hers across the room. She saw them spark and sizzle with relief, and she wanted to run to him and hold him.

"Ah, McAllistair, you've made it," Dwyer murmured.

And then Colleen was forced to realize that Bill Dwyer was holding a gun and Bret was not.

Chapter Thirteen

"Bret!" Colleen gasped, gladness warming her heart. But as instantly as the joy had come, it caught in her throat, strangling her. He wasn't alone; Sandy was behind him, holding a small pearl-handled pistol to his back.

"Sandy!" Colleen said with more incredulity than fear.

"Really, Mrs. McAllistair," Sandy said, sounding bored, "who else? Who else deserves the diamonds? They're mine. My grandfather died for them. My mother suffered all her life for them. I was sick of suffering. I'm not quite martyr material, am I, Bill?"

Bill Dwyer was laughing, seeming to truly enjoy what was happening, as if it were some kind of wonderful joke. "Not a martyr at all, darling. But then, martyrs are so boring." He waved his free hand in the air, indicating that Sandy should give Bret a prod toward Colleen. She did so, and Bret took Colleen's trembling body into his arms while surveying the pair.

"You're right," Bret told Sandy, sounding so calm and nonchalant that Colleen prayed that some of his strength would seep into her. "It was all so obvious. There were so many things I should have seen. Even when we left your town house, back in the States, you said you needed five minutes for phone calls. Those phone calls were to set Colleen up with Eli, right?"

"Right you are, McAllistair, but a little late."

"What about Rutger?" Bret asked her.

"I hired a professional," she admitted, casting Colleen a contemptuous stare. "I'm afraid that, with enough money, you can buy almost anything anywhere, including murder."

"You murdered Eli!" Colleen heard herself say suddenly. "When we were at General MacHowell's, I noticed that your feet were wet. You hadn't been out looking at the view. You'd been out hunting Eli!"

"Clever child, isn't she?" Sandy chuckled to Bill. Colleen felt a shudder sweep through her. This was the woman she had thought was so delicate and fragile. So sweet, almost nauseatingly charming. So beautiful. She was still beautiful. Tall and elegant, with sweeping chestnut brown hair. But she was about as fragile as a cobra, and her expression now betrayed that fully. Her eyes were cold and sharp and ruthlessly amused.

"I waited years and years, Colleen, to find a way to retrieve the diamonds and get my revenge. Ah, I can see your all-American mind ticking away, Colleen. Revenge, after forty years? Yes! They all escaped—Miller, MacHowell and Holfer. Only Sam Tyrell died a traitor." She smiled pleasantly. "I never knew Sam, but I watched my mother's slow destruction over it all. She was young and weak when my father seduced her, then left her in horror once he had discovered that she was the daughter of the infamous Sam Tyrell. I wasn't quite so weak. I learned to spend my time planning vengeance."

"And, of course, there are the diamonds," Bill Dwyer reminded her quietly.

"Yes, yes, the diamonds, darling, of course! Our little snoop did lead you to them, didn't she?"

Sandy swept over to Bill, casting a glance toward Bret and Colleen that was almost apologetic, as if she were a hostess forced to momentarily ignore her guests.

Even Sandy gasped when she saw the diamonds. In the dust, in the pale light, the Helmond diamonds glittered and dazzled, catching and reflecting the light. Brooches, necklaces, tiaras, bracelets, all shimmered in their casket lined with black velvet.

"Look at them, Sandy!" Bill murmured with love and awe, running his fingers through the collection of gems. "Plain yellow tints, blue tints, reds and greens, even blacks! Sandy, do you know how rare they are? And look at the way they're cut."

Sandy gazed at Bret. "Wouldn't you like to touch them, Bret? You came so close." She purred. "You were on to me, weren't you?" she asked suddenly.

Colleen stared up at Bret. He slipped his fingers through hers and squeezed, pulling her over to the diamonds and gazing down at them while he answered Sandy, still in a calm Colleen couldn't quite grasp.

"Umm-hmm. I began to doubt you when MacHowell died. It seemed rather convenient." He picked up a pendant and whistled. "This one stone must be ten carats. And I'd say it was almost a flawless blue, wouldn't you, Dwyer?" He shook his head, staring at the young man. "You were my problem, Dwyer. I just couldn't seem to clinch a few things because it never occurred to me that you could be involved. How did the two of you get together, anyway?"

Bill Dwyer scowled. "I don't have to answer any of

your questions, McAllistair—" Bill began, but Sandy cut him off sweetly.

"Bill! Don't be so gauche! If it weren't for the McAllistairs we could have spent years digging!" She flashed Colleen a convivial smile. "Bill and I met in college. I told you, I've been working on this for a long time! You see, I'd already assumed that the diamonds were in Austria. Bill very carefully pursued his appointment here. We just didn't have anything to go on." She laughed. "Rutger, MacHowell and Holfer had done such a wonderful job of disappearing! But then, through his diplomatic channels, Bill learned that Rutger was in the States. I was able to contact him—as the tearful, injured victim, of course—and then I learned that he planned to tell you everything. Well, I was quite upset at first. But then Bill told me about Bret's wonderful prowess at uncovering things, and we decided that involving you both would be a tremendous plus."

"Just like having a pair of bloodhounds," Dwyer said smugly.

"And we did do just about everything for you, didn't we?" Bret said dryly. "We led you straight to MacHowell and gave you the opportunity to kill him. Then we brought you right to the diamonds. Perfect. Or almost perfect. What about Rudy Holfer and his son, Wilhelm?"

"I can't handle everything at once!" Sandy protested with a little laugh.

"As soon as we shoot the two of you," Dwyer said flatly, "we'll worry about the Holfers."

"And your managing editor," Sandy said with a sigh. "He's a complication I wasn't counting on." She gazed at Bill. "And we can't shoot them all, darling. We don't dare risk your post until we're ready to do our own disappearing act. Tahiti is nice, don't you think, Bret? Though maybe there are too many tourists!"

"I'm sure you'll think of a lovely place to retire, Sandy," Bret returned.

"The ski lift," Bill said suddenly. "We'll wait until dark, then send the McAllistairs on a one-way trip down the pass. What do you think?"

"Lovely, what shall we do until then?"

"Hell, they're married!" Bill Dwyer chuckled with a guttural sound. "Let's let them spend their last hours together, confessing all their sins. We'll throw them in the oubliette."

"That sounds lovely," Sandy said. "How romantic! The doomed lovers can cling to one another until the final moment, and we can sit here and admire our diamonds!"

Dwyer was staring at Bret. "Let's go, McAllistair."

Bret laughed. "You just decided that you can't shoot us. Why should I do anything?"

Sandy smiled, and in that moment Colleen realized how coldly depraved the woman really was. "If you should force us to shoot, Bret," she crooned sweetly, "we'll start with your wife. And we won't kill her right off. Shattered kneecaps are terribly painful. A shot through the abdomen, the kind that can make you die, but oh, so agonizingly slowly…."

Colleen was certain that she was turning a ghastly shade of green. It suddenly seemed that there was no air in the stuffy bunker. She felt as if she would pass out before they could move.

"Where would you like us?" Bret inquired bluntly.

Bill Dwyer walked over to the hatch beyond the desk.

"Down, McAllistair. Quickly. Her first." He waved his gun at Colleen.

"Uh-uh. Me first," Bret countered.

"Let him go down first!" Sandy snapped. "What difference does it make?"

Colleen clenched her fists together while Bret fitted himself into the hole and climbed down the fraying rope ladder into the black void below.

"Now you," Dwyer said. He looked at Colleen, his eyes devoid of emotion.

Trying not to shake so badly that she'd lose her grip, Colleen started down. She bit her lip until it bled, knowing why Bret had insisted on going first. The rope was so frayed that it might break at any time; he intended to catch her if she fell. She had no idea if she was near the bottom or not; it was too dark to see anything.

Sandy chuckled above her. "The oubliette, Colleen. A forgotten place for forgotten souls. Enjoy."

Colleen answered Sandy with a loud scream; the frayed rope had broken in her grasp. She plummeted downward, but she didn't hit hard cement. Bret caught her weight and broke the fall; they fell to the cold, damp floor together.

"Shall we give them a light?" Sandy asked from far above.

"For what?" Bill Dwyer countered; then the trapdoor was slammed down, extinguishing all light.

Colleen felt Bret's body beneath her, heard the rasp of his breath as she felt thankful for the warmth and security of his muscled form. His arms moved around her, and all of a sudden tears stung her eyes. She loved him so much. He had always tried to be a step ahead of her, to catch her should she fall.

All their disagreements seemed so senseless now. So foolish. All the petty fights, the petty fears. Blackness and cold were surrounding them. All they had was one another amidst the dank smell and the haunting miasma of past suffering that hung in the air. Whether or not he had ever really loved her deeply, whether or not he would have stayed with her for an eternity, didn't matter. She suddenly felt that it was the most important thing in the world for him to know that she had been wrong, wrong not to talk, wrong not to tell him before that she loved him with all her heart, enough to reason, enough to compromise....

Enough to tell him the truth.

"I'm sorry, I'm so sorry, Bret!" she wailed.

"Listen, Colleen," he whispered, sitting up and bringing her along on his lap. Then he stopped and said sharply, "What?"

"Bret, I love you," she babbled in a feverish whisper, locking her arms around his neck, tenderly caressing the hair at his nape with her fingertips. "I love you so much. I never stopped. I was wrong to file those papers. I just thought that you wanted it. I mean, you walked out. But I—I believe now that you...that you were just determined not to let me get hurt. Bret, I think I'd do anything, anything in the world, to try again. To go back, to start over without all the misunderstandings, to start a family."

"What?" His arms tightened about her, cutting her words off cleanly. She couldn't see his silver gaze in the darkness, but she could feel it, narrowed and misted and demanding and tender all in one. "Colleen," he said hoarsely, "you don't have children as a part of trying again. You have them because you want them."

"I always wanted children," she told him, a little stunned at his intensity, especially since her words seemed rather moot, considering their circumstances. "You were the one who didn't want them, not with me, at any rate."

"Then what were you saying that night of the banquet?"

"Only that I hated to be poked and prodded and questioned about my life by nosy people!"

He started to laugh, which also seemed ridiculous, given their present circumstances. His arms tightened around her; he kissed her cheek, her throat, and then found her mouth. His lips were warm and passionate and warm and exuberant against hers. Thrilling and stirring and terribly sad. She was crying again when he released her to pull her back against his shoulder, stroking her throat tenderly with his thumb.

"Oh, Bret! We had it all. Everything. And I threw it away. And now...now it's too late."

"Hey, kid, never give up until the end," he warned her. "Never. But while we're on the subject..." He lifted her chin. She could barely make out his profile. "Sweetheart, the confessions don't all belong to you. Ah, Colleen! If I hadn't been so damned temperamental, if I'd ever really tried to understand your feelings! I did some awful things, too, babe. I walked out on you without really trying to make you understand. There were a dozen times when I could have pressed an issue, when I could have asked questions instead of taunting you or coming up with a sarcastic remark. You were just so convinced that it was always the story that mattered. Colleen, I am a journalist. So are you. But nothing, nothing in my life, has ever mattered as much as you. I love you, Colleen. I never stopped loving you, wanting you. I spent months trying to think of a way to prevent you from getting a divorce."

"Did you really?" Colleen whispered.

She couldn't see his slow, rueful grin, but she could feel it. She knew him so well.

"Really," he told her huskily.

"Oh, Bret!" she moaned, leaning against him, inhaling the scent of him, touching him, as if she could remember the sinewed warmth of his muscular frame for eternity. "Oh, Bret…"

He caught her chin between his hands and kissed her tenderly. Then, to her surprise, he found the rounded portion of her derriere and gave it a sharp slap. "Up!" he said huskily.

"What?" She was astonished. Up? They should have clung together, prayed together, held on for whatever time they had left.

"Up! We've got to find a way out. Hey, lady, do you think I'm going to let you out of a lifetime commitment when I've just gotten a confession like that? Not on your life! We're supposed to be in court in less than two weeks. We've got to tell our lawyers that they can take all their papers and stuff them. Come on!"

He was already up. Her derriere was on the cold cement floor.

"Bret, wait! What the hell are you doing? There could be rats down here, snakes, spiders…"

"It's too damned cold for anything to be alive down here. Come on!"

She could hear him checking the walls with his hands for an escape route. She stood carefully, hesitantly. Stretching her arms out before her, she found the wall.

"If I touch a rat or a spider," she warned him, "I'm going to rip out a nice sandy lock of your hair!"

She heard his throaty laughter. "That's my girl!" he told her. But as time passed, even Bret was ready to give up, disgusted and exhausted. It really was an oubliette, a forgotten place. Cold walls and cold floor and nothing more.

Held against him once more, Colleen felt her tears rising behind her eyelids. "Don't give up!" he commanded her. "We've still got a chance. A good chance. Don't forget, those two aren't really as hardened as they pretend. We may very well be able to escape them."

"Not hardened! They've both got guns! They've already been involved in three murders."

"Dwyer is a klutz," Bret said flatly. "Sandy is the brains, as they say. And she isn't a talented killer. She bought and paid for services rendered in at least one case."

Colleen sniffed. "She obviously killed MacHowell."

"The opportunity was handed to her on a silver platter," Bret announced with self-disgust.

"But the guns…" Colleen repeated morosely.

Bret seemed to hesitate for a second. He ruffled her hair. "We're smarter," he tried to assure her. Then his voice deepened gruffly. "And I told you that after that beautiful confession of yours, I have no intention of letting you out of a thing. We're going to learn to be a loving, talking, communicating—compromising—couple."

She couldn't help but laugh. "I think we would always argue. If we had the chance," she added wistfully, just stopping herself from sobbing.

"We will have a chance," he said firmly. "And I suppose we will argue. I think I do have a measure of male protectiveness...."

"You like to run the show!" Colleen sniffed.

"Well, yes, maybe. But you do have a tendency to fly off the handle like an idiot."

"I don't!"

"You do."

"Well, maybe," she conceded.

"And I only try to run the show when I feel you're in danger of jeopardizing what I love most in the world—you."

"Oh, Bret!"

She touched her lips to his, moist and caressing. Her tears mingling with the kiss; she played lightly with his tongue, then pressed against him in a fever, her breasts crushed to his chest, as if she could hold on forever.

He broke away from her. "We'll have to spend a great deal of time in bed. We never argue there. Have you noticed?"

"Oh, Bret!" She couldn't manage to say anything more. It was all so beautiful and too late.

The hatch suddenly opened far above them. Bret and Colleen blinked against the light, and listened to the argument ensuing between their captors.

"I still say we could just leave them down there," Bill Dwyer was insisting.

"Don't be an idiot," Sandy protested in turn. "Holfer will be right behind us. He'd find them, or else that editor of theirs or that snooping Arab. They've got to be in an accident. A natural accident. The ski lift is perfect."

"And how do you know it will snap?"

"The cables are frayed! The weight of a rat would

cause them to snap!" She stared down into the hole. "Get up here!"

Bret grinned up at her. "Sorry, Sandy. We can't reach the ladder anymore. It broke, remember?"

Sandy swore an inarticulate oath. A moment later a thick rope fell down to them. Colleen glanced at Bret and tried to be as nonchalant as he was. "I never was much at rope climbing."

"All you have to do is reach the hemp ladder. I'll be beneath you."

Bret gave her a boost up. She was so nervous that her hands were slick, and she slipped twice.

"If I have to," Sandy warned, "I'll shoot you."

"What the hell difference does it make?" Colleen muttered back. She struggled with the rope, then caught the ladder. Bill Dwyer reached down to pull her out of the trap. She shook free of his grasp as soon as she was standing and wondered fleetingly if she couldn't force him to fall down the hole. No chance. As soon as she had balanced herself, Sandy pressed a gun to her spine.

"Hurry up, McAllistair," the woman called down to Bret. "We might have time for one more touching reunion at the ski lift."

Bret crawled out under his own power. "You take her," Sandy told Bill, indicating Colleen. "He's more trouble."

"Sandy…"

"I don't trust him."

"Sounds like you don't trust me," Bill muttered, but he gripped Colleen's arm and shoved her toward the entryway she had discovered with jubilation such a short time ago. Colleen couldn't look back. She stumbled through the rubble and, with Bill still holding her, crawled out into the snow. She looked up at the sky. It was dark, with only the stars and a crescent moon to shine on the endless snow—and on the rusty ski lift that crept from cliff to cliff across the valley.

Colleen swallowed sharply as Bill prodded her along, straight toward the lift. It seemed strange that the cold air should feel so good against her face, that she could enjoy the crisp crunching of the snow beneath her feet.

"What happened to our last touching reunion?" she demanded, trying to keep the fear from her voice as Bill stepped past her to open the lift cage.

"Get in!" he told her.

She didn't have any choice; he grabbed her arm and shoved her.

But as she stepped into the cage, there was a commotion behind her.

"Son of a bitch!" Bill yelled. Colleen saw that he was staring across the snow, that Sandy was facedown in it and that Bret seemed to be flying across it toward them.

"Bret!"

He was carrying his own gun. Where had it come from? she wondered a little vaguely. Then Bill Dwyer was screaming again, his hand shaking too badly to aim.

Bret plowed into Bill, and the two men fell into the snow. Colleen started to sob in relief, but the sob caught in her throat with horror. There was a screeching sound, a horrible, shrill echo against the quiet of the mountains and the snow. Dimly she realized that Bill had hit the lever that started the cage.

The ski lift was moving. Shaking, trembling, still screeching from lack of oil. But it was moving.

"Bret!" she screamed.

He heard her. She saw him struggle to his feet and

reach desperately for the lever. He was just about to touch it when a second figure rose from the snow—Dwyer, pitching himself against Bret's back. The two fell again. Then Sandy was up, staggering after them, trying to find their weapons that were lost in the snow.

"Oh, God, no!" Colleen breathed a desperate prayer. She looked above her where the roof was rusted through. She could see the cage sliding along the cables. She could see the cables, worn and thin, catching on the pulleys of the cage and causing it to teeter like a stumbling drunk. "No!" she cried again, and she tore desperately at the door; it wouldn't give, no matter how frantically she pulled.

Below her she could still see the snow. Not far below, maybe ten feet or so. A long jump, but soon the snow would be a hundred feet beneath her, then two hundred feet.

And the crescent moon still showed Bret in the center of a desperate struggle with both Sandy and Dwyer.

"No!" She shook the metal cage, ripping the frozen flesh on her fingers as she clawed at it. Her minutes were evaporating into seconds, seconds that would fade so quickly.

Something caught her eye. A movement across the snow, not from the tunnel, but from the road below it. There was a figure streaking toward her, a figure dressed all in black, with a black ski mask hiding its identity.

Her heart seemed to lodge in her throat. Who was it, pelting toward them? Not toward the ski lift, as she had first thought, but toward the fracas in the snow. Could it be a third accomplice? Someone Sandy had hired?

As he slammed his fist against Dwyer's jaw, Bret,

too, saw the figure. He was so stunned that he barely
ducked in time to avoid Dwyer's counter attack. He
caught Dwyer with an upswing. A loud crack followed,
and when Dwyer went down this time, he was uncon-
scious. Bret struggled to his feet, but Sandy immediately pitched herself against him once more, like a wild
animal gone mad.

He wanted to kill her. To strangle her. Not because
she had so little regard for the value of human life, but
because every second that he struggled with her, Colleen's chances grew slimmer.

"Go!" a voice suddenly shouted.

Bret was amazed; the figure in black had reached
him and was hauling Sandy from him with a fresh and
forceful strength.

"Go save your wife!" the figure in the black ski mask
ordered.

Bret was only too happy to oblige. He was dimly
aware that more people were arriving as he struggled
through the knee-deep snow. He was barely aware of
anything until he heard another voice that he knew very
well.

"Bret, boy, move!"

It was Carly, his command filled with tension. The
snow no longer seemed an obstacle to Bret. He plowed
through it in desperation. The lift…in a matter of seconds it would be above the valley. And if the cable gave
way then, it would mean certain death.

Colleen, too, knew the danger. Frantically she continued to tear at the door, feeling as if the promise of death
were a blanket around her. She was becoming hysterical, and she could not calm herself. What did it matter if she did? No one would be able to save her. They

would hear only her scream when the air tore from her as the lift plummeted downward.

Then she gasped, astounded as she saw a pair of hands grabbing the woven metal floor of the lift. She saw Bret's face, his eyes silver in the night, his skin sheened with exertion as he hiked himself up by the strength of his arms.

"Bret!" she cried, grateful, terrified. It was bad enough to face the abyss herself. If he couldn't reach her, he would keep trying, and he, too, would die.

"Get ready to jump!"

Her heart slammed against her cheek. Jump! The snow was so far away! Suddenly all she could think was that his face looked so wonderful, that she was so glad to have seen him, his eyes, his care, his love.

"Colleen! Pay attention!"

He was balanced against the cage, grinding at the lock with a pocketknife. To her astonishment the door gave. It opened with a screech, almost sending Bret catapulting down to the snow below.

Almost.

"Your hand! Colleen! Give me your hand."

Panic closed around her. The ground was farther away than ever.

"Colleen!"

The anguish in his voice touched and warmed and awakened her to the promise of life. She stretched out her hand and felt his fingers winding around hers, strong and secure.

"Now!"

Colleen closed her eyes and jumped.

The snow rushed up to meet her, cold and hard. Her breath was swept away as snow clogged her nose and eyes and froze her cheeks. She thought she was dying. Her lungs seemed about to explode, but she gasped for breath, and it came to her. She opened her eyes and saw the beautiful crescent of the moon. She tried to move and she could. She was stiff, cold and sore, but nothing seemed to be broken.

A clattering thud rent the night and echoed in her ears. Colleen closed her eyes again, tears stinging them. The ski lift had fallen down to the valley below. She trembled. But for Bret she would have been on that lift.

"Colleen?"

She opened her eyes again. Bret was before her. A trickle of blood ran from the corner of his mouth, and his eyelashes were white with snow, as were his cheeks.

"Colleen?"

She smiled slowly, loving the anxiety in his eyes.

"Are you all right? Colleen?"

She nodded, still unable to speak. His hands cupped her cheeks. His lips touched hers, and they trembled. They should have been cold, but they were rich with heat.

She brought her arms around him. "Oh, Bret…"

He spoke against her throat, whispering things that were unintelligible, but understood, and she returned them. They were alive. They were both alive. Everything was beautiful and precious. The moon, the air, even the burning cold sensation of the snow. And Bret… his touch, his lips, his heat.

They became aware of footsteps plodding through the drifts. Bret broke away. He tried to help Colleen to her feet, but stumbled. She gasped as the black-clad figure came up to her, helped her stand, then retreated to remove the black ski mask.

"Wilhelm! Oh, thank God!"

She was going to sink back to her knees again, but Wilhelm supported her. The wind touched his hair and turned it gold and silver; his eyes were radiant blue against the darkness. "Mrs. McAllistair, Mr. McAllistair, you are all right?" he asked anxiously.

Bret had managed to stand on his own. He slipped an arm around Colleen's shoulders and nodded grimly, then reached out his free hand to grasp Wilhelm's. "Thanks to you," he said quietly. "If you hadn't taken Sandy off of me—"

He broke off because Carly, trying to reach them, had just pitched forward on his face into the snow. Carly cursed away, and Bret laughed, stepping forward to grimace at Wilhelm, who helped him raise Carly to his feet. Carly sputtered, spitting snow. Colleen laughed, too, and rushed forward to hug him, almost knocking him over again.

"What—" she began. "How—"

Wilhelm smiled and answered her calmly while Carly still swore softly at the snow. "Your Moroccan friend found me when everyone disappeared. He found a note in his room mentioning the oubliette. Living in this place, I knew it. I was able to find Carlton, and he insisted we rush here immediately."

"Thank God!" Bret breathed.

Wilhelm was staring up at the mountain. He pointed that way, still smiling grimly. "The authorities will take them from here. There is nothing else that we must do now." He shook his head. "Tyrell's granddaughter. Who would have suspected…?"

He shrugged and turned back to them. "My father

is waiting in the car on the road. He would like you to make his acquaintance. Will you do so?"

"Will I?" Bret chuckled ruefully. "Herr Holfer, I would do anything in my power that you asked. If you hadn't got here when you did…"

His voice trailed away. Wilhelm Holfer smiled with understanding, but quickly dismissed his role in the action. "Life is its own reward, is it not, Mr. McAllistair?" He didn't wait for an answer. He was already turning to Carly. "You will all be our guests at the schloss, please?"

"Yes, by all means," Carly replied. He stepped past Bret and Colleen, obviously quite pleased with himself and the outcome of the evening. "Come along now, you two," he said, speaking as if they were a pair of wayward children.

Then he was gone, following Wilhelm down the slope. Bret squeezed Colleen's hand and pulled her against him. She slipped her arms around his waist, hugging him tightly and silently saying a prayer of awe and thanks once more. She was alive. Bret was alive.

Miraculously they would have a future.

He whispered into her ear a little gruffly, "You made some commitments to me back there, lady."

"I know."

"You haven't changed your mind?"

"Not a bit. Why?"

He paused for a minute, staring down into her eyes. Then he shrugged, inclining his head toward Wilhelm. "Well, it seems that I was a rather faulty hero. I wouldn't have made it without Wilhelm Holfer. Tall, rugged, blue eyed and obviously intrigued. You haven't got any ideas about him, have you?"

"Ummm." She pretended to muse over his words.

"Colleen!"

She tried to bat her lashes innocently, but they were too clogged with snow. She laughed, the sound a little jittery with the aftermath of terror and her delight in being alive. "How did you get that gun?"

"I had it with me all the time. It was just that they had two of them. I spun on Sandy when she wasn't expecting me to have a weapon, but I couldn't use it on Bill because its range isn't all that great and I might just as easily have hit you."

Colleen leaned against his chest, trembling, smiling. "You'll do in a pinch," she told him.

"In a pinch?"

"For a lifetime?" Colleen whispered.

He smiled at her, trying to dust the snow from her face. Her eyes were radiant, her face pale and delicate and lifted to his with wistfulness and love. He shuddered, realizing how much he cherished her, that she was his life and had been his life even when they were apart.

"For a lifetime. Just try to get rid of me again!" he growled softly.

"Never," she promised.

Two HOURS LATER they were all at Rudy Holfer's schloss, bathed and dry, sitting before a roaring fire and sipping blueberry schnapps. Carly was there, shaking his head each time he thought of how close his prized pair had come to being a victim of Sandy's vengeance, smiling each time he realized that they were back together.

Ben was there, too, enjoying the schloss, the fire and the schnapps. He was very quiet, his eyes darting back and forth, absorbing everything around him.

Wilhelm stood by the fire, attending to his father.

And Rudy Holfer—eighty if he was a day, but sharp and keen of wit and hearing—sat in a wheelchair, his legs covered by an immense plaid blanket. Arthritis had crippled him. The strength in Wilhelm's face had come from his father. Lined and weathered, Rudy's was still an arresting face, with fierce blue eyes and character etched in by years of reflection and sorrow.

"I tried so hard to reach you without alarming you further," he said sadly. His thin hands shook slightly in his lap. "So very hard, yet…" He sighed, and Wilhelm's hand moved to his shoulder. "I had no way to assure you that it could not be me." His English was heavily accented, but fluent and easy. "Who would have suspected that Tyrell's granddaughter…?"

He raised his hands. "Those accursed diamonds have caused so many deaths! Would to God that we had never seen them, never heard of them! Would to God that I could have done something in this wretched life to atone for that crime!"

Colleen slid from the sofa to go to him, taking one of his trembling hands. "Herr Holfer, your determination to find the truth saved my life. Wilhelm helped to save both my husband and me tonight. I'm not sure what that's worth compared with the past, but it is very precious to me, and I am very grateful. I'm sorry that we condemned you for so long without anything to go on but suspicion."

He smiled and drew a finger along her cheek. "Ah, but that is understandable, is it not? When one looks at that war, it is natural for the German to be the villain, *ja*?"

She felt herself color. Behind her Bret laughed ruefully. *"Ja,"* he admitted to Rudy.

"Well, perhaps we must bear the blame until all of my generation are gone. We were to blame. We fell for the promise of glory given to us by a madman." He stared at Colleen again with eyes remarkably like his son's. "It was a bad war, but all war is bad. There has not been a good war fought yet. War destroys youth and beauty, mows men down like flowers. But you must believe that we were not all bad men. We were soldiers, fighting for a crushed land. A land to which I may never return. Those diamonds…" His eyes grew rheumy with reflection, and he shrugged. "They were transferring me to the SS. I knew what the SS did, but I did not know how to combat it. I was through with war at that point. Through with the promises, through with the madman pulling our strings. The diamonds were a new promise, a promise of escape. I was tired of watching a storm of death I could not combat. For a few moments there the four of us proved that little men do not fight wars. We had no war between us. Why would I wish the death of a stranger? That is the cause of war, my friends. Strangers kill strangers. And when it is all over, they are allowed to be friends. For that one day in my life—a day that proved that enemies are created, not born—we all paid the penalty for a lifetime. There is no forgiveness. I hope only to make you understand that I wished none of the horror."

"Herr Holfer," Colleen said, "good people do bad things. The world is not black and white. I believe you meant no harm."

He laughed. "Oh, I did intend to steal the diamonds. But I meant to be a thief, not a murderer."

"Father, they know that," Wilhelm told him.

"And we are eternally grateful," Bret added. "You persisted, no matter how we condemned and fought you." His voice was husky. Colleen turned back to him and caught his eyes on her, warm and glittering in the firelight.

Rudy looked at Carly. "You will have a fine story for your magazine, I believe. The truth. I will do anything that I can to assist you with understanding the past."

"Thank you," Carly said. "Yes, it will be a fine story."

"Father, you will sleep now," Wilhelm instructed him.

Rudy Holfer nodded. "Tyrell, Rutger, MacHowell and soon myself. We will be all gone. It will be history then."

"You mustn't say that!" Colleen protested. "You've got years ahead of you."

Holfer shook his head. "My heart is weak, and it is weary, too. Forty years of guilt is too much to bear. There is this life. There is the next. When it is time, I will be ready." He winked. "But we will get your story done first. Now, *Guten Nacht!*"

Wilhelm nodded to them all as he began to push his father from the parlor. "Please, you will make yourselves comfortable? I will see that Father gets to bed."

"Yes, yes, thanks," Bret replied, standing. But before Wilhelm could leave, Bret caught his shoulder. The German turned to him, and their eyes met. "I mean... *thanks*."

Wilhelm studied Bret, smiled and nodded, then left.

Bret walked back to Colleen, who was still in front of the fire. His arms enveloped her, and they embraced tightly. "I'll never be able to thank him enough," he whispered huskily.

Carly cleared his throat. "Ben, let's go up to bed, shall we."

Ben sighed unhappily. "For all there is a great ending! Except for me! Now you will send me back, and I will spend my days in a taxi cab again."

Carly chuckled. "What do you say, Bret? The boy seems to have a penchant for the States. Think we could manage to get him a job and work on the immigration department?"

"Sure, we can try," Bret said.

Ben whooped with pleasure. He hugged Bret and Colleen together, then hugged Carly so fiercely that he cried out.

"My dear boy, if you behave this way, I won't survive to give you honest employment! Now, let's leave these two alone."

Colleen and Bret noticed only vaguely when the other two left. They were too busy staring at one another, smiling. Bret slipped an arm about her, bringing them both down to the floor. The fire crackled around them; its warmth enveloped them.

Colleen touched her knuckles to his cheek, suddenly frowning. "Bret, don't ever leave me again." He started to speak, but she shushed him with a finger on his lips. "I know you'll have to go sometimes, just like I'll have to go sometimes. We're both still journalists. What I mean is…whatever happens, whether we're angry, hurt or worried, please, let's make sure we discuss it, that we never part the way we did before."

He caught the finger against his lip and kissed it tenderly. Then his teeth grazed over it, sending a delicious shiver of arousal streaking through her.

"Whither thou goest, I will follow," he teased her, but then he grew serious, leaning beside her and stroking her cheek while he warmed her with the loving heat of his eyes. "Colleen, I've spoken to Carly. We're going to try like hell to work as a team. There are going to be some bad situations we won't be able to avoid, but we're both going to make promises. Neither one of us is going to run around jeopardizing our lives again." He bent down to kiss her and spoke right above her lips in a husky tremor. "Tonight cost me years off my life! Our next story is going to be on the space program, and we're going to report it from the ground."

Colleen smiled, arching her body against his and running her fingers through his hair. "I'm not so sure about remaining on the ground."

"What?" he demanded with a frown.

"I feel ten feet above it already, McAllistair!" she said with a low growl. "I'm not invited to stay in a castle that often. Especially not with an incredibly sexy pseudohero who just happens to be my husband. Will you please take me upstairs and make love to this body you claim to cherish so thoroughly?"

He laughed and rose, pulling her to her feet and into his arms. "Claim to cherish! Just wait till you see how well I can cherish!"

"I am waiting. I have eternal faith."

Bret started from the room, striding swiftly toward the great staircase. He paused only once. "Pseudohero?"

"Perfect hero," Colleen purred softly.

"Thanks. That's much better. That will get you ravished straight through to morning." He lowered his head for a quick kiss that became longer. When they broke apart, breathless and laughing, he rephrased his statement.

"That, Mrs. McAllistair, will get you divinely ravished, absolutely cherished and deeply, deeply loved— for a lifetime."

"That's all I'm demanding. And everything I promise to give in return."

Bret grinned, then hugged her closer and continued quickly up the staircase, two steps at a time.

* * * * *

We hope you enjoyed reading

Undercover Connection

&

Double Entendre

by *New York Times* bestselling author

HEATHER GRAHAM

INTRIGUE

Edge-of-your-seat intrigue, fearless romance

From passionate, suspenseful and dramatic
love stories to inspirational or historical,
Harlequin offers different lines to
satisfy every romance reader.

New books available every month.

HARLEQUIN™

INTRIGUE

EDGE-OF-YOUR-SEAT INTRIGUE, FEARLESS ROMANCE.

Save $1.00

off the purchase of ANY

Harlequin Intrigue® book.

Available wherever books are sold, including most bookstores, supermarkets, drugstores and discount stores.

Save $1.00

on the purchase of ANY Harlequin Intrigue® book.

Coupon valid until January 31, 2019.
Redeemable at participating outlets in the U.S. and Canada only.
Not redeemable at Barnes & Noble stores. Limit one coupon per customer.

52616150

5 65373 00076 2 (8100)0 12402

"Four days and a wake-up," Trace McGuire, T-Mac to
his friends, said as he sat across the table in the chow
hall on Camp Lemonnier. They'd returned from their
last mission in Niger with news they were scheduled to
redeploy back to the States.

He glanced around the table at his friends. When they
were deployed, they spent practically every waking hour
together. In the past, being stateside was about the same.
They'd go to work, train, get briefed, work out and then
go back to their apartments. Most of the time, they'd end
up at one of the team members' places to watch football,
cook out, or just lounge around and shoot the crap with
each other. They were like family and never seemed to
get tired of each other's company.

T-Mac suspected all that was about to change. All of
his closest SEAL buddies had women in their lives now.
All except him. Suddenly, going back to Virginia wasn't

quite as appealing as it had been in the past. T-Mac sighed and drank his lukewarm coffee.

"I can't wait to see Reese." Diesel tapped a finger against the rim of his coffee cup. "I promised to take her on a real date when I get back to civilization."

"What? You're not going to take her swinging through the jungle, communing with the gorillas?" Buck teased.

Petty Officer Dalton Samuel Landon, otherwise known as Diesel, shook his head. "Nope. Been there, done that. I think I'll take her to a restaurant where we don't have to forage for food. Then maybe we'll go out to a nightclub." He tipped his head to the side. "I wonder if she likes to dance."

"You mean you don't know?" Big Jake Schuler, the tallest man on the team, rolled his eyes. "I would have thought that in the time you two spent traipsing along the Congo River, you would know everything there was to know about each other."

Diesel frowned. "I know what's important. She's not fragile, she can climb a tree when she needs to, she doesn't fall apart when someone's shooting at her and she can kiss like nobody's business." Diesel shrugged. "In fact, I'm looking forward to learning more. She's amazing. How many female bodyguards do you know?"

Big Jake held up his hands in surrender. "You got me there. None."

Don't miss
Six Minutes to Midnight *by Elle James,*
available January 2019 wherever
Harlequin® Intrigue *books and ebooks are sold.*

www.Harlequin.com

Need an adrenaline rush from nail-biting tales
(and irresistible males)?

Check out **Harlequin Intrigue**®,
Harlequin® **Romantic Suspense** and
Love Inspired® **Suspense** books!

New books available every month!

CONNECT WITH US AT:

Facebook.com/groups/HarlequinConnection

 Facebook.com/HarlequinBooks

 Twitter.com/HarlequinBooks

 Instagram.com/HarlequinBooks

 Pinterest.com/HarlequinBooks

ReaderService.com

 HARLEQUIN®

**ROMANCE WHEN
YOU NEED IT**

SGENRE2018R